THE OTHER ONE

Also by Julian Green

Diary 1928-1957
To Leave Before Dawn

Julian Green

THE OTHER ONE

Translated from the French by Bernard Wall

A HELEN AND KURT WOLFF BOOK

HARCOURT BRACE JOVANOVICH, INC.

New York

C .3

First American edition

Originally published under the title *L'Autre* by Librairie Plon, Paris

ISBN 0-15-170445-7

Library of Congress Catalog Card Number: 72-91843

Printed in the United States of America

B C D E

CONTENTS

PART ONE   9
21 April 1949

PART TWO   15
Roger's story: Summer 1939

PART THREE   113
Karin's story: March-April 1949

PART FOUR   277
20 April 1949

PART ONE

21 April 1949

THERE was happiness in the air that morning in spite of
everything. All were agreed on that. The sun was shuffling
off the remains of the endless Scandinavian winter – the last shreds
of fog, the cold in the side streets – so as to pour down all its rich
showy light on to the city. The shadows of the trees, on which
each individual bud gleamed like a jewel, were still clear-cut and
delicate as they spread over the stones. At the great dock's edge a
line of old houses looked across at the distant towers of the town
crowned in almond green. The black water with its strong smells
lapped gently against the boats in the port, and the seagulls
mewed in the timidly blue sky.

About fifteen or twenty people were standing in a half circle on
the quay, grouped round a waterproof sheet covering a body. The
feet, however, were sticking out, one with a brown shoe on it, the
other just a stocking.

A red-headed young woman was weeping, as was an undersized man whose hand she was holding as if he were a child.

'Someone must have pushed her into the water last night,' the
young woman kept saying. 'She wanted to live.'

'Don't be too sad, Marie,' the little man said. 'What happened
was that my sister came to take her away.'

Marie let go the man's hand and exclaimed:

'Don't go on telling me about her being in heaven, Ib. You're
too infuriating! She's dead, dead the day after her birthday.'

'It's the German Woman,' said a gentleman in spectacles. 'I
recognize her.'

'You've no right to call her the German Woman,' Marie said
with feeling. 'No one has called her that for a long time.'

'But she was often seen about in the big cars belonging to the
Nazis,' the gentleman in spectacles went on.

'Yes, and in those days she was very stuck up,' put in an old
woman scathingly. 'When I was walking, like everyone else, she

didn't even look at me as she passed by, and yet she knew me all right.'

'How spiteful can you get!' exclaimed Marie pugnaciously, pushing her hair from her forehead. 'She was punished, wasn't she? She's paid for it.'

At that moment a young man wearing a pale blue shirt and white linen trousers anxiously approached the group of onlookers, and with a sweep of his arm pushed his way up to the waterproof sheet and lifted one of its corners.

'Emil, don't look!' the young red-head protested. 'She wouldn't be dead if she'd married you.'

'She didn't want to,' he said as he straightened up. And then he collapsed on to the ground.

The ambulance arrived and took delivery of the drowned woman with a speed that testified to long habit.

'It always happens in the same place,' remarked one of the stretcher-bearers. 'It's as though there were some spell.'

'Here, the tarpaulin's mine!' said an old sailor in a red sweater.

And he began rolling up the heavy sheeting while Marie threw water over the face of the young man who had fainted. A certain hardness of his features showed that he must be approaching thirty, though his copper-coloured hair was all tousled on his forehead like a schoolboy's. He opened his large eyes finally and gave his head a shake at the very moment that the ambulance was disappearing.

'Karin!' he cried. 'She looked as if she were smiling.'

'Don't think about it any more,' advised Marie and burst into tears.

The young man leapt up. All around him men with their hands in their pockets were gazing at him in silence and not without a slightly contemptuous pity. He noticed this.

'Stop crying,' he ordered Marie, slapping at his legs to remove the dust from his trousers. 'You cry too much, you're always crying.'

The owner of the waterproof sheet turned to him and said: 'Now then, son, if you loved that young lady you shouldn't have left her alone at night.'

'That's enough, grandpa,' Emil said. 'At your age you can't understand things like this any more.'

The sailor took his pipe from his mouth. All the creases in his face rearranged themselves in a smile that obviously heralded a speech.

'When I was your age, my boy . . .'

'Come on, Marie,' said Emil, 'let's go to your place and you can make me a strong coffee. I haven't had any breakfast.'

'And I'll come too,' exclaimed Ib, the undersized man.

He waved his hands about like a child, though he was of mature age. His round, slightly moon-like face was similarly disquieting because of the unfulfilled childhood one could read in it.

'Who is he?' Emil asked Marie while she was drying her tears.

'He's Miss Ott's brother – Miss Ott, who died last month.'

'Ott,' shouted Ib. 'She loved Karin. She can see us, I'm sure.'

'Shut up,' Marie said. 'Don't start that again.'

'But may I come with you?'

'Yes, if you can behave.'

'It's a pity we can't take a slice of that big cake left at Karin's,' he said. 'It's really good with coffee, and a lot must be left over.'

The wind had begun blowing and the group of onlookers slowly dispersed like an audience after a show. The sun shone on the white stones where the body had been such a short time before. Marie cast a brief, sad glance in that direction. She seemed surprised at seeing nothing there.

'Poor Karin. How we've wept together, and more than once.'

And she slid her arm under Emil's and leant against the young man almost affectionately.

'A handsome young fellow like you,' she said, 'they always end up by finding some nice little woman to their taste.'

Emil made no answer.

They walked slowly towards a quiet street where the port noises were almost inaudible except for the harsh cries of the seagulls, which seemed to be calling for someone. In the April light, that thoughtful young man and his pretty companion inevitably brought to mind two young people in love.

Ib followed behind, looking to right and left and smiling at everything.

The inquest revealed very little. At that season, even in Denmark, suicides are not unusual enough to arouse a great deal of notice, and it seemed obvious that Karin had killed herself deliberately. There was no other way of explaining why she had fallen into the water fifty yards from her house, where she had been living for four years. The presumption that she had been drunk was dismissed. Karin never drank. There was always the hypothesis of murder, but this, too, ran into insoluble difficulties. Karin had so many enemies that almost the whole town would have had to be accused, and there had been no witness. In any case, public opinion was that death had rid the kingdom of one of its most unworthy subjects. With this something had ended. The German Woman, with her anguished face, would never again be seen in the public gardens.

A small body of people showed greater indulgence. They claimed that the guilty woman had redeemed her character in recent years and substantially atoned for what she had done. And then, as the war had been over for four years now, surely the slate could be wiped clean. Some of Karin's neighbours came forward as witnesses in her favour. A letter went to the newspapers but was not published. After a few days the deceased's furniture was auctioned off and the money collected went to pay her debts as well as the cost of her burial. Then, with the collaboration of the fine weather, attention turned to less funereal matters and those of a purely touristic nature.

PART TWO

ROGER'S STORY

Summer 1939

I

I HAD been waiting for so long that I no longer really knew what I was doing there, at the corner of that deserted street at eight in the evening, when I might have been somewhere else enjoying myself, for enjoying myself was the most important thing in my life. And indeed from time to time my thoughts did turn to quite other things than this rather absurd assignation. Why had I asked for it and why had it been granted me? It seemed obvious that we had no desire for each other. In that town where there was no shortage of beautiful girls I found this particular one I was meeting a bit commonplace. Grace, yes, she could be granted that, an attractive way of walking, both quick and light of foot, but there was nothing outstanding about her face except her fresh complexion. Ash-blonde hair, black eyes, a retroussé nose, and a small, very red mouth. This could have built up to an interesting physiognomy, but something was lacking. Denmark had made me very hard to please.

The street was straight and long and seemed to me more boring every minute with its almost identical red brick houses. The only thing I admired was the fiery glow with which the setting sun lit up the windows. Everyone was probably at dinner, and I felt hungry too. In my mind I ordered a menu in a good little restaurant of the district, the restaurant where I intended to take that ill-mannered girl who was keeping me waiting, and I was on the point of leaving when a hand touched my elbow from behind me, but so gently that I did not even jump. It was she.

I turned round and found myself facing a smile. Then I understood why I had gone on waiting – because of her smile.

'You've disarmed me!' I exclaimed. 'I was planning to make a scene.'

'We don't know each other well enough yet for scenes,' she said. 'Scenes come with intimacy.'

I burst out laughing in spite of a residue of irritation.

'And what about slaps, Miss Impertinent?'

'Oh, slaps. They're for much, much later. What on earth is the time? Is it six? Did we say six or seven?'

'It's eight,' I said, taking her arm. 'Have you no sense of time?'

'Time doesn't count, here. You've got a lot to learn.'

'And how about you?'

'Yes, I too. For instance, I rely on you to correct my mistakes in French.'

'Let's stop this ridiculous game and go and get some dinner. Don't you agree?'

She disengaged her arm and said, smiling again:

'We could just as well go and drink a glass of mineral water in a café near here where we could talk in peace.'

'But what would we talk about?'

At that moment a ray of sunlight struck her face as if to administer the smack I had foretold.

'You'd choose an interesting subject,' she said with a flicker of her eyelids, 'and I'd profit by increasing my vocabulary with useful expressions and – what do you call them? – gallicisms.'

Suddenly I felt angry.

'If you please we'll leave it at that. You'd do better to go back home. I'm surprised you're allowed to come out alone as late as this.'

'You'd like me to have a chaperone? In Copenhagen, in 1939!'

Since I had no idea what to answer, I made an undecided step as if to leave her. It seemed to me a good opportunity to rid myself of this girl who was really not quite pretty enough to attract me. A mocking laugh followed me.

Then she turned on her heel and slowly went off, perhaps disappointed that I did not chase after her. But she had wounded me in my vanity and I let her go, though not without a shadow of regret.

A moment later I found myself in a big amusement park where strollers became more and more numerous as darkness fell. By now I had lost my appetite, no doubt owing to my disappointing experience, but though I was blasé enough about the resources of this pleasure spot, I was determined to wrest from it some memorable adventure. There were plenty of pretty girls in this corner of the world, and I was young enough to lay claim to the best. This thought made me rejoice in spite of the rumours of war that had been circulating for the last few weeks and with greater and greater definiteness. What was the use of my youth? The threat of death hung over all of us who were of call-up age, but that evening I had made up my mind to forget the news. Everything lured me on. I lost myself in the most carefree crowd in existence and one, so it seemed, unthreatened by war.

After a stifling day the air was becoming cooler, and without any clear idea of where I was going I followed the strolling crowds who were laughing and chattering like children. I was almost completely ignorant of their language and could not understand their jokes, but I enjoyed the good-humoured atmosphere that almost amounted to infantilism (if the word were not unkind) because I loved this country to which I already owed so many happy moments. Even its frivolity delighted me because it took away the cares I would find again as soon as I got back home after the holidays.

There was a broad avenue, lit up by arc lights as far as the eye could see, winding in and out among lawns beneath a sky now deep blue and flecked with diamond dots. Moved by the magnificence of the night, I could not help finding our little earthly illuminations and this poor fête in the park a bit tawdry, but the demands of desire soon got the upper hand and I resumed my search because that was why I was there. Searching meant pushing my way through the crowds and casting a furtive glance on all those faces, none of which escaped my scrutiny. I flattered myself I could judge quickly, without ever making a mistake. I knew what I wanted, better, what I did not want. Occasionally when I saw a promising face I hesitated long enough to tell myself that it was such. But if I questioned myself, that in itself was a sign that I should not linger but press on towards the person whose beauty left me in no doubt and who was probably waiting for me in that half-light full of murmurs.

It seemed to me that everything breathed of love on that night of enchanting complicity. The thought of the menu that I had recently drawn up brought a smile to my face. Having dinner would have been a waste of time. My guts were gripped by another hunger than that of the stomach. Intoxication of the senses is no empty image. My head was getting lighter. I was burning. At the moment the crowd was too dense and bothered me a bit as I

...olled about. On the other hand I found it agreeable to be drawn towards places where something was happening, for there, so I thought, my chances of discovery would be better. I myself became the crowd, I moved on, I let myself be taken anywhere, and undoubtedly I did right. For soon I saw a large circle of light in the distance in the midst of which there rose two slender metal columns supporting (at about ten yards from the ground) a long horizontal bar announcing an acrobatic show. I was avid for this sort of thing, where the spice of danger enhances the taste for physical beauty, and anyway, even if I had wanted to, it would have been difficult now to extricate myself. Pushed forward myself, and helplessly pushing unknown others forward (contact with whom was anything but pleasant), I suddenly felt a discomfort which I endured as best I could. Even more than being imprisoned by numbers I was agitated by all the noise of incomprehensible words buzzing in my ears. Finally, however, we came to a halt not far from a barrier, and the show began.

I saw a young man and a young woman, clad in quite ordinary clothes, mounting the ladders at each end of the horizontal bar. The first thing they did was to wave to the crowd with that radiant yet mechanical smile that is a polite challenge to death. Both had brown skins, but though the boy was obviously Scandinavian the girl came from far away, and in the murmuring around me I heard Java mentioned. With airy lightness, and as if on a path, they advanced towards each other and touched hands. Such grace made me tremble. Then my heart was torn with sudden pity and I dreaded the false move that would hurl them to the ground – a dread soon dissipated when I observed their amazing assurance. What trick were they going to amuse us with next? Only the very simple would expect it to be something suitable for a church club. They undressed.

At first I was so innocent as to think that they would confine themselves to casting off, the one his jacket, the other her dress. These were dispatched into the void with contemptuous nonchalance. Shirt and blouse followed, leaving them half naked in the glare of the spotlights and producing a huge groan of admiration. Together with all the attentive crowd I then asked myself how far this audacity would lead them. It followed its course – hardly a 'normal' one, given the height at which this sort of tranquil drama was taking place. For will anyone laugh if I write that for two young people aged twenty it can be a drama to have to take off, he his socks and she her stockings, at ten yards from the ground, resting their feet on a very narrow iron bar, and all to amuse the crowd? This crowd was now watching with all the attention of fear, and if I just said that I had become the crowd, I can now say that we suddenly became those acrobats whose life depended on an incredibly precarious balance. No sound disturbed the silence of the night, and had I shut my eyes I might have believed I was alone, but my eyes stayed open as if their lids were glued. Meanwhile, with admirably slow and sure movements, that woman and that man were divesting themselves of everything that covered the lower part of their bodies whose very elegance seemed to indicate a frightening fragility. I felt at this moment that, in the mentality of the crowd, the curiosity of desire had insinuated itself into their anguish. We all held our breath as if indeed only a breath were required to throw this couple, offered to our horror-stricken contemplation, into the void. Yet they smiled for all that, clothed only in light, if we except the white frippery judged suitable to pander to our sense of modesty. In any case nothing could have been more chaste than that golden nakedness triumphant under a dark blue sky. They waved once more with raised arms. Then, with feline agility, they reached the ladders greeted by an enormous outburst of applause. A coat was thrown over their shoulders and they disappeared into a tent where they dressed again.

The crowd dispersed immediately as though fleeing from boredom as from the plague, and flowed over towards a corner of the park whither it was drawn by another spectacle – this time a comic one, with clowns. But I stayed where I was and, less than three minutes later, found myself confronting those bars that were being dismantled and those lights that were being extinguished. And the hallucination of the gymnastics that had just taken place started all over again in my head and I felt I could see them more exactly in recollection. Once more, but now more beautiful, that amber-coloured flesh shone in the depths of the night, and those perfect limbs carried out – but now for me alone – the perilous antics by which I was so fascinated. Once again I could feel my heart in my mouth – 'for if they fall,' so I thought,

'I'll die with them.' At such moments all sexual emotion was out of the question. It was even rather strange that no shade of desire arose to disturb that inner vision, and I was aware of this fact only because the mystery of it astonished me. The splendid nakedness spoke of something other than the body.

I remained motionless for a long time until I finally came back to my senses and decided to go on with my hunt where noise and lights betrayed the presence of questing onlookers, but I no longer felt the zeal that had spurred me on at the beginning of the evening. I was disenchanted by what I had seen. The hazards of adventure offered me something too far from my dreams. The temptation to seek out the acrobats (who, incidentally, had disappeared) came over me, but only feebly. The woman seemed to me beyond our world, like a statue or a ghost. I could not bring myself to imagine the contact of my flesh with hers. My imagination, I felt, was stricken with impotence about all that. Sooner or later I would have to content myself with more earthly fulfilments. After all, it was only perhaps those ten yards above the ground that had raised the recent show up into fabulous regions, but the effect was the same.

As I was twisting and turning these thoughts over in my mind I arrived at a sort of little artificial village with streets made up of temporary booths. There were showmen who would bring only the simplest strollers to a halt. Others, more demanding, paused for a moment to watch a huge cinnamon-coloured bear dancing; but the greater number stopped in front of a shooting-range where, for a coin, one could test one's skill with a gun.

Among those who fancied this were three sailors, drawn to everyone's attention by their white uniforms; they were aiming unsuccessfully with the guns handed to them and laughing at their awkwardness. One of them, stronger and better built than his companions, was displaying his figure to advantage in this posture and looking around him with insolent assurance. Judging by the long black ribbons falling over their shoulders, they were men from some foreign navy, probably Polish. I found myself near enough to them to hear the remarks they were exchanging in a language whose gentle, singing inflexions contrasted with the vigour of their rather rough faces.

Behind this trio stood a young Danish officer who, like me,

was watching the sailors' unsuccessful attempts. There was something arrogant in his bearing that compelled attention. His strong, thin face, his rosy cheeks and high cheekbones, above all his jet black eyes made him stand out from the common crowd. Tall and slim, he wore with elegance the rather dull uniform of modern armies and held himself apart in splendid isolation. I would not have called him exactly handsome, but you could not see him without wondering: 'Who is he? What's he thinking about all this? And why that proud, austere, contemptuous look?'

If I have paused a while to describe him it is because someone besides me was making similar observations. My hand gently touched the arm of a girl standing almost beside me but a little in front.

'What on earth are you admiring?' I asked her in French.

It was my little Danish girl of a short while ago.

'It could be the same thing as you,' she answered at once, without turning her head. 'I've been aware of your presence behind me for the past minute.'

'I'm not admiring; I'm looking. You must be amused by the silliness of those long ribbons over those thick necks.'

'Not at all; I like contrasts. But you're being rather a nuisance, you know.'

'So you're looking at something else? I think I know what – and who.'

'Then keep quiet and let me be. To begin with I'm not alone. The girl on my left is with me.'

And I noticed a serious young woman wearing glasses.

'Does she know French?' I asked.

'Not a word. She's a childhood friend. But if you go on talking to me I warn you I'll introduce you. We met just now. She's very nice but the most boring person you could imagine. Now, will you go?'

'You could easily leave her and have dinner with me.'

What whim made me persist in this way? At first all I had wanted was to tease her a bit, without any ulterior motive; but now her resistance was making me find her almost attractive. A further point was that she spoke my language; but she did not reply. She was devouring that young officer with her eyes. After a slight hesitation I leant towards her and said in her ear:

'If you stay where you are you're going to suffer.'
To my surprise she answered in a sort of murmur:
'Suppose I like that kind of suffering . . .'
'At least tell me your name.'
'What's that to you? For heaven's sake leave me in peace. My name's Karin.'
At that moment the young officer moved away and disappeared. Karin turned a distressed face towards me.
'Take me away,' she said.
'And what about your friend?'
'What friend? Oh, that lady? I don't know her.'
'But you said . . .'
'Please don't be so stupid. Sometimes I make things up.'
'Are you hungry?'
'I don't know. Come on, let's be off.'
We left the park and went to have dinner in a restaurant where small lamps with peach-coloured shades shone discreetly on the tables. The white table-cloths and drawn curtains gave the place an air of prosperous intimacy which, so I thought, would encourage confidences – for my companion intrigued me and I felt sure that after one or two glasses of a wine that I would choose myself she would tell me her life history, as people normally do when they have not yet lived. It was not that she really attracted me – I was hesitant on this point, which amounts to saying she did not attract me – but in her quick rejoinders, and indeed in her whole bearing, I felt there was something that concealed a little secret. I wanted to know what was going on in her mind when she had agreed to that meeting about which I myself was so half-hearted. And then just now, under the contemptuous eye of that Danish officer, I had been present at some sort of inner drama. My curiosity was aroused. I wanted to understand why I was sitting beside that young lady in front of a plate of crayfish and a bottle of Sauterne, for to tell the truth what astonished me most was my own behaviour.

So her name was Karin. In view of her youth – she was approaching nineteen – I again felt surprised that she was allowed to wander about the town as she liked after sundown. Yet I didn't say a word in spite of all the questions that occurred to me. I would also have liked to know how my guest earned her living.

But we were only on the first glass of wine. I admired the delicacy of the long brown hand which she placed on the table as though to submit it to my appreciation, for I sensed coquetry in this gesture, and the serious matter of sun-bathing came up in the most natural way imaginable. Did she sun-bathe?

'No time,' she said. 'And then I'm not eager to exhibit myself in public.'

I can hardly describe the primness with which she said that. All she let me see was her little-girl's profile and her slender fingers as they crumbled up a biscotte on the linen cloth. Her lovely black eyes redeemed the banality of her nose, which was a little too pretty, and of her pulpy, innocent mouth. She was one of those girls who, you feel sure, derive almost entirely from their mother, though this intuition cannot be corroborated. Risking a fairly discreet question, I learnt that her parents had died two years earlier in a motor accident and that her mother was German. She told me this detail with a shade of defiance on her face; and I then wanted to edge the conversation into more or less intellectual areas – but here, total silence. Karin read nothing, not even the newspaper.

'News floats in the air here,' she said; 'we see it every evening in blinding letters on the tower of the *Berlingske Tidende*.'

A sudden inspiration made me introduce the subject of travel and I wanted to know if she was curious about the Mediterranean. I knew the effect of those syllables on the Scandinavian imagination, and this time I was not disappointed. Her face lit up with the ecstasy of an inner vision, and she confided that she longed to visit Italy and Greece.

'Why Italy and Greece?' I asked. 'Why not Tunisia or Morocco?'

But she was not listening. The magic names she repeated as though to increase her intoxication had much more effect than the heady wine with which I vainly offered to refill her glass. The tone in which she mentioned the names of distant countries had an accent that almost resembled pain.

'Do you suppose that everyone is happy in those places?'

Once again I cunningly poised the neck of the bottle over her glass. She broke off her ecstasy and frowned.

'I've an impression that you want to make me drunk for reasons I don't know. It's a waste of time, you know.'

True, I did want to make her drunk and for reasons I knew well, but though she was not at all drunk she began to tell me about herself. I was ashamed of my behaviour, and to win forgiveness I offered point-blank to take her to visit the countries that so enchanted her. Her mouth opened slightly and revealed her teeth, as white as rice.

'Oh,' she said, her eyes swimming in such impossible happiness. Then she suddenly pulled herself together.

'You're joking,' she said coldly.

I was struck by the mobility of her face. I lowered my eyes and noticed for the first time that the material of her dress bore traces of wear beneath her breasts. She must have followed my eyes, for she moved her arm slightly forward to hide what I had seen. 'Anyway,' I thought, 'she isn't a prostitute.'

What could that matter to me? Why should I care about this meal, this groping conversation, or indeed my rather insincere offer no sooner made than rejected? It looked as though I were laying siege to a recalcitrant beauty. Above all, the travel gambit had been deplorably gross. I cut short that bizarre dinner as best I could, paid the bill, and waited for my guest to show a desire to leave. She had refused the liqueurs and we stayed at that table where the little lamp with the peach-coloured shade, like all the others in the slowly emptying room, spread a light intended to be one of complicity. Not far from us a spectacled gentleman was whispering something to a blonde young girl who was stifling her yawns. I did not want to become like that fifty-year-old. 'Better die,' I thought.

'Would you like to go for a drive?' I suddenly asked. 'We could go round the avenues in the wood.'

'No, thank you.'

'Or I could take you home.'

'It's not worth getting into a car to cross the square. I live nearby, behind the town hall. We can say good-bye here.'

While saying these words (and to what purpose, since she did not get up?) she turned her face to me and smiled one of those smiles that transfigured her so strangely. Suddenly she displayed a radiant and disturbing beauty. All the sweetness of her nature flowed from her great dark eyes. Something of my astonishment must certainly have appeared in my expression.

'You don't look very pleased,' she said. 'Didn't I do what you wanted? You wanted us to dine together . . .'

The opportunity to bring things to an end had been offered, but I didn't want that now.

'We're separating rather early.'

'I don't see what a few minutes could add to the evening.'

'Karin . . .'

'Who gave you permission to call me Karin?' she asked, laughing. 'I don't even know your name.'

'Call me Roger.'

'I won't call you anything at all! Roger. What a funny name! I haven't the faintest idea whether I even like it.'

'Tell me who taught you to speak French so well.'

'That isn't your business, Monsieur Roger,' she answered in a teasing voice.

'I could teach you one or two additional expressions.'

She glanced at me reproachfully and murmured:

'Why do you make fun of me?'

'Perhaps you would have preferred to spend the evening with someone else. How do I know? One of your compatriots. For instance . . .'

Did she guess that I was going to mention the young officer of a short while ago? She cast a withering glance at me.

'Forgive me, Karin.'

'Luckily, I've nothing to forgive you for,' she said and got up.

A moment later we were in the square dominated by the town hall tower. A huge murmur reached us from the pleasure gardens, whose lights threw a sort of halo over the black mass of trees on either side of the avenue. I did not want to take Karin's arm, but we walked a few steps as far as a poorly lit street. There she lowered her voice a little as though she were on the point of making a mysterious announcement.

'It'll be here,' she said.

'Here?'

'Here that we'll say good-bye.' And she added softly: 'Tak for mad.'*

An absurd and shameful thought crossed my mind. I had noticed the perfect roundness of her lovely neck. What could I

* Thanks for dinner.

27

take away from that evening save a kiss on her firm smooth flesh? Surely it was my right. (That was the shameful part.) I bent my head and rested my lips slightly below her pretty childlike ear. Karin jumped back as though I had burnt her.

'Oh, why did you do that?' she asked in a changed voice.

'But, Karin, what are you afraid of?'

She made no reply but walked quickly away and I saw her disappear at the end of the street. Possibly she expected to see me running after her, but I am not sure. In any case, this sad adventure came to an end in the most opportune way, so great was my fear of getting bored with the young lady.

'Good riddance!' I said out loud.

II

I felt both relieved and disappointed, rather humiliated too, rather shamefaced, and delivered back to my solitude. But it's time to talk about myself. My stay in Copenhagen was to end with the month of August and we were only in the middle of July. Why I had chosen this place for my holidays was explained, at least in part, by purely physical tastes. My parents, with the innocence of all parents, imagined that I was profiting by my leisure to study, and indeed I was studying, but not what they supposed. They thought I was serious. And I was, in the way that many pleasure-seeking men are.

I was twenty-four and though I wasn't rich I had all the money I needed at my disposal. My only lack was a knowledge of Danish with which to assure myself, or so I thought, of the finest adventures in the world. Unfortunately, I had practically no gift for languages, and dumbness becomes intolerable when the main business lies in persuading someone into an assignation or arranging where to make one. My trump card, and I say it without false modesty, was my thick, curly, ebony-black hair and the special colour of my eyes – a grey that sometimes turns to violet. It was this that drew people's attention. My position was like that of a blond in countries where everyone is dark. Obviously this natural advantage was extremely useful to me in ordinary meetings which only involved gestures; but I was aiming higher. Above all, I could not endure solitude. The power of Scandinavian beauty could alone have justified my presence in Denmark. But there was something else. Copenhagen was situated relatively far from Paris and truth obliges me to add that this mattered. People who remember the unendurable uneasiness dominating our lives during the last weeks of peace will understand the joy I experienced at waking up each morning in a country where the fear of war was not felt in the same way as in France. Who was threatening Denmark? I didn't read the French papers though they were easily available. I wanted to forget the nightmare blocking the future. Still a few minutes of happiness . . . I wanted to live. The call-up papers would come soon enough.

In the bottom of my pocket lay a letter written me by a Paris friend in answer to a confidential one from me. He knew Copenhagen well, and to help me out of my difficulties proposed a means that I found highly unattractive: '*Miss Ott,*' he said among other things, '*runs one of the best bookshops in the town. As she is crazy about everything French she will metaphorically throw herself into your arms. And since you are a handsome young man she may be tempted to leave the realm of metaphor, but this is unlikely, for she has solid principles. She is both pious and jingoistic and presents a façade beyond reproach, but I suspect her of having one or two sins which can only be small. You'll discover them if it interests you. As for me, I'm in her debt for meeting the ravishing Luisa, whom I've told you about. Don't make the mistake of taking Miss Ott for one of those women who promote situations conducive to love affairs. What she does is different and quite indefinable. It's a point of honour with her to open the doors of her beloved Denmark to a foreigner in distress. She likes flowers. She has some sort of massive respect for Mammon, but she is disinterested. Don't be taken in by her frank manner. If you say a single word out of order you won't see her again . . .*'

I knew this letter by heart, though it maddened me with its general vagueness. Nevertheless I read it once more before deciding to take the embarrassing step. I really must have been possessed to seek out that woman who I was told would be useful but who was definitely not a procuress. At the stage of effervescence I seemed to have reached I would have very much preferred a procuress . . . At last I crossed the threshold of that bookshop overlooking a charming, shady square – and what a half-hour of irresolution I had spent in that charming square, before crossing the road!

There was a faint smell of wax in the shop where at first I saw nothing but walls of paper-bound books and two heavy tables displaying art books. The blinds protecting the windows from the sun agreeably filtered the light. In the heat and tumult of the town this bookshop was a sort of oasis, an oasis of coolness and silence. Suddenly I felt reassured and relaxed. When a girl approached me and asked me what I wanted I gave Miss Ott's name.

'*Fransk?*' she asked with a smile.

I nodded my assent with some vigour. The word for 'French' I did at least understand. Some minutes passed during which I had leisure to notice a door in the corner of the bookshop, a raised door reached by three steps flanked by a brass handrail. How it shone, that brass handrail . . . But here everything shone, everything was redolent of prosperity, peace and the well-being of a life set in its own comfort and habits.

I waited. The young woman whose job it was to announce me had vanished through the door up the steps, and the time that passed enabled me to see that it was not so easy to disturb Miss Ott. I imagined her as being svelte and elegant, with the air of a governess full of secrets. Suddenly the door opened, and to my surprise I saw a woman advancing towards me who was heavy with at least forty years and who had a rather too rosy face – the rosiness not being one of health. Wearing a dark blue cotton dress, tight round her hips but floating around her ankles, and moving with a rather majestic slowness, she seemed a tower of middle-class respectability. When she was in front of me she looked me over with her grey-green eyes, which I could not help finding beautiful, and waited, for my mere nationality was not enough; she wanted to know what I wanted. After a moment's uncertainty I mentioned the name of my friend, and she nodded. A smile lit up her wide face and dimples appeared on either side of her mouth, which was still pretty. She motioned me to the open door and I followed her up the three steps which creaked beneath her weight.

I now found myself with Miss Ott in a rather small though comfortably furnished office looking out on to a little garden dominated by geraniums. She began by making a few remarks about my friend, of whom she seemed to have retained very pleasant memories, and I wondered by what ruses he had contrived to win her over. Seated in a black leather chair of sumptuous proportions, I observed the face of the woman leaning towards me over her work-table. With an effort of imagination I could see that she must have been pretty in the days when she was slim. For all I knew, someone might have killed himself out of love for her when she was eighteen. For she indeed had that slightly imperious look of women who have been adored. I felt her eyes seeking homage in the depths of mine out of habit, but it was more like a question than a prayer, and I conceived for her a feeling of pity mixed with revulsion caused by her small mouth, which was both prim and cruel. I thought of the murderous words that must have flowed from those lips so carefully touched up with rouge.

For all that, she expressed herself affably and the pleasant timbre of her voice in some degree redeemed her insistent gaze, which I found anything but pleasing. I was afraid she might find me to her taste and emerge from metaphor, as my friend had put it in his letter at that very moment lying crumpled in the depths of my pocket. Had this heavy lady but known . . . But I must admit that after a moment I became sensitive to the charm of her slightly affected modulations. She spoke our language perfectly but had the coquetry to hesitate at certain words, as if to draw attention to her choice. It wasn't very difficult to guess that she expected to be complimented on her linguistic virtuosity, and she was certainly not disappointed.

'Oh,' she said with a small dismissive gesture as though refusing a present, 'numbers of us here know French.'

'Precisely. If I could get in touch . . .'

She made a sign with her hand to show she had understood.

'You must feel lost in this country where the language is so difficult . . . Unless – excuse me – you speak Danish. You don't? Your friend suffered a lot from that situation until the day I arranged private lessons for him.'

'But I've got so little time here, Miss Ott. The easiest thing would be for me to get to know someone who knows French.'

'An exchange wouldn't be impossible. By that I mean that you'd speak French with someone who wanted a thorough knowledge

31

of your language, and she in her turn would teach you the . . . rudiments of ours.'

The smile accompanying these words displayed rather pretty teeth. I had a lightning intuition that she knew perfectly well what I wanted and was highly amused.

'My friend spoke extremely well of the person you introduced him to; a teacher, in fact.'

'Luisa? Luisa is a nice child, the niece of one of my school friends. But your friend is over-indulgent. Luisa has no university degree. She and he were satisfied with one or two hours of conversation every day in the park, one in French, the other in Danish.'

'What an admirable arrangement. Perhaps . . .'

There was a brief silence.

'Perhaps what?' said Miss Ott.

'Well, if Miss Luisa agreed . . .'

She gave a little silvery laugh, the laugh of a pretty woman, which made me want to split her skull with the heavy bronze paperweight adorning the table.

'Miss Luisa is in the country spending the summer with her parents.'

I couldn't help letting out a sigh of irritation.

'Don't be downhearted,' she said kindly. 'How long are you staying in Copenhagen?'

'Until the end of August.'

She seemed to be thinking, or rather dreaming, about something.

'Perhaps – I say perhaps – I could introduce you to a very good friend of mine . . . But, excuse me, would you feel more comfortable with a gentleman?'

She asked the question so directly that I suspected some trap.

'No, Miss Ott.'

'Then this girl I was referring to is very serious-minded, with a university degree.'

'Oh,' I said and wiped my brow, for even here the heat finally made itself felt. 'I wouldn't ask as much as that, Miss Ott.'

She leant back.

'Excuse me if I'm brutally frank,' she said in an unexpectedly powerful voice, 'but I have the impression that you're looking for a charming girl and that you're counting on me to find you one.'

Drawing myself up in my turn, I assumed a dignified air:

'Miss Ott, you must believe I'd never allow myself . . .'

This answer was doubtless the one she was expecting because we were obviously playing a sort of comedy intended to keep up appearances, and Miss Ott immediately became amiable again.

'I understand perfectly that a young man should enjoy the company of charming girls. And to be sure, there are plenty of them here.'

I now let out a laugh that I tried to make as light as possible, a laugh of careless youth – but it sounded horribly false.

'But they don't all speak French,' I protested, gesticulating.

'Oh, some do,' she said, laughing too. 'And I wager you've met one or two who gabble your language. But perhaps I'm being indiscreet.'

'Not at all.'

Karin . . . What compelled me suddenly to refer to her? Perhaps I was thinking about her without realizing it. I went on, raising my eyebrows with an air of indifference:

'Why, only yesterday I happened to run into a girl in the middle of the square in front of the town hall and, map in hand, I asked her the way somewhere, and she answered in very decent French.'

'So you see. Luck is on your side . . .' And she added with a series of light blinks: 'I'm sure that encounter was the prelude to a pleasant evening.'

'Not an evening, no. We parted after a few minutes and I lost sight of her.'

A silent voice within me cried: 'Liar! Liar!'

'The same luck may well make you find her again.'

'I don't know if I want to.'

'I suppose you're difficult to please.'

'Extremely.'

I flattered myself that with that single adverb I'd made her, so to speak, go back inside her metaphor. She looked at me severely and I detected a sort of cold greediness in her eyes.

'The young lady wasn't too pretty, I suppose,' she said between her teeth.

'Oh, she could have appealed to some people more than to me. She had charm, and large black eyes.'

'Large black eyes! That isn't so common with us, you know. And naturally you don't know her name.'

Miss Ott was certainly very inquisitive. I shrugged my shoulders and made no answer.

'Anyway, let me congratulate you on finding a young Danish girl with black eyes who speaks French in our town,' she said in a studied voice. 'The rare bird, my dear sir.'

Which implied that, because I had not taken her into my confidence, she took no further interest in my little sexual problems.

'The rare bird told me her Christian name – but I've forgotten it.'

'It was kind of her to tell you her Christian name after only a few minutes.'

'Elsa,' I said on the spur of the moment. 'She was called Elsa.'

A few seconds passed during which Miss Ott kept her eyes trained attentively upon me.

'I don't know any Elsa with black eyes who speaks French in Copenhagen,' she said finally, 'and I know everyone here.'

'You don't know Elsa.'

'Oh well,' she said in the tone of someone who is very busy and wants to bring things to an end, 'I've kept you too long already, my dear sir. But I'll bear you in mind regarding those private lessons.'

For a moment she seemed on the point of adding something, but, thinking better of it, stood up and gave me her hand with aggressive cordiality.

'I hope we'll meet again one of these days,' she said. 'Sometimes I have a gathering of friends at my home, quite informal, you know, in the Danish way. If you'd like to come one evening I'll let you know. What hotel are you staying at?'

I was living in the flat that my Paris friend had had before me, in the Sankt Annaegade.

'Oh,' said Miss Ott with a hint of respect, 'a good address. It belongs to a baroness.'

III

Disappointing though this conversation was, it should not have robbed me of all hope; but I was one of those men for whom only immediate pleasures matter. I found waiting exasperating, so that evening I decided to go prowling in a rather dimly lit public garden whose mysterious depths I already knew.

Quiet walks wound round great clumps of greenery and led down imperceptibly to a little lake where in daytime children sailed their boats. Tall trees, flowers and two or three artificial grottoes made the place delightful on a fine summer afternoon, but all traces of innocence disappeared at night. Where the burning sun had zoned off refreshing patches of shade over sheltered lawns, the moon ringed round areas of impenetrable darkness that evoked dreams of abysses. A few street lamps vainly cast luminous discs on the gravel, they dissipated only a small portion of those areas of darkness where the madness of the senses found a refuge and which the indifference of the local authorities rendered almost inviolable. More than once had I taken advantage of this situation, but the intoxication of brief moments left me unsatisfied.

The peaceful murmur of a waterfall led me towards those regions where I guessed my prey most abounded, and indeed I was soon almost brushing against silent and absorbed couples. It was the silence that struck me more than anything else. Except for the intermittent sound of footsteps on the gravel – for other people were hunting, like me – one would have thought one was utterly alone in this garden full of people. The areas immediately round the lamp-posts were, of course, avoided. One saw practically nothing except, now and again, the whiteness of a garment and also (I note this detail with admiration) the pale gold of hair.

In its general form recalling that of a funnel, with the concentric pattern of its walks, this place called to mind one of those naïve allegories of times gone by in which a picture of human destiny is presented, the pure ascending to the heights of the blessed while the lecherous are drawn by some invincible destiny towards the sevenfold-accursed depths. As for me in those distant years, I found it impossible to accept any distinction between good and evil where matters of the body were concerned. I obeyed nature and at the same time regretted that the sense of sin played no part so as to give spice to it all, for it risked becoming boring by the sheer fact of repetition. The need for novelty was becoming more and more of a tyranny to me, which was why even the most un-hoped-for strokes of fortune held no future for me.

I had reached this point in my reflections when I looked up – for I was at the lowest level of the garden – and saw Karin's silhouette above me, lit up by the yellow glow of a street lamp. It could not have been anyone else. She was moving as quickly as the upward slope of the land allowed, and making her way towards the exit. The grace and lightness of her step were unmistakable; and yet the moment she had disappeared from view I wondered whether I could have been wrong. Her presence in this place fitted so badly the image I had formed of her . . .

This thought kept me busy for a couple of minutes. I was astonished that Karin should have been alone and walking so quickly. It looked as though she were in flight. But what did the behaviour of that uninteresting girl matter to me? I was there to find something better. With this in mind I lit a cigarette, less for the pleasure of smoking than to announce my presence to the girls who, like me, were on the hunt, and also to get a dim look around by the light of the match.

By one of those chances that so rarely happen, my eyes fell on a face of extreme youthfulness, and in my surprise I dropped my cigarette, for, like many men of my age, I loved what was in-violate. The very young girl whom I immediately approached had features of a purity that made my heart beat faster, and, not without a certain respect which must seem ridiculous to some people, I did no more than stroke her hair whose resilient thick-ness seemed to leap to life at my touch. I did not dare go any further but asked her bluntly in her ear what she was doing there, and she replied wordlessly by putting her cheek against mine with a clumsiness that contrived to seduce me. Was I then, so simple? What followed repelled me so violently that I immediately drew away from her, put a ten-crown piece in the little hand that was resting on me, and made off. The fact is I would have been hard put to it to explain my behaviour, for vice had never frightened me. I liked vice, but sometimes was aware of sudden refusals within me that eluded all analysis.

On regaining the avenue I wondered how I would end my evening for there was no question of going back to my room on such a beautiful clear night. And I needed a walk. I could have walked till dawn . . . I was both displeased and surprised at my behaviour and was in a mood to argue with myself for hours. The idea of cutting short my holiday and returning to France entered my mind, but over France there lay that shadow . . . And then it would be too ridiculous to leave this town where human beauty reigned supreme at every street corner. The fact that I was not attracted by poor Karin, the girl who spoke French, seemed to me a teasing attribute of fate. With what clarity of detail I re-enacted our first encounter!

It was in front of the town hall, in full sunshine, my eyes nearly dropping out trying to read names on an official map without finding the one I was looking for, that this girl had suddenly passed within two yards of me. I stopped her with an imploring gesture and said one of the only Danish words lodged in my mind, and I'm sure I'm reproducing it incorrectly: '*Vaersaagod*'. She looked at me gravely with her hypnotic eyes and waited. At that I felt despair and put my map back in my pocket as if giving up all hope of making myself understood. Then an enchanting smile suddenly broke out on that serious face:

'*Fransk?*' she asked.

And so began a few minutes' conversation. I could see the girl enjoyed talking with me in my language and I felt an immediate sympathy with her, especially since I was not troubled by desire.

By some trick of my memory it was this recollection that imposed itself upon me as I was leaving that sinister park I have just been talking about. And so strong was the impression of that first meeting with her that it obliterated all the others, and now I would not even let myself believe I had seen Karin hurrying along the walk. It was so out of character for her to be there at all, in what amounted to an open-air brothel! And when I told myself that after all I was indifferent to all this it settled nothing, because I found I was no longer being very honest with myself in this matter. Truth obliged me to admit that for hours I had been thinking a great deal about that girl.

37

I walked a little further along the avenue, then crossed the bridge leading to the island where I lived in a large and beautiful room furnished with, among other things, a vast double bed, the sight of which drove me to distraction. To return there and solitarily stretch myself out beneath its coverings – what could be more melancholy for a man of my age and constitution? I imagined the tousled sheets after making love. I couldn't endure the idea of my bed being empty night after night. On the other hand, going out again and picking up a girl for twenty or thirty crowns – no. I could not do it and I didn't want to. Whom was I to tell all this to? To Karin? What a strange idea . . . I recalled her oddly prim air when I mentioned sun-bathing. Perhaps she had something to hide, an infirmity of some kind. But what could that matter to me?

I was now proceeding along a quiet street with old houses on either side whose shutterless windows watched me pass in the silence of the night. They looked so attentive that they made me feel uneasy as though I were really being watched by invisible spectators attracted to the windows by the sound of my footsteps. Finally I reached a little round square lit by street lamps half-hidden by trees, and those lights among the leaves produced an effect like Chinese lanterns. I am putting down these details because in the rather obvious charm of this setting something happened that nearly changed the course of my life: I had a feeling that a trap was closing in on me. It was useless hiding from myself that I was on the point of falling in love with Karin.

Everything warned me that this was a disaster. My youth was not going to help, I knew that. Had I been able to choose, I would never have cast eyes on her. But it so happens that we fall in love for reasons too deep for our knowledge. My love had originated in that most dangerous of emotions that sometimes attains the point of passion: pity; a pity that had imperceptibly changed into love with all the heart's fierce demands. Within a single instant I found myself feeling in turn suppliant and aggressive towards that slender young person so easily outmatched by the dozens of pretty girls I passed every day. It was not that I desired her. I still didn't desire her.

Fortunately, I did not have her address. That circumstance spared me the folly of sending her a letter and gave me time to look for a solution. I returned to my room and went to bed. In the darkness I was a prey to nagging insomnia and told myself that the cause of this disorder lay in my being deprived of pleasant sexual adventures. Tomorrow I would go and see Miss Ott and have a frank talk with her. My story about private lessons was absurd and she knew it. What's more, she had told me she knew everyone in Copenhagen. Her knowing look when uttering those words was unmistakable. I had failed in both subtlety and audacity. She had been offering me her services on condition I provided the formula. She did not want to be taken for what she was. The business had to be carried out with deep hypocritical understanding. And then for reasons I could not divine she had wanted me to talk about Karin and I had refused. It was there that my mistake lay. During the night, in the frustration of my desire, I resolved to forget Karin so as not to fall into the trap of an absurd love affair. What I wanted above all was pleasure, not love. Sheer sexual pleasure . . . This slightly pompous expression told the whole story, and to my mind it excluded a mere conjunction with a dumb partner. I wanted erotic chat, and that false but charming intimacy between two human beings who a minute before had not known each other, and soon would separate perhaps for ever. What a lot of pretty girls there were in this country. The Klampenborg beach was covered with them: they laughed and grew golden in the sun with boys as carefree as they. How could I be sure that a ravishing Danish girl was not all unknowing waiting for me there or somewhere else? This thought filled me with enthusiasm in spite of everything: to be within twenty-four or forty-eight hours of meeting the girl of girls who was calling for my love but did not yet know my name, nor I hers . . . I tossed and turned in my bed thinking of these things. I was hot. It was impossible to sleep.

I leapt up and went to the little balcony jutting out in front of my window. From here I could overlook the square I mentioned just now with its thick trees lit up from within; but more immediately striking was the proximity of a church whose tower was decked with a spiral that curled up like a ribbon, and this ribbon was so light that one had the feeling it would fly away at the first puff of wind. The moon brought out the details of this peculiar monument which was not lacking in grace. In less disturbed moments I had admired the architect's fantasy, though living so near to a building of this kind caused me a certain malaise. This surely would be the moment to explain that religion gave me feelings of instinctive horror, but I will return to this point. In the transparent splendour of the night I experienced the joy of being alive in spite of my agitation – of being young and breathing in the fresh air which gently stirred the clumps of leaves at my feet. At least that could not be taken away from me. My suffering diminished. Who could tell what happiness the future was concealing?

Suddenly I felt cold and, returning to my room, threw myself on the bed. At the very moment when I was sliding into sleep, an odd phrase came into my mind – it seemed like the end-product of a piece of reasoning whose intervening stages I had skipped: 'She is everything that you will want, but she is not insignificant.'

IV

The next day I got up rather late and had no hesitation in setting straight out for the bookshop. I had to settle the business, rid myself of Karin. A good sexual adventure would make me forget all about that young girl who was really scarcely pretty. When I pushed open the shop door I must have had a very determined air, for the assistant jumped when she saw me.

'Miss Ott,' I requested.

'Miss Ott is here,' said a calm voice.

I turned round and apologized. Miss Ott was examining some books in a shadowy corner of the shop which was in any case darkened by the blinds, for it looked as if the day was going to be boiling.

'You didn't expect to see me back so soon,' I said, advancing towards her.

'Yes I did. You're exactly like your Parisian friend: impatient. Shall we go into my office?'

A minute later I was sitting in the same chair as the day before. A grey cat crossed the little garden and ensconced itself in a shady corner to wash.

'I've been thinking about you,' Miss Ott said. 'I'm going to introduce you to someone. A woman . . .'

'A woman of what age?'

'The age is of little importance in the present case. The woman is no longer young, but she knows a lot of people. She has made a name for herself in literature.'

'I'm not interested in literature,' I said coldly.

'Do you prefer being with uneducated people?'

'I adore uneducated people, as long as they're young and very charming.'

'And who don't speak a word of your language? In that case, my dear sir, there's always the street.'

She uttered these words with such contempt that I felt I was blushing up to my ears.

'Forgive me, Miss Ott, but I'm imagining the physical appearance of the people who speak French in a literary woman's salon. I abominate intellectuals.'

She leant back in her armchair and began to laugh softly.

'Poor Fru Jensen! She's never managed to draw a single intellectual under her roof, but she provides little cakes and refreshing drinks in her garden and gets a whole motley band of both sexes who torture your beautiful French language.'

'How do they manage to know French?' I asked somewhat distrustfully.

'They're students.'

'Wearing spectacles, no doubt.'

'You really are impertinent, dear sir. Sometimes I like that, at other times I like it less. Today I'm feeling fairly indulgent.'

The way she looked at me while saying that! From half-closed eyes she seemed to be observing me through the slats of a sunblind. There was a moment's silence, then she asked with a smile:

'Have you seen Elsa again?'

'Elsa? I don't know . . . Oh yes, Elsa! No.'

' "No" meaning that her name isn't Elsa. Am I not right?'

'Do you suppose I can remember the names of all the girls I run into? It seems to me she said Elsa.'

'Anyway it's of no importance to me. I'm sorry that you should put up obstacles to calling on Fru Jensen.'

'You must forgive me, but I find literary circles repugnant . . .'

She shook her head from left to right and then from right to left like a disappointed little girl.

'A pity,' she said sadly. 'It was at Fru Jensen's that your friend met Miss Luisa.'

'Oh, in that case . . .'

'Oh, in that case, no, my dear young sir. You're being thoroughly capricious. Now a capricious young man can sometimes be amusing so long as he's not wicked. But to me you seem – how shall I put it? – an absolutist. That doesn't irritate me too much either. But it's going to be difficult to help you.'

'Perhaps you don't fully realize what I want.'

'Do you take me for a fool? There's no need to go into details about certain things.'

My heart began beating with hope. In order to enter fully into this woman's good graces, I made the shameful decision to sacrifice to her curiosity my poor conquest of the other day. It would be a way of freeing myself from that budding attachment.

'Oh,' I said, striking my forehead, 'Karin.'

'What do you mean?' she asked in a calm voice.

'The girl I met near the town hall wasn't called Elsa, but Karin.'

'I know several Karins. Didn't you say she had black hair?'

'No, fair. Fair hair and black eyes.'

'Ah yes. Black eyes – it's that that puzzles me a bit. And yet . . . but it can't be possible that you met little Karin . . . Our wild little Karin. That's amusing. I know her. Everyone knows her. I'm afraid I must get back to the shop now, my dear sir, but I'll think over your problem.'

She got up with a slight effort and I followed her.

'Karin,' she said dreamily as she opened the door. 'That's amusing. In fact very amusing. But Karin isn't the girl for you.'

She said this playfully and with a little gesture of her hand as if she were saying good-bye to someone or something.

'Anyway,' I said with a collusive laugh, 'she isn't at all my type.'

How contemptible I felt! There had been no need for me to say that. It was greeted with a pearly laugh that appalled me.

'I see, or rather I half see,' said Miss Ott with nicety, without specifying what she half saw. 'Don't lose hope, dear sir.'

The three steps leading down to the shop creaked under her weight, and I walked docilely behind her heavy contours as far as the street door, where she suddenly said, as she held out her hand:

'You ought to try Cook's.'

'Cook's?'

'To see if you have any mail, for example.'

'But I'm not expecting any mail at Cook's.'

'Ah, ah! You say that so charmingly! Good-bye for the moment . . .'

V

Cook's. She was making fun of me, of course. It took me nearly a minute to understand. Then, despite the heat, I went straight to the main square, which made me think of a page where destiny wrote things with letters consisting only of the passers-by. The strokes were anything but straight and many were unfinished; moreover, they were constantly shifting, but seen from above it all perhaps took on some meaning.

The agency in question was situated in a corner of the square where the sun, like a great tongue, had lapped up all the shadows. No midnight could be so sinister as this glare. When I entered the offices I could see at a glance that Karin was not there. Of course it was not Karin I was looking for, but I was unable to drive her from my mind. I was here purposely to try to efface the memory of her by means of some liberating adventure. There was nothing silly in Miss Ott's idea: if anyone spoke French in Copenhagen it was surely here, and who could say whether one of the employees . . . with the precision and speed of a true hedonist, I sent my eyes on a circular reconnaissance in search of a pretty girl, for in this dreamland there always is one lurking in some corner. Here in Cook's – oh wonder, oh Denmark! – I spotted two, both capable of delighting the eye of the most difficult of men, very serious-looking, bending over time-tables and folders, totally concentrated on the questions of the tourists who filed by. The first . . . But what would be the point of describing the gold lavished on that head with the prodigality of a *nouveau riche*, the delicate and inquisitive nose, the blue eyes, rather vacant, rather wild, but gorgeous? The young lady's solemn talk was all very well; in her veins there flowed nonetheless the blood of her ancestors who had leapt with cries from their long black boats so as to seize for ransom some half-naked Englishman. Today – and it was the only difference after eleven centuries – the Englishman wore flannels or tweeds and came himself to hand over his money to the Dane.

I was pondering these things while waiting my turn, having selected from the two employees the one who seemed to me the more disturbing, but after a minute or two I changed my mind and my place, only to change my mind yet again and take up my original position. The second of the girls I had picked out was certainly not to be despised. Her special feature was a look in her eyes that could put you on the rack, but I shall come back to this all in good time.

I waited patiently. The people in front of me were speaking English, a fact that gave me some uneasiness, and rightly so, for when my turn came I found myself confronting a pink- and amber-complexioned face that looked at me with a grave expression and made me stammer with desire.

'*Fransk?*' asked the sensuous mouth.

I gave an energetic nod. Whereupon, with a pencil held by the tip of a hand that I would have liked to devour with kisses, she pointed out a greying male colleague with enormous spectacles. My cheeks on fire, I withdrew backwards as though in front of a royal personage, and this was indeed the case up to a point.

Needless to say I passed beyond the bespectacled gentleman and calmly took my place in a small group at the other end of the large hall. Here the second Scandinavian goddess confronted my obsessed eyes. She was unlike the first in that she was smiling – she was smiling a lot. I felt as though my heart-beats were regulated by the frequency of her smiles. Oh no, I am not exaggerating. I am saying far less than the truth. I told myself that if she sent me back to the man with spectacles, I would implore her with clasped hands in front of everyone. But I want to try to describe her calmly. Her magnificent head of hair was of two clearly distinct tones of colour: butter and bronze. Experts on the subject will know what I mean. There were even black tints in the darker parts of that resplendent mass, a rich black shot with gold.

What a wonderful smell it must have had! I madly longed to plunge my face in it and cover my chest with it; for her hair was very plentiful and every time she bent her exquisite head, or raised it, or turned it this way or that, it seemed as though lightning was flashing across this bewitching head of hair which in my mind I was raking with my fingers. Her eyes, however, of such a deep blue that they appeared almost black, held my attention still more imperiously. They were at once grave and caressing and could lead a giddy young man quite a dance, and yet I detected something intractable in the sweetness of those large, stormy pupils. Here was a woman of the kind that likes to say No. Though I immediately decided that there was nothing to be done, I nevertheless mumbled a few meaningless words as she stretched her neck forward a little so as to hear me.

'*Fransk*,' I said, in despair.

'I understand,' she said with a smile, and in French.

'Oh, so you know French!'

'Here all of us know it a bit, but it's that gentleman over there who really deals with our French customers.'

I threw a horrified glance towards the bespectacled man and continued in a slightly imploring voice:

'It's just a matter of a small piece of information. How does one get to Klampenborg?'

'There's a coach every half hour,' she said, sliding a map of the town and the surrounding country towards me. 'You catch it there, do you see?'

What I saw most of all was her hand and her pretty fingers which were as yellow as the sand on Klampenborg beach. In a hypocritical gesture I bent my forehead over the map, and it seemed to me that my black and her golden hair nearly touched. Violently sensual thoughts assailed me with painful precision. My cheeks burning with emotion, I asked in a colourless voice:

'Where can one have fun here?'

She drew herself up straight.

'Do you know Tivoli?'

As if I didn't know Tivoli!

'No,' I answered.

And I wanted to ask her why she pronounced it Tsivoli, but I did not dare.

'It's that big park marked green on the map.'

'What did you say it's called?'

'Tsivoli.'

I would have liked to hear her say it twenty times. The word on her lips became gay like the sound of a cymbal, but she must have suspected something for she smiled and added quickly:

'It's best to go there after dinner. There are all sorts of amusements. But excuse me, I must take care of this lady.'

At that point I lost my head and heard myself say:

'Perhaps you might consent to go there with me, for instance to dine?'

She looked at me without raising an eyebrow, like someone used to this kind of proposal, and said:

'Go and discuss your idea with my husband, who is over there at the exchange counter, do you see? Next to the door. And now, Madame?'

Sick at heart, I made my way out, not without throwing a glance towards the exchange counter, as if to suffer more, and there I saw a small man already bald in spite of the fresh-coloured face of a well-fed child. His air of self-satisfaction infuriated me. The cause of his satisfaction was there, only five yards away, and what a good laugh she would have this evening when telling her husband about the fruitless overtures of the French tourist!

Outside in the square I tried to pull myself together. I told myself those two girls were probably not as lovely as my sexual hunger made me imagine. My desire had haloed them with heaven knows what mythological radiance. I recalled that I had noticed that the second girl, the wife of the gentleman in charge of the exchange desk, had a flat nose and uneven teeth. I had passed over that so as to profit from the rest, but there was certainly an element of delirium in my admiration.

Little by little I calmed down. I went to get my car where I had parked it in a nearby street, and returned home to sleep, for I was utterly exhausted as if I had been through some wild orgy, but my fatigue was only in my nerves and my head. I had had enough of the stupid life I was leading in a town where the paradise of sensuality open to everyone was turning, for me, into a sort of hell. Prostitution was nothing but a deception followed by disillusionment, always the same: I remained alone.

When I got back to my room I lowered the blind, took off my clothes and threw myself on to the bed with a kind of gluttony. The idea of sleep had become an obsession with me ever since my set-back of a short while before, and within a few minutes I fell into a deep slumber.

The ring of the telephone awoke me in the full heat of the afternoon. It was Miss Ott. I got the impression that her rather too melodious voice was hunting after me in the mists of my semi-consciousness and throwing its long phrases after me like lassoes.

'I hope I'm not disturbing you,' she began, 'and darkening one of the loveliest days of our Scandinavian summer.'

'Not at all. What is it?'

'Oh, I was afraid I might be interrupting something pleasant, a conversation or some other charming thing.'

Her tone was so frivolous and unnatural that my immediate suspicion was that she had been drinking, for my friend in Paris had told me she was prone to this weakness.

'You're interrupting nothing, I promise you. I was reading the paper.'

'You shouldn't read the paper at a moment like this. It's a useless and demoralizing occupation.'

'May I ask you what you wanted to say?'

'I've been thinking about you and your current problems. There oughtn't to be any problems for you, my dear young sir – and I'm not paying you a compliment – in our town which is always very welcoming and very . . . how would you put it? Help me to find the word I want.'

'Broad-minded?'

'Broad-minded is rather cold, rather abstract. I prefer the concrete now and again, and good human warmth.'

'Excuse me, Miss Ott, but I've got to go out.'

'I see, so you want to cut things short. Well, I'm having a few friends round soon, before dinner, including one of my best customers whom I'd like you to meet.'

'Why?'

'Your questions are rather abrupt, my dear sir. I'll explain. One of the richest people in England.'

'I'm not interested in rich people, Miss Ott.'

'How finely you say that! You're a real charmer, you know. At

47

this moment I'm at home, on my sofa, fanning myself. I'm feeling well, and happy – almost happy.'

'And beside you, on a low table, there's an exquisite iced drink.'

'Not on a low table: in my other hand, the one not holding the receiver. But I can see you've got second sight. So you'll be coming presently.'

'It's not certain.'

A short silence, then her voice came again, more clearly:

'When I ask you to come I know very well what I'm doing. I promise you you won't regret it.'

There was a whole world of double-meanings in her words.

'Fine, I'll come,' I said after a moment's hesitation.

'Promise?'

'Yes, promise.'

'Grand! Anyone at Cook's?'

'No.'

'Karin?'

'I haven't seen Karin.'

'The poor dear angel, may heaven bless and protect her.'

'Should I say amen?'

'Don't make fun. In any case, she's not at all your type of person.'

'I have an idea you've said that before.'

'Really? By the way, have you got my address?'

'13 Fasanvej.'

'Right. The second floor, remember. But do you know where Fasanvej is?'

'Don't worry about that.'

I knew the street called Fasanvej because I had followed and accosted various girls there who were as delicious as they were incomprehensible. There was a slightly mephistophelian ring to her laugh at the other end of the wire, as if she had understood.

'I'll be seeing you, then.'

Her voice was solemn, as if to remind me of my promise.

VI

It was towards seven that I rang Miss Ott's bell. She opened the door herself, her face a bit too rosy, her eyes shining as if at the height of battle.

'I've a whole crowd of guests,' she told me in a voice at once anxious and triumphant. 'I'll never be able to introduce you to everyone, but everything will be all right, everything always is all right in my house. Luckily, my brother's here to help. Ib!' she called.

Her voice was louder than the murmur reaching us from the depths of the flat. There then appeared a short little man with broad shoulders who so resembled his sister that it was almost hallucinating: the same florid complexion, the same sea-green eyes, the same paunch, or so it seemed to me. His ashen blond hair framed a forehead enlarged by incipient baldness, but he retained that air of prolonged youthfulness that I had noticed in so many middle-aged Scandinavians.

'Yes, yes,' he said with a benign smile, and he extended a plump, dimpled hand.

I had no more than got to the main room when I was seized with a desire to flee, but I was immediately hemmed in by elderly people, all very friendly, breathing the odour of cocktails into my nose. I saw them as through a mist. I did not know how Miss Ott had described me, but I aroused both curiosity and abortive attempts to talk French. A woman of a certain age with moist eyes raised a half-full glass to the level of mine at the same time wishing me heaven knows what, while chubby-cheeked gentlemen gleaming with sweat stared meaningfully at me as they repeated snatches of the latest news. I realized with horror that they were offering me sympathy, and when Miss Ott passed near me I said in a cutting voice:

'This is nothing more nor less than a trap.'

She seized my hand and led me into a small room serving as cloak-room.

'No,' she said, shutting the door. 'All these people will soon go. I give you my word that only the interesting ones will stay. Mr

Gore will be here any minute now. And he, let me tell you, is a wizard on the money market. No-one has ever discovered what his total income is and he may not even know himself. So he refuses himself nothing. Anyway, you'll soon be in a position to judge for yourself. You'll see . . .'

'The spectacle of his well-being is of total indifference to me. Do you mind telling me in so many words why I am here?'

'Oh, I'd prefer to leave the surprise to you.'

'What kind of surprise? I don't like surprises.'

She drew herself up as far as she could and, throwing back her head, assumed an air of enormous dignity.

'If you don't trust my judgement,' she said coldly, 'we'd better drop the whole thing now.'

'All right. I'm sorry. Can Mr Gore speak French?'

'He far prefers speaking his own language, but here I am, expressly to act as interpreter. He does sometimes manage to say something in French, a rather struggling French with an accent . . . how can I describe it? – a clown's accent. Nearly all the English speak French with a clown's accent. You'll be good enough not to smile at Mr Gore's accent.'

'I assure you I've been properly brought up.'

'Good God, how touchy we're being, you and I! Now let's have a final word about little Karin. She's a bit . . . not unbalanced, not mad, but strange. I implore you in all seriousness . . .'

'Why are you still talking to me about someone I don't care about? What's it got to do with our English millionaire?'

She gave the theatrical laugh I was beginning to know well, and which always betrayed embarrassment.

'Nothing, dear sir. I'm saying what comes into my head. But it's my job to watch over that child and she worries me. She's quite alone in life . . .'

'Is she a relative of yours?'

She gave another of her false-sounding laughs.

'You must realize that in Copenhagen we're all more or less related. Would you mind if we went back to my guests?'

'Let me stay here a minute. It's stifling in the next room.'

'Only a minute. I'm going to let some air into the room.'

'Come back for me when your Englishman arrives.'

She disappeared without another word. A sort of gust of Danish whirled into the room in the two or three seconds that the door was open. When it closed again I looked around me. The walls of the little room were adorned with engravings, one of which, larger than the others, depicted the bombardment of Copenhagen by the British fleet in 1807. On a long sofa upholstered in dark red plush, the guests' hats seemed to reflect the frivolity of their owners. 'What luck these idiots have,' I thought; 'Germany lets them be.' Rows of books on a shelf held my attention for a minute, but they were all in either Danish or English. Then suddenly I was seized by a nameless despair. I felt like an animal with a paw in the jaws of a trap. To leave the house and get back into the street would not have helped. There was death all around me. The trap was life. At the centre of life lay that pitiless mechanism that nothing could falsify. Death was inevitable. War was going to break out at any moment. In the sort of panic that possessed me I looked wildly for some refuge. Neither drink nor drugs had ever been able to dominate my mind. In my case, fear could be wiped out only by eroticism, but satiation soon came and fear was born again in the loneliness that followed, for once the intoxication was over I was alone even if the woman was still beside me. I believe that had there been a window in the room where I was, I would have thrown myself out into the void in spite of the horror that kind of death filled me with. Something was beating in my breast, not my heart but something in the middle of my thorax, and deep in my ears I noted that faint whistling sound I knew so well, the whistling of fear. I closed my eyes and leant against the wall. 'It will pass,' I said to myself; 'it's just an attack.'

Suddenly the door opened and I saw Miss Ott approaching me as in a dream, her glass in her hand. I held myself in so as not to cry out.

'What's the matter?' she asked. 'You're white.'

An absurd desire to embrace her took hold of me. In some incomprehensible way that heavy creature restored everything to its place. The jaws of the trap relaxed their grip.

'Nothing's the matter. I'm a little tired, that's all.'

'It's the weather. I'll give you a cocktail that would raise the dead. Oh, do you hear?'

And indeed the bell was ringing. She went out, leaving the door open, and I returned to the main room. I now experienced a base and shameful satisfaction at finding myself back with those people who were laughing and chattering in their guttural language. Even their banality had something reassuring about it, and I began smiling at them for no reason. A strong drink was offered me and I immediately accepted it. I was feeling relieved as if some unexpected good news were circulating in the world, when suddenly Miss Ott reappeared and made me a mysterious sign.

'He's here,' she said.

Her hand seized mine with authority and we pushed our way into the adjoining room, which was a dining room. An oak table took up almost its whole length, and countless half-empty plates of hors d'oeuvres testified to the guests' greediness. That was the first thing I saw, and then at the far end a window opening on to a garden where birches were shimmering in the setting sun; but Miss Ott steered me towards a rather dark corner and I suddenly found myself facing a little man who produced in me a violent reaction. Hatred, like love, has its lightning conquests. Ours, at any rate, was immediate and mutual. I scrutinized the physical appearance of this individual just as attentively as he scrutinized mine, and I noticed that his features were all close together as if there were a shortage of space in his face, enlarged by fat though it was. His eyes, nose and mouth were all small and as if brought together by avarice and ill will. We examined each other without a word while Miss Ott produced platitudes, then he articulated a phrase which translated exactly what I myself was thinking:

'We've already met somewhere.'

I thought so too, but by an imperceptible shake of the head I said No. He looked at me with contempt and incredulity and said a few words to Miss Ott which I could not catch. In spite of the revulsion he inspired in me, I had to admit that there was a keenness of intelligence in his expression that fascinated me. There could be no doubt that I was confronting someone of considerable weight even if his general aspect was as commonplace as that of a travelling salesman. Short, stout, wearing a navy blue alpaca suit, he remained motionless and seemed to be waiting for something from me, either a word or a gesture. He got nothing of the kind and an awkwardness immediately set in, for Miss Ott was as if petrified by awe and had no idea what to say. Finally she pulled herself together:

'What can I offer you to drink?'

'Nothing, Ott,' he answered curtly.

He called her Ott . . . She rubbed her hands together like a shop assistant facing a customer. Once again they exchanged a few words in English and I made as though to go, but Miss Ott detained me:

'Mr Gore would like to have a word with you, dear sir.'

With an imploring look she added: 'I beg of you,' and went off towards the main room, leaving me to a tête-à-tête with the financial wizard.

'I suppose you're here for pleasure,' he said.

His accent really was that of a clown, but I felt no desire to smile at it. The question was so abrupt that it became interesting.

'Partly,' I said. 'But I'm hard to please and find this town disappointing.'

'Ott tells me that you don't know Danish. Nor do I, but it isn't a serious obstacle. You're young, you don't know how to go about things.'

'If what you call knowing how to go about things only comes with age, I'd better tell you that it disgusts me. Lecherous old men fill me with horror.'

'We all say that when we're young. And suddenly along comes old age together with lust. Then you learn how to go about things.'

'I hope I'll be dead before that happens.'

He broke into laughter which caused the corners of his mouth to part and disclose a row of suspiciously white teeth. Without another word I turned on my heel, thoroughly determined, this time, to leave that sinister apartment. With some difficulty I pushed my way through the groups of guests and reached the passage leading to the front door. As I was passing the little room which served as a cloak-room I noticed that the door was ajar, and an impulse of instinctive curiosity made me risk a cautious glance inside because I thought I heard Miss Ott's voice talking to someone. I could not go in on the pretext of getting my hat – I didn't wear one in the summer – and moreover I was afraid Miss Ott would try to keep me. However, I pushed the door and stood, astonished, on the threshold. For right at the end of the room, her face turned to a little oval mirror fixed to the wall, a young woman was arranging her hair with slow, careful movements that looked like those of a statue, and it was of a statue that she did indeed remind one, as much by the beauty of her body as by the dignity of her bearing. On noticing my presence she lowered her arms and turned her eyes towards me, and I could see an angel's face against the light, the sort of face so frequently to be found in women of the Nordic races. But hers seemed to me to have a rarer quality. Her golden mass of hair, her pink and tanned complexion, her huge blue eyes – these certainly were attributes of Scandinavian beauty, but in the features of the girl who was looking at me there was something more: an almost intimidating gravity and – if one can still use a word that has become absurd through the abuses of it – a purity that could be compared to the innocence of a very young child.

Miss Ott gave a start when she saw me.

'Oh,' she said, 'don't tell me you're going.'

'No,' I murmured with a smile. 'I'm not going.'

'Ilse,' said Miss Ott in French, 'let me introduce a young gentleman who comes from France and likes our country very much. But how stupid of me! I'm speaking French to Ilse, who doesn't know your language.'

She said a few words in Danish to the girl, who gave me a slight nod. I advanced awkwardly, hoping that she would offer me her hand, but nothing of the kind happened. My heart began beating violently. 'What a nightmare,' I thought, 'I'm falling in love. This girl has everything in the world that I want, no one else matters now.'

Miss Ott drew herself up to her full height.

'Ilse,' she said in a motherly tone, 'is the daughter of one of my best school friends. Though she speaks nothing but Danish I wager you find her pleasing to look at. You'd do wrong to deprive yourself of the pleasure. But here comes Mr Gore.'

The Englishman had indeed entered without making a sound, and I had the unpleasant surprise of finding him suddenly beside me. His thin, dry, imperious voice broke in:

'Ott!'

She looked at him, bent very slightly forward and to my amazement left the room.

'Wait a minute,' said Mr Gore to me, closing the door. 'This is a better place for us to talk.'

With a sweep of his arm he let loose a cascade of hats, then installed himself on the sofa leaving Ilse and me standing.

'Do you like her?' he asked.

'She's charming.'

'That pleases her; "charming" is one of the only French words she understands. She's a good girl, but demanding, I mean sensual.'

In a flash I realized that I had before my eyes what Miss Ott had told me about: Mr Gore's happiness, and despite myself I made a gesture of horror. The angel, purity, innocence . . . I felt deeply ridiculous, but also, alas, ravaged by desire.

'You know,' said Mr Gore as he leant back and crossed his legs, 'we were talking just now about knowing how to do things. I myself always have the best because I give much more than anyone else.'

The effect of these words on me was sudden and violent. I must have turned pale. I was so stunned by rage that I found myself out in the passage almost without knowing how I got there, then on the staircase and finally in the street, where I began walking for all I was worth. I had forgotten about my car.

On reaching a quiet, spacious square where old people were taking the air, I sat down on a bench to try to pull myself together. My throat was dry with anger, less because of Mr Gore's grossness than because of his abuse of power, but truth obliges me to admit that I basely envied him the magnificent creature whom he had apparently made his slave. I have no idea what the people passing by thought of me when they saw me hiding my burning face in my hands.

'Ilse!' I said aloud.

What would I not have given to throw myself at her feet and adore her as an idol! I was suffering too much. That hour seemed to me the most difficult one to live through since my arrival in Denmark, and staring at the shadows of the lime trees on the ground I asked myself what I intended to do. There was no question of returning to France before the force of events made it necessary. But it seemed to me equally impossible to stay in this town. Among all the girls who had been offered to me – and I had

had plenty – not one of them seemed comparable to those I had not yet possessed, and probably never would. I would leave Denmark full of resentment and unsatisfied desires.

My car was quite near. I went to get it and found nothing better to do than go back to my room. It was still very early, but my plan was to sleep, just as a drunkard plans a spree. I was already half stripped when I changed my mind. It was too stupid to play a losing game in a town where everyone was winning. Slipping on my shirt with an absurd but instinctive gesture of modesty, I rang up Miss Ott.

'Oh, it's you, dear sir' – the voice sounded a bit distant. 'You left terribly early. You fled . . .'

'Yes; I do hope you'll forgive me, I didn't feel very well, probably the heat. Would you allow me to call on you now?'

'Certainly, if you like. I'm not dining tonight. Nearly all my guests have gone. We can talk alone. There'll just be my brother, but Ib doesn't get in the way.'

'Is Miss Ilse still there?'

A huge silvery laugh forced me to hold the receiver away from my ear.

'Is it Miss Ilse you wanted to see, then? She's gone already, with Mr Gore.'

'With Mr Gore?'

'That shouldn't surprise you. She never leaves him.'

I did my best to stifle a gasp of irritation and said calmly:

'If you'd really like it I'll be round in a few minutes.'

'I doubt if I shall be able to take Miss Ilse's place,' she said with a pert inflection.

An idiotic compliment came to my lips, but that woman had something about her that made me lose my patience, so I hung up without answering.

A quarter of an hour later I rang Miss Ott's bell and once again it was she who opened the door.

The flat smelt of tobacco, strong drink, and that indefinable odour that human beings leave behind them. In the dining room Ib was removing the plates from the long table and when he saw me greeted me with a broad smile.

'Ib doesn't live in Copenhagen,' Miss Ott said, 'but he pays me short visits from time to time. He's a simple soul, a sort of angel disguised as a civil servant.'

She went on talking while leading me into the main room and I had the impression I was seeing it for the first time, now that it was empty and no longer hidden by guests. Its general effect was of a red plush grotto, with its huge padded sofa and plump armchairs, all of the same dull but violent colour. On the top of an upright piano I noticed a winter landscape in a black frame; on a low table there was a large lamp crowned with a lampshade that diffused a light favouring intimacy. Doubtless the rather homely aspect within these walls could deceive an unsuspecting visitor, but I had what is called a twisted mind and saw sensuality everywhere. In addition I sensed something drearily lustful in the choice and arrangement of these downy pieces of furniture. I conjured up Miss Ott's secret love affairs.

'Sit down,' she said with a smile. 'No, there,' and she indicated a place on the sofa on which she had just sat down herself. 'Mr Gore was sorry about you leaving so early. He would have liked to have a longer talk with you. Mr Gore adores French people.'

'Will you let me tell you what I honestly think?'

'I won't just let you, I demand it!'

'Mr Gore is a swine.'

'All men are swine,' she said thoughtfully. 'Any difference between them can be seen only in the refinements of their tastes. Mr Gore is very exacting. Ilse is very attached to Mr Gore.'

'I suppose she's for sale.'

'Oh! Really!'

'Forgive me. Mr Gore gave me to understand . . .'

'Ilse earns an honest living; she's a model at one of our best dressmakers.'

'I find it monstrous that she should give herself to Mr Gore.'

'He has an irresistible charm for certain women. Besides, you should try to understand Mr Gore. Ilse is essential to his equilibrium.'

'His equilibrium?'

'Yes. His moral tranquillity, if you like. Ilse's presence liberates him, gives him peace. And I can assure you he needs peace. He has enormous worries. That immense fortune . . .'

'Precisely. Ilse must benefit substantially from that.'

'I find you very severe.'

'Severe! Not at all. I understand. I understand everything.'

Instinctively I turned my head towards the dining room and saw Miss Ott's brother at the far end of the long table busily finishing up what remained of the hors d'oeuvres.

'Don't worry,' said Miss Ott, who had followed my glance. 'Ib can't possibly understand a word we're talking about. The only French he knows is *"oui, oui."* '

'Ilse receives presents,' I said in a slightly strangled voice.

'Well, why shouldn't she?'

I felt slightly dizzy. I made a rapid calculation in my head.

'So she'll agree to my giving her one.'

Once again Miss Ott's crystal laugh served as a commentary on my words.

'She'll be appreciative, even touched.'

I felt I was on the point of saying what I shouldn't say. I was warned of the danger by an inner conviction which at the same time showed me that saying it was inevitable. It was a phrase I ought not to pronounce. It formed itself on my lips as if of its own momentum.

'I'm in love with Ilse.'

'Nonsense!'

'Did you understand what I said? I want to see Ilse. When may I see her?'

'I haven't the faintest idea, my dear young man. She gives all her free time to Mr Gore.'

'At that rate,' I said, getting up, 'I'll never see her. Is that what you mean?'

'There are other charming girls in Copenhagen.'

'Ilse is the only one who interests me.'

I thought I saw a gleam of triumph in her eyes and I suddenly thought of Karin. How little she mattered to me at that moment! But in spite of that I had a feeling that I was betraying her, and on a sudden inspiration I started thinking out loud, so as to see . . .

'I ought to have kept to little Karin. I'll try to find her again.'

Had my aim been more accurate than I had thought? Miss Ott lowered her head and seemed to be thinking.

'Poor Karin would only disappoint you. She runs away from life, she's afraid of men, afraid of everything. In addition she has moral difficulties.'

'But she speaks French.'

She shrugged her shoulders.

'You don't imagine that Ilse speaks French, do you?'

'Why did you let me see her if she's impossible?'

'Impossible I didn't say.'

I had no need of her syntax going off the rails to grasp that Miss Ott was upset. Drops of sweat shone on her forehead, which had become all pink. As for me, I felt I was blushing.

'Well, Miss Ott, if you think . . .'

She did not answer. Her large bosom moved up and down so obviously that I was unable to take my eyes from it. In the silence that followed I could hear the noise Ib was making with his fork.

'I would have done better never to have seen her,' I suddenly exclaimed with theatrical violence. 'I would have done better to have kept to little Karin.'

'Oh no.'

'Karin's free. She's not the slave of an elderly English multi-millionaire.'

'The word "slave" is very exaggerated,' she murmured.

'So couldn't you arrange . . . or facilitate a meeting?'

'I don't know. I've never done anything of that kind. What do you take me for?'

Her bourgeois spirit was fighting at the last barricades. I tried to help her make an honourable surrender.

'Be human, Miss Ott. I feel the greatest respect for you and I take you for what you are, someone with a noble nature.'

She drew herself up.

'No one really understands me,' she said with a sigh.

'But I understand you. I understand you and respect you. Can't you, for your part, make an effort to imagine what's going on inside me? I'm young, I've strong feelings. An hour ago I wasn't thinking about Ilse.'

'I know,' she said gravely. 'I was once your age.' And she added almost in a whisper, 'And I'm still capable of violent passions.'

'Be kind. Do something.'

'Unfortunately, I can't do anything. Mr Gore clings to Ilse like a tiger to its prey.'

I stood up.

'In that case,' I said coolly, 'the only thing for me to do is to give up that inaccessible girl and look for compensation elsewhere. I know perfectly well where to find it, and there at least I won't be made to suffer. Karin, too, has her charms.'

It was my last card and I threw it down not without a certain fluttering of the heart, even leaving the room to give greater eloquence to my words, and setting off down the passage towards the front door. It was Miss Ott's turn to get up and follow me. Was she angry or frightened? At any rate she was panting.

'As you really insist,' she said, 'I'll make a phone call.'

'Whom will you phone?' I asked.

She took on the air of a martyr and made no reply. We parted without a word.

VII

I had a feeling of having won the match. At the same time I suspected my rough words had shocked Miss Ott, and I thought of sending her two dozen red roses to appease the pricking of my conscience.

That evening I dined at Tivoli, in a café-restaurant brilliant with lights and buzzing with the harsh yet mellow Danish language. It was inconceivable to me how the human throat could produce sounds that seemed to me inimitable and make them pass for words. In vain did I stretch my ears in an effort to recognize a single familiar syllable, and all I heard was a noise like a rasping and continual swallowing. This imprisonment within a fortress of words finally became a torture. I found similar difficulties with the written language: I discovered I had ordered a dessert instead of a meat dish. At hotels the waiter translated. But not at Tivoli.

I almost regretted not having invited Miss Ott to dinner. It would have been a consolation to be understood by at least one person, however irritating she was in other respects. Irritating and mysterious. It was all very well recalling what I had been told about her disinterestedness: 'She's not a procuress . . .' It seemed to me obvious that she was, up to a point.

I tried to forget the bewitching girls at Cook's, especially the second, the one who knew French. Similarly, I tried to banish Ilse's face and figure from my memory, and when I say figure I am making a laudable attempt to keep within the bounds of decency. As for Karin, I wanted above all not to think of her. For what was she, poor Karin, compared with those goddesses? But deep down I thought of her in spite of myself, and that frightened me. The trap had snapped to, and thoroughly so. I felt pity for Karin. Everything had started with that. We ought not to feel pity unreflectingly.

'No, no, no,' I said aloud.

My neighbours – a fat man and his wife – looked at me. I blushed and signed to the waiter that I wanted to pay.

Once more in the milling crowd, I let myself be guided by it in the hope that it would lead me to some real, good piece of unexpected luck; moreover, I had the impression that my personality was diluted by numbers and that my suffering became diffused, as if it ceased to belong to me alone. I passed (but did not go in) a Chinese pavilion streaming with electric lights and filled with the blare of an invisible orchestra. I could not for the life of me imagine where I was in that park, when suddenly I recognized the shooting-range where passers-by tried their skill with the guns. It was the place where I had seen the Polish sailors with their long ribbons and also the Danish officer. The sailors were not there this time, nor was the interesting officer, but a few yards away I noticed a young girl whom I looked at for several moments before recognizing her. It was Karin. I had lived for hours with the memory of her, increasing her beauty in my mind perhaps, and now that she was in front of me she looked like someone whose name one can't even remember.

She was standing quite still, with that long-suffering yet vexed look of people who are waiting in vain. The strange thought suddenly crossed my mind that there had been some sort of interruption in the development of her intelligence. I don't quite know what this was based on – perhaps her little-girl's stance, perhaps her face that had remained too innocent – but I felt towards her the impulse that I feared so much. There was no question of

61

desire, but of tenderness. Slowly, as if she had guessed something, she turned her eyes in my direction and recognized me. Her mouth sketched a smile, but almost at once she pulled herself together and regarded me with a gravity full of reproaches.

After a moment's hesitation I went and stood beside her and said Good evening. She did not answer, nor did she move. If she had not had that child-like profile that so moved me in spite of myself, I would have gone off and my life would have changed; but this was a moment of destiny.

'You're displeased with me,' I said into her pretty little ear that pretended not to hear. 'I'm sorry I upset you that time but I can't regret what I did.'

She turned her head slightly towards a marksman who was shouldering a gun, and waited for the detonation which gave her a tiny start. Laughter broke out. The shot had gone wide.

'Aren't you talking to me any more?' I asked Karin. 'Are you still cross with me?'

That remark seemed to have gone home, for she hesitated a moment or two and then, with a kind of violence, directed her eyes towards me.

'No,' she said, 'not too cross . . .'

I took her hand in the shadow and squeezed it furtively.

'Let's get away from here, Karin.'

To my great surprise she followed me without raising any objection and we left the garden. When we were in the avenue I asked her if she wanted to dine, but she was not hungry.

Then I asked: 'Would you like to go down to the beach in the car?'

Her only answer was one of those smiles of whose power she was probably ignorant. I slid my arm under hers and we crossed the avenue. A moment later we were driving towards the outskirts of the town. After a torrid day the evening was becoming deliciously fresh, and when I saw the stars in the sky I felt happy. I would have liked to hold Karin's hand. Her silence inhibited me a little. Better wait. The trite remarks I started making about the summer evening produced no reaction.

By now the sea breeze was blowing on our faces and at the end of the road I saw the big seaside hotel with its long lit-up verandahs and its small orchestra pouring vain notes into the huge twilight. That ineffectual music followed us for a moment and then we stopped.

'Shall we go on with our drive, Karin?'

'No. I want to walk in the wood, but first along the beach for a bit.'

There were other people walking on the road bordering the beach. We took a few steps over the sand towards the sea in order to avoid them – the sea all milky under a pale sky. The smooth lapping of the water extended endlessly into the silence.

'The night's slow in coming,' I said, picking up a pebble.

'It won't come. It'll be like this till dawn.'

In this strange light that seemed to have originated in another world, I looked at Karin's face. Its various planes bore witness to an energy that I had not suspected until then, and I felt that she was observing me. Suddenly she bent down and picked up a fistful of sand in her hand. The grains streamed down between her fingers.

'I like this sand,' she said. 'It seems somehow to retain the imprint of all the bodies that have pressed down on it. Is that the way you put it?'

'If you like.'

'I can somehow imagine it, so golden that even when the sky is covered over you have the feeling that the sun is shining on all that flesh, sometimes so lovely.'

Various questions came into my mind that I refrained from asking. In Karin's tone there was a sort of exaltation in sharp contrast with her recent silence. I felt that she would speak of her own accord and that any questions of mine might make her fall back into her state of dumbness.

'As for me,' she went on, 'I'm tanned from head to foot, but I do my sun-bathing on the little balcony of my room. I cover myself with cream. For me summer consists of the scent of that cream and of one's skin being all warm, you know, a scent of fruit.'

The thought crossed my mind that she wanted to boast of her physical beauty, but I did not know her. She laughed softly and for the first time took my arm.

'I like the night,' she said. 'How about you?'

'I don't always like it, but I like this one.'

By now we were walking along the edge of the sea and, my confidence restored, I suddenly yielded to the desire to know something that had been puzzling me for two days:

'Why did you leave me the day before yesterday? Why did you run away from me?'

'I haven't the faintest idea,' she said in an astonished voice.

'You haven't the faintest idea?'

'No. And what a funny question! A typical question from a Frenchman who wants to know everything.'

'Were you frightened of me?'

She burst out laughing.

'Frightened of you! You really are extraordinary. Do you really suppose that people know why they do what they do or say what they say? Now it's my turn to be inquisitive: why are you so crazy about blue eyes?'

'I find them decorative.'

'You're evading my question. There's something else. You love blue eyes.'

'Did I say that?'

'I've a very clear impression that you love blue eyes.'

'I also love black eyes.'

'What a coward you are! You daren't say that you prefer blue eyes. And what do you see in blue eyes? They're vacant. To me they seem like holes through which you can see the sky.'

'Even that wouldn't be too bad.'

'Holes through which you can see an empty sky. But the sky isn't empty.'

'What do you think there is in the sky except emptiness?'

'I don't like your saying that.'

'In any case, dear Karin, you have black eyes.'

'Yes, black,' she said defiantly. 'I've got black eyes like my mother, who was Bavarian.'

'So it was your father who poured all that gold on your head to turn you into a true Scandinavian.'

'I don't know if that was enough. But blue eyes don't express anything, you know, neither love, nor hate, nor joy, nor anything at all.'

'Do you like compliments?'

'No.'

'Pull yourself together, Karin, and answer me: do you like compliments?'

'Yes.'

'There's nothing more beautiful in the world than black eyes and fair hair.'

'In your country so many men have black hair that it must be as commonplace as our eternal fair hair which you mistake for gold.'

'Anyway, I always enjoy hearing you laugh, Karin. You laugh like a happy girl.'

'I'm not happy, but let's not talk about that. Shall we go to the wood now?'

My hand brushed hers which she drew gently away and we walked in silence towards the huge dark mass which rose up like a fortress on the skyline. I had the impression that it was coming towards us in that light from another world.

Beneath the first trees Karin said to me calmly:

'I lied to you the other evening when I said my parents were killed in a motor accident. My mother's still alive, if you can call it that. My father threw himself into the water in the harbour two years ago. If you can't see clearly enough to walk, we can take the main path, but then we won't be alone.'

'My eyes are getting used to the dark.'

'Now and again you can see the glow from a cigarette. Don't pay any attention. They are people in search of any kind of adventure. The cigarette is there to say: "Do you want to?"'

'I know.'

'You shouldn't know.'

This was said in a half-severe, half-mocking tone which let me off answering. I confined myself to murmuring:

'But what about you, Karin?'

'Oh, I don't smoke,' she answered vivaciously.

The tree-trunks all around us suddenly emerged like huge people from the half-darkness. The earth at our feet was dead white.

'Do you often come out here?' I asked.

'Often, yes.'

'With friends?'

'Sometimes, but usually alone.'

'Aren't you at all afraid?'

'Nothing's happened to me so far. In any case, I'm not the kind of girl to whom things happen. Sometimes that makes me sad. But in fact this wood isn't dangerous.'

'Let's say it's no more than adventurous.'

'That's it. The adventurous wood, as in the stories of chivalry.'

I took her hand and this time she did not remove it.

'Now that you're holding my hand, what are you going to do with it?' she asked in a slightly ironical tone.

'I'm thanking the wood for my lovely adventure.'

'Do you mean I'm your adventure? Don't call it lovely too soon. It might well disappoint you.'

'Oh, Karin, I don't believe it. You're a mysterious person, but I understand you and enjoy being with you.'

'You didn't talk to me like that the other day.'

'It's that I've been thinking about you ever since.'

'You enjoy being with me, but what tells you that I enjoy being with you?'

'We're together in this wood and you're not taking your hand out of mine.'

'I'm taking it out!'

But I held it so tightly that she had to leave it where it was.

'I yield to superior strength,' she murmured softly.

'I wouldn't abuse it for anything in the world.'

'Do you think I don't know that?'

She said these words in such a sad voice that I was perplexed, and my hand relaxed its hold. After a moment I asked:

'Doesn't it seem odd to you that we met again this evening at Tivoli in the same place as the day before yesterday?'

'No. I'd still be there if you hadn't come. Anyway, nothing seems odd to me, you know.'

'Were you waiting for someone at Tivoli?'

'Yes . . . No. It's none of your business.'

'Karin, I know whom you were hoping to see.'

'You know nothing at all about it.'

'He hasn't come back. I haven't seen him again either in the gardens or in the town.'

'Whom are you talking about?'

'Why do you ask me? Karin, you're suffering.'

66

She took her hand from mine.

'I hate your romantic vocabulary,' she said, 'but this time you've hit the mark. Let's say I regret that I can't just disappear.'

'Disappear?'

'Yes. Tonight I regret having been put into the world, because I'm not like other people. Other people are happy, but not I. If it were possible to die without suffering, I wonder how many minutes I'd waver . . .'

'Karin, you must be mad!'

'You've no right to say that,' she said sharply. 'You're using words without knowing what they mean. I can assure you I've all my wits about me and I forbid you to doubt it.'

Seeing her thus stirred, I tried to calm her by taking her arm and she let me do as I wanted as if some sort of resistance in her were breaking.

'Talk to me or don't talk to me,' I said gently. 'It's enough for me just to be with you.'

A few moments of silence followed, occasionally disturbed by the crackling of dead twigs under our feet.

'I shouldn't have agreed to this walk in the wood,' she said in a more controlled voice. 'There are too many things I can't explain.'

'I won't ask you anything.'

'Just now you annoyed me because you came too near to the truth.'

'I didn't mean to be tactless.'

'But you're tactlessness itself,' and she gave a little laugh, only to go on at once in an almost cajoling tone: 'Since you know whom I hoped to see, describe him to me. Tell me what he was like.'

'But you saw him just as well as I did.'

'You don't understand. I want to see him again through your eyes. Then I'll have the feeling that he's appearing to me in the darkness.'

This last remark, put forward in an imploring voice, opened a sort of abyss in front of it. For it presupposed familiarity with a whole hallucinatory world and seemed to go far beyond my companion's age. It had not been said by someone altogether innocent.

'What are you waiting for?' she whispered.

'I admit that the young officer didn't seem to me so outstanding as he seemed to you. Besides, I hadn't the same reasons to admire him. But a little earlier, while strolling around in the park, I'd seen a boy and girl doing acrobatics. They'd taken off their clothes on a parallel bar about eight to ten yards from the ground. Both were exceptionally beautiful. The boy . . .'

'I know, I saw him. I didn't find him interesting. He was merely beautiful, whereas that officer . . . But you go on, please . . .'

'In order to see him through your eyes I'd have to cease to be myself. I found him a little bit stiff. Well built, certainly, well set up – a little too well, so it seemed to me.'

'What about his face?'

'Pleasant, but for that insolent look . . .'

Without a word Karin drew closer to me so as lightly to rest her head on my shoulder, and I had a feeling she was shivering as if with cold. Suddenly her hand clutched my arm with all the energy she was capable of.

'That was the man I wanted to love,' she said in a voice I had never heard before. 'Sometimes, when I think about him, I imagine that he's suffocating me, that he's killing me.'

Suddenly she began speaking Danish and I had a hard time recognizing the girl who, in French, expressed herself falteringly, sometimes like a child. Her native language, which I usually found so coarse, lost all harshness on her lips. Her phrases followed one another slowly, monotonously, as if she were reciting a text learnt by heart. For two or three minutes I listened to this mysterious discourse, then suddenly she seized my head between her hands and clumsily pressed her mouth on mine. A word immediately came to my mind: 'Virgin.' I wanted to hold her to me, but she disentangled herself.

'No,' she said, 'let's go back, I want to go back. Leave me alone . . . please.'

'You see, Karin, how I obey you. Are you still cross with me?'

'No, I'm not cross, but I want to get away from here.'

'We'll go and find the car.'

She touched my hand in a gesture of affection and we set out in the direction of the main avenue.

'You must find me odd,' she said. 'I hope we'll remain friends in spite of everything.'

'What were you saying just now?'

She seemed amazed.

'What was I saying?'

'Yes, Karin. After all, you were speaking Danish for several minutes.'

'Not too loud, I hope. I do occasionally talk like that when I'm preoccupied. But you'll never know what I said. Nor will anyone . . . Was there anyone near us?'

'No. Just tell me whom you were talking to.'

'Not to you, anyway. But don't take it to heart. And besides, I can't remember a word of what I said.'

'Karin, you're lying.'

'I do lie sometimes, but not tonight. Truly, I can't remember.'

'It seemed to me that you were reciting a poem.'

She gave a short laugh like a tiny cry.

'A poem? Oh no. But perhaps yes. A poem of hunger and solitude.'

We were in the central road from which we could see the long avenue leading back to the town. I looked at her. Her face was emerging from the shadows and I admired the avalanche of golden hair around that flawless skin and features so delicate that they might have been chiselled in metal. She noticed that I was observing her and fixed on me eyes that were larger and darker than in daylight.

'You wanted to know what I was saying just now. I can't remember everything. But there are phrases that I can recall. If I repeated them to you, you might never speak to me again.'

'That would surprise me. I'm not so easily shocked. Name any thought that's crossed the mind of a man – I've had it. When you get down to it, what man isn't obsessed?'

'What about women?'

'Women are different. Your obsessions aren't the same as ours.'

She laughed.

'If the other man had known what I was saying, he would have hit me to shut me up.'

I took her in my arms and covered her face with kisses, but she turned her face to left and right and struggled with such force that I gave up. We were both out of breath.

'I wonder why you see me, considering you don't love me,' I said all in one breath.

'Oh, you don't understand anything.'

In the car she did not open her mouth. I saw or thought I saw tears glistening on her cheeks. Back in town she told me to stop at the corner of a boulevard and a side street, then she touched my hand and threw a final word:

'Don't try to find out where I live.'

VIII

Next morning, after a very bad night, I was dragged from sleep by an imperious telephone call from Miss Ott. 'Come and see me before midday,' she said. 'I've something to tell you that should make you jump for joy.'

'Oh,' I said. 'What's it about?'

She hung up without answering. While I was in my bath my imagination had free rein, although my heart was a bit heavy because of Karin, but I lost no time and half past eleven was striking when I crossed the threshold of the shop.

Miss Ott conducted me to her office and closed the door. A cat was grooming its whiskers in the sun in a corner of the courtyard.

'It's about Mr Gore,' said the bookseller when she and I were alone.

I could not repress a gesture of irritation.

'I dislike that man intensely, as I think you know.'

'I do. Perhaps you don't understand him very well, for I assure you he has some rare qualities.'

'The main one being that he's rich.'

She looked at me solemnly.

'Will you kindly take back what you've just said?' she asked.

'I take it back, Miss Ott. Forgive me. I had a bad night.'

'Very well. I've been talking to Mr Gore about your feelings regarding Miss Ilse.'

'My feelings, that's saying a lot. My admiration . . .'

'As you like. Mr Gore consents to your inviting that young lady to dinner. She will accept. Do you know the Wivex restaurant? You do? Reserve a table for eight o'clock this evening. Does that suit you?'

'How can you expect me to say no?'

Miss Ott raised her eyebrows to indicate that in fact one did not say no to dining with Ilse.

'Mr Gore,' she added, 'expects that later on, either tomorrow or some other day, you'll pay him a short visit of thanks.'

'No. To begin with, he doesn't like me.'

'What do you know about it? You interest him.'

'You must understand that it'll be unpleasant enough as it is to drink out of his glass. It will diminish my pleasure.'

'Sometimes your expressions are very shocking. What you say is not my business. However, let me tell you that – to use your way of putting it – one always drinks out of someone's glass.'

I thought of Karin.

'Not always – even here.'

She immediately guessed what I had in mind, for she blushed.

'It will be altogether to your advantage to cultivate Miss Ilse. She knows how to be charming.'

'I want her to be more than that.'

'Really, sir, I don't know whether I can go on listening to you. Your only excuse is your youth. Ilse will be charming and more than charming, as you put it, if you promise to pay this purely courtesy visit to Mr Gore.'

'A moment ago you said it was a visit of thanks.'

'Yes, of thanks.'

'This bargain makes me sick. I'll have to think it over.'

'It isn't a bargain at all. And in any case you have the whole afternoon to think it over.'

A revolting idea crossed my mind.

'I hope your Mr Gore hasn't got some ulterior motive in wanting me to go and see him.'

She turned a baby face towards me.

'An ulterior motive? Here I cease to follow you.'

It was my turn to blush to the roots of my hair.

'Very well,' I said. 'Let's leave it at that. I'll think about it. Give me until five.'

'I'll give you until six,' she said in a regal tone.

Never had she seemed more mysterious to me than at this moment. I had the sudden impression that I was confronting someone whose motives were unfathomable. I really wanted to believe my Paris friend when he wrote that she wasn't a procuress and was disinterested, whatever her admiration for financial success . . . I suspected her of facilitating things with Ilse so as to deflect me from Karin. And as so often happened with her, she seemed to read my thoughts.

'As for the other one, dear sir, I'd like to confide a little secret.'

'What other one?'

'Oh, little Karin. She's to be left alone, do you understand? But I see that you don't understand. No one would seriously think of going after her. She doesn't want it. She doesn't want it for reasons that are entirely honourable. It would take too long to explain, and would be embarrassing . . . Karin isn't an Ilse. Karin would only be charming, never anything more. I'd like you to promise me that you won't see her.'

'But, Miss Ott, I don't even know where she lives.'

She appeared relieved.

'Sooner or later she'd say no to you, and you'd suffer.'

This sort of prediction was so near the mark that I was dumbfounded. Everything in Karin's behaviour was explained – or almost everything.

'Why doesn't she want it?'

'The Karin who doesn't want it is the stronger one.'

'You mean there's also a Karin who does want it?'

'How can we know? She's frightened. She's had misfortunes and one doesn't touch Karin. Besides, between ourselves, she isn't all that pretty. In our eyes, at any rate, she's looked on as rather commonplace. Nobody has ever known her to be involved in a relationship.'

'She's only eighteen.'

Miss Ott sketched a smile.

'At eighteen, with the ideas now in vogue, it's rare for someone not to have at least – tried. In our country permissiveness is total.'

'But Karin is to be seen at Tivoli. She looks around.'

'That's the Karin who isn't known, but the Karin who doesn't want it always has the last word.'

'How does she know French so well?'

'Her father taught it to her. He was a linguist like all waiters.'

I took the blow without flinching. I had imagined other things for Karin's father.

'Is her father dead?'

'Committed suicide two years ago.'

Karin had not lied. This gave me a slight feeling of pleasure.

'What about her mother?'

'Does that interest you? But it's more complicated. I'll have to tell you that some other time.'

'One last question. Has Karin a job?'

'You're thinking too much about Karin. She works for a big shop, as you insist on knowing, but you promise me not to try to see her?'

'I promise nothing.'

'In that case,' she said, reaching for the telephone, 'I'm cancelling the meeting with Ilse.'

'Miss Ott, I was joking. How do you imagine I could find someone again when I haven't her address?'

'What about Tivoli?'

'I don't want to waste my time looking for a girl I haven't the faintest desire for. I'm in a hurry, Miss Ott.'

'Then you promise?'

'Of course,' I said without the least intention of keeping my word.

IX

I left the bookshop in a state of mind hard to describe, not quite sure whether I was happy or not, for I felt strangely torn between the hope of an agreeable night and the sadness caused by the memory of Karin. Now that I knew she was poor, lonely and condemned to a joyless life she became dearer to me, but I still did not desire her. I desired Ilse. And I was going to have Ilse. The image of the glass from which others had drunk came back into my mind. Hundreds of unknown people had drunk from that glass and I did not care. What seemed to me harder to accept was that where I was going to place my lips, the filthy lips of Mr Gore had doubtless lingered at length. As for going to see him afterwards . . .

'It's enough to make one sick,' I said aloud as I sat down on a bench in the shade of the lime trees. The air was warm and seemed caressing. I watched the dappled sunlight at my feet as it moved with the breeze coming through the leaves. A faint smell of tar reached me from the port and made me dream of distant lands where life was not overshadowed by rumours of war. Here at least the threatening news did not affect me personally as in France. Blessed Scandinavia seemed outside the affair.

I forced myself to spend a tranquil day. Hence I avoided inflaming my imagination by going to look at the bathing-girls at Klampenborg. It seemed wiser to go to the museum, where I examined some dozens of pictures without really seeing them, for between me and those canvasses Ilse's body would suddenly appear, I would touch it, have its warmth against my cheek, and dizziness took hold of me. In those empty rooms – in Copenhagen when the sun shines people have other things to do than look at works of art, the works of art are on the beach – I wondered why I was here in this town where ignorance of Danish made me mute. I was a prisoner of my silence.

What had brought me here? Flight from war. And what kept me in this town? Fear and desire. In my imagination I foresaw the disgust that would follow a night passed in the company of a prostitute with whom I would not exchange a word. I could see in advance the number of fingers she would hold up tomorrow morning to indicate her price. Everything was mediocre, and even sad, but I wanted that girl.

I lunched alone in a restaurant where the menu was at least two yards long and reached as far as the floor. They served only fish and shellfish and the fixed price let one eat far beyond the satisfaction of hunger. If one could put away thirty little Norway lobsters then one put away thirty and paid the same as one would have paid for one. In the company of a friend it would have been fun. As it was I ate ten of those lobsters with no pleasure and went back home.

Under my door, surprise of surprises, there was a letter awaiting me – a few lines in rather childish handwriting: *'If you are free tomorrow morning, Saturday, we could go for a drive just outside the town. I shall show you where my parents used to live. I can't remember what I said to you yesterday, in the adventurous wood, but of course you must forget, you must forget everything except Karin.'*

I was absurdly touched by the final words, by which I mean that I suddenly pressed my lips to the signature, for that at least did not hold out against me. The blood rose to my face. Was it not obvious that Karin loved me? She had evidently come herself, during her lunch hour, and slipped the note under my door. Had I been there I would have opened the door immediately, seized her brown hand, and dragged my prey into my room by force . . . There followed five minutes of emotional delirium. I talked out loud, I threw myself on the bed calling Karin's name into the pillow, sometimes with tenderness, sometimes with frenzy, as happens in novels. The only thing lacking was a torrent of tears which I was unable to produce.

Nevertheless the irony of the situation did not escape me. I was perhaps in love with Karin, but I had an assignation with Ilse, because I desired the one and did not much desire the other. These thoughts stayed with me for the rest of the day. Then just before half past seven I parked my car opposite the Wivex restaurant on the other side of the boulevard.

For some wily reason I was wearing rather large dark glasses, and, as was then the custom, a hat whose brim, when pulled low over the forehead, had the effect of making me unrecognizable. Hence I could spy on Ilse's arrival without her knowing. Her punctuality was quite extraordinary for a Danish girl, but I immediately realized that I had to interpret this not as a mark of courtesy towards me but as blind obedience to the orders of Mr Gore. I was being lent a slave.

And indeed Ilse had the haughtiness, insolence and contemptuous look that slaves have for everyone other than their masters, and how gracefully she walked across the boulevard just as the town hall clock was striking eight! I watched her with the eyes of a madman. With every step she took the splendour of her body could be divined beneath her light silk skirt. I found it extraordinary that no one seemed to notice her, that no one followed her, and I trembled to think this temptation might come to someone, but, tonight, she was mine. 'You're mine,' I whispered, 'mine from head to foot.' With the aim of prolonging this intoxicating moment and deliciously titillating my desire, I did not stir from the car, but watched the girl enter the restaurant, turn her head to right and left, then sit down at a somewhat secluded table to wait for me. The girl to whom no one could say no was waiting for me, perhaps surprised that I was not yet there, for up in the still-blue sky the hands of the great clock were pointing to five past eight.

Perhaps Ilse was already vexed with me for being late. This thought pleased me. I was making her pride bleed a little. She was becoming visibly bored (I saw all this from my hiding place). Again, as before, she was looking to right and left. I laughed without attempting in any way to conceal myself, then suddenly, in the grip of a panic hunger at the thought of the prey offered to me, I started up the car.

I was stopped almost at once by the traffic lights and had to let long trams and a number of cars pass by which seemed to snap their fingers at my impatience. When the road was finally clear I shot forward and parked my car not far from the restaurant, towards which I then ran, only slowing down two or three yards from the door so as to walk in with perfect composure.

On reaching the door I halted, glued by horror to the spot. A man of a certain age, dressed with care in a navy blue suit, was sitting at Ilse's table, at my table, and was talking to the young woman in the animated way that one does when one meets a girl-friend with whom one has lost touch. The most shocking thing about it was Ilse's delighted face as she returned smile for smile and seemed completely at her ease.

I advanced as one does in nightmares, each foot weighing sixty pounds. It was a long, wide room, broken up by tall windows draped with muslin curtains. Scattered all around were low lamps softened by rose-silk shades. The tables were not too close together and were totally concealed by white table-cloths whose folds reached down to the thick red carpet. A band was playing appropriate music at a discreet distance behind an imposing group of palms. I was in the best restaurant in town, and I was not only there as in a nightmare, but I myself was a potential nightmare for this chosen haunt of the rich. Everything suggested that I should not make a scene. Yet I advanced towards *my* table from which I never took my eyes, and soon I was so near it that Ilse and her companion turned their heads towards me in wordless interrogation.

'Ilse,' I said in a strangled voice, 'Mr Gore . . .'

She looked me over in silence and raised her eyebrows. I wondered if she even recognized me. I leant towards her.

'Please,' said the navy blue gentleman firmly in English.

'Mr Gore,' I repeated.

'Yes, Mr Gore,' said the unknown man, still in English.

And he pointed to himself to give me to understand that he was indeed there through the good graces of Mr Gore. This lie unnerved me. My head was swimming. I retreated to the strains of Boccherini's minuet which I hate and which gave me the feeling that I was being shown the door with mocking politeness.

Suddenly I gave a start and returned to my senses. I was at the wheel of my car parked alongside the pavement. My watch told me that it was seven minutes to eight. I had been asleep for three minutes, worn out by the nervous fatigue caused by my day of waiting and comings and goings, and I had been dreaming. Relief drew from me the sigh, no, the groan, of a man who sees himself rescued from some frightful despair. I crossed the boulevard with no further hesitation, parked my car near the restaurant and rapidly entered.

It only needed a glance to assure myself that Ilse had not yet arrived. What could be more natural? As a matter of fact there was no one there yet and my only problem was my vast choice of tables covered with rich white cloths – but not quite so long as in my dream. Similarly, the room was rather smaller and less sumptuous, the windows smaller, the ceiling lower, and for the moment at least no music could be heard. A head-waiter with a wide white shirt-front approached me and led me to a table not far from the door, but I needed something more private: an alcove . . . But there was no alcove. I shook my head and looked all round the room, followed by that fat man who was puffing with impatience. Finally I sat down on a velvet-upholstered banquette that I would soon cede to the noble posterior of my guest. The head-waiter offered me a menu which he accompanied by the habitual *vaersaagod* and I embarked on a sort of lively pantomime to indicate that I wanted to wait. He smiled.

'I understand,' he said in an attempt at French.

Why did he smile? His long, heavy face with grey cheeks and blue chin reminded me of the face of an old offender at the magistrate's court.

It was fun being here after all, in this weird and delightful country. I watched with interest the arrival of a smart young woman followed by a gentleman of ripe years, 'so ripe,' I thought to myself with a laugh, 'that he's soon going to drop.' By all the evidence, a grim amorous adventure. The woman, dressed in peach-coloured silk, displayed magnificent arms and just a bit more of her lovely breast than was proper, and there was something else provocative in her appearance, for her skin and the silk were of an almost identical shade so that she looked naked. No wonder her escort was devouring her shamelessly with his bloodshot eyes. He was stout, massive, hideous, where I was young and slim, and the woman, casting sweeping glances of charming hypocrisy around the room, seemed entirely of the same opinion. At certain moments life is full of savour. Who could say that the expectation of happiness is not happiness itself? I felt within me a very special sense of good-will towards the world because of Ilse, who was going to appear any moment now and sit down in front of me – or perhaps beside me on the banquette. But the places were set facing each other. A pity. And by the way, what time was it? Twenty past eight. That could hardly be called late, I told myself, as I crumbled my roll.

The restaurant was filling up. The waiters were carrying dishes and the head-waiter was unhurriedly moving his heavy presence this way and that. All around him there arose a humming of those words that remained incomprehensible to me, but the general tone indicated good-humour and here and there laughter mingled with the clatter of forks. Nearly all the diners seemed to me ugly except for the peach-coloured woman who, however, did not look at me. I waited. I had to be patient, but I had the disagreeable impression that people were smiling a little about me as I sat before my empty plate, because they could guess that some ravishing creature was making me pine. Pine? The word was a bit strong. One does not pine for a woman who sells her charms, and yet . . .

Somewhat blatantly the town-hall clock struck half past eight. Once Ilse had taken her seat in front of me I would tell her in

78

French what I thought of her, but I would say it with a smile. I would be coarse, even filthy, I would assiduously drag her in the mud in our admirable language which she surely did not understand. A certain pleasure crept into the preparation of this vengeful tirade, and that helped the time to pass. In spite of everything I noticed that drops of sweat were falling from my forehead when the clock struck again, because I was beginning to understand . . .

It was hot in this restaurant. The ventilators were doing nothing. I could hear the diners talking in louder and louder voices and their laughter reminded me of barking dogs. I would give Ilse ten more minutes, and after that I would go. Or no, I wouldn't go. I would order a good meal.

I waved my menu to attract the head-waiter's attention, but I had long ceased to exist in his eyes and it took him two or three minutes to realize I was still there. At last he came to a halt in front of me like a funerary monument.

'*Vaersaagod!*'

'I think you understand French.'

'Yes.' He mispronounced the word.

'Would you be good enough to translate this menu.'

It was a laborious business. He leant over me, breathing beer fumes into my face which in their own way scented the dishes he described to me. I was suffering. My recent nightmare was as nothing compared with this one. Instead of Ilse's smooth and golden face, I had next to mine this evil-smelling jowl, and because something was still lacking to the cruel singularity of my situation I suddenly saw Miss Ott's questing face turning to right and left in the restaurant. When at last she spotted me, half-hidden by the head-waiter, she stopped dead and put on a solemn look, then advanced towards me as you approach a sick person's bed. Resting the tips of her fingers on the table-cloth, she looked at me for a moment and smiled sadly:

'Dear sir, how spiteful life can be!'

I looked at her. In her deep blue cotton dress, and with that little black hat on her head, she gave the impression of a gigantic bird of ill-omen. And there was great dignity in her attitude – that, too, I noted in my confusion. Instinctively I rose to my feet.

'Has anything happened?' I asked.

79

The head-waiter straightened up and held the menu to his heart with a patient air, but curiosity made him screw up his eyes.

'I don't know if it's possible to talk here,' Miss Ott said, 'although you've chosen a rather withdrawn table.'

People were beginning to notice this fat person, so still and serious.

'May I?' she said, looking down at the empty chair.

I abandoned the upholstered banquette and she installed herself in it, very discreetly, I must say, and as if she would have to go in a moment. After all, it was Ilse's place . . .

'Ilse isn't coming,' Miss Ott said. 'That's almost certain.'

'In that case,' I said in an icy voice, 'it's useless for me to stay here.'

'I suppose you haven't dined.'

'Of course I haven't. Anyway, I'm not hungry.'

She leant a little towards me with a thoroughly maternal expression.

'You're wrong not to eat. Eating is comforting, you know. Then I don't want to cradle you in false hopes – is that the way you put it? – but it's not altogether impossible that she may put in a late appearance. Do you like shellfish?'

'I don't like anything,' I said savagely.

Ignoring my protests, she addressed the head-waiter with a speed and superabundance of vowels that seemed to stick in her throat. The head-waiter chimed in in his turn and there was a sort of gargling of indistinct noises.

'They recommend the Norway lobsters,' Miss Ott said.

'I won't eat.'

'And yet there's just a small chance that the girl will decide to come, and she can only find you here. That's why you must eat something while you're waiting. Don't you agree?'

'Be so kind as to order for yourself.'

'That's done. But it's especially important for you, my dear sir, because as for me, you know . . .'

She assumed an ethereal air but for all that unfolded her napkin with a quick, adroit movement which bespoke a very ready appetite. Perhaps she thought I had not noticed anything.

'What makes you think Ilse's going to come?' I asked in an imploring voice that made me ashamed of myself.

'I'm afraid of shocking you.'

'But tell me all the same.'

'There are certain words a lady shouldn't say. You must spare me indiscreet questions.'

'I beg of you.'

'A short while ago Ilse was dressing to come to this meeting with you. I have to tell you that Mr Gore isn't always very generous with her. It's a peculiarity of his character. However she wanted to come to this appointment and was getting dressed. I was there.'

'What do you mean by "there"?'

'At her house. Then Mr Gore suddenly turned up. A whim, if you follow me. We had to open the door because it was Mr Gore. He bawled his name through the door. When he saw Ilse in her lovely little frock . . . How can I describe its colour?'

'What do I care about its colour?'

'But you would,' she insisted, raising her voice. 'It's the same colour as the dress the woman behind you is wearing.'

'Peach,' I said without turning round.

'Yes, but a bit more subtle.'

At this moment a waiter with a snub nose put on our table a black bottle and two small glasses.

'Take a drop of aquavit,' Miss Ott said, sending the waiter away with a gesture. 'It'll be so good for you.'

She filled the two small glasses without waiting for my answer.

'Here,' she explained, 'gentlemen swallow this in one gulp, but I don't advise you to go that far if you're not used to it. To return to Mr Gore – he will certainly apologize.'

'I don't care a damn about Mr Gore's apologies,' I said rudely.

'I don't understand,' she said, her small glass half raised.

'Then I'll translate: Mr Gore's apologies are a matter of indifference to me.'

'I see. You know, very rich and important men of his type – he's worth millions of crowns – are often totally unpredictable in their behaviour. They have whims like monarchs.'

She drank a sip and went on:

'When Mr Gore saw Ilse in that pretty frock he had a whim. But it must all be over by now. So I would guess you'll have Ilse a bit later.'

By now I was sure she was drunk, if only slightly, because she was losing her customary propriety and her French was getting shaky. Setting down my glass, I plunged my gaze like a knife into her sea-green eyes softened by alcohol and muttered in a voice trembling with rage:

'I'll never see that whore again, do you hear?'

'Whore?' she repeated with a laugh, pretending not to understand the French word I'd used. 'Oh, I see what you mean. You're getting interesting!'

A dozen dishes of hors d'oeuvres were put in front of us by two snub-nosed waiters. Miss Ott emptied her glass and filled it again. Meanwhile her hand hovered over the dishes to indicate the ones she fancied.

'Mr Gore finds you interesting too. But look, you must eat something. Here, have this and this and this. Aren't you feeling any better? The aquavit will pull you together. Followed by beer. It's a major principle with us: first aquavit, then beer to put the fire out.'

She signed to the waiters to go away.

'I feel such sympathy for you,' she went on, 'and I understand you. Everyone in Denmark feels sympathy for the French, especially now because of the news. But there won't be a war. Mr Gore is sure there won't be a war, and he knows. For heaven's sake, drink.'

I drank a sip or two. Anger had dried my throat.

'You mustn't pass judgement on Mr Gore,' she went on, lowering her voice with a serious air. ' "Judge not." So you must not judge Mr Gore. Mr Gore is rich. Good. Millions of crowns. Good, very good. Mr Gore likes attractive girls. I say nothing. I remember the mote and the beam. Don't you, too?'

This little speech seemed to me so unsuitable that I could no longer hold back the words that came to my lips:

'Look, Miss Ott, it's pointless quoting me texts that I don't believe in. Above all here. You're talking to an atheist.'

She paid not the slightest attention to this remark but went on:

'I'm having some more eel, I'm having more of everything, and you aren't touching a thing. In our country there's an abundance of all the good things of this world because we're faithful to our ideal. One day I'll introduce you to an old friend who's very strong in theology. He understands everything because he has problems like the rest of us. Tell me about your problems,' she said, putting down her fork so as to rest two fingers on my forearm.

I freed myself at once.

'Excuse me. I haven't any problems.'

A tear glistened in the corner of her eyes.

'*I* have,' she said. 'Miss Ott has problems, but she keeps them to herself. They're her secret. However, this evening I'm feeling happy, here, with you. Oh, I'm not just being complimentary. Don't go imagining . . . But then I must admit I don't often have the opportunity of dining in a place like this.'

This last phrase was uttered softly, like a confession, and suddenly I felt sorry for Miss Ott. Though she did not live in penury, she could not afford the luxury of a meal at Wivex. This supper was for her a minor festival. She smiled at me in a way that she thought seductive, but it seemed to me so ugly that I averted my eyes. The pretty woman in her did not want to die.

'Will you let me ask you a question?' she said.

'Of course.'

She wiped her mouth and her fingers and made a visible effort to overcome a certain hesitancy.

'Have you seen Karin again?'

'No. I told you I'm not interested in Karin.'

I regretted my words the moment I said them, for at last an opportunity had been provided for me to learn something. Miss Ott sighed.

'Karin is a good girl,' she murmured.

'Why did her father kill himself?'

'For love. A very stupid business really. He became crazy about a girl who said no and whom he could very easily have had. Is "crazy" the right word?'

'Yes, crazy.'

'I find that extraordinary, because we say it too. Anyway he jumped into the water. His wife took the shock very badly.'

'Is she still alive?'

'Yes, but she doesn't recognize anyone. Her husband's escapades didn't prevent her adoring him.'

Her eyes sought a compliment for the elegant gerund she had used. I managed a smile.

'The poor man lacked all character, all faith. She had faith, but that stopped nothing . . . That bit of lobster on your plate. Yes, I want it, in the name of all the seas that wash our Denmark!'

Out of inertia I let her do as she wanted.

'She was a believer to the very depths of her soul. She may well be so still in her lucid moments. Are you a believer?'

'I'm nothing,' I said firmly. 'Religion bores me to death.'

She raised her eyebrows.

'Of course,' she said, 'a Frenchman . . .'

'What sort of work does Karin do?'

'She's very gifted in her own way. She makes designs for wallpaper. She's employed by a big store but she works at home.'

'What big store?'

Her eye took on an extremely cunning expression.

'I'm not going to say anything about that because you're too interested.'

'Does she live alone?'

'Alone with a canary and her rather mad ideas. With *her* you're wasting your time, my dear sir.'

'How often you've told me that! What are her rather mad ideas?'

Miss Ott dabbled the tips of her fingers in a bowl of water that had just been placed in front of her. Then she laughed:

'I'm sorry, dear sir, but you've forbidden me to talk about religion.'

X

I took leave of Miss Ott a quarter of an hour later and, leaving my car in its parking place, returned home on foot. The night was luminous beyond all dreams. From time to time a gentle breath of wind blew over my face, and I walked the length of the old port asking myself whether a more peaceful place existed on earth, a place where even shadows seemed to invite happiness.

Yet I was dissatisfied with my stupid evening nevertheless and knew full well that the years would not remove the bitterness of that failed appointment. My conversation with Miss Ott left me with a sense of disgust, especially her glib references to religion. There was something in me that rebelled at the thought of a faith enslaving mankind, and having to talk about it in that restaurant where I was waiting in vain for a prostitute only heightened my vexation. I was seized with a desire to leave this town next morning and forget Ilse's name for ever and the names of all those beautiful blondes whom I could touch only with my eyes. These streets already contained too much of my suffering.

Just as I was approaching Sankt Annaegade I saw someone coming towards me whose step I recognized at once.

'Karin!' I called out.

She stopped dead and waited till I drew level with her.

'You're going to ask me questions,' she said, laughing, 'such as why I'm here. The answer: Entirely by chance. I came out to get some air, that's all.'

The rays from a street lamp cast a violent light on her face so that it looked like that of a statue.

An odd phrase came into my mind.

'Karin,' I exclaimed, 'you're almost . . .'

'Almost what? Almost pretty, I suppose.'

She said exactly what I was thinking.

'Almost dangerous,' I said, taking her hand. 'Dangerous through being beautiful.'

'How badly you tell your lie!' she said, laughing.

'But I assure you . . .'

I began laughing in my turn. It really looked as if she had expected me. My sadness suddenly vanished. I went on:

'As you don't want me to ask any questions, all I'll say is that chance arranges things well, because it's by chance that I met you.'

'Oh, chance . . . It amused me to know what kind of house you were living in.'

'Would you like to come up a minute? I'll show you the balcony.'

'Are you mad? I don't go up and see people just like that.'

'I hoped I was something more for you than "people".'

'Don't be so silly, Mr Frenchman. What one says is unimportant. Try to understand what isn't said.'

'But there's so much you don't say.'

'Exactly.'

'So you insist on being enigmatic?'

'I'm as simple as a child's school-book. But you're becoming boring and I was hoping for distraction. Would you like a short walk beside the canal?'

We walked for a few minutes along by the painted houses on which the trees cast their shade as to if wipe out an evil memory. With a movement I could not control, I took Karin by the arm and said:

'It's true, what I said to you just now. This evening you're lovelier than usual.'

'You're not going to make me a proposal,' she said with a laugh. 'I warn you it's useless.'

'Useless because you don't love me at all.'

'Since it's you who are asking the questions *and* giving the answers, all I can do is keep quiet.'

'Karin, you're exasperating!' I said and stamped my foot.

She burst out laughing like a child.

'You, stamping your foot! It's rather ridiculous, you know. Suppose someone saw . . .'

I took her in my arms and kissed her on the mouth, but she struggled so hard that I let her go. She was stronger than I had imagined.

'You're stupid, plain stupid,' she said, vigorously wiping her lips. 'You've no real desire to kiss me, and as for me I don't like it.'

'Would you dislike it less if I were that officer of the other evening?'

'Leave the army alone,' she said in a calmer voice. 'If you want us to stay friends you won't start again with your – how do you say it? – your fussing.'

'I wonder why we see each other.'

'I've my reasons just as you have yours.'

'And supposing I was in love with you?'

'But you're not in love. I'd know if you were, you see.'

'Then why do you see me? Don't tell me it's to improve your French. That would make me see red and I might beat you!'

'You wouldn't dare. You'd be too afraid of losing me for good, because you'd like to add me to your collection, have the little Danish girl no one else has had.'

'No one?'

'That's what I said.'

'No one, Karin?' I insisted.

She made no answer but took my hand and gave me her lovely smile.

'Be kind,' she said. 'Don't bother me any more with your questions. After all, you ought to know that women loathe questions. We'll go and sit on this bench and you'll tell me about yourself. To tell the truth, I don't even know who you are.'

'I'd much prefer it if you told me about yourself.'

'Very well, I'll tell you about myself. Listen to the lapping of the water against the boats,' she said when we were seated. 'I sometimes come this way when I want to be at peace. I love the night, the smell of the canal, and that little lapping noise. You'd think the water was giving affectionate little pats on the hull of the boats.'

So to please Karin I docilely listened to that sound, at the same time deploring that in this solitary spot I could not clasp her to me, not from desire but from a burst of tenderness. This was what I could not make her understand without perhaps wounding her, for at that age one does not willingly hear it said that one is loved chastely and that desire, if it comes, will come only later. In my case, I was almost certain that it would come once I had forgotten Ilse, and, as often happened, Karin had a confused intuition of what was going on in my head.

'I'm sure,' she said, 'that you've already made some brilliant conquests in our town.'

'Conquests – no. But I'd be lying if I told you that I've been good every day. There are certain facilities . . .'

'Did your facilities have black hair and eyes?'

'No. The regulation golden hair and blue eyes. Blue eyes, but I also like black eyes, some black eyes.'

'You're a libertine. Is that the word you use?'

'Yes, in old-fashioned novels. But as for you, you prowl around Tivoli.'

'I don't like *prowl*. For me, Tivoli means despair. I play with fire without ever getting burnt.'

This phrase seemed to me so literary that for a moment I

ceased believing in Karin's sincerity, and remained silent. Once again she suspected something.

'You aren't saying anything,' she said.

To my surprise she sought out my hand in the half-light and murmured:

'Do you really think you're in love, Roger?'

It was the first time she had called me by name. I bent down and put my lips to her hand.

'As for me,' she said without moving, 'I can't do without you. It's not quite the same thing.'

I stayed still, my lips pressed to that delicate scented skin, attentive to the soft and rather uncertain voice as it unfolded above my head the phrases of a strange declaration:

'When I talked in Danish in the adventurous wood, I said things that we never say. I'm hungry and thirsty. I'm hungry and thirsty for love. I'm lost, Roger. You see, I'm telling you this calmly and I couldn't say it to anyone but you, because you're going away, and if there's a war we'll never see each other again.'

She stroked my hair with her free hand.

'So it would be better if we didn't love each other,' she went on, 'but I would have loved you in spite of everything . . . The last day we'll come back here and you will kiss me.'

For long minutes I rested my head on her knee, feeling happy and hopeless at the same time. Suddenly she whispered:

'Get up.'

I obeyed and saw that she was smiling at me.

'Perhaps there won't be a war, Karin. In any case, you've nothing to fear here. Why do you say that you're lost?'

'Oh, nothing will happen to me, I know. I'm safe in my own country. I wasn't talking about that. My mother too was afraid of not being saved. She fell ill. She thought she saw a sign, some sort of terrifying sign in my father's death, and now she no longer knows who she is. Yet she was innocent. But not I.'

'You're a virgin, Karin.'

She gave a mirthless laugh.

'What things you say . . . A virgin. My body, yes, but that's all.'

And as, with her, irony always triumphed at some moment or other, she added:

'You haven't had the chance of coming across what you call a virgin in Copenhagen in 1939.'

Some strollers came in our direction. We got up and walked a little way under the trees.

'My father hadn't a trace of faith,' Karin went on. 'I loved him very much, but he frightened me because he hadn't faith. When he drowned himself I had a terrible shock. I can't remember whether I told you. He drowned himself in the canal.'

'On the other side of the town?'

'No,' she said softly, 'about three paces from the bench where we were sitting.'

She pointed to the water gleaming through the trees. Instinctively I stopped and she looked at me calmly.

'What surprises you about that? Sometimes I sit there and think about him. I wonder what can happen when one goes . . .'

'Do you mean when one dies, Karin? Nothing happens. Nothing at all.'

'If you want to joke, let's talk about something else.'

'I wasn't joking. I love you too much to joke.'

We walked on again, in silence now, and soon we found ourselves at the corner of my street.

'I'd like you to understand me,' Karin said abruptly. 'Sometimes life frightens me. I'm not thinking about the world's news, but about all the things in life, and among them some which are close to my heart.'

'Love?'

She gently shrugged her shoulders without answering.

'Love attracts you, Karin, as you told me just now.'

'I like what destroys me.'

And with almost no transition, she added:

'Don't forget you're driving me to the country tomorrow. I'll meet you here at seven.'

'At seven or nine?'

'If it bores you to stand and wait, you can always sit on our bench.'

In the space of a second I had a glimpse of the scenes which her caprices would cause me to endure if I had an affair with her, and at this moment, as if to disarm me, she smiled at me like a child.

'A child,' I thought, 'that's all you are.' And I had to control myself so as not to take her in my arms.

On returning home I went out on to the balcony to look at the stars and the full moon which was shining with wonderful brilliance. The cold mysterious light fell obliquely on the neighbouring church with its weird corkscrew curling round its spire. Like gigantic ink stains, the trees formed clumps of darkness between the white roofs and the little grey streets like metal ribbons. A confused murmur reached my ears from the centre of the town, but it deepened rather than disturbed the silence of the night. I felt at peace before this landscape that had become so familiar to me. And yet a sort of melancholy joy took hold of me at the memory of my conversation with Karin, of her tenderness and her refusals. 'Obviously,' I said to myself, 'there are two obstacles preventing her from giving herself to me: religion and fear of men. I'll demolish those two obstacles. Sometimes love is begotten by desire. The opposite is equally true. Once she's mine, passion will unite us and, if there's no war, I'll stay here. Listen, Karin . . .'

I began talking to her in a low voice with my hands on the balustrade as though she were near me, I begged her, I reasoned with her, I brushed aside all her objections with a phrase, then I enclosed her in my arms as one protects a child, with that voluptuousness of the soul that devotion procures. Finally I went back into my room and slid between my sheets. The image of Ilse came into my mind but I drove it away without too much difficulty by recalling some of Karin's words, her voice, and her smile which enraptured me.

XI

'Smile at me, Karin.'

She obeyed but nevertheless took me to task in a firm little voice:

'You mustn't call me *"tu"* but *"vous"*. We've only known each other for five days.'

' *"Tu"* will come later.'

'Perhaps on the last day.'

'Is it fun to make a man suffer?'

'So it seems, when one's in love.'

'And you're not in love?'

'I explained myself on that point in my little monologue in Danish. Shall we go?'

Ten minutes later we were driving through a market town not far from the sea – of a blue paler than the sky and visible at the end of the straight streets. White houses stood in their gardens where the flowers seemed to jostle one another on the lawns in the light shadow of the birches. Here everything spoke of happiness and peace. I would have liked to stop, but Karin pointed to the road with an authoritative finger.

'Go on,' she said.

Once free of the town, we rolled along beside the milky blue waves. Here and there peasant houses stood at the corners of long meadows where pale yellow cows were grazing. Finally there appeared prosperous-looking residences, encircled by trees and lawns and revealing the presence of city people weary of their town, then a double row of fancy villas and a scrupulously rustic inn whose sign, in the shape of a huge pretzel, glittered goldenly in the setting sun.

'Let's stop and have a glass of beer,' I implored.

'Put such an idea from your mind. To begin with, Danish beer is good only at Easter, when it's brewed in a special way. And furthermore, we must see our house at the best moment of the afternoon. On you go.'

I couldn't help admiring her imperious tone. Sometimes it is delightful to obey.

Meadows and still more meadows, then, leaving the sea, we took a road gently rising through woods where the sunlight scattered its rays like seeds in the green depths.

'Will we be there soon, Karin?'

'We are there. Stop in that drive there on the right.'

Then between two walls of black pine trees we walked up towards a tall, wide iron gate whose bars were growing rusty. Karin started to run and pushed open this barrier with both hands. Then she turned to me, her face lit up with happiness.

'Come on, hurry up!' she cried.

To the left and right of a long drive overgrown with grass,

birch trees planted haphazard held the last rays of the sun in their leaves. As I did not walk quickly enough for Karin, she came back and took my hand.

'It's here that I used to wander when I was a child,' she said in a voice that slightly trembled. 'I loved these trees, I used to lean my cheek against their white bark, which seemed to me as soft as human skin. Look, their leaves are fluttering though the air is scarcely moving.'

While talking, she led me towards a house standing in the middle of a large gravelled terrace. It was white and square and had the massive prosperous look of buildings of the last century. It could have been thought beautiful, with its high windows and green painted shutters, all closed, and the abundance of ivy that clothed it on one side like a tattered black shawl. The five or six treads of the scrolled steps led to a main door whose upper section was decked with an ornate grille protecting a pane of glass that enabled us to look through into the entrance hall.

'It's all we can see,' said Karin sadly. 'The door has been shut since my father's death and the house is for sale. There, on the right, perhaps you can just make out the beginning of the stair-case, but it's very dark inside already . . . When I was seven or eight, this was the moment when I was frightened, just before the light was put on. Do you see it?'

I did not see it. She let out an impatient little sigh.

'If only you knew how happy I was here . . . I had a room on the second floor from which you could see the sea and almost all the villages we have come through. In winter you could see the spires of Copenhagen and the almond-coloured roofs. My father let me come and go as I pleased . . .'

Listening to these strange ramblings I felt moved by the dangerous pity I knew so well, because the girl seemed to believe so deeply in the accuracy of all the details she was giving me in this headlong and rather feverish way.

'My father was in the diplomatic service,' she said as we went down the steps again so as to walk round the house . . . 'He and my mother had large numbers of guests and then, at night, the house shone like a lamp, like a diamond! It was like a festival. I hid myself so as to see everything. I loved the noise of all the talk reaching right up to my room. I used to crouch on the stairs. The ladies were in full evening dress, and among the men there were officers in uniform under the light of the chandeliers. The men-servants circulated in fine blue and gold liveries, with great silver trays laden with glasses and crystal decanters which seemed to sparkle like fire. I remember one evening there was a ball. The gusts of music were even louder than the noise of the voices, and I could hear the whispering of dance-steps sliding over the parquet of the drawing rooms.'

We were at the far end of the terrace from where we had a view of a white sea glimmering in the tawny twilight. There was a brief silence and Karin said in a low voice:

'When my father died, everything came to an end in a single day. As for the house, it was emptied with incredible speed, as in a nightmare. My mother disappeared.'

The brutal temptation came to me to tell Karin that I did not believe a word of her story which suddenly irritated me on account of the credulity its narrator ascribed to me, but surely the credulity was in fact on her side rather than mine. For she was not talking like a liar but like someone intoxicated by her story and convinced of its truth. If I informed Karin that I had not been taken in I risked causing her grave harm. And then, I couldn't help finding this dreamlike past that she had invented for herself absurdly touching. And as none of us is altogether simple, my pity was accompanied by a sort of disgust, an almost physical disgust at so much innocence. My sudden impatience could not have been explained in any other way. And then, above all, I was furious at feeling thus touched. Did she guess all this?

'You're not listening to me very well,' she said suddenly.

Instead of answering I took her arm and walked her a few steps along the big drive.

'Do you want to go?' she asked.

'Yes. It's beginning to get dark.'

'Why don't you say anything about what I've told you?'

'Because I haven't anything to say about it, but I'm thinking about all those things.'

She leant very lightly against me.

'It's done me good to tell you all that, Roger. I've never talked about it to anyone except you. Let me say good-bye to the big house.'

And turning her head over her shoulder, she remained for a few moments in that position while I wondered what part sincerity could possibly play in it. Here again, she seemed to sense the presence of a doubt.

'I'm sure my story must seem surprising to you.'

She looked so forlorn as she said these words that I wanted to smother her in my arms. We were alone in the drive and as we walked down it the setting sun fell straight upon us, gilding the forehead and lovely cheeks that I would have liked to cover with kisses, but I feared her sudden anger and contented myself with taking her hands which she left in mine. I then felt an irresistible impulse to bend right over and hide my face in them, and almost without realizing it found myself kneeling in front of the girl who was now quite still. A minute passed, then I heard her slightly faltering voice say softly:

'Why are you going back to France? You should stay here. You've nothing to fear here.'

I stood up.

'But you're talking as if war were certain, Karin.'

'I heard some Germans in the street this morning. I understand German just as well as Danish. It's war, all right.'

'Are you afraid?'

'Yes, I'm afraid. Afraid for you.'

'But you're not afraid *of* me any more. Karin, you love me.'

She did not answer. I would have liked to linger with her in the rather sombre setting provided by the pine trees. I felt that here she could have given herself to me, but at the same time I was apprehensive about what she might say. What I knew about her religious scruples made me edgy. I could not accept a human being's harbouring within him a terror of a phantom he called God. Arguments that I saw as irrefutable came into my mind and I suppressed as well as I could the desire to embark on a discussion from which I nevertheless flattered myself I would emerge victorious. Imitating my companion's silence, I put my hand in hers and we went down towards the drive where we had left the car.

Night was falling as we got back into town and I asked Karin if she would like us to have dinner together in the Tivoli gardens.

'Oh no,' she said. 'This evening Tivoli means nothing to me.'

'How about somewhere else?'

She shook her head violently. I suddenly saw her as obstinate, recalcitrant. Nothing remained of her recent tenderness.

We were at the very place where she had agreed to meet me two hours earlier, under the lime trees near *our* bench. The first lamps were beginning to shine among the leaves.

'I've an idea that you're not happy.'

'Yes I am,' she said defiantly.

'I'm wondering if you're still a little afraid of me after all.'

'Why are you always saying that? There's nothing very alarming about you.'

She smiled without showing her teeth, with a teasing gleam in her eyes. I should have taken advantage of the opportunity offered me just now under the pine trees. Perhaps it was this that she was insinuating.

'Are you regretting all you told me when we were out there?' I asked.

'Oh,' she said, shrugging her shoulders, 'surely you don't believe I can remember everything I told you . . .'

Had I put my finger on the sore point? She was no doubt holding against me her lies which were so at odds with the image she had of herself. For a couple of seconds I despised her. She read that in my face and gave me that wide smile that I loved only too well.

'Thanks for the lovely outing,' she said, and began to move away.

'Where are you going to have dinner?' I called after her.

'You don't have to worry about that!' she threw at me in the same tone.

I saw her walking briskly away under the trees and at that moment, for a reason I could not immediately grasp, I felt a violent desire for her. Perhaps it was her naturally graceful way of walking. And then I had told her too much that I loved her. Now it was absolutely true, and desire had come just as I might have expected. To all this I should add that for some days I had been deprived of all physical pleasure.

My first impulse was to catch up with Karin in my car, but this would have been an additional blunder. No girl can resist the pleasure of saying No to someone who implores too much. With a heavy heart I left the car where it was and went up to my room.

I suddenly had a headache. Without turning on the light, I went to get some air on the balcony dominated by the spiral steeple in the still-pale sky. Below me the street lamps lit up the pavements in front of the painted house-fronts and I took in these details attentively in an effort to drive Karin from my mind. I had behaved like a fool. I should have caught up with her just now. I should have taken her by force in the garden of the house up for sale, when we were alone, but then I didn't desire her enough. Perhaps that was what she wanted: to be taken by force, but I was seeing everything hours too late. No one could be more clumsy than I with girls who obsessed me.

I returned to my room in a rage and kicked over a table with books and papers on it, then hurled myself on to the telephone and rang Miss Ott at her home. Luckily, she was there.

Still in a state of confusion about her failure, as she had promised me the charming Ilse, she let flow a torrent of excuses into my ear, but I cut her short.

'You're aware that Karin doesn't interest me at all in the way you know about, and you're right to want to protect her, but this evening I happen to want to talk French with that girl. Try to understand me. I'm feeling very lonely. Where can I get hold of her?'

'I've mislaid her address. But if you want to spend the evening with someone who knows French . . .'

There was a terrible silence which meant: 'Haven't I made my point?'

I hung up. In the rage that followed I started talking out loud and in such a shrill voice that I did not recognize it. 'What a town! It dangles the world's loveliest girls in front of my nose but only gives me a virgin who says No!' My mind was quickly made up. I went out. Prostitutes were not difficult to find. There were always four or five of them round about the city's main hotel. Others walked rather too slowly along by the canal bordered by the oldest painted houses of the quarter, and they stopped obligingly at the faintest wink. In this archaic setting their youth formed a contrast of whose seductive power they were totally unaware. The street lamps, reflected in the black water, cast a rather uncertain light, and one had to get quite close to the pretty loiterers before one could assess their quality. My natural timidity did not lend itself to this game. I preferred to take up my position near one of the large granite posts linked to each other by huge chains which served as a parapet at the edge of the harbour. I didn't have long to wait. Despite my youth, everything about me proclaimed the votary.

Back in my room two hours later, I threw myself on my bed, my face in the pillow. I felt as though I still had in my hands and my whole body the odour of the gorgeous flesh that had been offered to my gluttony. I relived everything in my mind. It was not a memory but a real hallucination. Once more I was in a room bleakly lit by a single bulb above the bed. The threadbare carpet had lost all recognizable colour and the purple velvet curtains hiding the window were streaked with yellow. There was that . . . And there was also the sordid basin and the chipped jug on a white-wood table, and, most distasteful of all, on the wall to the left of the door there was a huge engraving representing some sort of religious scene. But at the time I had not seen those things, I had eyes only for the smooth and amber body gleaming under the strong light of the electric bulb.

Afterwards . . . Afterwards, as was always inexplicably the case with me, I would have liked the floor to open and swallow up my partner. How slow she was getting dressed again! With her two open hands, fingers widespread, she gave me to understand the number of crowns she wanted, as though the price had not been agreed on beforehand, beside the canal. I gave them to her at once. It was then that I saw in a single glance and in all their eloquence the blood-red eiderdown, the carpet, the jug, the edifying engraving, the faded curtains, the whole commonplace setting for a crime. And now, by myself, I fed my memory once more with that brutal, panic joy, not really savoured at first in the impetuosity of desire – and this, now, was surely the best moment.

I slept till dawn. The birds were chirping on the balcony and woke me up. I leapt out of bed. My first thought was that I might find a note pushed under the door; but no, there was nothing. I don't know why I had counted on it and the disappointment was bitter. For some minutes I ruminated over my sadness. Why should I hide it from myself? I was madly in love with Karin. Now that my body was calm, I was better able to take stock of the extent of my growing passion, and the idea of returning to

97

France filled me with horror, as did my adventure of the night before.

Though it was still night rather than morning, I ran a bath and plunged myself into the hot water as if to wash my body clean of all the caresses it had received. From my ears to my toes, every square inch of my body was then extravagantly soaped in a sort of frenzied disgust. With vengeful hand I spread the snowy foam over my limbs and even as far as my face and hair. I would have liked to use up three cakes of soap in this purifying fury whose meaning became plain to me only much later.

I was distrustful of prostitution, less because of the possibility of disease than because I felt it ignoble to have recourse to these facilities before the age when one has ceased to please. In my eyes they sullied me, made me old, filled me with shame. Morality – I have surely no need to emphasize the point – played no part in all this. In my eyes a street girl was worth more than many supposedly respectable people, but I was too lacking in courage and clear-sightedness to admit to myself that prostitution attracted me with the same violence as a man prone to vertigo is attracted by an abyss. It was only much later that I understood that.

In my bath I fell asleep again. I dreamt that I was slipping naked into a marble vault. The water growing tepid dragged me from this nightmare.

When I was dressed I heard the bells ringing from the neighbouring church. Their sound was so true, firm and moderate, so unbragging and unbigoted, that for a moment I forgot my prejudices against faith and listened to that ancient voice sounding all around my head.

It occurred to me that as it was Sunday I could have a look at the interior of this church once the service was over, for it was considered to be one of the most interesting in the region. In fact I owed it a visit in view of my future as an architect which I so easily forgot in my sensual reveries. 'An animal,' I thought, 'that's what this town has made of you; enjoying a woman, that's all you ever think of . . .' These reflections made me smile for, as I told myself, a Christian moralist would not have reasoned otherwise. Was I to attribute this oddity to the influence of a peal of bells? This beating bronze certainly plunged the listener into a bygone world that had its own charm and eloquence, but I was happy to have cast it off after the mystical flights of my earliest youth.

While mulling over these things, I ate without much appetite the breakfast I had had perforce to prepare for myself. After the sound of bells, the sound of singing reached my ears in the still-cool air. I was just going to shut the window, thinking this was really enough, when I recognized one of Luther's chorales whose beauty seemed to me incontestable, even gripping. 'These,' said I to myself, 'are the emotional means that religion makes use of to assure its hold over the individual.' I shut the window after a moment or two and turned the knob of my little radio to listen to some light music, and then – the temptation was too great and I gave way to it – to catch the day's news. It was always possible that the news might be better. My radio was certainly not much good. Paris produced nothing but cracklings, whereas Germany sounded very near and brought me the hysterical voice that was making nations tremble. My heart stood still. I could not understand a word, but it would only be about death, about our death. It was not the end of the world, but it was the end of Europe, the Europe of our youth and our hopes. I switched off the little box.

Half an hour later I was standing by the church door from which the faithful of both sexes were emerging, chatting – they were nearly all of a fairly venerable age but this did not prevent some of them from having a resounding good humour. Perhaps I'm being over-severe. It's characteristic of men of pleasure to be severe when confronted by the religious phenomenon. I searched for the seriousness of faith on all those faces, for conviction, for the mark of the absolute. I found only intemperance and dissimulation or sanctimonious stupidity beneath the colours of an impregnable digestion. What struck me most was the vulgarity of their features, and all combined with the solid quality of their clothes which I noted with an inexorable eye as they passed. 'So that,' I thought, 'is the outcome of the Gospel in the twentieth century.'

As the crowd thinned I slipped into the church and almost cried out in admiration. Immense transept windows lit it up from both sides, through which the sky could be seen behind the poplars. Oak benches polished by time formed a dark mass in contrast to the bare white walls. Two blue elephants made a semblance of supporting the dark wood organ-loft whose lavish ornamentation made ample amends for all that was austere between those walls.

As discreetly as possible I made my way towards the baptismal fonts whither I was drawn by a magnificent gilt wood crown, when suddenly I stopped dead. Four or five people were passing fairly near me, going towards the door. One of them was Karin. She was not alone. Another girl, as blonde as herself, but prettier, was talking to her in a low voice. We were separated by the whole length of the benches, for I was keeping close to the wall, and Karin certainly did not see me. Her face, which was usually anxious or mocking, was steeped in a serenity that I had never seen on it before, a sort of peaceful joy that made a stranger of her. A stranger, that was the word that crossed my mind. Yet it was certainly she, and my first instinct was to go and greet her, but something held me back and I let her leave.

As the church remained open I lingered there for a moment or two, no longer to look and admire but to recover from my astonishment and, as it were, digest it. The very same Karin I had seen at Tivoli, her eyes glued to a young officer's face, came here to make her devotions. Tivoli itself could just pass, because the whole city went there, but the girl's presence in the secret garden of sensual pleasure was less easily explained – if it really was she whom had I seen there. The word 'hypocrite' came to my lips, but I suppressed it at once. The radiantly happy face I had seen a moment ago was not that of a hypocrite. So here there was something that eluded the usual arguments about people's sincerity, a mysterious contradiction to which I had no key.

While contemplating without seeing the monumental crown that glittered in the sunlight, I suddenly had the idea of running after Karin, following her, discovering where she was going with her friend. But as so often happened with me, these inspirations, whether good or questionable, came too late. Too late? Possibly not. I rushed out of the church like a madman and went in the direction of my street, then changed my mind for no particular reason and went towards the opposite street. The Sunday strollers looked with curiosity at this tourist, so hurried and yet so undecided, and soon I found myself by the port and near the bench where we had sat, she and I, when I had kissed her hands in the shade with an almost religious fervour. Did I hope to find her there all of a sudden? After a moment's hesitation I sat down at one end of the bench as if to leave room for Karin, and I looked at the water dancing in the sunlight. An old lady in black sat down beside me after some minutes and amiably articulated a Danish phrase which she accompanied by a gesture towards the clouds. I immediately got up and left.

I spent a gloomy day, divided between the wish not to leave my room, because I hoped Karin would telephone, and annoyance at not being able to go to the beach where the brilliance of a triumphant sun was drawing the whole youth of the town – except Karin, as I told myself.

I had a beach of my own. Having bought a bag of peaches, a bottle of beer and some sandwiches the day before, I could lunch at home. But first I carefully dragged my folding-chair to the end of the balcony and stretched myself out on it. In this way I could tan my skin on both sides, but alone. Alone. I began exploring the abysses contained in that word. The light dance music emanating from my radio only increased my desolation. From time to time I closed my eyes and fell into a half-sleep which the church clock shattered whenever it chimed the hours or half-hours, but from time to time I forgot my worries and savoured that special voluptuousness that comes from the simple fact of being alive and young. The massive caress of the heat on my body was like a simplification of all my problems: I was my body and nothing else, I wanted it to be like that, I wanted my body to be a refuge against the despair and complications of love, I didn't love anyone any more, I belonged to the sun, to the breeze that gently stroked me from my feet to my head.

After lunch I read five or six pages of a detective story and dozed till the end of the afternoon, not far from the silent telephone. The colour of the sky slowly changed and the murmur of noise from the town proclaimed the end of a torrid day. Perhaps Karin was there where I could have seen her if I had taken a walk in the adventurous wood or under the trees in the square outside my window. Who could say that she was not waiting for me just at the end of the road, on a bench? Perhaps she too was counting on chance to bring about a crossing of our paths. This game of hide-and-seek wore out the soul, because soul there was.

Ten times I leapt over to the door because I thought I heard the rustling of paper pushed into the room, but of course I was mistaken.

By now it seemed pointless to hope for a telephone call. To kill the evening I left my house and started wandering round the wide square in front of the town hall. Karin lived somewhere around here, but the cruel caprice of chance doubtless intended that my presence here or there would lead to the girl's absence – she would be looking for me elsewhere. 'Elsewhere,' I repeated to myself like a madman, 'where is elsewhere?'

There was no question of having dinner. I was not hungry. Passing in front of a cinema, I bought a ticket and made my way into an almost empty auditorium where films incomprehensible to me were being shown, but in the coolness and half-light I felt calmer and after a few minutes I was asleep. The noise of foot-steps all around me woke me up. The lights forced open my eyelids. Out I went.

Back in my room I undressed in the twinkling of an eye and threw myself into bed with a sort of greed. Had I been able to throw myself into the valley of death as easily, I would have done so without hesitation. I did not want to suffer.

That night, fear engulfed me. For weeks I had been holding it at bay with all the dark forces we have at our disposal for re-sisting fate, but suddenly I gave way. It was around two in the morning. At that moment I was wrenched from sleep by the memory of something Karin had said the day before and which had lodged itself within me, even within my dreams: 'It's war, all right.'

Despite the air coming in at the wide-open window, it was too hot in my room and I was bathed in sweat. I reared up at once to take off my pyjamas which were sticking to my skin, but once naked I started to shiver. It took me a few seconds to realize that my teeth were chattering, not with cold, obviously, nor with fever, but as a result of the abject and degrading fear that had seized me by the stomach. This had never happened to me before. I had always thought I was brave, but I was not. In vain had I protected myself against daily reality by refusing to read the French press which arrived in Copenhagen every morning, and in vain had I congratulated myself on not understanding the presumably alarming news that flashed at night from the tower of the

Berlingske Tidende. Why was I in Denmark, in the first place, if not to escape? Of course there was the attraction of bodies, there was the multitude of fair heads, but how well desire slotted in with a sickening horror of death! Karin had told me I was going to die. She knew nothing about it, but she had spoken as a substitute for destiny. It was useless for me to flee before a menacing future. Even here, in this land of refuge, my destiny joined up with me to say: 'Here I am.' And it was Karin herself who had provided fear's answer: 'Stay here in our country, don't go back.'

These minutes transformed me into another person. I did not want to switch on the light because I did not want to see, above all I did not want to see myself, but after having groaned so often with pleasure I was now groaning with indescribable dread. Panic swept over me like a wave. I was only sorry that it did not kill me, but after fifteen minutes the crisis came to an end. I left my bed to go and get some air on the balcony. My hands were still trembling when I rested them on the rail. Meanwhile, despite myself, my strength was returning and with it the power of reasoning. For the moment no peril was threatening me. Peace was still reigning throughout Europe and not a shot had been fired. I could come and go freely wherever I wanted . . . The stillness of the things around me comforted me a little and I raised less hostile eyes to the great corkscrew tower. That long grey arrow in the sky had something reassuring about it that I could not analyse. Perhaps it was simply that the magic of the past offers a refuge to many simple souls: the faith that does not move. There was no room for it in me, but the happiness I had seen on Karin's face came back to me and for a moment I envied her.

When I got back to bed I felt completely calm and went to sleep not to reawaken until nine. A surprise was awaiting me. There was a piece of paper under my door. It contained only one line and there was no signature: '*I shall come tomorrow evening.*' Karin had come during the night.

The following day was difficult. To the ever-renewed anxiety caused by the threat of war was added the fear of not seeing Karin that evening. Words she had said kept coming back into my mind as if to kill all hope: 'For a Danish girl, an engagement doesn't count . . . I only lie when I'm forced to . . . If you think I can remember what I told you yesterday – or just now . . .' The memory of her teasing voice accompanied me on my endless walks through the town. I wandered around like a ghost, noticing nothing and nobody. Sometimes I let myself sink on to a bench or go into a café. Somehow the time dripped by. It seemed to me that each hour presented me with the following one like an object passed from hand to hand. In the full daylight, indeed in the brilliance of the sun as it devoured the main square, I was suddenly seized by the anguish of the previous night on catching sight of the *Berlingske Tidende* tower where *Mene Tekel Upharsin* was written in Danish every evening at the approach of dusk.

There was a small square not far from there where I went to seek refuge, but in order to reach it I had to pass in front of a kiosk where they sold French newspapers whose headlines seemed to me to become bigger every day. Hitler's resounding demands, troops massed on the German frontier – how could I avoid seeing these headlines which seemed to bring their load of terror towards me in leaps and bounds, like soldiers dressed in black? Denmark had already received its first French exile, its first deserter. When finally seated on a bench in the square, I closed my eyes and gradually my heart-beats slowed down as yet again I started madly hoping that everything would sort itself out. I seemed to see Karin's smile behind my closed eyelids. As night fell I regained my room.

XII

She arrived at nine o'clock, tapping at the door with the tips of her fingers. As soon as I saw her I knew that something had happened to her. Without a word she came in and sat at one end of the long yellow sofa that cut across the room. Her features and disordered hair gave her the look of someone just emerged from battle and in the silence I could hear her breathing. Instinct advised me to say nothing for the moment and I contented myself with going and preparing her a fruit juice in the kitchen. After a minute she called me softly. I went back and handed her the glass which she took automatically and put to her lips.

'Last night,' she said gently, 'I knocked several times at your door. Were you here?'

'At what time?' I asked, sitting down in front of her.

She frowned and waited so long that I thought she had decided not to answer, then said in a tone resembling a reproach:

'At two.'

'At two! Of course I was here. I had a bout of insomnia around midnight, then went back into a deep sleep.'

'You should have heard me. I knocked ten times. I needed to talk to you.'

'Tell me now . . .' I urged, leaning slightly towards her.

'Now it's no longer the same. I'm no longer the same. It's too late.'

At this stage I was certain that she had come to give herself to me. However, I made no movement and then suddenly realized she was crying. She was looking straight over my shoulder, but what filled me with a sort of dismay was the quantity of tears that fell from her eyes. It was as though a bowl of water had been thrown into her face.

'I hate you,' she said in a dull voice.

Instead of asking her why, as she probably expected, I leant back in my armchair. She went on:

'I'd better tell you everything that's weighing on me. You must know. I've hated you from the first minute, from the day you spoke to me in the square. My whole being rose up against you . . . You'll forgive me all these polite remarks,' she added with the smile I loved.

'Is it to tell me these things that you've come tonight?'

'I didn't want you to have misconceptions about me.'

'But surely all these things could have been said in daylight, Karin? For instance in the adventurous wood.'

She put her hands over her eyes.

'Here,' she said, 'where you live, in your room, I calculated they'd do you more harm. And don't talk any more about the adventurous wood. There's no adventurous wood.'

'So,' I said gently, 'you doubtless wanted revenge for your . . . I don't know what.'

'Not exactly revenge. I wanted to give you a false hope – for the fun of it.'

'But aren't you exposing yourself to danger by coming here?'

She smiled again.

'Danger with you? Oh, no. You aren't a violent man, Roger.'

'Not like the other one, I suppose.'

She knew what man I meant, and with a gesture I could not help admiring she threw her empty glass against the wall. In the silence, this sudden clatter made me think of a flower suddenly blossoming. Keeping absolutely still, I asked after a minute:

'Do you want never to see me again?'

She shrugged her shoulders.

'That's not the point. And anyway, you can't understand anything about the sort of person I am. You're blinded by reason.'

She added a little more calmly:

'It was stupid to break that glass. Will you please pick up the pieces?'

And faced with my hesitation she adopted an almost coaxing tone which she knew to be irresistible:

'Surely you can do that for me. Can't you? It worries me seeing all those broken splinters.'

Blushing, I finally bent down in front of her and picked up the fragments one by one as they gleamed under the light, and threw them one by one into a newspaper.

'There,' she said serenely, 'and there, over there, there's another. And now in my turn I'm going to ask you a question, though usually I never ask questions. Why did you say the other day that the sky was empty?'

'I don't remember having said that.'

'Oh yes you did. It was about blue eyes. You compared them to an empty sky.'

'But the sky *is* empty.'

'In what way do you mean that?'

'In all possible ways, Karin.'

'Are you an atheist?'

'Of course.'

As I was busy picking up the last piece of glass, I was kneeling in front of her, and when I raised my head I saw that her black eyes were aflame as if contemplating hell. She was resting her head on one hand and seemed to me to be of a strange beauty, a beauty that had nothing to do with the one that lit up her face in moments of light-heartedness. It was not a child who was looking at me, but a woman of formidable nobility and severity, notwithstanding which I felt a stab of pity towards this being who was losing her youth in the darkness of superstition. Something within me cried out: 'Save her from error! Snatch her from the useless tragedy of faith . . . You have the light. Give it to her.'

Perhaps she guessed what I was thinking. My conviction is that she guessed everything.

'Why are you looking at me?' she asked.

'I am looking at someone I didn't know until this minute – and someone who hates me.'

'Do you understand why?'

'Yes. You can say what you like, but you find me dangerous.' I thought she would burst out laughing, but she remained silent without taking her eyes from mine.

'Dangerous for whom?' she asked finally.

'For that faith which you carry like a burden and prevents you from moving forward, Karin, and prevents you from living.'

'Put out that light,' she suddenly commanded.

I obeyed. In the darkness that the moonlight could not dissipate I did not see her at once, but little by little I made out the contours of her face and her hands, which she held crossed. She began talking in a low, sweet voice which seemed in harmony with the darkness.

'I live surrounded by men and women who don't believe, because they have never known how to think. But you, you're one of those who do think and yet reach the conclusion that the sky is empty. You're mad.'

'Karin, many people who think would be tempted to say the same to you.'

'I know. I look as if I'm deluded and can't prove that I believe.'

'So?'

'I don't need proofs. But look, you're still kneeling. Get up, it's a ridiculous position.'

Again I obeyed, but this time so as to sit down near her and take her in my arms. To my great surprise she put up no resistance. A sort of stifled cry rose from her breast like a cry of pain too hard to bear.

'I hate you, but I love you,' she whispered. And she added even more softly: 'I didn't want to love you. We don't choose.'

XIII

At dawn, as I was slipping into sleep, I felt her arms round my shoulders hugging me convulsively.

'Don't leave me, Roger,' she said in a low voice. 'War is certain. If you go back, you're lost. Here, you've nothing to fear.'

Suddenly my heart beat violently.

'War isn't certain. And then, what would I do here? What would I live on?'

'I'd find you something.'

In the grey light seeping into the room, our words had a tone that disturbed me as if we were talking in a prison. The voice went on, a child's voice:

'If you go, I'll kill myself, I'll take poison.'

She wept gently on my chest, I had the scent of her hair on my face.

'Why did I meet you?' she said plaintively. 'Why did you have to talk to me on that square which I hate now? You only had to ask me the name of a street and my fate was sealed. This night I've discovered a world I didn't know, and then you go.'

'I'm not going at once. There'll be days and days, and other nights like this one.'

Without answering, she put her arms tight round me like someone drowning and her body closed on mine with panic violence.

She spent the whole of the following day with me in a state of nervous excitement that in turn frightened and enraptured me, for at times she broke into giggles which she could not explain, and at times gave way to equally mysterious fits of crying. Sexual pleasure threw her into a sort of delirium that I found still more disquieting. At these times she displayed certain aspects of madness and I had to use all my strength to keep her still. In her slim little body which seemed so frail there dwelt a furious and almost superhuman energy.

Once calmed down, she fell into a silence from which I could not draw her whatever I did. She lay stretched on the bed staring at me yet not answering any of my questions. Sometimes I had a momentary impression of being face to face with a total stranger.

Her eyes were different. Their depth was lacking and was replaced by an extraordinary radiance, as if an abyss of sadness had produced a surplus of happiness that overflowed into her great black pupils. Perhaps even more astonishing was the subtle transformation of her body which seemed to be surrounded by a sort of halo. But that is not quite the word. For it was not so much an illusory luminous glow surrounding the contours of her head and limbs as a prodigious embellishment of her whole physical being. She was surely aware of it herself, for whenever I said an adoring word her face lit up with the smile that had enraptured me on the first day, then suddenly tears flowed down her cheeks and she frowned.

'Don't go,' she implored.

'But I'm not going, love.'

'Stay here, stay here with us for ever. If you go, I'll die and so will you, you'll die far away from me.'

The following days passed like a delicious dream in the middle of a nightmare. For the news was becoming more and more ominous, but we, Karin and I, were a refuge for each other. When I was in her arms I forgot my terror, and when I was in her arms she felt she was going to keep me for ever. Though all around us Europe was tottering on its foundations before slipping into the abyss, it seemed that this little corner of land where we were was protected from disaster, and I felt a growing temptation to flee by staying here. I loved Karin with a fury that swept away all the arguments my mind used to produce in the days when my heart was not yet committed. Now I no more belonged to myself than she belonged to herself.

I took her away from town and we went to hide our restless passion in villages where the voice of the world arrived in an attenuated form, villages that seemed not to belong to our century with their little thatched cottages and empty roads. We played a game suggested by the horrors of the time: we pretended we were living in the past, in the age of the stage-coach, and that history had forgotten us. A peasant room, a red eiderdown on the bed, a copper candlestick on the table, seemed to us a setting conducive to peace of heart and the insatiable joy of our bodies. Now and again I asked Karin what she thought about this happiness we were stealing from fate.

'I've forgotten the person I used to be,' she said. 'Everything has changed now I love you. I don't mean the universe is different, but I'm someone else.'

'I also loved the Karin of those early days, with her weird ideas.'

She was silent a moment. She had surely guessed that I was thinking of her faith, which I now assumed to be dead.

'My weird ideas,' she went on as if talking to herself. 'It's better not to look at that side of things, Roger.'

Then almost at once she laughed like a little girl and, with that disconcerting facility she had for switching from one subject to another, said:

'Do you know whom I met the night I knocked at your door? You don't? Can't you guess? The other man.'

'The other man?'

'Yes. The young officer. He saw me just as they were shutting the gates at Tivoli – because it was at Tivoli – are you listening?'

'Of course.'

'He followed me along the Aa Boulevard. I must admit I'd stared at him a bit. We went like that as far as a rather empty street, and there he kissed me, without a word.'

'And what happened then?'

'That's all. But it lasted some time, I must confess. He held my head in an iron grip as if he wanted to devour my face. In the end he frightened me. Such rage, you see . . . Then suddenly he let go to get his breath and I escaped.'

'Why do you tell me that?' I asked calmly.

She laughed.

'To make you a bit jealous. You think I'm too innocent. Anyway, what I've told you may not be true.'

'When *do* you tell the truth, Karin?'

'Do you mind not asking questions? What is true is that I'm now with you.'

She curled up against my shoulder and whispered:

'If only you knew what a wicked look he had . . .'

These words made me wildly angry. I drew away from Karin, pulled her head back by the hair and slapped her on the cheek. She turned a dumbfounded face towards me and said: 'Oh!' A slightly artful expression slid into her eyes and she looked at me as if she had never seen me. Suddenly she burst out laughing:

'That's the slap you promised me on the first evening we met!'

Without answering I put my arms around her shoulders and pressed her against me.

The next day was a Sunday and the bell of a Lutheran chapel chimed in the clear air while we were finishing our breakfast. We were alone in a long low dining room that I shall see for the rest of my life. The sun struck the wall on which it seemed to have deposited the window behind us, complete with window panes and transparent curtain.

'If you'd like,' I said softly, 'I can go and walk in the woods for an hour. And meanwhile you can go next door . . . to church.'

I had said that to salve my conscience and in the most respectful way possible. She placed her long, delicate hand on mine:

'No,' she said simply. 'That's all over. I'm not leaving you any more.'

Yet we did leave each other – on the day after the Soviets signed their pact with Hitler. She did not say good-bye. I had taken down my suitcases and said I would come up again, but I had hardly got out of the lift when I heard her childish little voice shouting down:

'It's not worth your coming up again, don't you agree? It'll be easier like that. You write to me as soon as you get there. I'll come down in three minutes and give the key to the concierge.'

Suddenly she shouted in a voice that seized me by the throat:

'A telegram, Roger! You'll send me a telegram, won't you? As soon as you get to Paris . . .'

And she banged the door shut.

PART THREE

KARIN'S STORY

March–April 1949

MY room. It is too familiar to me for me to know what it looks like. I could not describe it, and in any case I wouldn't want to. I wouldn't say that I have suffered too much in it – that expression would sound really too romantic – but I have been too bored in it. Because of that I'm oddly attached to it. I would find it painful to leave it for another – another what? another prison? But it isn't a prison. I can go out as I wish, I can come and go. No one is watching me, but no one sees me. It is as though I didn't exist. The town is haunted, it has a ghost and I am the ghost. That makes me laugh to myself. The postman doesn't see me, the butcher's boy doesn't see me, nor do women, men, no one. With children, it's different. They see me and wave to me. It is said that children have psychic gifts, but there is always a mother or a nurse to pull them by the arm at my approach, and the mother and the nurse always have that dead-pan look which for four years has been reserved for my benefit, ever since that decisive moment when all the church bells started ringing together.

I knew what that meant. I was afraid, but I went out in spite of everything, because I am not a coward. I thought: 'They're going to kill me because of what I've been doing during the occupation.' I would have preferred them to kill me at once, to get it over. I walked in streets full of people as in a dream. They moved aside as I passed by, no one touched me. It was as it was when the Germans were there; no one looked at me then either. People looked through me as they looked through the young officers who were with me in their lovely silent cars. On that day, the day of the shouting and rejoicing, I thought I was going mad. They left me alone. I thought the police would come and that I would be taken to court. Nothing of the sort happened. I went into shops and bought what I needed: not a word was uttered, the price was on the ticket. Automatically I said good-bye and the answer was silence, not the silence of indignation or of dumb anger, but an empty silence. I telephoned to my former employers. In a clipped and distant voice they told me I could take up my work again at home, as before the occupation. I asked for details as to terms. They rang off.

Why am I writing this? Because I feel less lonely when I write. I feel I am talking to someone. Writing is like talking aloud to oneself, but I don't know what I want to write. Do I want to tell the story of my life? That would be to die all over again.

There had been that letter that I had torn up and then stuck together again so as to be sure I hadn't imagined it. Let us begin with the letter.

That happened a month ago. I had prepared my big envelope for the shop. The messenger was to come and collect it at nine as usual, and it was half past eight. I was sitting near the radiator in my dressing-gown and reading yesterday's newspaper while I drank my tea. The news didn't interest me one bit and from time to time my eyes wandered. A bunch of marigolds in a pewter pot on the small table threw a beam of light into this room, which was rather dark, in spite of the three windows which turned it into a sort of lantern. In the corner a big grandfather clock inherited from some ancestor who was a clockmaker sounded its deep tick-tock that I no longer noticed. White curtains, blue carpet, white-wood furniture and a multicoloured bedspread – all this was gay, not to say gaudy, but not very serious. More severe, perhaps, and more beautiful was the dresser in burled elm which comes from my mother's family and has survived all bankruptcies and forced sales. It is tall and narrow with two small ornaments imitating the capitals of a column to the right and left of the upper section. I love it stupidly just as it is, as if it were a person. It has a village simplicity and a sort of distinction that make it unique. And then there's that long table placed obliquely so as to cut across a corner of the room, near the door. It is there that I do my work, and when I'm behind that table I have the feeling that nothing can ever harm me.

I began by saying that I would not describe my room, but it fascinates me like the rooms of one of those old royal castles one sometimes visits. One sees nothing in it, but one looks at walls and furniture that have seen something. On that March morning, things were going neither better nor worse than usual when, towards a quarter to nine, I heard the rustling of a letter falling into the box. This noise in itself was an event because I hardly ever received a letter. I ran to the door, picked up the envelope and opened it. Only two lines, typewritten: *'Karin, don't refuse to see me. I've come back here for you alone. I have something to tell you. I'll ring you. Roger.'*

The letter slid from my fingers. I looked at that white paper at my feet on the blue carpet. 'You're mad,' I thought, 'you've gone mad. The dead don't write.'

For a moment I remained motionless. My head was buzzing. For the first time I heard deep down in my ears a faint whistling sound, so sharp and delicate that it seemed like a minute cry coming from outside and far away, the cry of some supernatural terror. Roger had been killed in the war and here was this letter.

At last I bent down and picked it up. The paper had no heading. It was ordinary paper of rather poor quality. On the stamp of the envelope I read the date of the day before. Slowly, and with a movement I am unable to explain properly to myself, I tore that letter up into four pieces and threw it into the waste paper basket. If I had had an open fire in my room I would have burnt it.

What was I to do after that? I went and looked out of the window from where I could see the port in the distance with its black boats against a white sky. The pavements were glistening under the rain and from time to time a fog-horn uttered a long hoarse cry. Seagulls were swooping down into the void and throwing out their sharp, mournful calls. I was going to see and hear all that till the day of my death. There was nothing else for me on this earth, and that letter stirred up so many memories that it seemed to come from an unreal world. Yet there it was, in four pieces, two steps away.

For a moment I struggled against an idea that came to my mind. Apart from me, Roger had known only Miss Ott in Copenhagen. If he was still alive, she might have seen him and given him my present address . . . The only other explanation was that some practical joker who knew French wanted to make fun of me and cause me a little suffering. I had reasons to be distrustful. My long-ago love-affair with Roger was no mystery to anyone. Those two typewritten lines seemed to me suspicious. The handwriting of the signature did not resemble Roger's. And yet . . . And yet in spite of everything I had to telephone, dial the number that I remembered though I had not used it for four years. For a few minutes my pride held me back. I had not forgotten certain words that I had heard over that instrument, and yet I had to know.

Standing with my ear glued to the receiver, I now waited as if in a nightmare. The bell rang out in the depths of the horrible little flat of scarlet plush. Once, twice, three times. Perhaps Ott had left for her office . . . And suddenly the dry and peremptory voice which I immediately recognized asked who was at the end of the line.

'It's I, it's Karin.'

The line went dead. I am not the type that breaks into sobs. I burst out laughing. A wild hilarity forced me to sit down. In my mind's eye I saw that strong sturdy personage hanging up the receiver with a theatrical gesture. She had taught me a lesson, another one: Karin was not to be answered.

I felt myself blushing – with rage or shame, as you like – and that seemed to me absurd. My over-emotional reaction gave too much credit to that dubious little woman who was setting herself up as a judge. And anyway, I knew she was a coward. It would not be difficult to get the better of her, even on the telephone.

I called Ott again. She answered almost at once, with impatience, for she was in a hurry to go out. In a rapid and threatening voice, which made me smile to myself, I said:

'Karin again. If you value your peace of mind you'll answer my questions. This morning the postman brought me a letter from a foreigner whose name I don't want to mention, but you know whom I mean. Have you been in touch with this man, or have I got a practical joke on my hands?'

'There's no practical joke.'

'Have you seen him?'

'I saw him yesterday.'

'Did you talk about me?'

'Hardly at all. You should realize that elementary shame . . .'

It was my turn to hang up. The gesture afforded me perceptible pleasure, but a pleasure too brief for my liking. I would have preferred the motion of hanging up to last for hours. How could a procuress speak of shame! She had always been a bigot, but the war and the occupation had turned her into a rabid nationalist. However, I had plenty of other things to think about. Roger . . . Why that strange phrase: 'Don't refuse to see me'? Refuse to see a man!

I should have been at my table working for the shop, instead of which I telephoned the manager's office and left a message that I was unwell: that day there would be no drawings. It didn't matter to me if I gave up a few crowns. Perhaps Roger might come today? I was in such an anxious state that I talked aloud to myself. Why was he in Copenhagen? Did it mean that he was still in love with me? I was not asking as much as that. What I was asking . . . Suddenly a cry escaped from my breast, a cry in which I didn't recognize my own voice. It was three long years since I had really kissed a man . . . I cried out in a frightening way, and each time the silence closed in round my cry as if to smother it, for it was scarcely a human cry.

I wanted to throw myself on to my bed, but first I took off my dress so as not to crease it, because I foresaw that I was going to roll about howling. It was ridiculous, but that morning everything was ridiculous. The mirror reflected the image of a slim and still pretty woman, yes, as pretty as a schoolgirl. I was only twenty-seven and by a miracle – after all that had happened – no deep line marked my face. I tried out a smile, the sort of smile you give a man; I thought of Roger, of the dinners in the country inns, and I smiled. Nothing doing. It reached no higher than my mouth. My joy and my inimitable light-heartedness had gone.

By now I had lost all desire to cry out or toss about on the bed. I put my dress on again and sat down, suddenly exhausted. Had Ott told Roger my story, what she doubtless called my filthy goings-on? Perhaps I should not have hung up so quickly for, after all, she could tell him everything, stop him from coming . . . Why didn't he call?

The morning slipped by. The idea of preparing my lunch just crossed my mind but I put it aside. I got up, walked to and fro, then sat down again beside the telephone. Slowly the light changed around me, withdrawing from one whole half of the room where the shadow seemed to come up like fog.

Sitting still at last, I became absorbed in a sort of contemplation of my life since the day I had met Roger on the town hall square. Had I truly loved him? Perhaps, yet the grief of the farewells had been short. In my desire to see him again today I could perceive nothing but sensuality. I was too clear-headed to see hunger of the senses as love. It remained to be seen what ten years had done to him. The war years had settled nothing, but I could not show myself difficult. And why did he want to see me again? Out of love? I shrugged my shoulders. He had written to me less than three times.

Night was falling when the telephone rang. I let it ring a short time, then asked casually who was speaking. And then, from the depths of 1939, there came the voice that set my heart beating.

'It's I, it's Roger, Karin. Did you get my letter?'

He addressed me as *'vous'*.

'Your letter? Yes, I did. But I must admit I didn't understand it at all. What are you doing in Copenhagen? Are you here on business?'

'Not at all. I'm here because of you. I must see you.'

'Is it urgent? I'm very busy just now.'

'Couldn't you spare a moment this evening, Karin?'

'This evening? No, I'm afraid not. Or perhaps I could manage just a few minutes if you came at once. Where are you?'

'Very near the town hall.'

'You remember the draw-bridge that goes up and down several times a day?'

'Of course.'

'Follow the avenue to the end. I live in the last house, on the port, the ground floor. But don't be late. I shan't be able to give you long.'

'I'm coming now, Karin.'

Putting back the receiver, I nearly fainted. That unchanged voice which had said my name and said it three times, that voice was like the body of a living person, it had the same warmth and volume. 'If I've already reached the point of hallucination,' I thought, 'it's a bad beginning.' And I dragged myself in the half-light as far as the bathroom, where I dabbed my face with a damp towel, an odd gesture, perhaps, but my forehead and cheeks were on fire.

A moment later, I was seated in my room. I had unfolded the screen to conceal the bed and put on my blue silk dress, the one that suited me best, though it looked rather severe. A lamp placed on the round table lit up the room, sufficiently, but not too much. I knew about the importance of gentle and discreet lighting. Now all I had to do was wait. It was the hardest part. I was in a state of such nervous over-excitement that when I heard the ring at the door it was all I could do not to cry out.

I looked through the little peep-hole before I opened. My disappointment was extreme. The man I saw was not the one I had left ten years earlier, and as though guessing I was looking at him he lowered his head. For a few moments I wondered if I would open up, but then I did.

He came in.

Where was the boy of before the war, handsome, almost too handsome, with his mass of black hair curling over a too-low forehead? And where were the pink cheeks, the beautiful big mouth over which I loved to pass my finger, the round, full, smooth neck? I saw in front of me a man with a grave, rather haggard face. The hair was much thinner and thus framed a higher forehead, and the greedy lips had become so thin that they seemed no more than a line. Of course he was still handsome, but the sensual child of time gone by was dead and I had the impression of seeing his father. I read my age in his features, in his eyes that looked sadly at me.

'I've changed,' he said.

'Yes.'

'You haven't.'

'No use lying just to please me.'

'I'm not lying, Karin.'

It was only then that I noticed the great cloak that was wrapped round him, the sort of cloak shepherds wear. 'That,' I thought, 'is for dramatic effect. He wants to *be* something or someone. I don't know who, or what, but it's a garment for effect.'

'Take off your coat and sit down,' I said. 'After all, we have a little time.'

He took off his cloak and folded it carefully before putting it on a chair. His black suit didn't surprise me: I expected it the very moment I saw the ample and funereal coat by which he seemed to set such store. I had to admit that the colour that he had chosen for his clothes suited him to perfection, but it completed the transformation wrought by time. If there was a hint of coquetry in his get-up it was subtle, for one does not age through being light-hearted and all this black made him look oddly as though he were forty whereas really he was no more than thirty-four.

Seated at some distance from me, a respectful distance like that of a first visit, he smiled in a shy way I had never seen in him before.

'Are you surprised to see me, Karin?'

'A little, yes. I confess you were rather far from my thoughts after all this time.'

'Ten years! It's ten years in July, isn't it?'

'I suppose so, I haven't counted. I'd like to know . . .'

'To know why I've come here, Karin?'

With what sweetness he pronounced the syllables of my name. His voice seemed to gently stroke my face. I could not help being sensitive to the magic of that caress and found it hard to talk coldly.

'Well, yes. I can't believe you've made this journey without some serious reason.'

'The reason is too serious for me to want to summarize it in a few words. Would you like us to put off this conversation to some other time?'

Surprise prevented me from answering at once.

'Some other time?'

'I mean some day when you've more time to give me. I'm perfectly free myself, and since I'm here only to see you I can come back whenever you like.'

The firm and courteous tone in which he said these words suddenly made me uneasy. But much more disturbing were those he went on to say after a silence that seemed to me endless.

'I'd like to dispel from your mind a suspicion that might have crept into it. However great the affection I feel for you, Karin, the motive for my journey and this visit is not of an emotional kind.'

I took the blow without flinching. Today as I write these lines,

I flatter myself that my visitor had no inkling of what was going on in my mind, nor of what hopes he was dashing by talking like that, for, and I say it humbly, he may well not have been the seductive young faun of 1939, but he was still a man. From the place where I was sitting I looked at his grave, resolute face to which I was now becoming accustomed, his broad shoulders, his slender but powerful hands. And I had a sudden fear that all this would be taken away from me before I could even launch a campaign to keep it. I had to act quickly.

'Very well,' I said with a smile, 'as you've reassured me on this point, I don't see anything to prevent us carrying on with our conversation. My chores can wait. But, to begin with, do you smoke? I've forgotten.'

'No, Karin.'

That could mean: 'No, you haven't forgotten,' or 'No, I don't smoke.' This was characteristic, but I didn't press the point.

'Perhaps you'll drink something?'

'Nothing, thank you very much.'

What worried me most about this new Roger was a hint of the intellectual – and I didn't like intellectuals – but his gaze, which had become deeper, was that of a man who had certainly suffered. Despite all our memories, it was more natural to call him '*vous*' than I would have expected.

'How did you stand up to the occupation?' he asked gently. 'It must have been terribly hard.'

I got up. So Ott had not betrayed me, or perhaps he knew and wanted to set a trap for me.

'No,' I said, going over to one of the windows to draw the curtains. 'It wasn't very hard because we weren't at war.'

'I was thinking of moral suffering.'

I gave a slight jump, sensing something . . .

'Moral suffering?' I said as I drew the curtains of the second window. 'I suppose your friend Ott must have made you a little speech on the subject: it brings out all her eloquence.'

'I've only seen Miss Ott for a few minutes, just long enough to ask her how to find you. By the way, it wasn't too easy. And then, I can't really call Miss Ott a friend.'

'Nor can I, Roger.'

The name slipped from my lips and made me blush. As I almost had my back to my visitor, I delayed a little so as to tidy the folds of the curtains before going on to the next window. But from the corner of my eye I could watch the man whose name I had un-wittingly used. He was looking in my direction.

'It's nice to hear myself called that by you, Karin. I feel I'll be able to talk to you more easily.'

When I went back to sit facing him I had outwardly regained my composure. Between that man and me there was the round table with the lamp that only feebly lit up our faces. I would have happily switched it off so as to hear without seeing, for his voice was that of the boy of former years. He waited a moment and then went on:

'We change in the space of ten years. Ideas, behaviour, in fact everything. You yourself, Karin . . .'

'Yes. In 1939 we were still children.'

'If you want to put it that way.'

I wondered what he was going to say – 'After all, he must have passions,' I thought. 'Perhaps he doesn't like my blue dress.'

'I don't disown what I was in those days,' I said in a clear voice.

'I've always like your frankness, but it's not a matter of dis-owning. What I have to tell you is difficult. You're looking at a man who has little in common with the one you knew before. Only his name is the same.'

'And his voice,' I said eagerly. 'The voice hasn't changed.'

'That may well be. I'm not very aware of it, but it could never say the same things.'

By now my one idea was to stop him from going on along these lines, because I foresaw embarrassing disclosures.

'Roger, let's leave all that. Things said in the past can only revive regrets. I was happy – worried, but happy.'

'Worried?'

'Worried as you were because of the threat of war.'

'But you had another worry, you had discord within yourself.'

'I don't know what you mean.'

'Perhaps I should confess that one day I saw you in church. You didn't know.'

For me that sentence was like the lash of a whip.

'Oh no!' I protested. 'Don't talk to me about that. There are certain words I can't bear to hear any more.'

'In that case I'll leave you, Karin,' he said, rising. 'May I write to you? Perhaps I would explain myself better in a letter.'

'No,' I said, getting up too. 'Don't go.'

I didn't really know what I was saying, but certainly Roger was aware of my confusion, because he came towards me and took my hands in his with an authority that reminded me of the old days.

'Poor Karin!'

I would have liked to cry. Indeed, no means would have seemed to me unfair so as to get what I wanted, so as to reawaken this man's affection – for I knew he was susceptible to pity as I was myself. But unfortunately for years now I had lost what is called the gift of tears, so precious to my sex. However, Roger must have seen the despair in my eyes and perhaps the admiration too, for by now I found him handsome.

'Why "poor Karin"?' I asked.

And I tried to smile as in the past, but he immediately looked down.

'We'll see each other again tomorrow,' he said briskly. 'I'll come back at the same time.'

A twinge of pride prevented me from trying to keep him. I disengaged my hand and said simply:

'Come a little later. Towards eight.'

'Would you like us to dine together, Karin? You would choose the restaurant.'

Dine in a restaurant! They would have refused to serve us, because of me. I shook my head.

'I never eat in the evenings.'

'Very well,' he said with slightly contrived good humour, 'that'll make two of us not eating.'

And so saying he picked up his cloak and threw it over his shoulders. A few moments later the door had shut behind him and I was alone.

Alone. Never had I been more cruelly alone. For the first time in four years someone had entered my solitude and gone out again, and a man at that. I did not count the very brief intimacy with Emil. Emil had brought me no more than purely physical happiness, a sort of dazzlement of the senses. Nor did I count the casual and infinitely less significant encounters which I don't want to think about any more. Roger was a different matter. In the past he had wandered through my head and my heart as he pleased, and that night all those things started leaping to life again in the magic light of memory.

I had the idea of taking a short walk in the avenue to calm myself down, but it was possible that Roger might ring. Better stay by the telephone like an obedient slave all ready to answer her master's first call. That was how it was.

I put on some water to boil to make tea. If I told Roger not to come before eight, this was so as to seem independent, but he was sufficiently intuitive to know what power he had over me. Men sometimes have flashes . . . Oh, why so much fuss about getting into bed? The bed was there, behind the screen. I had prepared everything.

I pictured to myself all that might have happened if only I had been cleverer, but though it didn't show, I had lost my head on seeing that man. And yet it isn't difficult to seduce a man, or rather re-seduce him, and this one was the most sensual I had ever known. The whole German army couldn't produce his match in ardour. I should have pretended to be gay instead of presenting myself as his equal in seriousness. How he used to love hearing me laugh! I should have laughed. All I could do now was groan with anger. 'Fool!' I said out loud. 'Fool!' I had made conquests of dozens of young officers, yet was incapable of getting the man, who had taught me love, to kiss me.

And now the problem was to get to tomorrow, rather as one takes the road to get to a distant place. A thousand little things would help, a thousand small actions, anything, no matter what. For instance I thought I might use the vacuum cleaner on my room – I had been meaning to do it for a week but it bored me . . . Inept!

I poured the boiling water into the teapot, but I no longer wanted to drink that tea. The mirror above the chest-of-drawers sent me back the reflection of a wild, wild woman. More than anything I needed to comb my hair. So I ran to the bathroom to set all that in order a bit, and spent a good fifteen minutes giving myself a normal hair-do and a face capable of pleasing. The mirror did its best to tell me the truth: I was fairly pretty but lacked that freshness and velvetiness of the skin, and above all that mad look that are the hallmark of youth, true youth, not the youth of women who are still young, but pristine, inimitable youth.

'Admittedly, this evening I feel tired,' I told the mirror . . . And yet if someone had taken me in his arms, I would have become what I used to be.

Seeing Roger made me remember the young Danish officer I had watched with him in the Tivoli gardens. Under his forage cap, which he wore tilted so far forward that it touched his right eyebrow, his contemptuous face had produced a sudden and devouring hunger in me, a delicious torture which I never tired of. When the man had gone, I had followed him in my imagination until that fantastic moment, six days later, when chance put him again in my path and that wicked greedy little head had bent down over my face to devour my mouth. And thinking of it now, ten years later, made my head spin. I dropped my comb, threw myself back in my armchair and closed my eyes in a fit of dizziness. I saw everything again. My room vanished around me and I found myself again in a world that had disappeared for ever, I breathed the before-the-war air, and if I spoke to someone in the crowd they answered with a smile. I was free; I was not, as now, shut up behind thick walls of silence.

I took off my dress and my under-clothes. The luke-warm cup of tea helped me to swallow my sleeping-pill.

The next day was a hard one. I had work to catch up with because of the events of the previous night. If I telephoned the shop and said I was still ill I ran the risk of a routine check-up, done at home, and if there was the faintest suspicion of fraud I would have twenty-four hours' notice. I had been told often enough that I kept my job only through the kindness of the management. Those upright gentlemen were sorry for me. This allowed them to exploit my talent monstrously in full tranquillity of conscience, but I had so many motives for dying with rage that I preferred not to dwell on that one. Through missing one meal out of two I would finally put aside enough money to run away – but in how many years, and in what physical condition?

Seated at my long table, I quietly drew the face of a little girl playing croquet with a boy in a garden more than half of which

I still had to adorn with delphiniums, lupins and gillyflowers – the whole to be delivered before seven. I took great care with the little girl's features, and with furious application made her the kind of mouth that demanded to be bitten and would land her up as a victim – deep in some wood! In the same way the flowers amiably jostling each other along the walls grew in soil fertilized by deep resentments. It was in the garden of anger that my children were playing. Anger found its place in all my designs, poisoning earth, air and water, but no one noticed it; on the contrary, the customers loved my style, wanted laughing scenes, abundant vegetation, dreamlike and yet realistic landscapes. I gave them all that in my own way and more of it than they asked for. No compliment ever came from my employers and my work remained strictly anonymous, but then, I was paid enough to feed myself and I had a roof over my head. What more could I ask?

What more could I ask? One March night I had left my room and dared to go down to the port. This brief sentence tells a long story about the hours of anguish and privation that had finally forced me to leave my room, but one cannot tell everything. Sometimes in our endless winters a gentler air blows – as it did that night – making one believe for a few hours in the return of spring. A nature such as mine becomes drunk with that caress from heaven which seems like a call to the joy of life. My heart and senses were possessed by a hunger for love and the vague hope of some wonderful encounter.

I walked beside the low little houses with brightly coloured fronts lit up here and there by the street lamps – apple-green, blood-red, orange, blue. The last of those houses, and also the smallest, was painted black, but there was certainly nothing else funereal about it. It was here that the sailors come from afar went to drink till dawn, and the establishment's success was partly due to the smallness of the room where men and girls were squeezed up together in the warm half-light. I could hardly have avoided being attracted by this place of ill-fame. I had in me the stuff that makes a prostitute. I had said that to Roger in the adventurous wood, but I had said it in Danish.

Yet there were many reasons forbidding me to cross the

threshold of the little black house. One of the girls would certainly have recognized me, and then what insults thrown at the intruder! She had spent the occupation in the cars and beds of German officers. Did she now want to insinuate herself among the sailors? I knew how much those women had it in for me for my behaviour – as much through a patriotism which they ostentatiously displayed as through the feeling that they themselves had been cheated because they had not dared profit by the occasion, whereas the German Woman, as I was called, had cynically sold herself to the enemy. That was how they saw these things, not knowing that, far from selling myself, I gave myself.

A huge noise of song, laughter and altercation burst from the bar each time the door was opened, and light filtered through smoke fell on the stones in front of the inn. I stood in the shadow like a beggarwoman – and I was a beggarwoman, expectant, patient, waiting for the men as they came out. Almost all of them were reeling and unfortunately went off in twos and threes, which prevented me from accosting them, and then it must be admitted they didn't seem to me very attractive in spite of that uniform for which I still have a weakness.

Finally, towards one o'clock in the morning, there emerged a young Swede of the merchant navy. I can't bring myself to describe him except to say that he aroused in me the uncontrollable fury of desire that produces the most reckless of actions. Like all the others, he could hardly stand straight, and he stretched out his hand as if seeking support. I was there at once, sustaining with all my strength the weight of that limp but robust body which at every step threatened to stretch its length out on the ground.

The man was so totally drunk that he failed at first to notice my presence, convenient though it was. I held him by one of his arms that I wound round my neck – I, too, drunk in my fashion – my body touching his from his shoulders to his dangerously sagging knees. Even I felt in danger of collapsing under that swaying load.

However, we managed to reach the corner of the port behind the black house, deserted at this hour but garishly lit up. What did I want exactly? I have no idea, I didn't want to know, but at that moment, horror of horrors, my companion turned away from me and made as if to vomit. I drew back, ashamed and utterly sober, and saw him leaning panting against the wall. He was groping along the stones with his hands, searching for the support that had upheld him a moment before, and, moved by pity, I grabbed his wrist and led him a few yards further on. He was younger even than I had thought. There was something of the child in his profile, which I found touching. Turning a little towards me, he asked me in a thick voice who I was and what I was doing there. The few words of Swedish that I knew came to my help:

'No one,' I said. 'You've never seen me.'

'Danish?'

'Perhaps. German if you like.'

He shook his head like a baby.

'It isn't the same thing,' he stammered, 'but I don't mind.'

He made a great sweep with one arm which nearly sent him to the ground, but saved himself by putting a hand on my shoulder. I saw that the fresh air was beginning to bring order into that angel's head which otherwise would have come to a bad end.

'You're not bad-looking,' he said after a moment. 'But me . . . not a crown in my pocket.'

'I don't need crowns.'

'Aren't you a . . .'

'No,' I said, interrupting him.

'Then what are you? A young lady . . .' (He burst out laughing.) '*Froken!*'*

I couldn't help devouring him with my eyes. He then said a phrase I would never forget, for it summed up a whole part of my life with all its suffering:

'*Froken*, why are you looking at me like a child looking at a Christmas tree?'

Emotion struck me dumb and I could only smile. He then examined me quietly for nearly a minute, then guessing – or thinking he had guessed – he mumbled in confusion:

'This evening, not possible. Too much alcohol. Too much aquavit.'

His great hot hand clumsily took hold of my face which seemed to be wholly contained in his palm, and he added in a lower voice:

'Don't worry, pretty miss, another time, you'll see.'

'Another time? When?'

'When the boat comes back.'

* Miss.

130

Whereupon with those great rolling steps that men learn at sea, he slowly made off into the shadows. I saw him passing a bit further on under the harsh glare of a street lamp, then he turned the corner of a house and disappeared. For no definable reason I still waited a moment, then finally left the scene of my humiliation and went back home.

I shall not attempt to talk at length of the hours that followed. On my empty bed I gave way to despair, the despair of a wretched animal driven mad by hunger. People can smile at such things. As for myself, I like to treat the tyranny of the senses with a certain irony – the tyranny that extends as far as the heart and its infinite need of affection. There is always one part of my being that makes fun of the other, my brain deriving amusement from the furies of sex, but there are times when we are almost entirely sex. I am well aware of the monstrousness of this situation, but I was reduced to it by the cruelty of the people who wanted to punish me. Besides, despite my fiery temperament (which I acknowledge) I was altogether normal. There were thousands of women of my make-up on this earth, which men had turned into a hell of vengeance for me.

This misadventure made me wary and even more unsociable than I already was. There is this to be said, since I have embarked on the path of confessions: that deep down my sensuality was no more than a thirst for affection. It was this that had been quenched in physical frenzy. With what annihilating joy would I have folded my arms, which now held no one, round a being I could cherish! There was something in me that refused to make of a man an instrument of sexual pleasure. My soul demanded much more than that. Surely every woman would understand me. Is it our fault if their constant pangs of bodily hunger throw men into a state nearing madness? Because it is with half-mad people that we have to deal. If they could only see themselves at certain moments . . . As for women, they never entirely lose their heads and can only observe the appalling misunderstanding when they see lust trying to pass itself off as love. On this point they cannot explain themselves, since men use the same words as they do, but to indicate things of a different nature. Women love and men love, but only their bodies are united. There are sublime exceptions, I know, such as are treated in poetry. I am not denying that these unique moments occur, but, speaking generally, for a man variety is the rule and the bed is the tomb of love, or rather of one love after another. With what self-sufficiency does the king of creation bestow a plural on this word where he himself is concerned! His precious loves . . . and the fact that he can't count them makes him think that he's a great lover, whereas in his headlong rush he misses out on love in the singular. But I would never finish if I tried to say everything.

After the set-back of the Swedish sailor, there followed the compensation of my brief liaison with Emil, nephew to the baker's wife. Let me first describe the baker's wife herself. I am not interested in where the moralists situate good and evil. To me that woman resembled my former idea of a true Christian more than anyone else. She alone refused to treat me as guilty. She alone talked to me in front of those shocked mutes who punished me by their silence. By doing so she ran the risk of offending her customers, but she defied everyone, and so great was her authority that no one dared reprove her. She was not particularly religious. Vaguely Lutheran, she put in an appearance in church on important feast-days. But it was not religion I asked of her; I asked her, seeing that she was willing, to be merely human. In my eyes, her kindness redeemed the hypocrisy of the whole town. But I don't want to give vent to my indignation or I might wax eloquent.

Mrs Jensen, for that was her name, was a pretty woman with rather unmanageable copper-coloured hair, a pert little nose scattered with freckles, and in her round face something indefinably golden which made you think of the magnificent crown-like loaves in her shop. Her incipient plumpness did not prevent her from being quick and agile in her movements, and her whole personality breathed a natural gaiety that disarmed the most crabbed people. A few delicate little lines which looked as if they had been traced on her face with a fingernail indicated a pronounced taste for pleasure, and it is certain that her husband, a fat and rather sleepy man, was not over-severe where conjugal fidelity was concerned, though Mrs Jensen was anxious not to be found out.

One day when we were alone in her shop she asked me if I didn't get bored in my solitude. 'They're very harsh towards you,' she said. 'What's done is done. The Germans have gone and you've suffered enough as it is. It's a shame to see a pretty girl like you languishing in her house when fine young men would be happy to keep her company.' I asked her why she was talking like this. 'No reason,' she said with a wink, 'no reason, my little Karin, but sometimes I put myself in your place.' While saying this she was filling a bag with croissants, and she added as she handed them to me: 'Tomorrow my niece Johanna will bring you a little treat, with my love.' These words were said in a conspiratorial tone which made me laugh in spite of myself.

The next morning I had forgotten all about it – or nearly – and the whole day passed without the arrival of that promised little treat. I was not too disappointed, for I knew Mrs Jensen's feather-headedness and how she often said whatever came into her mind. Another day passed, then towards the end of a Saturday evening heavy with the languors of May, there was a ring at the door bell. I slipped back the peep-hole and saw a man with lowered head. I half opened the door which was held by a chain and asked who was there. 'It's from Mrs Jensen,' was the answer. 'She was going to send you something by her niece, but Johanna is afraid of going out alone at this time of night.' His voice was young, warm, rather low. 'Leave the package at the door,' I replied, 'and be off.' Suddenly he raised his head. 'You really want me to go?' he asked. At first I saw only his eyes, then his whole face. We looked at each other silently for a few moments through the tiny window, and I opened the door.

How to describe that man . . . No, I don't want to suffer all over again in that way. He was like a personification of the sun, but what do these words mean? He was something other than that, something more, he was all that I had imagined in my loneliness. It was as though I had invented this being who was so strange and yet so Danish. My hunger endowed him with an almost prodigious beauty. He made fun of me and my adorations. Even at the moment of ecstasy, I was thinking of the time of separation which would inevitably come, for in three days he was to leave for Jutland, where his parents had a farm. In the summer he worked at the harvest and I imagined him stripped to the waist, his great arms clasping the sheaves like a god of plenty in the ocean of corn. 'But we have machines, you little idiot,' he said and laughed. 'It's not sheaves I clasp in my arms.'

He left the house at dawn and came back the following evening. The day after that he took advantage of my being asleep to go out of the house and I never saw him again. Although I had expected something of the kind, the blow was so hard that for a moment I thought of suicide, but I was afraid of death as children are afraid of the dark.

All that happened in 1946 and we were now in 1949, but I did not know myself deeply enough even yet: privation of happiness taught me what there still was to know. I felt my heart hardening. Finally there was that visit that I can only describe as extraordinary . . .

As soon as Roger had gone I thought of writing him a letter, a fiery, voluminous love-letter. I wrote it with great freedom because I hadn't the faintest intention of sending it, but I wanted to rid myself of various obsessions by this means. Moreover, it gave me strange pleasure to see in black and white certain phrases that it was impossible to say. In this way I liberated myself.

Once again, with the help of the imagination, I found myself at dawn in a bed that was not mine, offering myself shamelessly, if you like. A grey glimmer came from the balcony and as if in a hallucination I saw the gleam of a man's chest and shoulders – a man who surely no longer existed and yet had talked to me the previous evening. The letter was seven pages long. I slipped it into the table drawer where I kept my pencils.

Roger kept the appointment. His punctuality could only amuse a woman, above all a Danish woman. It used to annoy me in the past, but this evening I could hardly resist throwing my arms round his neck. As soon as he came in I saw he must have had a ghastly night. His ravaged face was that of a man at the end of his tether, a situation on which I secretly congratulated myself, for I know how a state of exhaustion can be turned to one's advantage through leaving one's adversary disarmed. He took off his cloak and I immediately asked him if he'd like a cup of tea.

'Yes, very much,' he said in a dull voice. 'Thank you.'

He kept his eyes stubbornly averted from mine. Without another word he sat down in an armchair and rested his chin on his hand. How much play-acting was there in all this? I did not doubt he was tired, but I felt he was making the most of it.

From the kitchen, where I was boiling the water, I could watch him without his knowing. The lamp-light seemed to caress his face and gave him the mystery of a portrait. His eyelashes made a shadow on his pink cheekbones and the hand concealing the lower part of his face was still beautiful. I had kissed that dormant hand more than once while Roger was asleep.

As a result of dreaming over those things, I nearly got scalded by the jet of steam escaping from the kettle. I had been very naïve, just now, when I said that I had resolved to love that man: I'd never stopped loving him.

His silence and stillness worried me a bit. What was he thinking about? What did he know about me? I poured the water into the teapot without a sound, then I too waited motionlessly. Perhaps he had dozed off. But no, for I saw between his black lashes a thin line of light of a colour that still astonished me. Roger was the only man I had ever known with violet eyes. For a sight of his smiling at me again or paling with anger or desire – because love, with him, often took on the face of anger – for this I would have consented to anything.

I prepared the tray and went in to put it on the little table. My visitor gave the tiniest jump, raised his head and looked at me with a smile as if to excuse himself.

'I do believe I was going to sleep,' he said. 'It's so nice in your house and I feel tired.'

'Stretch out there, Roger. Yes, I mean it, on the sofa.'

I tried to put as much sweetness as possible into my ironical voice of a little Danish girl, but with a gesture he cut short all effusion.

'Tea,' he said.

I liked him talking in that way, I liked him to take command. Nevertheless I told him he must wait a few minutes.

'You surely don't want to drink hot water?'

It was almost the exchange of a married couple.

'Karin,' he said, 'I've something to tell you that will surprise you, and I'm not sure that you'll understand, or not at once.'

'You never had a very high opinion of feminine intelligence.'

'That's not what I meant.'

He got up. I admired his figure, the curve of his back, which hadn't changed. Oh, I would have done anything for this minute to go on when nothing tiresome had yet been said, for I had dark presentiments of what was going to come. I got up too and assumed a look of surprise.

'Don't stay standing,' he said. 'Sit down, Karin. It's I who need to walk up and down.'

He stared at the carpet as if searching for the words he was going to say, then raised his head without looking at me.

'Since I left you in 1939, I've changed,' he began. 'I'm no longer the same person.'

'You told me that yesterday.'

'Yes, I know, but yesterday I was a coward.'

'A coward?'

'Yes, a coward. I left you without telling you the real reason for my visit, the reason for this trip. I wanted first of all to know the sort of situation you were in yourself.'

'I don't understand a word.'

'Well, I wanted to know whether you've been able to keep your faith, or rediscover it, through these difficult years.'

Without realizing it I was immediately on my feet.

'But I lost the faith!' I cried. 'Thanks to you I freed myself from it.'

He became very pale.

'That's why I'm here this evening, Karin. Because of me, you have ceased to believe.'

'If I'm grateful to you for anything, it's certainly for that, that and the rest.'

'The rest . . .'

This vague word which had escaped from me signified love, our love. I wanted to clarify my thought. He didn't give me time. For the first time that evening he looked me straight in the face and smiled a little sadly.

'I'm not repudiating what happened,' he went on. 'May I ask you to listen to me for a minute?'

My heart was beating so fast that I had to sit down. Everything I had feared, guessed, sensed the night before was now coming true. I said nothing. He sat down in his turn and let a few moments pass.

'In 1939 I was a complete atheist and I knew you were a believer.'

'What's your proof? I never talked to you about religion.'

'I saw you in the Church of Our Saviour.'

'What are you getting at, Roger? All this is painful.'

'Painful, yes.'

I heard him sigh. Now his wonderful eyes were looking for mine, but not with the former tenderness that was so dear to me. All I could read in them was anxiety.

'Because you were a believer, or because I thought you were, it seemed to me impossible to obtain from you what I wanted.'

At this moment his pallor gave way to a sudden blush.

'It's a sort of confession I'm making to you,' he murmured.

'It is indeed.'

'That faith that separated us, Karin – I wanted to destroy it.'

'You were highly successful. Is that all? Let's make it short, do you mind?'

'Make it short? But I've got to talk to you, I've got . . .'

'You're not going to ask me to forgive you for seducing me!' I exclaimed with an effort at a laugh.

'That's all I've been doing since I came into your house.'

Embarrassment turned me to ice and I could not help finding this man ridiculous with his repulsive humility when the memory I preserved was of an imperious young lover.

'Your tea's getting cold,' I said at last.

He pretended not to hear.

'Karin, do you want to know how and why I've changed?'

'Do I want you to tell me the story of your conversion? Frankly, not much. Not tonight in any case. You must give me time to get used to it.'

'Get used to what?'

'To the idea that you're no longer what you were, and then, yes, to forget – because I can't forget.'

'Nor can I.'

It was the only human cry he had uttered since we had met again, but it was a cry with an accent of despair.

'Memory is intractable,' he said. 'It's the price we pay.'

I could hardly withhold a smile of triumph. All was not lost.

'You have to understand that religion has become completely foreign to me,' I said gently. 'I don't see its usefulness in life, in mine at any rate.'

He looked at me for what seemed an intolerably long moment.

'But you, Roger,' I said bluntly, 'you must have suffered.'

'Four years' imprisonment in an officers' camp. Others have suffered much more than I.'

'Were you ill-treated?'

'No. The worst was being deprived of freedom – and the cold. I got rheumatism in my right arm which makes it difficult to use this hand, for instance for writing. That's why I sent you a type-written letter. I can type.'

'Your signature's different.'

'Yes, it's quite an effort to form letters. But tell me about your-self, Karin, since you don't want me to talk about the change that has taken place in me. Are you satisfied with your present life?'

'Oh, I can't complain. I earn my bread as I used to.'

He had the look of a policeman.

'Don't you feel lonely?'

'Why should I feel lonely? I've got friends.'

'Friends . . . I wasn't thinking of that. You don't seem happy, Karin.'

He knew something. Ott had betrayed me. I was going to lose him. I would have thrown myself on my knees to keep him, even if he talked about my conscience – and I felt that's what he was going to do.

'Well, no, I couldn't say that I'm happy,' I answered docilely. 'Sometimes life seems to me rather grim.'

He turned away his eyes, bashfully.

'I'd like to help you find peace, Karin.'

'A sermon,' I thought to myself. 'Here it comes; he's going to drag my soul in that horrible literature, whereas I'd like to tear off my clothes and see him tearing off his.' I could imagine the scene. There, behind the screen. It would have been so easy . . .

'But I'm perfectly contented,' I said rapidly. 'In spite of every-thing, I like you being here, Roger. And then,' I added in a tone I wanted to make roguish, 'it's nice speaking French with you, Roger, as in the past. Do you remember the adventurous wood?'

Was I losing my head? He took me up at once with his mania for accuracy.

'Karin, you were speaking in Danish in what you call the adventurous wood.'

'At a certain moment, yes. That's perfectly correct. And when I think what I said to you in that language . . . How mad I was in those days, wasn't I?'

A smile which was more of a polite grimace passed over the lower part of his face. With an almost ceremonial air, he rose.

'If you don't mind, I shall go now,' he said. 'It's late.'

'Late has no meaning in Denmark. When shall we see each other again?'

I hadn't the strength to get up.

'See each other again, Karin? Why?'

'Well, I can't believe you made this long journey to ask me if I was happy. There must have been some other reason.'

'Yes. I told you what it was. I wanted . . .'

'To ask me to forgive you. I know. Right, it's done. In any case, I don't know what there was to forgive you for. You realize that that isn't serious.'

'You forget what I told you about the change that has happened to me, Karin. I hoped to tell you about it.'

'You mean your conversion? But what's that to do with me? There, leave your pilgrim's cloak where it is. I'm sure a conver-sion is a very good thing, a very fine thing even. Sit down, Roger, please. Explain it all for me.'

He did not move. A cold gaze fell on me from his eyes, which had narrowed with concentration, as if he were examining an insect.

'Do you really want me to explain, as you say? Will you listen?'

'Oh, I'll listen, and I'll try very hard to understand. I'll be intelligent. Perhaps you'll persuade me.'

I felt as if I were vomiting these last shameful words. Roger looked me over in that frightful silence he made too much use of. I pushed a lock of hair from my forehead in a rather wild gesture.

'Are you serious, Karin?' he asked me. 'Are you . . . yes, sincere?'

I raised my face to him, trying hard to put on a noble and upright air.

'Roger, I promise you.'

'Then I'll come back,' he said simply.

And he went. His footsteps faded away down the street.

For a long time that night, as I lay in my bed, I listened to the tick-tock of the grandfather clock advising me to be patient. 'That a man should pay a second visit to a woman,' I thought, 'doesn't mean much, but if he pays a third one, then it means he's caught.' What mattered was to know why he was coming back. Having taught me unbelief in 1939, he doubtless now wanted to try the opposite operation, reconvert me in the other direction, win one of those spiritual victories which so flatter male vanity. I laughed aloud under my sheet. Every man has a poor fool somewhere inside him. What matters is to find out where.

I had made my Frenchman's eyes shine with the hope of what he called a change. For the moment, at least, that was enough. If only my poor Roger had known how far I was from that degrading Catholicism where idolatry was contending for him as against simple honesty. To think that he, so proud, such a scoffer in the past, should bend his knee in front of plaster statues . . . In spite of that I would listen to him, I would listen to my little apostle. The crucial thing was to drag things out so that he would visit me more and more often. When would he come?

For my part I had made him suffer in 1939, but he had had his reward. Certain details came back to my mind: his fervour as a lover, the things he said, his total disregard of any kind of modesty . . . And the tenderness, the tenderness I needed more than anything, the great tide of sweetness, afterwards . . .

Would I ever get to sleep? Rather reluctantly I swallowed a sleeping-pill. Thus I annihilated pleasant reveries, but one needed rest, one mustn't lose one's looks with wakeful nights.

Roger did not come the next day, nor the next. I was not too surprised. 'Wait,' advised the grandfather clock. Apparently the method of trial by humiliation was the one he judged to be most effective. The sinner had to have time to reflect on the state of her soul, dispose herself to receive the grace of a heavenly reprimand, for the convert was surely not going to treat me kindly – but he was surely going to come.

A letter came, instead. I read it standing, then sat down to read it again:

'*Karin. For the last two days I've been in bed with a nasty influenza that attacked my throat as I was leaving your house. I'm not complaining about it too much. It enables me to make a more careful examination of conscience. Perhaps you don't realize the full import of our new meeting, which must wipe out the other one, the one of ten years ago. If you pray for me, who am the real culprit, you will help me find peace once more, and if I don't ask you to do this, it's because you're not yet capable of it, but I'm hoping, my little Karin, and I give you a brotherly embrace. Your Roger.*

'*P.S. Don't ring up. There's no point.*'

I put the letter on my knee. Like him, I felt that my throat was being attacked, not by our good old Danish influenza that I knew so well but by resentment and indignation. What shamelessness and egoism were contained in those ten or twelve lines! In them I recognized the converted playboy who wallows in the delights of his guilt and with monstrous insensitivity asks his accomplice of yesterday to help him find peace, that precious inner peace that will wash away the memory of his escapades. All he retained of our ruined love was a hint of warmth enabling him to call himself *my* Roger, whereas he was already the Roger of another.

I had a sudden thought: God takes men from women . . . I laughed out loud, and if one can laugh with fury, well then, that was it, I laughed with fury and nervous tension. And then came that mawkish formula at the end, that brotherly embrace . . . It was not in a brotherly way that I wanted to be embraced. I wanted to be thrown on a bed, ill-treated, raped if possible, in a word I wanted violence and not pious sighs, lowered eyes, the tip of a cold nose just touching my cheek by way of a kiss. And that was what this letter, this obscene letter, was offering me!

Yet there was something else. Roger was ill. I could not help imagining him in bed, alone in his hotel room, his handsome head making a hollow in the pillow, and the sentimental idiot slumbering within me suddenly came to life, its heart swelling with pity. How well I would care for him, my poor goose! I would read him stories, serve him with miraculous brews of camomile, cool his forehead with eau de Cologne. He wanted to be brotherly with me. I could be his mother. In fact, I loved him when he was ill and, as it were, given over to me. Oh, to be sure, I wouldn't take advantage of the situation, but he would see how good I could be, what treasures of charity lay in my heart . . . I would edify him before seducing him.

On a sudden impulse I dashed to the telephone, nearly upsetting it. He had said: 'Don't ring up.' That naturally meant: 'Do ring up.' The number confided to me by the letterhead of the notepaper gave me his voice after a few moments, a rather hurt voice, almost a child's voice.

'I forbade you to ring me, Karin.'

'But after all I would have been very inhuman if I hadn't. How are you feeling? You sound as though you're talking from the depths of a well.'

'It's getting better. The worst is over, but I'd forbidden you . . . '

If he had but known the pleasure he gave me by repeating that word! It was rather like the Roger of the past talking to me, the tyrannical, unbeatable Roger. I faced up to him.

'Forbid me as much as you like. I'm coming to look after you.'

'You won't be able to. I've given orders for nobody to be let in.'

Alas, that was not necessary. For a moment I had forgotten how well known I was. The German Woman would have been shown the door.

'Have you read my letter properly?' enquired the sick child.

'Read it and re-read it.'

'Would you do me a favour?'

Sensing some pious blackmail, I pretended not to understand.

'You want me to go to the chemist's?'

'Not at all. I've everything I need. You won't make fun of me, will you, Karin?'

'Of course not, but speak plainly.'

'After you've rung off, I'd like you to say a prayer.'

My face grew red with irritation.

'Roger, if you weren't ill you wouldn't mention such embarrassing things on the telephone. I haven't got faith. Consequently prayer is impossible for me.'

'I said: say a prayer. It's very simple.'

To think of that mouth, from which eroticism used to flow like a river, articulating a phrase like that . . .

'Anyway, Roger, I could never perform such a hypocritical action.'

'To say a prayer is not necessarily hypocrisy. I've heard a prayer said by an atheist in a play in which he was playing the part of a believer.'

'That's not at all the same thing. An actor pretends.'

'An actor doesn't pretend. He is his character all the time he's on the stage.'

'I refuse. I'm not an actress. Try to understand me, Roger. Look – I'm the actor who refuses his part because he doesn't believe in it. It's a question of simple honesty.'

'I understand very well. Let's leave it at that.'

'Ask me something else, my little Roger . . . I . . .'

It was the first time I had called him 'my little Roger' since 1939. The answer was immediate, and icy.

'I've nothing else to ask you, and this conversation is rather tiring. If you don't mind, we'll say good-bye.'

And he gently hung up.

I was dumbfounded, furious like someone suddenly gagged. 'Fool,' I said out loud, 'you've lost him! You should have said Yes, thirty-six thousand times Yes.' But I had been right to refuse. Did he think he could convert me by using little ruses like that? What God did he believe in? A God with whom one could cheat? Because it was a cheat he was proposing to me, a subterfuge. Something in me cried out that I had given the proper answer to that mealy-mouthed fanatic. Unfortunately, I was in love with the fanatic, and that was why I walked up and down my room for ten minutes and then passionately seized the telephone again and asked for Roger's number.

'Roger.'

'Yes. Is that you, Karin?'

'Yes, it's I. I've thought it over. And I promise you I'll try.'

'Thank you, Karin.'

'When am I going to see you again?'

'I don't know.'

'But we are going to see each other, aren't we?'

My voice sounded as though I were mewing. Everything in my conduct seemed to me unworthy.

'See each other again?' said my tyrant. 'Perhaps, if I think I can really help you.'

'Oh, you can, you can!'

'I'm not as sure as you are.'

'But I shall do what you want.'

'I hope we're not going to re-open that argument. I don't feel strong enough.'

'Promise that we'll meet again when you're better.'

'I promise you I'll think it over. Forgive me, Karin, but I'm tired.'

This time it was with a firmer hand that he hung up.

Alone again, I began inveighing against him as my father used to do on discovering someone had cheated him. 'You're a swine, Roger! However many times you make the sign of the cross on your chest, you'll always be making it on the chest of a swine. If I'd been able to foresee all this when you threw yourself at me in 1939 . . . May you fall into my clutches again one day, my little Roger, and I'll really put you through it!'

I would never have talked like that before the war, but the occupation had turned me into someone else. I felt it keenly at that moment and fell silent. My young officers in field-grey had not taught me sweetness, and the ostracism from which I had suffered since their departure had not exactly improved my character. Today I was a savage. But to let myself get into this state for a man . . . it really was rather ridiculous. I carefully combed my hair and pushed back the heavy lock that kept falling over my nose. Thank heaven I still had all that hair which he used to admire so much, which he plunged his face into, the colour of brass, with surprising dark streaks – and my features had not changed. My cheeks had lost their schoolgirl roundness, that was all. The schoolgirl was dead. Instead, there was a maenad.

That day passed, then another. Not seeing Roger removed him slightly from me and the temptation to ring him became weaker, then suddenly at dusk one day I was seized with a violent desire to hear his voice. When I had dialled the number they gave me his room and the bell rang once, three times, ten times. I went on waiting, my throat dry, then called back the porter.

'Ah, yes, he's gone out. The key is there.'

So he was better and I was going to see him again. My heart beat with a mad joy as if all happiness had become possible again. I very nearly danced, there, by myself. He was going to come back! He was going to come back to save my soul! Because the attraction of a soul operated on him like the attraction of one body on another. I would be serious, I would not play the naughty little girl, I would obey.

Suddenly I remembered the absurd promise I had made him, the prayer I was supposed to repeat. If he turned up suddenly I wanted to be able to tell him that I had kept my word. And I would not want to lie – not about that, at any rate. In vain had I lost my faith . . . But it was difficult to explain. I would have had to go back to my childhood, and my childhood must not be touched. It was necessary to be loyal about certain things.

A prayer. To tell the truth I knew only one, the one that Christ himself had taught. With all the violent contradictions that teemed within me, one thing remained from the past: I liked the person of Christ, but all women love Christ. I persuaded myself that he, alone among men, would have understood me, that he wouldn't have been horrid to me like the others. He would even have loved me in his own way. So I was quite happy about reciting his prayer, I would recite it in memory of him and as if he could hear me, as if it were possible that, though separated by nineteen centuries, he could hear words said in Danish by an unbeliever.

All the same, what I was going to do was a little embarrassing. It seemed vaguely edifying somehow. Outside, darkness was falling and I had not yet turned on the lights. It was better in the darkness. I got to my feet in honour of the occasion and murmured in a low voice: 'Our Father . . .'

And that was all I could say. My mouth was half open, my tongue perfectly ready to form the words I knew by heart, but nothing came. I was struck dumb. Nothing like this had ever happened to me before. I began to laugh out of nervousness, but my laughter sounded false in the silence. It was certainly not the laugh of a happy person.

I shrugged my shoulders, switched on the light, then went to sit at the long table to resume my work. Beneath the light of the lamp covered with its huge shade, I found once more that imaginary world that helped me forget the other one, the one so lightly called real. With the help of my pencils and brushes I escaped. My agile hand seemed animated by a life independent of my own, and yet, far from guiding the pencil, it seemed as though my hand followed it, as though the pencil were magic. The truth is that these drawings had become such a habit with me that they almost made themselves. I did the same flowers over and over again, and the same faces, though the range was wide – some very innocent, others not, and the innocence was there only to serve as a contrast.

That evening I put my pencils down after half an hour because I was tired. Usually I was sturdier, but I was suddenly overcome by disgust for my whole life and regretted that I had not died ten years earlier, before the war, before Roger had loomed up before me in the town hall square to ask me the way. If I had never met him I might perhaps have remained the girl I was, rather naïve despite her impudence, pious when she felt like it, and the German occupation would have left me unscathed, instead of turning me into a girl breathless with admiration before the young men of the *Reichswehr*. Roger had delivered me into their hands. Asking my forgiveness altered nothing; it did not give me a husband, for instance.

'A husband!' I exclaimed out loud with a little laugh of surprise. 'I, married to some fair, blue-eyed boy . . .'

The possibility occurred to me from time to time, but just now it seemed particularly preposterous. I was not made for marriage, I was made for some attenuated form of love affair.

The night was going to be icy. However, I decided to go out, to go anywhere so as to escape from my room. Wrapped in my thickest overcoat, I followed the boulevard as far as a road crossing it where I was sure I would meet no one. The stars were shining like splinters of glass in the black sky, each in its own solitude which seemed even more mysterious than my own.

I went along beside houses whose shutters concealed men and women with whom I fancied I could have had a good time, but had I been so foolhardy as to ring at one of those bells I would have risked seeing even the most kindly face turn sour with contempt, for I was the girl who had given herself to the enemy (of course I was not the only one, but the one who had been most seen and paying for the others who had been quieter and more prudent); I had sought my satisfaction from handsome Germans, while in our Denmark there lived the most charming boys in the world, but ones who could only offer me, besides their youth, a glass of beer in a café.

This was the sermon I read in the eyes of people from whom I occasionally implored a glance. I was used to humiliations, I drank them in – if I can so put it – in long draughts every day. With what joy would I not have consented to be whipped for one whole day in full settlement, so that afterwards I might be allowed to re-enter normal life and kiss people! It was a refinement of cruelty, this not touching a hair of my head.

The only people who sometimes cast a sly glance at me were the schoolboys who were too young to have really known the war. And certain thoughts came into my mind on such occasions. Yet such easy prey hardly tempted me, and I was afraid of the scandal, for young boys talk and boast. In two or three years something would perhaps be possible with them, but while they would grow more handsome with time I was not getting any younger.

It did me good to mull over these things in the fresh air of night rather than turn them over endlessly in the sickening stuffiness of my room between the sideboard, the grandfather clock and the bed. I wandered from one street to the next, unafraid of any encounter. Sometimes a drunk would stagger towards me, and I would cross over the road. The idea suddenly occurred to me that I was in prison, but my prison was outside and everywhere in this town, whereas freedom was living and drinking and chatting behind walls and well-closed doors. For a good half-hour I walked in solitude, stunned with a fatigue not only of the body, and as if emerging from a maze I suddenly found myself again in the avenue at the end of which I saw my little house.

It was low and square, not white so much as grey, and topped by a black roof that gleamed under the harsh and watchful light of a street lamp. To tell the truth, this dwelling that had been assigned to me was a cottage sharply isolated from the neighbouring houses – it, too, in quarantine. I looked at it from afar with a mixture of horror and affection, because after all it was my refuge and on entering it I escaped from the world. But now, when I was still about ten yards from my door, I came to a sudden halt on the other side of the road which I still had to cross.

Someone was waiting at the door, walking up and down . . . The silhouette was too thin to be that of my loathsome enemy, Ott, and in a way I would have preferred it to be she, because at least I knew her. Had I some unknown watcher on my tracks?

Anger made me cross the avenue in three seconds and I saw the person in question leap to one side as I ran straight towards her.

'Who are you and what do you want?' I cried.

The face she raised to mine was that of a very young girl with cheeks pink with cold. A scarlet scarf enveloped her head and gave her the look of a peasant.

'I've come to tell you to watch out,' she said in one breath.

'Watch out for what and whom?'

As I had my hands on my hips in an attitude of defiance, I must have frightened her, because she did not answer at once.

'It appears,' she said at last, 'that someone's visiting you.'

'What do you mean, someone? A man? A woman?'

'A man.'

'Are you a spy?'

'Not at all. I've been sent by my aunt, Mrs Jensen.'

'What is all this? What has Mrs Jensen seen?'

'She's seen someone wandering around here almost every evening.'

'A man?'

'No, a woman.'

I immediately thought of Ott.

'Someone short and stocky?'

'I don't know.'

'But what was Mrs Jensen doing around here?'

'She came to see, she's afraid they'll make trouble for you.'

'Why didn't she come herself this evening?'

'She came down with influenza this morning. Everyone's got influenza.'

'She could have telephoned.'

'She doesn't want to.'

'Perhaps she doesn't dare?'

The girl shrugged her shoulders.

'How did she know that someone was visiting me?'

'Everyone knows.'

'You must tell your aunt not to worry about me. Good night, little one.'

I held out my hand.

'Good night, miss,' she said, without appearing to see my hand. And she went. I called to her at once and she turned round.

'Wait a minute,' I said in a gentler voice. 'Come here. Didn't you see that I held out my hand?'

Silence. She looked at me solemnly. I understood everything in a flash: even though she had come on behalf of the baker's wife, who liked me, the child herself had been taught to hate me. I tried to smile, to reassure her.

'What's your name, my little girl?'

'Johanna.'

'Why don't you want to shake hands with me, Johanna?'

Very gently I took her arm.

'Leave me alone, miss, please.'

'Tell me why you don't want to shake hands with me, Johanna.'

In the blinding light of the street lamp I noticed the delicacy of her features, her short nose, her full, innocent lips, and on her cheeks the imperceptible down of tender youth. There was another silence during which my eyes gave battle to those of an intractable child. Neither of us lowered our lids or gave way. I was the first to speak.

'How old are you?'

'Fourteen.'

'If you are kind, Johanna, people will be kind to you. If you're unkind, you'll be unhappy. Are you unkind, Johanna?'

'No.'

'Then why are you waiting to shake my hand?'

A final look was cast at me and then she abruptly turned on her heels and fled. With trembling fingers I put the key in the lock of my door and entered my house. Once in my room, I collapsed. Something had broken within me. I had held on for years and suddenly I found myself prostrate on the floor. A hoarse voice that I did not recognize, though it was my own, was shouting in the silence:

'Shake hands with me, Johanna! Shake hands with me, Johanna!'

How long did all this last? I don't know. Exhaustion suddenly overwhelmed me and I wasn't even aware of falling asleep.

It was twenty past ten by the clock when I woke up. I had slept for more than two hours. My shoulders and ribs were hurting as if I had been beaten, and I had to get on to all fours before I could get up, my hair falling over my face like curtains. The scene in the street flashed back into my mind: Johanna's pretty little face, her clear, pitiless voice, her eyes icy-blue and devoid of expression. She was as hard as innocence, that child who had broken me down. I regretted, now, that I could not throw myself on my knees before someone to ask for help, but there was no one. I was no longer one of those who deceive themselves and imagine that God is in their room, listening to them. They believe he's really there, the poor simpletons. Unfortunately, it is not true.

I have no clear recollection of how the night passed. Yet I remember that I made some tea and turned on the radio in such a way as to hear just a murmur and not be completely alone. Songs either sentimental or smutty hummed stupidly around me.

The next day was difficult to live through, but what day was not? I did my marketing as usual, selecting and paying without a word being said to me except for the price of what I bought. It would have been utterly pointless to smile, even had I felt inspired to. A cold, austere face looked me over, and I went off as quickly as possible. Once home, I worked.

That day the weather was sullen. Occasionally I heard the boats moaning sadly in the mist, and through my window a grey light barely enabled me to see the outline of passers-by behind the muslin curtains. The thought that Roger would never come back gradually took possession of me. It was no use hoping. Hope only nourished suffering. Of course tears would have given me relief, but you cannot cry just when you want to. Mrs Jensen was surely right: I was being watched, they unquestionably wanted to prevent the man I loved from coming to see me. What could I do? After a good hour of hesitation and struggle, I did what I was bound to do sooner or later, I took up the telephone and dialled the number I knew by heart.

They gave me an answer that I could have given myself, for I had known it by intuition since the day before: he had gone. Had he left an address? None. Was there a message for me? For whom? I had to give my name, and then they rang off without answering.

I returned to my table. Now certainty had wiped out even a shadow of hope. If I had not made that call, I would still have been able to hope a little.

After a moment the telephone bell made me drop my pencil and let out a cry. But there was nothing to get excited about. It was the shop letting me know that the cyclist would call rather earlier than usual to fetch my drawing. I had finished my work, they could come when they liked. Having hung up, I went and lay on my bed.

It was five in the evening and the day was already drawing in. A pale shadow was gradually covering the white ceiling on which I kept my eyes fixed. I had not had any lunch, but I was not hungry, and I didn't turn on the light. 'If you were a little braver,' I thought, 'you'd kill yourself.' But I was afraid of death.

Though the room was well heated I was cold and slid under my eiderdown.

Another ring, this time at the door. I leapt up. It would surely be the cyclist from the shop. I must have been asleep because it was quite dark. The only light came from outside, from the street lamps, and the light they cast into the room was eerie. In my panic – but why this panic? – I bumped into the furniture looking for the light. The bell rang again.

It was not the cyclist, it was Johanna. Upright in her hand as one holds a candle, she was holding a bunch of flowers wrapped in transparent paper. The bunch, or rather the flower, was white. I looked at the child and her face seemed like an angel's in a picture.

'Johanna!' I cried.

She handed me the flower in silence.

'Is it from your aunt?'

She shook her head to say no, and smiled. I had never seen a lovelier smile on a human face.

'Do you mean it's from you?'

No answer.

'Johanna . . .'

I would have liked to say something, but she didn't wait and ran off as on the previous evening, leaving me dazed with this flower between my fingers.

It was a branch of lilac. Lilac in March, in Copenhagen – at which florist and at what price could she have found it? It was a beautiful greenhouse lilac, heavy, snowy, like a hint of spring that had strayed into our winter night. I put it into a yellow stoneware vase which I filled with fresh water, and for a minute I walked it up and down my room as I looked about trying to decide the place where I would have it constantly before my eyes. I finally chose the mantelpiece . . . I put my face close to this cluster of tiny flowers, and with its exquisite scent I breathed in all the happiness of my childhood. I felt I was being born anew. Mankind was less cruel than I had thought. At all events, there was Johanna, who was sorry . . .

Two days later the postman brought me a typewritten letter which I opened with beating heart, and at first I read the words dancing before my eyes without understanding them. I had to cross the room and sit down so as to pull myself together.

'*Dear Karin, I've been rather more ill than I thought at first. I ought to tell you that my long period in a prisoners' camp has aged me and I have weak lungs. Now I'm better I'll come and see you one evening. I've been thinking about you. Roger.*'

'Dear Karin . . .' I looked over at the white lilac. Roger had put: 'Dear Karin.' Coming from him, this letter was almost a love letter. My life was changing, the world was changing. The phrase about the weak lungs alarmed me for a moment, and moved me.

Then after a quarter of an hour I began to sing. I have a true voice and a pleasant enough tone, but I only knew the tunes I had been taught as a little girl. It gave me pleasure to hear them that morning while I was soaping myself in my bath.

If my face, and above all my eyes, bore the mark of difficult years, my breasts and arms and my long legs all preserved intact the beauty that had intoxicated my Frenchman in the past. I tried to forget that hands other than his, more brutal, had caressed me. I thought only of him.

He came two evenings later, an hour after dinner. Thinking he perhaps did not like my blue dress, I had put on a white one with narrow green stripes; it was younger and gayer without being showy. My hair fluffed out around my forehead, but what did Roger see of all that? He looked at me furtively and with an inexplicably discontented air. All trace of colour had disappeared from his emaciated face. Without removing his cloak, he went and put his hands on the radiator.

'Good evening, Karin,' he said. 'I'll talk as soon as I've got a bit warm. Could you make some tea?'

So I went into the kitchen, leaving the door open, and from where I was I could see him in the mirror that occupied a panel to the right of the sideboard. Standing absolutely still with his head bent forward, he seemed to me old, but it was always the same: first, disappointment because of the magic memories of the twenty-four-year-old boy who came to me in my solitude, then, after a few minutes, I fell in love all over again with the new Roger. The young man was dead and I was captivated by someone else who had the same name.

'Well, Karin,' he said suddenly in an impatient voice.

So the young man wasn't entirely dead!

'I see you're still the same,' I answered, 'but water only boils at a hundred degrees, you know. Anyway, here you are.'

A minute later we were sitting at the little table and the tea was steaming in the blue cups.

'Do you really feel better, Roger?'

'Yes, but your winter will kill me. I've no idea how you endure it.'

'Spring isn't far away. Look at this lovely lilac.'

'You're making fun of me, Karin. That flower comes from a greenhouse. You get very nice presents.'

Who was talking about presents? I understood his insinuation perfectly, it took me back ten years, and I burst out laughing.

'A very pretty young lady gave it to me.'

'Really?'

'Yes, really. The niece of the baker's wife, if you want to know the whole story.'

He raised his eyes and gave me a sharp look, then smiled and turned away his head. He didn't believe a word I said, any more than he used to. In those days he would say: 'Only your body tells the truth,' or, if by a marvel he believed me, it was always when I was telling a lie.

'Very well,' I said, 'if you don't like my jokes you'd better know that it was a man who gave me the lilac.'

He looked at me in silence.

'Thanks, Karin,' he said. 'I prefer you to tell the truth.'

'Even when the truth displeases you?'

He gave a slight shrug of the shoulders.

'A young Norwegian,' I went on in a delirium of silliness because I was so happy, 'a serious boy, very nice, tall, with blue eyes, but rather dark blue.'

'Please. These things have nothing to do with me.'

And after a silence he went on:

'Well, Karin, I would have liked to see you sooner but I was in two minds. I wondered whether it was fair.'

'Fair?'

'I thought perhaps you still felt too much affection for me, a revival . . .'

The humility of voice and look ill concealed the male self-satisfaction of this remark.

'Too much affection, Roger? Let's not exaggerate.'

I was sorry not to have a cigarette so that I could have blown smoke into the air when I said these words, but his horror of tobacco deprived me of this pleasure.

'All right, I'm mistaken,' he said, 'and I prefer it to be like that. You make my job easier. Yes. I'm leaving.'

'You're leaving?'

'In a week or ten days. I'm thinking of making a retreat in one of our monasteries in Provence.'

I was suddenly repelled, and got up, biting my lips. I had the feeling I was in love with a monk.

'A monastery!' I said at last.

'The word seems to shock you.'

'You can do what you like.'

'When the war ended,' he said without looking at me, 'I was like you: I didn't believe anything, anything at all. I simply picked up my life where I'd left off: work and pleasure. You understand me. I liked my work, but I couldn't do without my pleasure. It played an enormous part in my life.'

'When you say "pleasure", you mean sexual enjoyment, women?'

My voice was a bit drier than I would have wished it to be, and I was losing control of my words.

'Of course, Karin.'

'Speak frankly. You mean you slept around a lot?'

He looked me straight in the face with extraordinary intensity.

'As you say, Karin. I slept around a lot. After four years of privation, it was the only thing I thought about, and I sought out all the easiest women. Is that clear?'

'Very clear.'

'One day when I was travelling in the provinces I happened to go into a little Romanesque church, the sort that France abounds in.'

I sat down.

'You're going to tell me the story of your conversion. I don't know that it interests me too much, you know.'

'At first I saw nothing at all. It was a summer's day with a blinding sun outside. In the church you would have thought it was night-time and the air was deliciously fresh. After a moment I made out the pillars, then the vaulting, and finally the altar. I thought I was alone, but I was wrong. A few yards behind me there were two women.'

'Two women? Good heavens!'

'Two very old women, dressed as peasants, in black, both absolutely still, kneeling like rocks and looking straight in front of them. I just glanced at them and didn't think any more about them. What interested me was the barrel vaulting, the capitals decorated with foliage and sirens, all very simple and solid, beautiful as only the Romanesque can be. When I'd seen what I wanted to see, out I went. It was in the full sunlight that something happened to me. I was just getting back into my car when I remembered those two women and I thought about them for quite a few minutes.'

He stopped. I was becoming attentive in spite of myself.

'I retraced my steps and went back into the church, and again I had to get used to the darkness. Why was I there? Out of curiosity. Those women intrigued me. They were still on the same bench, in the same attitude, looking.'

'What were they looking at?'

'I told myself what you would have told yourself, Karin; that they were looking at nothing. It was this that had struck me. I thought religion had turned them into morons. The comparison with cattle in a meadow was irresistible and made me smile. To test the accuracy of my analogy I passed in front of them, not once but three times, and their faces, and especially their eyes, didn't move. I was ready to believe, and ended up by being sure, that they hadn't seen me. Their features were seamed with age and gave away nothing, but suddenly I got the idea that they were looking at something – or someone. It was like lightning tearing across the night. For some minutes I remained in a corner of the church, not really knowing where I was. One thing seemed certain: between those walls and under that vaulting there was a presence, a presence not perceptible to my eyes. That's all. I went out.'

There was a brief silence, then I heard myself automatically pronouncing words that he himself had said to me years earlier.

'All that just existed in your mind, Roger.'

'In my mind, certainly, in myself, Karin, but elsewhere too, everywhere, the presence was everywhere.'

What was his proof? I decided to say nothing. The thought of a theological argument with Roger repelled me. I listened in a sort of resigned despair. He was escaping from me.

'It isn't what you told me in 1939,' I murmured finally.

'No. At that time I didn't know, I didn't understand.'

I got up again.

'In 1939 you convinced me.'

He got up too and came and took both my hands.

'Karin, forget what I said in 1939,' he said in an agitated voice. 'I was mistaken, I wanted to have you for myself alone, it was desire that spoke.'

His face was so near mine that I could feel his warm breath on my cheek.

'Desire, Roger? In those days you called it love.'

'Yes,' he admitted with a guilty air which revived my indignation. 'You must try to understand me. I was a different man.'

'What about now?'

Gently he let go of my hands.

'I don't know what I'd give to destroy the wrong I've done you.'

'You mean what you'd give to convert me? Or rather to re-convert me? Is that what you're saying?'

'Yes, Karin.'

A voice whispered to me, 'Here's your chance.' I assumed an air of dejection and said simply:

'It's impossible. You're leaving.'

We were facing one another as in the old days. It was no use telling myself that we had changed. It was and was not true. I was Karin and he was Roger. Why didn't he throw himself upon me? He said nothing. Once again I asked him the question he hated:

'Roger, why did you come back here?'

With a groan of impatience he turned away his head and pushed a book that was lying on the table.

'Let's go and sit on the sofa,' I said. 'You'll talk to me about yourself, and also about my soul, if you like. It might do me good. Yes, Roger. There, sit down there. There's nothing to fear from me, I assure you, nor for me to fear from you. We aren't in 1939 any more. So?'

The sofa on which we took our places was large enough to keep a respectable distance between us, but I was far too clear-headed not to see that if 1939 was far away, it was nevertheless 1939 that I wanted to revive. Roger had sat down awkwardly, in that indefinable way of visitors who seem to be apologizing to the seats for the liberty they're taking in sitting on them. He paused a few moments, then said in a low voice:

'When I went out of that church, I'd been converted without really knowing it. The rest followed quite naturally.'

'The rest?' I asked softly.

'The rest, by which I mean the discovery of the Gospel and the return to the Church. But that couldn't interest you, Karin.'

'Everything that concerns you interests me!' exclaimed the hypocrite.

He gave a shy smile.

'Some other time I'll tell you the details about those things, if you like.'

'Yes, but you're leaving.'

'Karin,' he said, with a motion of his hand towards me, 'I'll stay. I'll stay as long as it's necessary.'

Lowering my head to conceal my joy, I let out a big sigh.

'I did have faith once,' I said at last, pink with embarrassment, for my duplicity made me feel uncomfortable.

The silence that followed was of the edifying kind.

'My little Karin,' murmured Roger.

I trembled in spite of myself. The voice, the tone, the tenderness were of 1939. I felt a kind of disgust at succeeding so easily and by such means.

'You see,' he went on in a joyful and almost inspired way, 'one can imagine that one's lost the faith and yet keep it in the depths of one's heart.'

I looked up.

'Do you believe that, Roger? Do you really believe it?'

'Yes, I believe it,' he said forcefully, leaning towards me and searching my eyes with that fanatical look of his. 'Even when I used to talk to you against the faith there was something in me that struggled to dismiss my arguments.'

'And yet you won. You finally achieved what you wanted so much.'

'Let's not think about that any more.'

Not think about it! But it was all I did think about, I saw everything again, the room, the disordered sheets, the frenzy of dawn.

'It's easy enough to say that, Roger.'

'You'll forget,' he said with a beatific smile.

For one or two mad moments I thought he was going to favour

me with a brotherly kiss, for he was leaning towards me. The psychology of the sofa, if I can so put it, was giving results. Yes . . . No . . . Was he going to kiss me? He didn't kiss me. I suddenly emitted a cry that I could not withhold:

'One doesn't forget one's first love!'

He threw himself back.

'Karin, it must be forgotten.'

Perhaps he would secretly have liked to hear me say that this was impossible. We must always make allowances for male vanity. I did no more than give the slightest shrug of one shoulder. In a faintly worldly way he went on:

'I can't suppose that my presence . . .'

This phrase was left in mid air, heavy as it was with all sorts of things. Filthy and disgusting fellow, I was thinking, your presence puts fire into my blood and you're beginning to suspect it. Just you wait.

'My little Roger, your presence today affords me pleasure without danger. Let's be frank. The man I see tonight is no longer the young man you used to be.'

That past-historic really pleased me. I would have liked to repeat my sentence.

'Splendid!' he said with a forced laugh. (I had touched his sore spot.)

'. . . But the young man,' I added, 'won't let himself be forgotten, even after all this time.'

It was some slight balm on the wound, and by the same stroke we rediscovered a vaguely erotic atmosphere. Roger looked down.

'The young man is dead,' he said.

'Ah!'

Silence. One might have thought that we were mentally burying the young man and that this took time, and time to pass on to another subject, but in fact the young man was there, alive, imperious, sensual. I knew it just as Roger did. It is impossible to kill memory. I resolved to make an effort to strike the right note.

'That amounts to saying that since your conversion you are being very, very good.'

He blushed.

'Forgive me. Perhaps I'm being terribly tactless . . . But don't you find it difficult?'

'Find what difficult?'

The voice was icy. I put on a confused expression and, lowering my head a little, looked up at him from under.

'Chastity.'

He got up and took a few steps in the room.

'Well, no, not really. At first, perhaps . . . At first, yes, I admit. At first there's an inner struggle. But that first period is already far away.'

'Oh? And what do you mean by far away, Roger? It interests me.'

He gave a short laugh and stared at the tips of his shoes as though to ask them for an answer.

'Three years.'

Three years . . . It was almost like me, for very different reasons. Probably thinking the conversation was taking a dangerous turn, he stretched out his hand towards his cloak. I pretended not to notice this gesture.

'Three years, Roger! You . . . It's impossible. Oh, I'm not saying I don't believe you, but it seems so extraordinary . . .'

'Yes and no, Karin. Sometimes we do things that seem beyond our strength, but then we're helped, you see?'

By now he was swathed in that garment I detested because the heavy material added to the obstacles separating us.

'Why are you going? You're leaving me alone just when I need the presence of someone like you.'

'I'll be back. This evening I feel tired. It's the effect of that horrid influenza.'

'When will you be back? Soon?'

'Yes.'

'I need you, you know. Do you understand?'

He was standing in front of me in his cloak as in a sentry-box, seemingly undecided, and silent. I calculated that this was a right moment for a huge compliment.

'May I confess something to you, Roger? I admire you for having the courage to remain chaste for three years. As for me, I couldn't do it. I feel I'd die . . . if I couldn't lead a normal life.'

The look he gave me allowed me to gauge the enormity of my

mistake. There was one thing that I ought not to say, and I had said it. I felt myself flinching, reeling before the eyes fixed on mine.

'Why do you lie, Karin?' he asked.

He knew. It was obvious. I was probably the only woman in the whole town who was *not* leading a normal life. Who had told him? Ott's name immediately crossed my mind. Or perhaps he had received an anonymous letter revealing my behaviour during the occupation. I was being watched. The baker's wife had sent me a message to be on my guard. What should I do now? Go out? But where to? It seemed more reasonable to take a sleeping-pill and go to bed, but then I ran the risk of not hearing the telephone if Roger rang me up. And why should he ring me up? I didn't know. But anything was possible. Why hadn't I thought of asking him for his new address? I thought of running after him in the street but immediately dismissed the idea. That was not the way to catch a man.

'He'll come back,' I said out loud. 'He'll come back to convert me.'

I imagined an impossible scene. Throwing myself on my knees before him, I was making a full and heart-rending confession of my vileness (that was the most suitable word), of my vileness and abjectness (the same remark). Now I was really repentant and would talk about my salvation. Finally there would be a grand dramatic scene that would settle everything. I would invoke the sinners of the New Testament, I would go far in that direction. The words came of their own accord, they rushed to my lips. I had to talk, and talk quickly . . .

I was in my armchair and suddenly got up to look for my coat. The only thing to be done now was to find Roger at all costs. If necessary, I would make a scene in the street.

In the street . . . There I suddenly found myself, walking more and more quickly, then running, then walking again. It was less cold than the night before, but misty, and the street lamps were enveloped in a sort of white smoke. I couldn't see five yards ahead of me. Black shapes rose abruptly and stopped or slowed down as I passed, men and women who doubtless found my haste strange.

A boy called out some sarcastic remark. Perhaps I was recognized, but that didn't bother me. Suddenly I made out a telephone booth and ran breathlessly and shut myself in.

The strangest thing about this nocturnal ramble, and the saddest, was that deep down I knew perfectly well that I would never come across Roger in this way. He had left too long before and I didn't know in what direction, but it gave me consolation to pretend. One ends up believing what one pretends to believe, but in the glass booth where I had taken refuge I stopped believing in this childish game altogether.

A sudden impulse made me ring up Ott. My hands dialled the number as if they were someone else's hands. A slightly impatient voice answered and asked who was speaking. I paused for the pleasure of annoying that woman and if possible of frightening her, then gently, without a word, I hung up. She was at home. For the moment, that was enough for me.

For some minutes I waited for the tram in the mist. A great calm descended on me like a grace from heaven. I now felt more tranquil, almost at peace. Only a detail disturbed my inner serenity: I regretted that I had not slipped my small revolver into my pocket, not that I had any intention of eliminating Ott, but I wanted to strike her with a salutary fear. I would have to deal with things in another way. While walking to and fro at the tram-stop, I pondered my plan of campaign.

The tram arrived, almost empty. A man who had obviously been drinking was dozing in one corner, and as far away from him as possible two muffled-up old ladies were talking in undertones. I was reassured by the glance they gave me: I had not been recognized. I had in any case turned up my coat collar, and now I bent my head forward as if I were dozing off.

A quarter of an hour later I was climbing the steep, ill-lit staircase where I had not set foot for ten years. A small electric bulb cast its bleak light from the ceiling of each landing, and I noticed that the red carpet of pre-war days had been replaced by linoleum imitating wood, but I recognized the smell of cooking which at all hours of the day and night floated between walls that were rarely penetrated by air.

When I got to the second floor I stopped and stood motionless on the doormat. Froken Ott's visiting card had yellowed a bit in its tiny brass frame. It was a curious moment. Time seemed to have evaporated and I was once more the charming little scatter-brain of 1939. I pressed the button very hard with my finger and heard the old-fashioned bell ringing discreetly behind the thick curtains. A silence, then the quick step of that woman whose inquisitiveness would have sent her at the trot to the ends of the earth. As I knew she would look through the peep-hole I blew my nose and held my handkerchief over the lower part of my face while slightly bowing my forehead.

'Who's there?' she asked.

'Oh, Miss Ott,' I said in English and in a rather deeper-than-usual voice, 'you don't know me. I have an introduction from your friends in Croydon: Mr and Mrs Picken of Beddington Lane.'

'I'm afraid you're mistaken, miss,' she replied in the same language. 'I've never heard that name.'

'Oh dear! And here I am alone in Copenhagen with this letter of introduction. May I at least show it to you? Perhaps there's another Miss Ott hereabouts . . .'

'Not to my knowledge.'

'Then I'll go, Miss Ott, but all the same you do live in Fasanvej and it's Fasanvej that's written on the envelope. I can't understand it.'

'Let me see the letter.'

The door opened ever so slightly and I slipped in my foot, then by pressure I forced it back on its hinges.

'Do forgive me,' I said, still speaking English, 'but I'm ab-solutely exhausted. I've only just arrived by air.'

Ott did not recognize me at once for her hallway was only lit up from an adjoining room. Without violence, but with a firm arm, I pushed aside that fat little woman and closed the door behind me.

'Oh, it's Karin!'

'Of course. Now let's both go into the sitting room. I've got some things to tell you.'

'Get out, Karin. If you stay, I'll call for help.'

'You'll do nothing so silly. Do you want to end your days in peace?'

'Wretch!'

I could see she was trembling all over and I put my hand on her arm.

'It's all right, Ott. I won't do you any harm, but a little conversation is absolutely necessary. Shall we go into the sitting room? Excuse me.'

And pushing her in front of me I forced her to the end of the passage and soon found myself with her in that little sitting room I had so often seen in my dreams, certainly not as a place of delight, but as the theatre in which my destiny had been in part played out.

The room's ugliness far surpassed what my memory had retained. It was smaller than I remembered, but, this detail apart, I recognized the crimson plush armchairs, their arms decorated with braid and tassels. I also recognized the engraving above the piano and the foul lace covering the small table – and the photograph of that pretty woman, a cousin (so Ott had said), who had died before the war and was ravishing. In the corner to the left of the piano I noticed two more photographs of the same type; they were doubtless cousins too!

'Ott,' I said, smiling, and taking off my coat, 'it's years since we met here. Not since that nice party in May 1939, wasn't it?'

'I don't want to talk about that. What have you come here for?'

'Shall we sit down?' I suggested, taking a seat in an armchair near the door.

A moment's hesitation and she let herself down on to the sofa. I had the impression she was swallowing hard.

'Now, will you tell me why you're here?' she repeated in a hoarse voice.

'Ott,' I began, crossing my legs, 'I could say a lot of unpleasant things to you – as you could too, I'm sure. But we're not going to have a quarrel because it would be very bad for you. Your face is rather redder than it used to be and I think you've put on weight, haven't you? Perhaps I'm being tactless. Tell me, Ott' – and with what contempt I hurled this name in her face – 'are you having me watched?'

'Watched? I don't understand.'

'I was warned the day before yesterday that I was being watched. Is it true?'

'I don't know. I don't know anything.'

She was panting like an animal and the noise she made fell on my ears like the sweetest music. Turning a little to one side, I stretched my arm towards my coat which I had put on a chair, and plunged my hand into one of the pockets. All colour immediately left Ott's face and she looked white as a sheet. I had a dead person before my eyes. This sudden transformation awakened my pity.

'Ott,' I said, laughing, 'what are you thinking? I'm looking for my handkerchief. Did you think I had a revolver?'

She shook her head.

'Of course,' I said when I had blown my nose, 'I easily could have one. There are such awful ruffians in the streets since the war. Are you going to answer my question? I am being watched. I want to know by whom. Aren't you going to say anything?'

Silence. She crossed her hands on her stomach with all her strength.

'Is it you?' I asked softly.

'No,' she murmured.

'I'm sorry to see you in this state. Pull yourself together. I repeat that you've absolutely nothing to fear. Merely answer this question: Have you told my French friend about my present situation?'

'Situation?' she repeated.

'To put it more bluntly, have you told him about my conduct during the occupation?'

'No.'

'You mean he knows nothing about it?'

She shrugged her shoulders.

'Ott, you're lying.'

Another silence. I suddenly got up and went to look at the portraits of the young beauties to the left of the piano, and from the corner of my eye I saw that she was watching me. The position I had taken up blocked her access to the door. After a few moments I turned and gave her an ironical wink. Those pretty girls . . . She understood perfectly. She was the most cowardly of women, but she was no fool. In any case her emotional peculiarities were not my business. I just liked teasing her a little.

'Ott,' I said, resuming my seat, 'we're going to have a civilized conversation. You have betrayed me. You've told the Frenchman everything. Don't get alarmed. I couldn't care less about all that. He knows, and what's more he now knows that I know that he knows. It doesn't matter. Now let's turn to more serious things. The moment I leave here you're going to pick up that telephone and make a report to the authorities. But you would be making a mistake, my little Ott, for if any restraint is put on the little liberty remaining to me, if for instance I am forbidden to receive the Frenchman in my home, do you know what will happen?'

She made no answer.

'Answer, Ott. Do you know what will happen, what will happen to *you*?'

She shook her head.

'Very well then, you'd better understand that I have friends in town whose existence you know nothing about' – what a story I was inventing! – 'friends who are very determined, admirers if you like, because you can hardly suppose that I live like a nun in a convent. But to repeat: if there is any serious interference in my private life, and in particular regarding the visits of my Frenchman, it's you whom I shall hold responsible, and in that case . . .'

I paused for a moment to assess the effect of my words. Ott did not budge. Now she had a strange resemblance, not to a corpse, but to a fat doll. Her eyes were fixed and unblinking, and from the corners of her half-open mouth there flowed two thin threads of saliva.

'And in that case,' I resumed, 'nothing will happen, by which I mean that nothing will happen for a while, and you'll forget all about it. Then one evening, perhaps in the street, perhaps elsewhere, perhaps even here where you are at this minute, someone will steal up to you behind your back – probably – and will blow your brains out with a revolver shot, exactly as one breaks the shell of a boiled egg with a spoon.'

I paused for a moment, then burst out laughing.

'With a spoon, Ott!'

She looked at me from eyes bulging with terror and her lips began to quiver. It just crossed my mind that she was saying her prayers.

'Come, forgive me if I'm frightening you, but it's only fair that you should be warned. Put yourself in my place. I'm attached to my Frenchman. Shall you and I make peace?'

She said nothing. I wondered if she was going to faint or have a heart attack. Most certainly that pink-shaded lamp had shone on merrier scenes than this.

'Are you feeling ill? Do you want a glass of water? Answer!'

I got up.

'Oh . . . oh . . .' she said.

'How queer you're being. Do you want me to go?'

Her face crinkled up like a ball of paper that is squashed, and with an immense and visible effort she managed to whisper:

'Yes.'

'That's not very nice, my little Ott. Don't you remember the day you invited me to come and see you? I was eighteen. You were kind to me that afternoon. I didn't understand. I was so stupid . . . And you wrote me such nice letters! But, goodness, Ott, what's the matter with you?'

She was crying now. Tears of fright were rolling down her round cheeks. I sat beside her on the sofa.

'Ott,' I said, 'I didn't mean to hurt you, but you know what a brutally frank person I am, and I've really got to defend myself. And then I become bad. I realize that. Dry your eyes. Have you a handkerchief?'

One of her tears whose passage I was watching with fascination ended up by falling on to her neck, which was ringed round with parallel wrinkles. Not a pretty sight.

'You've no handkerchief, Ott? I don't dare offer you mine. Do say something, won't you?'

Slowly she uncrossed her hands and put one of them like a claw on the arm of the sofa. I knew she wanted to speak, for she opened her mouth so that her whole tongue showed, but not a sound emerged. I got up and said with a smile:

'Do you know what you need? A good cordial. I'll fetch something from the dining room. I can see bottles on the sideboard from here.'

This was only a ruse on my part. In fact I wanted to know what she was going to do, and from the dining room it was easy to keep an eye on her. There were liqueur bottles in a row on the sideboard beneath an oval mirror. Without turning my head I could see Ott struggling to her feet. She succeeded at last, and with an unsteady step, like that of a woman who has been drinking, she laboriously reached the little passage leading to the front door. I joined her there, and, putting a finger on her shoulder from behind, caused a jump which resembled a convulsion.

'Ott,' I said laughing, 'my adorable old troll, you probably want to open the door and call for help. Let me assist you.'

And I opened the door but barred the way, my hands on my hips and my elbows sticking straight out.

'All right,' I said, 'I'm waiting.'

As I had foreseen, she opened her mouth wide without being able to emit the cry for liberation, for fear constricted her throat. In her little face rendered hideous by rage, I saw her eyes becoming bloodshot as she fell against my chest. I only just had time to clutch her in my arms so as to stop her from collapsing on to the carpet. Dragging rather than carrying her, I finally stretched her out on the red plush sofa. She had fainted, which gave me the right to administer a dozen good slaps on her face which at least restored colour to a corpse. To be frank, this operation gave me only mediocre pleasure. Of course I enjoyed the emotions of revenge, but on the one hand my victim knew nothing about it, and on the other her soft cheeks inspired me with a certain disgust. In her swooning state the old lady was really frightful. With her mouth open and her eyes turned upwards, she made one think of a dying animal. Suddenly she shuddered and looked at me, and this earned her an additional and resounding slap.

'Leave me alone,' she whispered.

'I've saved your life getting your circulation going again. A bit longer and you would have stayed where you were, my dear.'

'Oh!' she groaned.

'Shall we make peace? Shall we shake hands, Ott?'

She did not move.

'Shall we shake hands?' I repeated in a piercing voice.

Once again she started trembling and swallowing her saliva, but it was so easy to bring fear to the soul of that woman that it was hardly more interesting than cheating at a game with a child. I heard her short, panting breath. Her eyes heavy with hatred, she raised her right hand, and I felt it heavy and cold in mine. I had the unpleasant impression that I was holding a potato, in spite of which I feigned extreme satisfaction.

'It's the first time for ten years, Ott. We're reconciled now, aren't we? And you'll leave my Frenchman alone. Say yes.'

She was silent.

'Say yes,' I screamed, 'or I'll get angry.'

'Yes,' she whispered in a sigh of rage.

I let out a joyful 'Ah!' and very gently let go of the old woman's hand, or rather I placed it like a precious object on her thigh.

'And now,' I said with a smile, my smile for major occasions, the smile that used to captivate Roger, 'now, Ott, I shall go.'

And without taking my eyes off her, I put on my coat. She made an effort as if to get up.

'Don't bother,' I said. 'I know the way. Good-bye. Perhaps I'll come back some time.'

Once at the door and with my hand on the door-knob I looked back at her and saw that she was still outstretched, but she was moving one arm in the gesture of a child.

'You've promised not to do anything silly,' I said, my finger upraised. 'No indiscretions on the telephone, or else . . . You remember what I said about the boiled egg and the spoon? There, be good, my little Ott, and sleep well.'

Two minutes later I was in the Fasanvej, exploding with laughter. I returned home with a feeling of deep security. Had I not been right to follow my instinct and pay this nocturnal visit to my main enemy? I now realized that in fact it had been solely for this that I had gone out, not so as to run after Roger, whom I had no chance of finding. Now at last I was at peace: Ott would obstruct me no more in my relations with my Frenchman. I had played my hand well. She was dying of fright.

It was late and the mist was growing thicker. Through this pallid veil, yellow patches of weak light disclosed the presence of the street lamps, and several times I only just avoided bumping into drunks who suddenly reared up in front of me like towers, hilarious in this sort of white obscurity. No more trams. I walked home in twenty minutes.

As soon as I had shut the door of my room behind me, I switched on all the lights as if for a celebration and sang as I undressed. Laughing uproariously, I imagined her state at that very moment. She would have recovered from her panic and be drinking a small glass of aquavit, or perhaps . . . I stopped laughing. A thought I was ashamed of came into my mind. In spite of her fear and fury, I had seen several times in the eyes of that woman the old gleam of times gone by, when she used to talk to me in such a humble and caressing voice and I pretended not to understand. Tonight I had smiled at her as I had smiled at Roger and had said I would come back. With what ray of hope had I lit up her solitude? But above all she was surely trembling. That evocation of the egg-shell was not the kind easily forgotten. Why did she suddenly seem less funny?

When I was younger I would not have behaved as I had behaved tonight. I had become malicious. No, I had been made malicious by people and circumstances. The Karin of 1939 would have found it ignoble to make use of the weapon of fear on someone so vulnerable as that absurd old woman. But one had to defend oneself, I thought, as I slid under my bedclothes.

I switched off the light. Sleep did not come. After a while I switched on the light again and did an odd thing. I rang up Ott. What did I want to say to her? I hadn't the faintest idea. Take back what I had said about the boiled egg and the spoon? It would perhaps be imprudent to gloss over that phrase, which could be useful, but it was because of it that I could not sleep. The telephone rang. The line was engaged. The wretched old woman was making a call. She was telephoning at half past eleven at night. But to whom? The police? Very unlikely. Probably to a friend, because she was frightened of being alone, but she would not betray me, of that I was sure; too cowardly to run the risk of the violent end I had predicted for her if she talked. I could sleep, and sleep in peace.

Having turned off my light, I closed my eyes and counted the minutes by the ticking of the clock. Why? How do I know? I waited a good ten minutes, then turned the light on again and dialled the number. Engaged . . . She was still talking, but what could she be saying? It seemed to me odd – I won't say actually disturbing. In no circumstances did I want to give way to that uneasiness which so quickly turns to anxiety. If that old woman wanted to spend all night gossiping over the telephone, she was free to do so. As for me, I wanted to sleep. With this in mind I took the strongest sleeping-pill I had and in less than a quarter of an hour had fallen into a deep sleep.

I dreamt that I was deep under water and struggling with all my might to get back to the surface. My efforts were so terrible that at last they woke me up. In the darkness I saw the squares made by the windows, a pale line round the drawn curtains, then the furniture dimly appeared: the sideboard, the low armchair near the small table. Roger had sat in that corner gazing at me with that undecipherable look he now had. Did he suppose I had forgotten the things he had said to me in the past when we lay naked one against the other?

I suddenly got out of bed and turned on the light to see what time it was. Two thirty-five. In the bathroom, where I went to get another sleeping-pill, I saw myself in the glass above the wash-basin with my hair all awry and my eyes wild. My mother came into my mind: those visits to the mental home suddenly brought to an end by her death. She used to look at me with an absorbed air and in a polite voice ask me who I was. I did not want to become like her. I was afraid of doing or saying things uncharacteristic of myself. Just now, with Ott, I had behaved like one possessed. With Roger I promised myself I would be reasonable. He knew I had slept with the Germans. Ott had told him. So much the better: it would allow him to be magnanimous. If necessary I would throw myself on to my knees, hide my face, and pray . . . No. That I could not do.

'No, that I can't do,' I said aloud, the glass of water in my hand.

One had to draw the line somewhere, and this was where. To begin with, I could not pray. I didn't want to encroach on the things of my childhood: faith, the Bible. I had abandoned them, but in their way they were still beautiful. The other day I had not been able even to pretend to pray, I was not prepared to commit such base treason – and yet . . .

I closed my eyes and saw him, I saw the face of my first love. The voice was the same, and a voice is magic. If only I could get him to kiss me in the dark, if only we could love each other in the blackness, what did all the lies on earth matter to me? I would lie and lie and lie.

By now I was back in the bedroom again, holding my glass from which I had not yet drunk. I was talking out loud, making an incoherent confession to Roger, unloading my most disturbing faults under the guise of repentance. But out of modesty I would first propose that we turn out the light. In the darkness I would know what had to be said.

This peculiar monologue fell into the muffled silence of the room I had so rudely dragged from sleep. Everything around me seemed strange and vaguely alarming because of having the light on in the depths of the night, and because in the midst of the furniture that woman was standing motionless – the woman I saw in the mirror and who held me in thrall, as if by not moving herself she prevented me from making any motion.

I put the glass of water briskly to my lips and swallowed its contents almost with greed, despite the bitterness of the tablet I had dissolved in it. Now I could be sure that I would sink into sleep and so stop suffering. I switched off the light and threw myself into bed. There I found the warm hollow and curled myself up in it with a shiver, for my room was cold; all that remained was to wait for the blessedness of sleep. My limbs were already becoming heavy when a cry made me leap up.

It came from outside and my first thought was that it was a dream: I had distinctly heard my name. Someone not far from my house was calling me in a long-drawn-out voice that I did not recognize. It could not have been a dream. I was out of bed with a bound and at the half-open window. The wind was blowing, dispersing the mist, and I saw the lights of the quay and the masts of the ships swaying slightly in the dark sky, but I scanned the melancholy scene in vain – there was no one. After a moment I got back into bed.

'After all,' I thought, 'I'm not the only Karin around the place. If some drunken man has lost *his* Karin, let him find her!' I did not have to wonder for long whether my sleeping-pill was going to carry through its interrupted task, for I felt myself slowly sliding into irresistible annihilation when the cry I had just heard came again, this time less loud and almost under my window. But I did not get out of bed again.

I dreamt that a face and two big hands were pressed against the window, as if the shutters had not been closed, and the face was in turn that of my father emerging from the depths of the water that drowned him, that of a soldier I had loved who had been killed in Russia, and finally Roger's, but a haggard and tragic Roger. This phantasmagoria lasted only a few seconds. I woke up five hours later feeling refreshed and, for no known reason, filled with a vague and powerful hope.

Four days passed, then the morning postman came to still all impetus towards the future. With hands trembling with joy I opened a letter which gave me the following message to meditate upon:

'*Karin, I'll come and see you towards evening the day after tomorrow to say good-bye. I've decided to return to France in a week and carry out the project I told you about, but if you could keep a fairly long time free, we could discuss certain important things. There's surely no need for me to specify what these things are. The man who will ring at your door on Thursday evening will come solely to help you rediscover the lost land. What I want, Karin, is your happiness, the one the world doesn't give. I would like your soul to open out to joy, the joy I have in my heart while writing these words. Roger.*

'*P.S. I'm adding a piece of news to my letter which I think will mean something to you, though it concerns someone for whom you had a low opinion. Miss Ott died suddenly five days ago tonight, in the little sitting room where I had visited her a week earlier. I was intending to go and see her again, but neighbours told me what had happened. She was found on her sofa near the telephone and she had taken off the receiver. She must have had a weaker heart than was thought, and she died in solitude but not, as I am convinced, in despair. You know as I do that she was, in fact, a believer. R.*'

The letter slipped from my fingers and I got up. Five days ago tonight . . .

'I killed her,' I said aloud.

My ears were buzzing and I was suddenly cold. The blood ebbed from my hands and face and for a few minutes I felt unable to move, frozen by fear. I seemed to see the little woman lying on the red sofa with her hands on her breast and her mouth open, the telephone at her feet. She had wanted to call for help but had not been able to.

With a violent effort I bent down and picked up the letter and went into the kitchen. I had to pull myself together, calm myself down, above all think clearly. This woman had died a natural death. She had a weak heart. I knew nothing about it. Emotion had killed her because she was liable to an accident of this kind. We had had an argument but had left one another peacefully. I had insisted on making peace with her.

I put on some water to boil for my tea and thought: 'Everything is all right at the moment. The poor old woman suffered too much from loneliness and age, entirely aside from those passions which become so disturbing with the years, but I'm sorry I teased her. She had forgiven me. We had made our peace.'

Through the window above the stove I saw, as always at this hour, men coming and going on the quay and the masts of the ships bending at the will of the wind in the dull grey skies of an endless winter. No one on earth knew that I had been to see Ott. When this certainty had really sunk into me I regained my calm. I prepared my breakfast and sat at the little table. Roger was going to come. That was the most serious item of news for the time being. As for those farewells announced in the ponderous tones he now affected, I took it on myself to head them off. As he wanted religion, he would have it. The recipe was familiar to me. I would be the perfect model of a soul appealing for help and unable to be left to its own devices.

On re-reading his letter I found it weak and faintly suspect. He wanted to see me. What woman would not have sensed something?

While I was washing dishes in the kitchen a moment later, I was thinking of all that when a name came distinctly into my mind just as if it had been whispered in my ear: 'Ott.' I shrugged my shoulders. If I had been the cause of this woman's death, my conscience was less burdened than hers, on which there weighed all the hatred deployed by the old scoundrel in my pursuit. She had killed my youth.

That night the weather became milder. It seemed possible that the first breath of spring was driving away the cold from our skies and I could not help seeing in this a presage of happiness. There was within me a sort of predisposition towards hope which always prevented me from going under.

The next day, towards five in the evening Roger rang my bell.

By an oddity of my rather perverse nature I took pleasure in making him wait. My eye glued to the peep-hole, I noted his still and patient stance and detected a sadness in his eyes which rather tore at my heart. But once I had opened the door he put on an amiable expression and offered me both his hands with a smile.

'Karin,' he said, 'I want this visit to leave us with a happy memory, because it's the last.'

'Come in,' I said, and I smiled too.

When he was in the centre of the room he took off his cloak and folded it with careful movements and an absorbed expression. I did not find him handsome that evening. It would be easy to stand up to him.

'Dear Karin,' he began, sitting down in *his* armchair (we already had our habits . . .), 'I realize that I didn't talk to you as I should have the other day. I feel I probably seemed too solemn, not to say severe, didn't I?'

He put the question cheerfully. I let it fall into silence. He joined his fine hands and looked straight in front of him.

'Today,' he went on, 'I want to bring you joy, you understand? I said that in my letter. But why don't you sit down?'

This last remark was accompanied by a furtive glance towards me. I took a seat almost at his feet, on a low chair, and looked up at him with the face of a good pupil. He must have been agreeably surprised by the humility of my attitude, for he leant a little towards me with that same smile that seemed to be attached to his face like a mask, but my silence worried him. Dusk was falling. Of all the various lights, this was the most propitious; it favoured the language of love. Perhaps Roger was vaguely aware of these dangerous beginnings.

'Aren't you going to say anything?' he asked.

'I'm waiting.'

'I'm wondering if you're happy. I'd like to go away with the deep certainty that you're happy.'

He said that with an adorable clumsy gesture as if offering me a bouquet. Much against my will, I felt myself recaptivated by his charm, by the charm of his voice and his very awkwardness. But I was torn in two. The convert irritated me and it was unfortunately the convert whose turn it was to speak in the uncertain light of dusk.

'Don't be afraid that I'll preach you a sermon. I've neither the right nor the desire to do so, but I want to talk to you about yourself, yes, Karin, about . . . your soul.'

At this point I stopped listening. Something in me rebelled against the use of certain words, and though I went on looking meekly and attentively at the man who had been my lover, I was remembering the uncouth young officers who used to tramp about and whistle in my untidy room. That, as I knew well, was vice, and what I wanted was affection. A terrible apathy had fallen on me these last few minutes. If I was not loved, there was nothing to do but die. The man in front of me had loved me. I wanted to shout out, but I controlled myself.

'Karin, are you listening?'

I could not help feeling a thrill. His warm voice in the half-light enfolded me as in the past.

'Roger,' I said suddenly, 'why don't you look at me? Are you afraid of me?'

'What do you mean, Karin? Would I be here if I were afraid of you?'

He was now looking me straight in the eyes as if to challenge me, but in the depths of his magnificent pupils I could read nothing but his determination not to *see* me: his look was empty. So finally I turned away my head, my cheeks burning. Without really knowing why, I got up, and so did he. I've no idea what we were expecting to happen as we stood facing each other, but it was I who spoke first and the words came from my lips as if of their own accord.

'I've something to tell you, Roger. You saw Ott before she died. Did she tell you about me?'

'Yes.'

'At length?'

'Yes, at length. She didn't hate you as you thought.'

'She must certainly have told you lots of things about me.'

'She told me what everyone knows, Karin.'

'But things you didn't know before you came to Denmark?'

'Yes, I did know them. She had written to me – with great sadness. Now that she's dead I can talk about it. Her letter had a decisive effect on me.'

At this moment I began trembling and had to lean against the small table.

'A decisive effect?' I echoed in a flat voice. 'What do you mean?'

'I mean I sat in judgement on myself and recognized that I was guilty with regard to you. It was I who set you going along the path you followed. I aroused your dormant sensuality. Had you not known me you might not have acted as you did.'

'Roger, you have judged me, you too.'

He must have been very agitated for he didn't notice that I used the '*tu*'.

'I judge no one. In my eyes you're no more guilty than I.'

'But I've been punished!' I cried. 'They've been punishing me for four years and they're still punishing me. They've robbed me of my youth, they've deprived me of love. Do you realize what that means? Try to remember what you were in the past.'

'We must pray,' he said, stretching his hand towards me as if to thrust me away. 'I've suffered, too. God is the only refuge in such cases.'

'Not for me. I don't believe in God.'

He looked at me wildly.

'Karin,' he said, 'that's because of me. We're lost, Karin.'

I said nothing. Turning his back on me, he went towards one of the windows. Though the lights from the port were shining through the panes, it was dark in the room. As if talking to himself he murmured:

'Your conversion was the sign I was hoping for, the sign of forgiveness and salvation. I'll never be able to forgive myself.'

'Isn't it enough that your God forgives you?'

'You can't understand. I'm not sure of his forgiveness, I'm no longer sure of anything.'

Our voices in the darkness sounded different from in the light: they reminded me of blind people looking for each other. Instinctively I remained motionless, my eyes fixed on Roger's tall silhouette.

'The other day,' he went on in a calmer tone, 'you promised to obey me.'

'Yes.'

'Will you do what I tell you? We're going to kneel down, I

here, and you there, where you are, and you'll repeat after me the prayer I'm going to say.'

'Roger, I can't pray.'

'Then I'll pray alone.'

And I did indeed see him kneel down and pray, but in silence. His round head was outlined against the pale light of the window. Long minutes passed, long and embarrassing, before he got up and groped his way towards the chair where he had put his cloak.

'I'm going, Karin. I think God will have pity on both of us.'

He looked for the door. I got there first.

'You'll come back, Roger?'

'No.'

He pushed me gently aside and opened the door.

'Roger,' I said, 'if you don't come back I'll kill myself.'

He said nothing but turned his head towards me. Never in my life had I seen so much sorrow in a man's eyes. His gaze told me what no human lips could have, and I said nothing. In the light of the street lamp slanting down on him, from the side, his ravaged and suffering face seemed determined to stamp itself on my memory for ever.

'I'll kill myself,' I repeated softly.

His lips moved, but I did not hear what he said except for the word 'cross'. The blood was beating in my temples and the lights from the street seemed to be darkening. Suddenly he was not there any more and again I found myself in my room behind the closed door.

I hadn't the faintest intention of killing myself, but I wanted to be dead, I called on death. Suddenly my knees gave way and I fell to the floor. Lying absolutely still like that, I understood what was meant by a broken heart. My years of humiliation were nothing compared with my present anguish. In spite of everything, I wanted to live. There was no logic in my mind. My one idea at the moment was to stop suffering. After a while I got up and went to the bathroom, where I prepared a sleeping draught. It was a tablet wrapped in silver paper and I found it hard to swallow tablets. So, as usual, I took a hammer and with a light blow reduced the tablet to powder without tearing the silver paper.

A moment later I was in bed, but sleep was slow in coming. In vain I imitated all the positions of sleep – curled up on one side or flat on my back with arms flanking my body. My mind did not want to sleep. My eyes wide open in the darkness, I saw again that unhappy child's face, the pupils enlarged by despair, saying it was impossible, it was finished. Once again my heart was wrung and I felt a bar across my chest, just beneath my breasts. 'No, never!' I thought, and slipping out of bed I ran to the bathroom to repeat the performance with tablet and hammer, the comic side of which did not escape me even at that moment. So the second tablet joined the first and this time the dose knocked me out.

I was dragged from sleep by a dream. I saw myself lying passive and motionless on my back. Above me hung a black object that was slowly moving. It took me some time to realize that its oscillations were bringing the object gradually lower, and that in coming closer to me it was assuming a more distinct shape. Suddenly I saw it was a cross, a huge cross, exactly as big as myself. It stopped an inch or two from my body and seemed to be measuring it. I began to howl with terror, but what I thought was a howl turned out to be a very weak cry like that of a small animal caught in a trap. Throwing back my blanket, I found I was bathed in sweat. 'What an idiotic nightmare!' I thought. 'Of course it's the memory of the word Roger said when he left me, because I'm not really one of those women who dream of crosses.'

The day stretched out before me like a desert that had to be crossed at whatever price. I washed and got dressed. 'It's finished,' I repeated from time to time as though answering someone. Finally I picked up the telephone and on the off-chance, without believing anything could come of it, called the only number Roger had consented to give me. Of course they told me he had left. When? Five days ago. 'Are you sure?' They rang off.

I went out on to the quay and looked at the water below me. It was green turning to black and gently lapped against the hulls of the boats. One would have said it was stroking them as one strokes an animal. My father had drowned himself further on, under the trees. Nothing in the world would have made me throw myself into the water as he did. I wondered yet again how he had found the courage to take a step forward into the void. One step and the water smothered you. I drew back with instinctive prudence, distrustful of what I might do as the result of a sudden impulse, and I went home where my work was waiting for me.

For there was always work, hundreds of little pencil strokes with which my hand had to blacken the thick paper, even if my heart was breaking. This evening the cyclist would be there at five thirty. Owing to recent upheavals I was behindhand. I had already been excused a second time, over the telephone that had the manager at its other end, and a warning had been given me in tones of icy politeness. So this morning I felt I was drawing in a bad dream. Sometimes my vision got blurred and I had to pause for a while.

I had left my window open. The sky above the black chimneys was a timorous blue and the intoxicatingly sweet air seemed charged with memories, as if across the world's brutality child-hood was carving a path towards me. Suddenly I put down my pencil. I could not draw any more. If the little girl was dead, the grown-up woman had no business to be on the earth today. An absurd thought, no doubt. But I felt I was dying of grief. I had let Roger go. I should have kept him – I could have. I was convinced now that it was he who had called to me the other night. 'Impossible,' asserted my reason. I shrugged my shoulders, put my elbows on my work-table, leant my head on my fists, and let out a groan which horrified even me. I groaned like a woman being dragged to the torture chamber. Supposing anyone heard . . .

I got up quickly, closed the window, drew the curtains – not only of the window I had closed but of the others too. Why? One drew the curtains in the houses of the dying. There was a sort of mad logic in all that. I myself was dead, after my fashion. I was in another world. Anguish had made me cross its threshold.

At long last the thought that had been wandering about within me for hours came to a head in my mind. I went to the window in front of which I had seen Roger on his knees, but I didn't at all want to kneel down myself. All I did was to say out loud: 'Listen, make that man come back . . .'

The sound of my voice had a strange effect on me. For in fact I was talking quite alone. Millions of men and women talk alone every time they pray, but to tell the truth I was not praying. Prayers begin with *Lord* and finish with *amen*. I went on because it did me good to hear the voice that was mine and that kept me company in my loneliness. It could not be helped if I was talking to someone who did not exist. The truth, the piteous truth, forced me to admit that I was trying a recipe, that I was resorting to a superstitious practice in order to influence destiny, because everything had gone wrong. It was not a matter of play-acting, but rather of magic. My voice spoke again, urgently:

'I ask you to bring back that man who left me last night. I ask for nothing else, neither for freedom nor for riches. Only for the presence of the man I love. I am unhappy.'

'That's enough,' I thought. But no, I had to go on, I had to argue with emptiness. I closed my eyes and made an effort to believe that an invisible and all-powerful person was there before me, in the night of my shut eyelids.

'Help me,' I said softly. 'Don't ask me to do what I can't do, don't ask me to kneel and believe like a real believer. It's already hard enough that you never answer, for after all no one has ever heard of your answering. If you didn't exist, there'd be the same silence. It's this silence of yours that's so unacceptable. It's the reason why people don't believe. As for me, I ask you to answer by giving Roger back to me. That's all. Do you want me to kneel? If that can bring back Roger, then I'm quite willing. Considering the point I've reached, talking to you out loud and by myself in this room . . .'

So, blushing slightly, I knelt down.

'Supposing someone saw me . . .' I murmured.

The answer came immediately, in the very depths of my being: 'Someone is seeing you and watching you.' 'No,' I thought, 'that's the little girl talking, the Karin with her child's hair down her back. I'm not deceived. God talks in another way.'

Suddenly I lost all patience and, hitting the floor with the flat of my hand, cried out:

'Do something! Lord, I command you to do something!'

I do not know how the day passed. Towards half past five the messenger rang the bell to fetch my work, but I had only two drawings to give him out of four. The messenger was an ugly, greying little man (they did not risk sending me an Adonis, though there were some). I had known him for more than a year. Normally he did not speak, in accordance with the atrocious ban, but on this occasion he looked at me from under his peaked cap with his small, red-rimmed, pale-blue eyes and asked me if I was all right. With his bristly moustache and lined cheeks, he seemed to me so unattractive that I usually did not look at him. Yet there was something friendly in his voice that surprised me and the thought crossed my mind that he had designs on me.

'Why are you bothering about my health?' I asked.

'You don't look well, miss. If you telephone the management that you're not so good, I'll say for my part that you look poorly.'

'Thank you.'

He buckled his big black satchel that almost reached down to his knees and paused for a moment in the doorway. I thought perhaps he expected a tip as reward for his advice and fetched my purse from a drawer in the big table, but he guessed what I was doing and shook his head to say No.

'You may have caught cold,' he said, 'but the weather's settling down. Don't worry. Things will get better.'

'What makes you think things will get better? Nothing can get better for me.'

'Yes it can.'

I shrugged my shoulders, gave him a slight nod, and shut the door. That poor fellow with his ageing scragginess caused me an almost physical malaise. I could not forgive him for being so ugly. Yet I was sorry to have seemed so cold towards him. He had tried to be kind – which was totally abnormal. Next time, in a week, I would talk to him a little.

In a week Roger would be far away. Why had he come back to Denmark just when I had got over thinking about him? Everything started up again in my head – the questions without answers, the good ideas that came too late, the opportunities lost because I never understood in time what was being offered me. I should have kissed Roger. I must have been mad not to press him against me as in the past, when I felt his breath on my face.

I telephoned the management and made my excuses to the *voice*. It let me talk and merely said: 'If you're temporarily unfit for work, we'll advise by letter after an enquiry.'

That night I stayed up till dawn. Seated at my long table I did the drawings that were lacking. They were neither better nor worse than the previous ones, so it seemed to me. My hand knew what had to be done. As dawn broke I collapsed into bed.

Six hours later I was up again. A glance at my work revealed that all the boys had Roger's eyes and one of the little girls, half hidden by a friend's shoulder, had Ott's face. Hadn't I noticed this while drawing? That spiteful and attentive look and the little cherry-coloured mouth – I recognized them with horror, yet not without a hint of admiration for the faithfulness of the likeness. Without further delay I rolled up my work and went into town.

There was a wave of happiness in the air that morning. Our Scandinavian spring has the force of an explosion. It's a victory over the icy hell into which we are plunged for long funereal months. The sun was flowing over the roofs and caressing people's faces, some of which would have seemed to me the purest in the world but for the mocking eyes that distinguish us from other peoples, for there is no use looking for angels in our country: the angels are further north, in Norway, but we are more amusing.

I was thinking these thoughts while walking down the long street leading from the town hall to the market – the market which is called 'new' while being very old. And I was telling myself that in our country there was no place for suffering on a fairy-like morning such as this. The women were chatting all along the pavement and the boys were laughing or pulling faces of delight at the return of the sun. In a few weeks everybody would be lying flat on the sand at Klampenborg – where I had been with Roger.

There was a lively contrast between my memories of the past and the personage in front of whom I found myself a moment or two later. The office was one of exemplary austerity, and I spread out my drawings on the table where they received a cursory glance from the assistant-manager in his black suit. Had that man ever sun-bathed, I wondered, and what on earth would he be like naked? As straight as a church tower, thin and desiccated, he had a perfectly regular face topped by the remains of fair hair which he must have combed with the fanatical care of men destined to total baldness. Pointing a disdainful finger, he now signed to me to roll up my drawings one by one after he had seen them. There was something horrible about his arrogance. I wondered if a woman had ever kissed that long tight mouth. But who knows – perhaps he was adored. I could not help observing him as I observed all men. He had a smooth complexion the colour of ivory, or, more prosaically, of cold chicken, and his eyes were of that china blue that is generally admired. At eighteen he would probably have seemed to me tolerable, but today I looked at him with horror. However, something occurred to modify my opinion ever so slightly.

Having established that the four drawings were there on the table, he put his hands behind his back and made me a speech of which every syllable is still present in my mind.

'We'll take no notice of your delay, young lady, because everything is now in good order. Let me add that the regularity of your work over the last four years justifies some increase in your wages. You'll be informed of this in due course by the accounts department.'

I looked at him in stupefaction, not so much because of the words that fell from his lips as because of the smile that accompanied them. I had never seen him smile, I had never seen anyone in the store smile at me since the war. He added:

'I've no doubt your manner of life will soon improve, young lady. There'll be a little enquiry beforehand just for form's sake, but nothing that could bother you.'

Without giving me time to answer, he dismissed me with a sign of his head and I went to the door. Outside, I walked first in one direction, then another, as if I had lost my way, and in fact it did seem to me suddenly that I was in a foreign city. I went towards the new market and sat down on a bench to try to rally my thoughts. Without a doubt something was happening around me. I had been sensing it vaguely for several days: a confused, strange hope. It was unusual for my salary to be increased and for the assistant-manager to smile at me, but what difference could that make? What difference could it make that the sun was shining right down to my feet and that a bird was singing just above me in the trees sprouting with pale green buds? Roger would soon have left the country, so whom was this festival for, this virginal blue sky and this cheeky sunlight? With some embarrassment I recalled my formless prayer of the night before and my dictatorial thump with the flat of my hand on the floor – that ridiculous appeal . . . My absurd prayer could not have been heard. A sigh of exasperation escaped from me involuntarily and I saw that passers-by were glancing at me. I went and sat down in another corner of the square, a corner where there were children playing.

One of them was so tiny, I remember, that he went staggering along the pathway as if drunk. His great pink blond head seemed too heavy for his small body and he stopped in front of me, his mouth open, staring at me with blue eyes in which nothing could be seen but abysses of innocence. I smiled and held out my hand which he touched with his and gratified me in his turn with a wide toothless smile. At that moment a grey-haired woman – doubtless his grandmother – came and grabbed him by the arm, giving me a reproachful look over her shoulder as she led the little boy towards a bench where several people were sitting. Whereupon I was visibly the object of censorious remarks, for these were accompanied by the contraction of the eyebrows I knew so well. So off I moved yet again and left the square to go towards the port.

I tried to look at this scene with the eye of a tourist seeing it for the first time. The black, blue, red and green housefronts made a row in the sunlight. At my feet the sun sketched a large inky patch round the paving-stones. The water smelt strong and the city noises reached me on gusts of wind that dishevelled my hair in teasing good humour. Two boys with open collars passed by and with a wink offered to show me the curiosities of the town. I turned away without answering. One of them, with his ripe-corn hair, pink complexion and blue shirt, seemed to me absurdly pretty, like so many of the boys here. For him, the war had not existed and so he didn't know who I was.

I went and leant against one of the boundary-pillars marking the entrance to the canal. If Roger could have come back, if only for an hour, I would have stopped suffering. Where could I go to feel less pain? I remembered that two minutes away there was a little café just next to the Royal Theatre. Perhaps I could sit there for a while, unless they asked me to go somewhere else, as had happened one day, owing to my being recognized.

I entered the café with confidence. Fortunately, it was empty and

I sat on a seat enabling me to turn my back on the street. I felt safe between those walls. Great mirrors reflected doors and green plants as if competing with each other, and also, in a corner, the top of my untidy head. I put a little order into my hair and saw my hand multiplied by three making the careful gesture that pushed back the rebellious lock. At that moment three waiters came out of the mirrors and immediately reduced themselves to one who approached me and asked me what I wanted.

'Mineral water.'

I did not find him handsome, but he had an excellent figure which showed itself to advantage in his rather indiscreetly tight suit. It was a relief to see him disappear and come back again with a small bottle: he at least had not recognized me. I suddenly wanted to talk to him, to say anything so as to be less alone, so I risked a remark about the beauty of the spring morning. He agreed with me – no more. I regretted his tipped-up nose which made him look like a clown, but he had a nice smile as he poured my water into the glass, the faintly self-satisfied smile of waiters used to advances, and I blushed. How could I be so trivial when I was feeling too unhappy to live? What did it matter to me if the waiter had a good figure? Perhaps even today I would take that step into the void if I had the courage. Had I not told Roger I would kill myself? I took several coins from my purse and told the waiter he could keep the change. A fresh smile, much more definite this time, and his bold hand just touched mine in gathering up the coins. I drew back my fingers as if he had burnt them and he moved away.

A stout man then came in, sat down at a certain distance from me and ordered a beer; then another even stouter came to disfigure the back wall. Both cast appreciative glances in my direction. Not without disgust I imagined their amorous advances and wondered how they would dispose of their stomachs. Perhaps when they were twenty they were slim and agile like the handsome boy I had seen at the port. What a hideous farce life was! I drank down a gulp of water and left.

Back home, I took an aspirin and tried to put some order into my thoughts. 'A little enquiry . . .' The assistant-manager's words came back into my mind. At first I had not given them much attention. I had had other worries, because Roger was leaving, whereas I and the assistant-manager were staying. The word 'enquiry' smacked of the police. Suddenly I lost my nerve. I picked up the telephone, rang the shop and asked to speak to the assistant-manager, but such a favour was not so easily granted. I was informed that my request would be handed on to him and in due course I would receive a communication by telephone. I pressed the point: I had seen the assistant-manager an hour before, I said. I was told to ring off. And in any case they rang off at the other end without waiting for my answer. And what was I going to say to the assistant-manager? I had no idea, I never did have any idea what I was going to say. First I acted, then I started thinking. Now I must wait.

'Wait!' I exclaimed as I contemplated the sideboard, 'but I've been doing nothing else for four years. I'm sick of it. I've had enough of it. Why don't you do something? Are you asleep?'

I was not talking to that piece of furniture. Truth to tell, I did not know whom I was talking to: to things, to God, to death, to everything? As it happened I did not have long to wait. A quarter of an hour later the telephone rang and I seized the receiver so quickly that it fell from my hands and I had to pick it up from under the table. I was on all fours when I answered. Yes, I was there. Yes, it was I. Who was speaking? Oh, the assistant-manager . . .

The icy voice asked me what I wanted.

'It's about the enquiry you mentioned to me. Couldn't I know . . .'

'You've got nothing to worry about. The enquiry will be conducted according to the rules.'

'But couldn't I know what it's about? If there are questions to be asked, I'd be grateful if the management would ask them as soon as possible.'

'Are you in such a hurry? Will you hold on, please.'

I had never dreamed of not holding on. I was trembling shamelessly. What had I started up by telephoning? What stupidity was I committing? Two mortal minutes passed, then a voice spoke, not the assistant-manager's any more, but one I had heard in the past, just once, and never forgotten: the voice of the manager himself, calm, low, to the point – terrifying.

'I'd like you to come to my office at four forty-five.'

'Yes, sir. Yes, sir.'

I collapsed into my armchair and closed my eyes.

By four o'clock I was walking up and down the pavement in front of the shop. What were they going to say and what was I going to answer? I had a mental conversation with an imaginary person who understood everything. I explained my case, I implored him to intervene, and little by little this imaginary person became Roger – and sometimes God. 'When one talks to him, he exists,' I said to myself.

At four forty-four I was in front of the door on which the manager's name was written. I knocked and entered. I had put on my navy-blue cotton dress scattered with little white flowers, an irreproachable get-up.

At first my confusion prevented me from seeing the manager other than as a black mass seated against the light and behind a desk on which there was nothing but a telephone, but I heard his voice telling me to take the armchair, and this my hand gropingly found. Mutely, I sat down.

'As you want to hurry up this enquiry, we'll go ahead at once with questions and answers. Do you agree?'

His voice seemed to me quite kindly, almost reassuring. I said of course I agreed, and then I suddenly saw the man who was talking to me. He did not look at all evil, quite the opposite. In his broad, rather too highly coloured face there was a basis of good humour. He had pale, smiling eyes set in a network of little lines. His lips were full and greedy and his nose was a real Danish nose, plainly facetious. All this was in contrast with what followed.

'I assume that you know what has happened to Miss Ott?'

At this name I felt my cheeks and hands getting cold as if the blood were draining away from them. I must certainly have grown pale.

'She's . . .'

'That's it. She's dead. Did you know her well?'

'I knew her a little. We hadn't seen each other for a long time.'

'The authorities found a certain number of letters in her flat.'

'The authorities?'

'That seems to surprise you. She was an informer for the authorities. Didn't you know that?'

'Yes, like everyone else.'

'Very well. Now, it's beyond all question that her death was due to natural causes. Miss Ott was alone. She felt an attack coming on and tried to ring someone up, probably her doctor. Are you following me?'

'Yes, certainly, sir.'

'There's nothing disquieting in all this, but I must tell you that I'm carrying out an enquiry – an entirely private little investigation, but serious all the same. Are you prepared to answer all my questions?'

'I am.'

Suddenly I felt a great flow of energy throughout my whole being – this had happened to me before at the onset of danger. In a completely calm voice I added:

'That woman detested me.'

'She did and she didn't, but I didn't ask you the question. In one of the drawers of her desk she had neatly put away several letters typewritten in French and dated from Paris.'

He let a few seconds elapse, doubtless to assess the effect of his words, but I had entirely recovered myself by now.

'And . . . ?'

'These letters were answers to other letters which of course were not found at Miss Ott's, but it was easy enough to reconstruct their drift. She had given her correspondent a detailed account of your conduct during the occupation.'

'I think I told you she detested me.'

'Detest is too strong a word, but let that pass. She was a patriot and held herself bound to make certain denunciations. But she wasn't without humanity. However, that's not the main point. Do you know who this French gentleman to whom she wrote was?'

'I can guess, sir.'

'Perhaps you will be glad to know that he took up your defence with outstanding generosity.'

'I am glad, but it doesn't surprise me.'

'He was of the opinion that by and large you were not responsible, and this for reasons which he preferred not to disclose. What, in your view, could those reasons be?'

'I've no idea.'

'The tone of his letters is very elevated. Moreover it is manifest that this gentleman has formed a very favourable impression of you. Can I go on believing that you'll answer all my questions?'

'I'll answer as far as I can. After all, there are limits.'

'Yes there are limits. I won't tell you that this gentleman has been in Copenhagen for some time, for in fact you receive his visits, usually towards the end of day.'

'I'm sorry to learn that I'm spied on, sir.'

'Watched, let's call it watched. In the present case such surveillance cannot give troublesome results – on the contrary.'

'I don't understand.'

'Is it reasonable to suppose that between you and this French gentleman there's a bond of a sentimental kind?'

Having previously turned pale, I now blushed, which did not displease me, as the blush of surprise could be taken for a blush of modesty.

'I leave the responsibility of your suppositions to you, sir.'

This phrase was well said. It was not lacking in a certain dignity and at the same time a climate of comedy was introduced. But what sadness there was at the bottom of it all! Roger was going to go . . .

'We Danes,' said the manager with a smile of complicity, 'we understand these things very well.'

I got up.

'May I take my leave, sir, if you have nothing else to say to me?'

'I'll go with you.'

This remark was the most amazing of all. To be shown out by the manager . . . He got up, crossed the room and opened the door. We went along the long corridor leading to the lift and it was he, not I, who pressed the button, as if even this tiny effort should be spared me. We had to wait a few moments during which I saw that the manager was silently, but smilingly, regarding me with an amused air. Finally the heavy apparatus reached our floor and once again it was he who opened the door.

'Good-bye, Miss Karin,' he said and held out his hand.

As though in a dream I touched his enormous hand and smiled as well as I could.

'Good-bye, sir.'

If my calculations were correct, this day must mark the end of Roger's stay in our town. The thought that he was still in Copenhagen, and that I could still reach him, aggravated my sadness and I nearly wished him far away, for then the vain hope of a chance meeting would no longer torment me.

As I was not in the least hungry, I went to sit in the great amusement park where so many memories of better days still lingered. At that time of day there were very few people in the walks. Birds were singing in the bud-covered branches of the trees and the heart-rending gaiety of their chirping seemed to me a mockery. In spite of everything it was going to take time for my suffering gradually to subside. What distressed me most was the uselessness of this terrible ordeal. Had Roger stayed in France instead of coming to Denmark I would not have given him a thought, and what good had he done me? None whatever. He had appeased his conscience by asking my forgiveness. In this I recognized the selfishness of men. So long as he was at peace, Karin's torment counted for very little indeed and my poor convert was going to his monastery with a light heart.

Towards the end of the afternoon I went back home and drew the curtains across the windows so as to rest on my bed in the half-light. It was the best thing I could do, for I was completely exhausted, and sleep came almost at once.

I was wakened by noises from the port. Shafts of light from the street lamps came through the gaps in the curtains and traced luminous bands on the floor of my room. I jumped out of bed and ran to one of my windows overlooking the quay. At first all I could see were men coming and going and talking in loud voices, then when two or three of them moved aside I realized at once what had happened. A woman was lying on the ground, half covered by a green tarpaulin, and I could see her legs in peach-coloured stockings like the ones I was wearing. She had no shoes. She seemed rather small. It was the usual drama that I had seen five or six times in my life, almost certainly a suicide. In our country spring is a festival, but it is also a season of despair. Driven by what is called morbid curiosity, I pulled aside the curtain to see as much as possible of the gruesome spectacle. The woman seemed to be young and her legs looked like mine. She at least had had the courage to take that step forward. She had done it in my stead. I was that woman, I had drowned myself. At that moment an ambulance arrived with a howling siren. Now there were too many people for me to be able to see. I drew the curtain and went back to my bed.

It was there that a strange idea came to me. I gave way to it as if obeying an undisputed command. A minute later I was sitting at my table, near the lighted lamp, writing a letter that could not possibly reach the person for whom it was destined since I did not know his address: '*Roger, writing to you seems to bring back your presence, and without it I can hardly breathe. I love you and I'm suffering. It might kill me to see you again, but I'd like to die like that, to die of joy.*'

At this point I realized I was addressing the Roger of 1939, the one who no longer existed. However, I went on, though slightly more hesitantly: '*Don't tell me you've changed and that nothing is possible any more. If I could only hold you to me you would see that time can be obliterated by love. Come back to the world of the living. Religion can only bruise your heart. It is I who will give you the human warmth that allays suffering. We'll re-discover the lost garden . . .*'

But to what purpose was I writing these things if he would never read them?

I threw my letter into the waste paper basket and was starting to undress when the door bell rang. That sound in the silence of the night made me jump and I admit that I didn't move for a while. It was nearly ten. A few moments passed, then the bell rang again. Finally there was a discreet knock, then sharply and with a sort of urgency that turned me to ice:

'Karin!'

It was not possible. And yet it was. I recognized the voice and opened the door.

He was standing outside, bare-headed, and seemed unable to cross the doorstep. From his pallid face his eyes stared at me with an intensity that was the most alarming thing of all. I heard a voice that seemed someone else's although it was my own:

'Roger, what's happened?'

He opened his mouth but I saw that he could not speak. So I took him by the hand and brought him in. He let himself be led like a child. The idea occurred to me that he had gone mad. Suddenly he took me in his arms and put his cheek against mine. He was crying. I felt his tears wet on my face.

'I thought you were dead,' he gasped. 'A woman has just drowned herself. I thought it was you.'

He let go of me and sat down in the corner of the sofa, then put his finger to his eyes and carefully dried them.

'I've been such a fool,' he said at last. 'I couldn't bring myself to leave. Don't judge me, my little Karin!'

'Judge you!' I burst out, sitting down beside him. 'I asked for you to come back, and you have come back. It's like a miracle.'

'You asked?' he said, looking at me.

'Yes.'

'There's no miracle, Karin. I've been outside here almost every night. The miracle is that you should have asked. Will you give me something to drink? I'm cold.'

Cold! It was so warm I had left a window open, but I closed it now and from the sideboard got a decanter of light wine that I nearly dropped – my hands were so trembling with emotion.

'It's all I've got,' I said, putting the decanter with a glass on the side table. 'Would you rather I made some tea, or coffee?'

He looked at me as if thoroughly confused.

'No,' he said, 'nothing. I don't want anything, I don't ask for anything.'

'You're upset, Roger,' I said, going over to the sofa. 'What's happened?'

He took my hands and raised imploring eyes.

'I should never have come back, Karin. My great mistake was writing to that woman, Miss Ott, for news of you, because I was so furious with myself . . . You've no idea what a convert's scruples are like. When I examined my whole life . . . Will you sit down beside me, Karin?'

So I sat on the sofa. He kept my hands in his.

'Yes. In that careful examination of all my past life, how could I not see you, Karin, when it was you and only you I was looking for?'

'You were looking for me?'

'Oh, naturally I didn't admit it to myself. I was in the middle of a religious crisis at the time, but I hadn't forgotten you, quite the contrary, and I had plenty of things to blame myself for: I had dragged you into evil.'

'Don't talk like that. Love isn't evil.'

'I was fascinated by love, by physical love, even at the height of my impulse towards God. I wrote to Miss Ott to find out what had become of you. At first I just wanted your address so as to write you a letter and ask your forgiveness, but deep down it wasn't that that I really wanted.'

'You mustn't hark back to those things, Roger.'

I gently put my arm round his neck. Now he was mine. All I had to do was to wait.

'Miss Ott's answer was like an arrow in my heart,' he went on. 'I suffered from what she told me, but I also saw it as a pretext for this trip which then appeared as a positive duty. Writing wasn't enough. I had to see you, Karin, to try to give you back the faith that I had caused you to lose. Oh, I was sincere all right, but at the same time, without wanting to admit it to myself, I was cheating, Karin, I was cheating.'

Once again his eyes shone with tears. Had I any need of a plainer avowal? I had him completely in my hands. Trembling with indescribable happiness, I took his martyr's face in my hands and placed my mouth on his.

Once the lights were out I had the sensation of sliding with him into an abyss. It was not the Roger of 1939 whom I was clasping to me but almost a madman whose delirium frightened me. For something else, whose meaning at first escaped me, was added to the extreme of desire. The words of love he showered on me could deceive no one but himself. I soon realized that this man who was out of his mind with passion (whereas mine was perfectly intact) was nevertheless in revolt against me. I did not doubt that he was in love, but he was suffering from it as if it were a form of torture in which sensual pleasure itself was a stretch on the rack. He knew nothing of tenderness and I had nothing but that to give him, but I had a lot of it and in the end it subjugated him. I enfolded the poor sick man in all the gentleness a woman is capable of when she rises above herself, but I no longer desired him. He had changed too much. Moreover I could not play at being Messalina as I had in 1939. In those days he was easy to deceive. Now it bored me to deceive him. I gave myself over to my real nature.

When the moment of physical passion was passed, we both fell asleep almost at the same moment, but I was awake at dawn and with an almost instinctive gesture stretched out my arm. I was alone in the bed. It took me a few seconds to realize it, to believe it, then I called out but without getting an answer.

Yet I seemed to hear noises, and when my eyes were accustomed to the half-light I saw Roger bending over in a chair doing up his shoes. He stood up, fully dressed, and came into the middle of the room.

'I'm going, Karin,' he said. 'I've been up for half an hour but I didn't want to go without saying good-bye. I don't want you to suffer.'

'I shall suffer and so will you.'

Standing still like that in the uncertain light, he reminded me of a tree. What was he thinking? Why did he not say anything more? I looked at him in the act of destroying my happiness.

'Roger, let me ask you one question. Do you believe you're lost because of what happened last night?'

'No.'

'Perhaps it's I who am lost?'

'Oh no, Karin.'

'You're going because you think I'm dangerous for your salvation?'

'Only as I'm dangerous for yours. Yes.'

'But what are you going to do for me to be saved?'

'Do you really want to be saved, Karin?'

I didn't answer. There was something so embarrassing in an exchange of theological propositions after the excesses of the night . . .

'Since you're going anyway,' I said suddenly, 'give me another half hour, the time for me to get dressed and prepare coffee.'

He seemed to be hesitating so I profited by his silence to slip on my dressing-gown and go like an arrow to the bathroom. It was all so quick that I had vanished without his realizing it.

'Put on the light if you like,' I shouted through the door above the noise of the splashing bath-water.

I rather hoped the electric light would dispel the meditative atmosphere engendered by the semi-darkness and restore the commonplace in all its force.

'Karin,' he replied, 'I assure you I don't need anything.'

His childish weakness could be detected in this remark. A resolute man would have made straight off.

'Put on the lights!' I shouted again.

'No!' he said with sudden energy.

He preferred the dark. It probably enabled him to act out better for his own benefit the little drama of the repentant sinner. I imagined him with his hands over his face. While I was in the bath I calculated my chances. On the sensual level they were non-existent for the moment. He had said everything he needed to say the night before, and this morning the soul was in possession. Perhaps the splashing of the water would arouse in him who knows what forbidden thoughts . . . Men are so primitive! But no, it was absurd, and distaste for this somewhat shameful situation descended on me. But I rose above the distaste. A few hours had to be gained. Then hunger and massive desire would be reborn. Having offered my body, I would now offer my soul with the same shamelessness. It was very base, what I was doing, but then I was in love.

A quarter of an hour later I left the bathroom – freshened, but without scent. Scent would have been a mistake. With exemplary tact I put on my blouse and selected from my wardrobe a navy-blue silk house-coat which seemed to me to strike the right note for the occasion. In my schoolgirl voice I softly uttered Roger's name.

'Yes, Karin.'

Noiselessly I unfolded the screen so as to hide the disordered bed, then drew back the curtains of one of the windows. Daylight entered the room and spread a joyful golden glow over the carpet. I would have liked to see a favourable omen here, but Roger's face was enough to revive all my uneasiness. It looked unhealthily pale and there were shadows in the hollows under his cheekbones. At the noise made by the curtain-rings sliding along the rod, he turned towards me and smiled.

'Forgive me for making you get up so early,' he said.

I went into the kitchen to put the water on to boil, then came back to prepare the table. He was sitting in silence on a straight-backed chair but seemed so calm that I could not help hoping yet again. Hoping what? A thought suddenly crossed my mind like a flame: 'Don't take his paradise away from him.'

I was arranging the cups and saucers on the cloth, but I suddenly stopped, spoons and knives in my hands. He looked up at me as if in interrogation and I went back into the kitchen. I was so disconcerted that I did not notice the water was boiling. 'After all,' I said to myself, 'isn't that exactly what he did to me in 1939 when he took my faith away from me?' What did it all mean? What was the point of my life? And how could I ask myself such tremendous questions while preparing breakfast?

When I came back I noticed I was trembling.

'Help yourself, Roger.'

He obeyed me with his characteristic clumsiness, which only made him dearer to me. If ever a man needed love and protection, it was he. Needless to say, drops of coffee made large stains on the cloth. He apologized. His voice was so humble that it made me want to run away, to hide absolutely anywhere. His pride must have been bleeding. I even doubted whether he had much of it left. I, for my part, had an inflexible pride, but he moved me – if I can so put it – horribly. Anyone but I would have shed tears and perhaps won the game with an unfair weapon, but I could not cry. I saw him raising the too hot cup to his lips and foresaw a disaster.

'My little Roger, wait a minute.'

He put down his cup and asked:

'Why, Karin?'

'I don't know. I wanted to tell you something.'

Tell him something . . . I had nothing to tell him, and I was tired of this struggle. What was the use of holding back a man who wanted to go? He was no longer mine, he belonged to another. I made a final and cowardly attempt to play the card of religion. I would have drawn a cross on the floor with my tongue if he had asked me to!

'I believe I told you that I had prayed.'

'Yes.'

'I thought it might interest you. But perhaps I'm mistaken.'

'No. I'm convinced now that you have the faith. It got in your way so you tried to get rid of it, but it's still there. My own case isn't very different.'

'Everything's starting again,' I thought, and in a fit of exasperation shrugged my shoulders.

'Drink your coffee,' I told him. 'You can see it's getting cold.'

He gave a polite smile which made me lose all patience.

'But after all, Roger,' I burst out, 'we did make love last night, didn't we?'

I had never felt so vulgar, so heavy-handed. Unhurriedly he drank a sip and put down his cup.

'Yes, Karin. And what does that prove? In this business I'm the main culprit. I shouldn't be here. In fact that's the reason why I'm going.'

'How simple it is! You're leaving me alone here with my difficulties.'

'I'm not leaving you alone.'

'Now we're at the heart of mysticism, if I'm not mistaken. But do what you will, your conscience will reproach you for having abandoned someone you could save.'

'I thought about all that last night – afterwards, you understand? My salvation is inseparable from yours, my little Karin. But just now when I heard you having a bath – it's difficult to confess it, but I was tempted to open the door.'

'I wouldn't have sent you away.'

'Exactly. I realized that things weren't working out at all, and that I'd have to leave at the first possible moment.'

'So you put up a heroic resistance, like a saint.'

'Don't make fun. I felt deeply ridiculous and pathetic.'

He hesitated a moment, then took from his pocket a small piece of paper which he showed me with a sheepish and yet imploring air.

'While you were washing I wrote down – not without pain, let me say – I wrote down the address of a Catholic priest in Copenhagen.'

This remark so enraged me that I snatched the piece of paper from his hands and tore it up. In the ensuing silence we sat and stared at each other. My eyes, I am sure, were shining with anger.

His were shining too, but with tears, because he was able to cry, he had the gift.

'I was too hasty,' I said at last, 'I'm sorry. But there's a traditional Protestant inside me. You must try to understand.'

Whereupon he took from his pocket a handkerchief that nearly made me burst out laughing, because it was a large blue-check handkerchief of the kind associated with country people. But life, being a rather mad novelist, is fond of these comic and inopportune details. He blew his nose very softly.

'I'm tactlessness itself,' he said. 'You must forgive me. The priest I'm referring to is the parish priest of the only Catholic church in Copenhagen. He's a very fine man. I'm just telling you that on the off chance.'

The peasant handkerchief disappeared into his pocket. I wondered where he had found it and what it signified. Was it a sign of rejection of the world, of Satan and his pomps? I hid my face in my hand so that he would not see my smile. He probably thought I was moved.

'Karin,' he said, 'I want you to keep a good memory of me. The real Roger is not the one of last night. The real one is talking to you now.'

'I liked the other one very much,' I said in a low voice. 'Are you going to drink your coffee?'

He drank obediently and I saw his eyes looking at me sadly over the brim of his cup.

'We could have been happy together,' I murmured like a prayer.

'Not now, Karin. It's too late.'

'One has to feel very strong to withdraw from the world, Roger, and you're not very strong. You came back here because you couldn't resist it.'

'I know, but now it's finished.'

Suddenly his face lit up as if he had been struck by an inner revelation.

'I came back out of weakness,' he said in an exalted voice, 'and God has made use of my weakness. I've come on God's behalf to save you, Karin. There you have the purpose of my trip.'

He got up.

'If you pray, Karin, God will talk to you. You've no more need of me.'

A phrase escaped from the depths of my heart.

'I'll always need you. I love you.'

He looked at me in surprise.

'But it's the same with me, Karin. I've never stopped loving you.'

'One day you gave me to understand the opposite.'

'I had to protect myself.'

'But now, now . . .'

'Now?'

'Don't go, Roger.'

'If I stayed we'd suffer too much. I don't belong to myself any more.'

He turned away with a sorrowful sigh and said:

'I'm going to ask you something very simple: will you give me a glass of drinking water? As in the past, you remember, after coffee.'

A glass of water? Yes, of course I remembered this habit of his. I went into the kitchen and opened the cupboard, fool that I was, then put the glass under the faucet. At that moment, too late, I realized.

'Roger!' I yelled.

No answer. I dropped the glass and went back to the room. It was empty. Through the open door I saw him walking away with huge strides along the boulevard, wearing the great cloak I had made such fun of. It occurred to me to run after him, but I desisted, probably out of pride. In any case, it was over. I shut the door. 'It's you who've done that,' I thought as I crossed the room. Without knowing why, I went towards the bed where the sheets thrown back in a semi-circle made me think of a wave. Suddenly the room grew dark and I fell forward, on to the very bed where we had made love.

Like the preceding days, this one was radiant. I think it was the light that brought me out of my fainting fit and I looked around me for a minute or two without really understanding, then memory came back with a rush, and with it the bar across my chest, but this time I was resolved to struggle against the old suffering.

'Gone,' I thought. That was all. He might as well have never come. What was there left of him, after all? A memory testified to by the eloquent disorder of the bed. I summoned all my energy and tugged off the bedclothes and re-made the bed with clean sheets, throwing the others into the laundry-basket in defiance of my nature which was even more sentimental than sensual. Then with a heavy heart I got down on my hands and knees to find those bits of paper I had thrown under the table: the address Roger had written with such care on a page of his notebook and I had torn up. I reassembled the pieces, smoothed them out, then stuck them together again. And now, my mouth half-open, my eyes dry, but my head buzzing, I read and re-read those two handwritten lines, the very last he had written with me in his mind, the good-bye in fact.

In order to escape the room where all was redolent of him, I went to the public garden already teeming with mothers and children. There I chose a quiet corner, though happy cries reached me even so. They somewhat interrupted my suffering and that did me good. The important thing was that time should pass, that day should lead to night and night to day until grief was worn away. Passing women looked at me with a curiosity I misinterpreted, imagining they had recognized the German Woman, but this time they had other reasons. I was sitting under a vast lime-tree covered with a delicate lace of tiny leaves, and was admiring as if in a dream the extreme intricacy of the shadows cast by the branches on the ground, when I noticed I was still in my house-coat. At that moment I heard a lowered voice articulating (as it moved into the distance) a French word that had long since passed into our language: 'Toquée.'

I am not a woman who loses her head for so little. In any case there was nothing very incorrect about my attire – it was unusual more than anything. So getting up with feigned composure (for all was really tumult and agitation within me), I moved off at a measured pace and a few minutes later found myself at home.

Having done my housework and restored order to my room, I once more abandoned myself to my thoughts, in the course of which I made the happy discovery that I loved Roger much more when he was away from me. I felt both calmer and less amorous when I had him in front of my eyes and even in my arms. Not because he disappointed me, but I needed his absence so as to be back with the Roger of 1939. So was I in love with a ghost? No, never.

Then I suddenly changed my mind. If I were given back the Roger of just now, with his ascetic face, I would have been satisfied with him, I would have protected him, enfolded him, defended him, served him . . . I would have knelt down and prayed like him, so as to please him. I tried to recall the way he executed that mysterious gesticulation, the one he made before praying and also after. I had certainly seen him do it, but something eluded me: first the hand on the forehead, then on one shoulder, but which? I stood in front of the mirror in the half-darkness and tried to make the sign of the cross like Roger. The right shoulder or the left shoulder? My reflection worried me, it turned everything round. And in any case, what did it all amount to?

I spent that day in a state of languor or, better, in a sort of numbness. The thought of preparing a meal made me feel sick. I nibbled at a roll and left three quarters of it, and that was my lunch. In some sort of automatic effort I sat down at my worktable and took up my pencils. Though my hand was inert, or almost, it managed to draw some features in which I recognized the face of the man I would never see again, surrounded by huge flowers that I found idiotic. The eraser rubbed it all out. Oh if only I could have cried, what a river, what a flood! And what a deliverance!

That was a strange night. I lay on my back in my bed and looked at the ceiling whose whiteness I guessed at rather than saw. My constant care not to behave like someone suffering from delusions stopped me from talking to myself, or rather from talking to an absent or a present Roger. I imagined him in France, given over to his devotions, probably on his knees and talking out loud (yes, *he* was) because he thought in this way that he was talking to someone. 'I'm not leaving you alone,' he had said to me. Oh, Roger, what cruelty! You're leaving me with someone I can neither see nor hear and who never answers . . . Except, yes – he had answered in his fashion by bringing Roger. I believed that and at the same time disbelieved it, because religion seemed to me to border on madness.

Was it possible that after all there was someone keeping me company in his fashion in this darkness? At any rate one could talk to him like a believer. So in a hoarse voice I asked him why he was unkind to me. It was not a prayer, it was a legitimate question. Had I asked to come into the world? Then why? Why? If you were really there then you'd do something for me. If you do nothing, it's because there is nothing or because you're unjust, and if you're unjust I don't want to have to do with you. How long do we have to suffer before you give us a sign? Are you all-powerful cruelty or all-powerful goodness? What place does love have in your system?

These thoughts occupied my mind for a while, and though I had taken no sleeping-pill, fatigue suddenly overwhelmed me and I didn't wake till dawn. A bird's song reached my ears through the half-open window and at first I thought I was in a garden, then the song was continued as I dreamed. My heart beating with joy, I walked in this airy song as if beneath trees. Where are the words to describe such things? Quite simply, there was no more unhappiness, I was out of reach, in a security beyond description, but I had to keep my eyes shut and hold my breath. 'To die,' I thought, 'to die now . . .' It seemed that everything was motionless within me as it was around me, that there was a halt in time's atrocious journey.

I only said that to myself later, when I had come back to my senses and saw myself in that wretched room. I tried with all my might to rediscover the enchanted world, but succeeded no better than when we try to capture a dream whose transience defies the memory. I remembered, but no longer possessed, the joy.

'What happened?' I asked myself while I was dressing. 'Where was I?'

Now I was no longer smiling about Roger's faith. I would have liked to have the same, just as simple and solid, a faith that settled everything. This thought had only just crossed my mind when it was followed by another which made the comb drop from my hand: 'True faith unsettles everything.'

I was sitting down. I stood up. It seemed that someone had spoken, that this sentence had been said to me. I felt like an animal hemmed round in its last refuge. It suddenly seemed ridiculous that little Karin should be overwhelmed by such fantastic ideas because a flighty person from abroad had talked to her about religion – both before and after making love, especially after. What sorcery was there in those signs of the cross and those prayers?

'I don't want it,' I said aloud.

I felt very strongly the horror that Catholicism inspires in so many of us Scandinavians, and this movement of revolt did me good, but I needed time to calm down. My daily work enabled me to regain a semblance of equilibrium. Without this slavery to bridle my imagination a little, I would have let myself follow my natural inclination and become lost in the cruellest of sentimental daydreams, for after all I was in love.

In love with Roger, yes, but also just in love. That was the crucial point. I wanted to love. I had been denied it for four years, and this Frenchman reappearing from a world of memories had at a blow re-opened my wound. The craving for happiness was slowly killing me. Then while I was sketching futile garlands and brooding on my broken and ravaged life, I suddenly remembered those extraordinary moments I had lived through early that morning, and the thought slid into my mind like a sort of inner whisper that this had been a sign, the very sign I had asked for the night before.

The next day was my birthday: I would be twenty-eight. I noted this without pleasure, but without sadness, because now it didn't matter to me – and who else was there to care? After the morning marketing came a solitary lunch, then an afternoon spent more or less at work and the usual walk in the less frequented parts of the public garden. Like everyone else, I had seen the lady coming out with her sunshade on top of the tower near the town hall – a presage of fine weather – and the general good humour affected me a little in spite of myself, because I felt that in the opinion of the world I had no right to it. They were on one side and I was on the other. They left me alone and I think that in their view this was much more than I deserved. I was used to it.

Seated on a bench, I was reading a popular novel without taking in a word, for my attention kept wandering towards something else that I did not understand. Finally I put the book down. Nothing interested me, nothing ever could interest me again in this world. That at least seemed to me certain, but behind this idea there was another slowly forming in my head. I wanted to tell Roger what was happening inside me. He had refused to give me his address, but someone perhaps had it: the parish priest of the little Catholic church.

To cross the town to go looking for a Catholic priest . . . The enormity of the thing seemed overwhelming. It was simply impossible. What would I say to the man? How would I explain that I knew Roger? It was hard to imagine a more embarrassing situation. A girl going to a priest to ask him the address . . . I didn't dare finish the sentence. The address of her lover, because that was really what it was all about. Suddenly I began to laugh all by myself, not a gay laugh but an exasperated one. In spite of everything I did what I did not want to do. Leaving the public garden, I took the tram that went near the little street where the church was.

There was nothing about the church that seemed worthy of interest. With its dark-red-brick façade and the modest cross of white stone surmounting it, its aspect was as commonplace as could be. It looked as if it were apologizing for being there, on our Protestant soil, for it was true that our country did no more than tolerate its presence. But was I not in the same situation? This absurd thought, like so many others that came into my mind, seemed to me overwhelmingly true: they tolerated my presence. My own foolishness made me shrug my shoulders: Danish and Lutheran – that's what my parents had made of me.

All the houses in this sun-baked street were utterly ordinary; low, unadorned, not rich, not poor, boring. The church had slipped in among them like someone hiding in a crowd, for that discreet little white cross did nothing to draw the attention. For a minute or two I walked along the pavement in a state of indecision. Passers-by looked at me with embarrassing curiosity. Suddenly I went towards the oak door and entered the church.

My irritation at finding myself there was almost at once succeeded by a modified surprise. At the far end of the long white interior there were, of course, painted plaster statues of holy persons to the right and left of an altar on which a sort of little house was to be seen with white curtains trimmed with gold braid – all things to be imputed to idolatry – but through the windows with their many-coloured stained glass there filtered a light of rainbow sweetness which gave the place a rather childish atmosphere of mystery.

It was the first time I had put my foot inside a Catholic church. It struck me as very poor compared with the Church of Our Saviour which I saw in my mind's eye with the blue elephants supporting the organ-loft and the great crown of gilded wood shining triumphantly in the baptistry. Nothing like that between these walls. Not enough money, no doubt. I made various ironical remarks to myself and yet I was less displeased to be there than I would have supposed. To begin with, I appreciated the quality of silence, and then I was alone – I was relieved to see neither priest nor anyone else on those dark-wood benches.

But then, in a corner, oh horror! I turned away my head: the appalling piece of furniture my father had laughingly described to me once, the sentry-box with its grille and olive-green serge curtains . . . I was sorry that was there because, seated at the back of the church, I was beginning to get used to this rather naïve décor; I don't say I was beginning to like it, but I was tired and was resting, that was all. And I must admit that when I stopped looking at the confessional I soon experienced a feeling of peace. By a whim of the imagination, I started thinking about my room and saw myself again in that hell. Hell, those natty curtains, the blue carpet, the bed, the ghastly little kitchen where I cooked my cutlet. In my disarray I closed my eyes and leant forward till my forehead touched the back of the bench in front of me. I did not want to suffer any more, nor to go back home. Little by little my mind became calm again and I opened my eyes. I now looked at this peaceful church with an emotion akin to gratitude.

Why did the door have to open at this moment to let in two people? The noise they made disturbed me. There was an old man whose long overcoat reached almost to his ankles and a little boy he was holding by the hand. Both passed near me and went up the central aisle and knelt down before the altar and its little house with white curtains which they bowed to in a sort of dive. The child lost his balance and toppled over. When he got up he glanced at me over his shoulder and laughed with such innocence that I wanted to go and kiss him, but he and the old gentleman took their places on a bench and once more knelt down.

Long minutes passed. The child was not praying. From time to time he threw me a collusive glance accompanied by a smile and I saw his face on which the light fell like a caress. It was at this moment that I would have liked someone beside me, and as life delights in bitter irony, there suddenly was someone, I mean the sacristy door softly opened and a man in a cassock came towards me as if he wanted to ask me something, but it was not to a man in a cassock that I wanted to talk. To begin with, this garment aroused violent antipathy in me, and then the priest's face seemed to me too refined not to be cunning. I must admit that I had looked at him rather quickly. His eyes were light, his cheeks hollow, and his nose pointed and inquisitive – a Danish nose.

The priest knelt down without a sound two benches away from me. I saw him praying, his head in his hands, in a way that I thought professional and conventional, whereas the old man was praying with simplicity, his head raised towards the altar as if addressing himself to a person standing there. The presence of the priest in a cassock deprived the church of its enchantment; it now seemed quite ordinary in my eyes owing to that absurd black garment. Nevertheless, I said to myself, not without sadness, that man in black is certain to be the priest Roger told me about. As if he had read my thoughts, the man got up almost at once, genuflected quickly, and went back to the sacristy leaving the door half open. I felt entirely Lutheran confronted with this so subtly prepared trap. I was being given a sign. What was I waiting for? But how could I fail to recognize in this the style of all the foxes Rome has unleashed on the world so as to catch souls? I hesitated, in a rage. If the cassock in the sacristy hoped to convert me, it was grossly deceived. What I wanted was an address. And then I wanted to talk about Roger. In that way the magic of language would make him be present, up to a point. Overcoming my disgust, I rose from my place and went towards the sacristy.

The man was there, sitting in a wicker chair in front of some gleaming cupboards. That was all I saw at first. He was reading a black book which he closed and placed on a small table before he

got up. In all his movements I noticed an assurance that immediately antagonized me, for it seemed obvious that he knew I was
going to come, but then he smiled and I felt everything changing
within me. The devil take men and their airs and graces! This one
had a smile I could not resist, because it was all tenderness even in
its discretion. I could not help thinking that this man must have
caught many women with this dishonest weapon. Despite my
feelings, I found his appearance pleasing, though he was no longer
all that young. The hair around his temples was greying, and semi-
circular lines made a sort of parenthesis on either side of a mouth
that revealed irregular but white teeth. After a moment or two I
said in a brisk voice that I wanted to talk to him. He murmured
softly:

'I was expecting you.'

He was expecting me! The blood rose to my face. With a light
step the man passed behind me and closed the door, then we both
sat down two yards from each other in the middle of that small
room smelling of furniture polish. Through the curtainless
window I could see the street, whence we could no doubt be seen.
Thus I had nothing to fear, for I was distrustful.

'You were expecting me, sir?'

'Yes, indeed,' he said in a louder voice because the door was
shut and our words could no longer disturb the devotions of the
people in the church. (Oh, how all that was *arranged*!) 'I was
informed of your visit by a foreign visitor.'

Just think of Roger's complacency, his certainty that I would
come! Just think of the complacency of all men!

'A Frenchman?'

'Yes, a Frenchman.'

'Yet I wasn't at all sure that I'd come.'

'He hoped you would. He told me so just now.'

'Just now . . . You mean he didn't leave this morning?'

'No. At three this afternoon. And before he left he called on
me.'

He went to confession, I thought; he told everything to this
man in black.

'I suppose,' I said after a pause, 'I suppose he told you about
me.'

'He confined himself to saying that I would probably have a

visit from someone whom he then described in detail. I recognized you at once.'

A great uneasiness took hold of me and I moved a little on my chair in front of this totally still man who kept smiling. Gathering my strength I said in one burst:

'I want to write to that gentleman – where should I write to?'

'Give the letter to me. It will reach him.'

'Can't I have his address?'

'The way I'm suggesting to you is the only one he authorized me to use.'

'In that case, I'll think it over.'

I said this as frigidly as I knew how and stood up. So did he. This was the most awkward moment of our interview because, having got up, I had to go, yet I wanted to stay. Why did I want to stay? I wondered. Moreover, having produced an effect by rising, I somehow felt I had to produce another.

'Do you know who I am, sir?'

He stopped smiling and looked at me quietly. How could he not have known? Everyone knew. I answered my question myself, in a sharp, cutting voice:

'I'm Karin, Karin the German Woman.'

'As far as I'm concerned, and above all for him who will judge us and who loves you, you are simply Karin,' he said gently.

'I want to tell you something.'

I had absolutely nothing to tell him just then, but I had begun to lose my head. But yes, I did have something to tell him after all:

'I'd like to talk to you about someone.'

He pointed to the chair I had just vacated. We both sat down again.

'Someone,' I repeated. 'You can guess whom I'm referring to. I want to talk to you about Roger.'

Having said these words, I mentioned my meeting with the Frenchman on the eve of the war and, in a fairly discreet way, what I called our relationship. Yielding finally to the irresistible temptation to put oneself in the centre of the picture, I imperceptibly started to pour out confidences from which the person of Roger was excluded, for it was really about myself, about myself that I wanted to talk, whatever the cost to my pride.

For the first time in my life I savoured the pleasure of accusing myself so as to deliver myself of an intolerable burden. In this way I put the whole town, which had brought such heavy charges against me, in the wrong. The mere fact of my admissions re-established a sort of equilibrium. In the matter of my behaviour I did not spare myself, I sketched in everything in the clearest and yet the most acceptable terms. Between those astonished walls the young enemy officers were conjured up in all their insolence. How many had there been? I counted three dozen. Once more I was driving with them in their long, contemptuous cars, letting myself be seen by the indignant pedestrians. Had I been aware of doing wrong? This was the only question put to me by the man in black, and I heard it with a shudder and made no answer. The truth was I could have said Yes.

I continued, after a silence, in a rather lower voice. The light was gradually fading from the sky and all I saw of the man's face was the outline of his jaw and cheekbones, for he had his back to the window. His stillness and attentiveness – apparent even in the angle of his shoulders and his whole body – made me feel he was listening to me as though to someone dying. This respect of his, added to the half-light in which we found ourselves, encouraged me to go on. In the full glare of day I would either have said nothing or said something else, but for some time now I had felt I was descending into a womb of welcoming night where I breathed more easily. I admitted that with the exception of the man who had originally seduced me, no one had ever cared about me, then suddenly there had been this invasion of young wolves who had created a void around them in a conquered town. I had not been afraid to look them in the face. Their elegance had dazzled me. Especially their gloves . . . Why their gloves? It seemed that I had committed treason in a sort of intoxication.

Having brought my story to an end – or almost, because there was still last night – I fell silent and waited. With one part of myself I was observing the cupboard doors gleaming with the reflections of the lights from the street, but there was another person within me to whom these things were a matter of indifference and who was amazed not to be suffering any more. I had the feeling of having stripped in front of this man; the exhibitionist was satisfied.

'Am I to understand that you've said all that you wanted to say?' asked the man in black.

'All.'

A long minute elapsed. My interlocutor's silence made it plain that he expected yet another avowal, the very one I could not make: the night with Roger that I was keeping for myself. How long were we going to stay facing each other like this? Just when the situation was becoming intolerable he asked me in an almost affectionate voice:

'Do you regret having confided in me?'

'Far from it.'

'In that case, if ever you have anything else to tell me, here I am.'

I didn't like that 'anything else' because I knew what it meant and I knew he knew that I knew, but I pretended to have misunderstood and said almost rudely:

'Don't hope to convert me! There's too much anarchy in my head for me to turn into a Catholic.'

He laughed cheerfully.

'Well, don't let your anarchy prevent you from coming to find me if you need me, Miss Karin.'

The trap . . . Those ways which were sometimes serious, sometimes gay. I sensed the cunning. Why, then, did I stay instead of leaving? Why did I ask an incautious question?

'Perhaps you wonder why I came?'

In the light cast by the street lamp I saw the expression on his face change and become serious.

'Do you feel calmer since talking to me?'

'Calmer, yes.'

'Don't look for any other explanation, Miss Karin. You came here to find peace.'

Peace. I did not like that word, which smacked of piety. If only he knew that in making my confessions to him I had had the feeling of challenging the whole town in the person of one of its most respectable (it had to be admitted) representatives . . . It was my turn to laugh, but my laugh sounded hollow.

'Frankly, I don't know why I came.'

It was becoming rather absurd, this conversation in the twilight with a priest who probably wanted to go and have his dinner but did not know how to get rid of this importunate woman. I suddenly stood up and so did he, but without haste.

'Did Roger talk to you about me?' I asked abruptly.

I had great hopes of this unexpected question. The answer came immediately, very calm.

'Yes, he did in fact talk to me about you.'

My heart beat faster. At the moment of leaving I had admitted the real reason for my visit.

'May I know . . . well, just in a general way?'

'He hopes that one day you will give yourself to God.'

My disappointment was concealed only by the darkness.

'Is that all?'

'It's all I can tell you. You must try to understand.'

'Yes, I know. Your well-known secrets of the confessional.'

Silence.

'Once again,' he said in a low voice as though to put himself in tune with the darkness, 'don't hesitate to call on me.'

'Even in the middle of the night?'

To this odd question he answered soberly:

'Of course. We keep the same hours as doctors.'

A little ashamed of what I was admitting, I whispered:

'There are sometimes difficult moments during the night.'

'I'll give you my telephone number.'

Passing in front of me in the blackness with the skill of a bat, he opened the door leading into the church and switched on a light. The glare was dazzling and I turned away my head. He had purposely not lit up the sacristy to begin with so as to spare me the brilliance. But after a minute he crossed the room and almost at once a lamp was shining on a table, a modest little lamp with a soft light favourable of confidences. I could not help admiring the setting which was both clever and naïve. A painter as an expert would have appreciated the discretion of the lighting. Bending over the table, the priest wrote his number on a piece of paper which he then handed to me with a smile of charming (I must admit it) kindness. Perhaps I was too susceptible.

'Talisman against anguish,' I said as I took the paper.

And I gave him my hand. He took it in both of his and held it for a few seconds.

'God is there, Miss Karin.'

'But God isn't there like a human being who talks and whom one sees.'

'Well then, I'll be there, I'll be there too, for you need the one who is nothing as well as the one who is everything.'

We went back into the church, which was now empty. Lit up by bulbs to the right and left of the altar, it had lost its mystery and poetry. It was as bright as a kitchen. The man in black bent his knee in the central aisle and then accompanied me as far as the street. His thoughtful face gave me a final smile in which he tried to inject some gaiety. I went off without a word.

Once home, I drew my curtains and lit just the small bedside lamp which shed a rather feeble light over the room. I thus achieved lighting more or less comparable to that of the sacristy a short while before, though I did not notice this at once. In my confused state I had no clear idea of what I was doing and blushed when I realized I was talking to myself. And what was I saying? I prefer not to think about it but I know that I felt uneasy, happy (yes, happy) and irritated all at the same time. The word hypocrisy kept coming to my lips and suddenly I got a fit of the giggles and collapsed on the bed. With my face in the pillow I heard the muffled outbursts of irrepressible merriment. They sounded like shouts. After five or six minutes I was exhausted and fell into a heavy sleep.

It was eleven at night when I woke up, and I sat on my bed pressing my fists against my eyes to think things over. What had happened? Nothing. I was at home as usual. A glance round my room assured me that everything was in its place. I might be changing, but this context of boredom and failure (as it seemed to me) was exactly the same. It told the story of my life, my wasted life. I was through with it, as I was through with myself. What do these words mean? I no longer wanted to be the person I was. I seemed to see the future as a succession of years all identical with the one I had just completed – the twenty-eighth. I could not bear the thought that things would go on like this until I died, that every minute would bring me nearer to being a lonely old woman working for the shop. I was frightened.

Surely the most sensible and reassuring thing would have been to get undressed and into bed. But that was impossible. I went over and sat beside the telephone. And it was here that what I do not hesitate to call my martyrdom began. One may smile about these things and about my exaggerated vocabulary, but I was suffering. I would have liked Roger to be there even if he had to start his Catholic preachifying again. I regretted, too, that I was not in that little church where I had felt so at peace. It was definitely ugly and its plaster statues jarred on me, but it had something – don't ask me what. And then there was the man in black, so reserved, so concerned, with that smile which he used both discreetly and skilfully. Oh, the trap, the emissary from Rome, the little lamp for confidences, the unpretentiousness of the décor, the smell of wax, the gentle measured voice which contrasted with my screams – for I had let out two or three screams – the tranquillity, in fact everything . . . I was not going to become a Catholic! Again I burst out laughing and stopped immediately.

I did not want to be alone; solitude seemed to me dangerous. It was a quarter past eleven. I dialled the number that the man in black had given me and immediately hung up. What I was doing was stupid. To disturb a priest at this hour . . . What would he think of me? A woman wanting to be converted? Or a neurasthenic? I decided to keep calm and that lasted five minutes during which I forced myself to think about my work, then suddenly I heard myself murmur in a small wounded voice: 'I love you.'

Those were the words that I had said to Roger and I said them again now when he was far away, making for the monastery where they love only God. And now what did I hope for from that telephone? I was afraid of myself and of what I was going to do. For instance, I was sure that sooner or later I would ring up the man in black, and the longer I waited the more inconvenient it would be to make a call at midnight or at two in the morning . . . I was capable of it. The best was to get it over. In a sort of rage I dialled the number and held my breath.

The telephone had only rung once when I heard a voice saying 'Hullo.' At first I could not utter a word and the voice repeated patiently: 'Hullo.'

'It's me, Karin,' I brought out finally. 'You told me I could.'

'You've done the right thing, Miss Karin. Is something the matter?'

The voice was so peaceful that it seemed to spread waves of sweetness through the night all around me.

'Yes, I'm afraid so. Will you say something to me?'

It was an absurd request! My face felt hot and I wanted to ring off, but once again the voice surrounded me with its human tenderness.

'You mustn't be frightened. You're like a child lost in the woods. The child should ask Our Lord to take her by the hand and lead her out of the wood.'

I stretched out my finger and pressed the switch of the small lamp to put it out. The voice seemed much more present in the darkness. I felt the man was beside me.

'Our Lord is a person,' the voice said. 'Talk to him as you would to a person.'

'To tell him what?'

'The words will come of their own accord.'

'I'll try – but don't go away yet.'

'I'll stay as long as you want.'

'It's easier for me to talk to you now than it was in the sacristy. Solitude unsettles me. I certainly ought to be used to it by now, but tonight it's difficult to bear. Your voice is reassuring. When I listen to you I have faith.'

What had I said? And yet it was true. I felt the faith of the man in black as we feel the warmth of a fire.

'Will you say your prayer and then call me back?'

'But I can't keep you up all night.'

'That's what I'm here for. Tell God you love him.'

'But I'm not at all sure that I do love him.'

'Say that you love him, Karin, and you will love him.'

I hung up noiselessly and switched on the lamp. It was then that an inner voice cried out to me: 'You're lost, Karin! The trap is closing in on you. You must pull yourself together. It's now or never.'

I was so astonished that I remained for a moment open-mouthed. Then I looked across to where Roger had said his prayer. I turned out the light and went and knelt where Roger had knelt. My heart was beating so fast that I had to wait several seconds. At last I said simply:

'I love you.'

But I was speaking to Roger. I must not deceive myself. I tried hard to imagine God but could not. What God did Roger pray to? Suddenly I thought not of Roger but of someone else. In the darkness I could perhaps persuade myself that he was there and that he was waiting for me to talk to him. 'Supposing it were true?' I said to myself. 'Supposing he really was there, not at all like a ghost but in his body as he appeared in Judea? I would have loved and followed that Other One then, I would have kissed his feet, I would have covered them with my hair. A woman did it in the past and I could have done it too.'

'I love you,' I whispered as if I were afraid of being heard and misunderstood . . . This strange thought whirled in my head for a moment and suddenly it seemed silly because my heart was breaking with love and there really was someone. I remained trembling and silent, unable to utter a word, but I was not afraid. Three paces away from me in the darkness someone was standing. I knew it as I knew that I myself was alive and on my knees, dumb with joy.

It is here that one might speak of delusion and I feel quite incapable of arguing the point, but an inner certainty cannot be changed. I did not believe: I was certain. Someone had come near to the German Woman to tell her he loved her. If I had to die for that truth, I was ready to do so, because it was more important than anything. The world around me dissolved like a bad dream, I was drawing breath in another world where only love existed, and that world was the true one.

Time passed and I found myself alone again. The presence was no longer there, but the memory of it remained and would never leave me. I stayed on my knees for nearly half an hour, restored to the world but for ever a prisoner of the invisible kingdom.

Next morning towards nine I was in the sacristy. The priest wasn't there and I had to wait in the church. It seemed to me every bit as commonplace as the day before, but I loved it, I accepted everything, the plaster statues, the little house on the altar, the stained-glass windows, dreaming about what had happened the night before, happy, having exhausted the resources of my brand-new piety in the recital of the *Our Father*. The sound of footsteps and cloth drew me abruptly from my thoughts and I saw the man in the cassock walking up the central aisle to the altar. He knelt down and stayed in that position for a few minutes, then came towards me and signed to me to follow him.

In the sacristy he immediately asked me how I was.

'Last night something happened to me,' I said.

Seated opposite him in that setting of cupboards and wicker chairs, I hesitated to tell him about the amazing moment.

'I hope you're not going to think I'm mad.'

He smiled.

'That's something that no one mad would ever say.'

After a silence, I began talking. He heard me out with an attentiveness that made me scrupulous as to my choice of words, because I wanted to tell the truth as simply as possible. His face was slightly bent towards me and I felt he was listening with his whole being, not only with his ears but with his forehead and his eyes . . . When I had finished my story he sat in silence for a moment and at first I was afraid he didn't believe it. So I started to say in a lower voice:

'Perhaps you think it was an illusion . . .'

'No,' he said eagerly. 'Our Lord does not play with souls. He waits until our heart is ready.'

'Mine is ready, sir. Will you baptize me? I want to be a Catholic.'

I stood up while speaking and so did he. I could see that he was moved for he lowered his head, then raised it again to say:

'I'll have to instruct you first and you'll have to learn the catechism.'

'Can't you baptize me straight away?'

'No. In any case I need the bishop's authorization.'

When he saw my disappointment he added with a smile:

'Don't worry, Karin. You're already a Catholic by intention.'

'Will you give me a catechism?'

He opened one of the cupboards and extracted a little cloth-bound book. I saw that there were a dozen of them piled in a corner. 'A fly trap,' said an inner voice. I put the thought aside and took the little book with a sort of greed.

'It isn't big,' I said, 'I'll soon have learnt it.'

'I'll explain it as we go along.'

We agreed on a day when I would go and see him for my first instruction and when I left him I was radiant. I felt I was going back to school and was a child again. I found a strange enchantment in this unforeseen situation which transformed my life. I almost ran – but why run, I suddenly asked myself. So as to go where? Home? To get back to work in that hopeless woman's room?

A small public garden nearby offered me its tranquil walks and a bench under a tree. Some children were playing on the grass. Through the still-delicate foliage the sun threw golden splashes on the ground which moved to and fro at the whim of a warm breeze. I didn't choose a bench but a chair in a withdrawn corner. 'Let's recapitulate,' said the inner voice calmly and sensibly. It was just what I wanted; I wanted to get things straight. What was happening to me was so extraordinary, especially as I usually kept so cool. I marvelled at the adventure I had thrown myself into. 'Poor little Lutheran fly,' the voice went on, 'there you are glued to the papist fly-paper.' I made an involuntary movement, as if my ears had really heard those words. It was true, all that was true. Common sense was talking at last. My reveries had led me astray. I could not even say that I had been blinded. With my eyes wide open I had gone straight to where I was expected. The man in black, his coaxing smile, his tact, his courtesy and his kind words, and the little book he had given me . . . How could I have? I asked this question again out loud and two women who were passing turned round, two greying women, one dressed in navy blue silk with a white collar and little cuffs, the other in black with a pleated skirt, both highly respectable. They stared at me for a moment, but so gravely that I wanted to apologize, to explain everything. They would have taken me for a fanatic.

Roger was at the bottom of all this business. I had tried to find Roger and then, since that was difficult, Roger's God, or rather God plain and simple who took Roger's place – but I loved Roger and who could take his place? The lucidity of this reasoning astounded me. What was I doing sitting in that public garden with a Roman catechism on my lap? Leaving my chair, I went slowly towards the iron gate, slowly because I wanted to remain very calm. Surely it was obvious that I had just escaped the mental derangement I feared so much? God had had pity, yes, God. I believed in God. The secret pleasure of having foiled Rome made me smile and as I was passing by a waste paper bin I disdainfully dropped the little catechism into it.

Rays of sun were caressing my face. A child almost threw himself into my legs with his hoop. How beautiful and friendly my life suddenly seemed to me! Today was my birthday . . . Twenty-eight years old. One day perhaps I would have put aside enough money to go and live in France. Why in France? Alas!

There remained a word to be written to the man in black. Once out of the garden I crossed the avenue and went into an almost empty café and sat down on a red leather seat. Everything was white and bright in this place which I knew well. The trees lining the avenue were reflected in a huge mirror. I ordered a liqueur to reward myself for my new orientation. For in fact I suddenly felt in a jolly, almost farcical mood. My Danish blood was talking in its turn. 'Something to write on!' I shouted to the waiter as he moved off.

I had to take care with my letter. I wanted it to be over-whelmingly polite, then I changed my mind and envisaged it as dry, angry, or else as a little bit ironical and condescending. Would I go as far as to tell the gentleman that I had played a trick on him and that he, not I, had fallen into the trap? What spoils the fun in a case like this is that one cannot see the face of the addressee at the moment when he's reading the letter. I laughed to myself – perhaps rather shamefully, in spite of everything – at that vulgar thought! And now they brought me the pretty little golden liqueur and a writing pad.

'Has Mademoiselle got a pen?' asked the waiter.

No, I hadn't. Whereupon he eagerly offered me his. He was as blond as butter, baby-faced, fresh, with a blue, collusive eye, and was hanging around me. He seemed about eighteen.

'Fine, thank you. I'll give it back to you presently.'

'Sir, this letter will probably surprise you, but it is time for common sense to take over again. Don't take seriously the whims of a young woman who, having lost what she held dearest in the world, was looking for who knows what mysterious consolations in faith. I have been misused for too

long and now it is fitting that neither of us should be, neither you nor I. I shall stay what I am. You can go on working for the extension of a kingdom that I will never enter for the simple reason that it doesn't exist. Karin J.'

It was not exactly what I wanted to write. The great insolence of rebellion hardly showed, and it lacked sparkle. To tell the truth, my temper evaporated at the memory of that man who was so polite and probably so good, but I had to put an end to the mummery. Then I suddenly had a desire to do something unusual.

I called for the waiter who came immediately and I paid for my drink. While he was slowly pocketing the coins without taking his eyes off me, I asked him where he came from and he mentioned a village in Jutland.

'Are you a newcomer here?' I asked as I wrote the address of the man in black on the envelope.

'I came three weeks ago.'

'Why do you look at me like that?' I said, raising my head.

He blushed. Suddenly he was no more than twelve and he started to laugh without answering. A wild desire to be kissed took hold of me. Suddenly I desperately wanted all the joy the world could offer me. I stood up and smiled at the waiter whose freshness and even silliness had managed to disturb me.

'Have you lost your tongue? What's your name? Your Christian name?'

'Willy.'

'Well then, Willy, you're a booby, a nice booby, but a booby all the same.'

As I said these words I felt myself ageing. The invitation was plain enough . . . I only needed to make a gesture and the booby would respond, but I was ashamed. Now I had to go, I could not stay on behaving like one obsessed. My night with Roger had reawakened my sexual instinct. Because of that I was staring at this baby-faced boy whom I would not even have noticed but for this sudden perturbation of the senses. To make my misfortune worse, I had fallen on a moron. There are not many of them in our country. Perhaps I had to do with the only one in our town.

'You come from the country,' I said as I picked up my bag.

'Yes, miss.'

He must have smelt good. His round full neck did not fail to hold my attention for a moment. Then, without another word, I looked away and went out.

In the street I was assailed by monstrous images. It was no use trying to dismiss them, back they came with intractable insistence. It was no longer only affection that I wanted, it was love in its most animal form. I could feel the blood pulsing in my throat. Perhaps never before had I experienced the tyranny of nature to such a degree. To return to the café would have been so easy, and yet at the same time it was impossible – my pride did not allow it. Willy apparently had no idea that I was Karin the German Woman and was probably burning with the same desire as I myself, but I had lacked skill. The stupid incident exasperated me. I boarded a passing tram and made the journey home as if in a feverish dream.

I was far indeed from suspecting the surprise awaiting me! Back in my room, I walked up and down for a while in a state of painful agitation that tired my body without bringing me peace, when suddenly I noticed (was it deliberate?) that in my comings and goings I was avoiding treading on a certain fairly clearly marked-out space – the place where I had knelt last night, or rather a little in front of this actual spot. And then I began acting in a strange way, pulling my work-table towards me in such a way that no one would walk on the place where I imagined that an invisible person . . . but I did not want to follow my thought through; as usual, I was acting by instinct.

Less than half an hour had passed when I heard a knock at the door and through the peep-hole saw Mrs Jensen holding a large bunch of primroses. Her face was lit up with a smile. I opened immediately and she took me in her arms.

'I wanted to be the first,' she said laughing. 'Take these flowers, Karin, and happy birthday!'

Wearing a pretty white linen dress patterned with forget-me-nots, she seemed the very picture of joy with her chestnut hair even more dishevelled than usual and her laughing blue eyes.

'Thank you, Mrs Jensen, but what's happening?'

'No calling me Mrs Jensen, Karin. You must call me Marie. It's all over, my little Karin, you understand?'

'No.'

'Right, then I'll tell you,' she said, sitting down. 'Sadness is over and done with. No one's against you any more. Oh, they're going to come and I won't have time to explain. You've had a terrible time, Karin, but you've never complained . . . and we're not savages. Today we're making things up with you.'

She stammered a little as she spoke and it was hard to follow her.

'Karin,' she said, suddenly placing her hand on mine, 'who is the gentleman who's been coming to see you this winter? Am I not being inquisitive! Is he French? I mean the gentleman with the cloak.'

'French, yes.'

She burst out laughing.

'You've always liked handsome men, but we prefer him to be French. You've been very much watched recently, you know. I warned you. We still didn't know who the foreigner was. It was poor Miss Ott who told everything and when they found out that your lover was French . . . What's the matter, Karin?'

'Nothing, Mrs Jensen.'

'Call me Marie. Have I said something to upset you?'

'Nothing at all. I'm going to put your pretty flowers in water.'

She followed me into the kitchen.

'You see, Karin, the Frenchman wiped the slate clean, so we're doing the same.'

'I see. And if the Frenchman hadn't wiped it clean, when would all of you have done so?'

'I wiped it clean at once, Karin, as you know.'

'Yes, Marie, you're the only one with a heart.'

And putting the vase down in the sink I threw myself into her arms.

'What's the matter, Karin? Are you crying?'

I was not crying, but sobbing. One whole part of me was viewing this scene as utterly absurd, the other was savouring those tears which were rolling down my cheeks for the first time for years.

'You're not unhappy, are you, Karin?'

'I don't know. One can cry without being unhappy.'

'That's true, but you're making me cry as well.'

This absurd situation went on for some minutes. Then with one hand over the baker's wife's shoulder I tried to dry my face.

'But Marie, there's no reason for you to cry,' I said between sobs.

'None,' she said in the same broken voice, 'but it's so lovely from time to time!'

This remark brought me back to myself. I reached out for my bag on the small table and pulled out a handkerchief.

'We must put an end to it, Marie,' I said, drawing away from her. 'I had a moment of weakness. It won't happen again.'

I blew my nose.

'Anyway, we've had a good cry,' she said.

She said it as she might have said: 'We've had a good lunch.' I found her innocence touching and slightly distasteful at the same time. I noticed the wild locks of hair on her white neck. It seemed to me that everything about her that was gentle, kindly and a bit foolish was situated below the head, where nothing much went on; but her heart moved me. Once again I gave her a hug as if wanting to be forgiven for my trenchant judgements, and of course there was a fresh effusion on her part. I had the feeling that I was clasping a gigantic spaniel to me, the more so as when she wept her noises were evocative of that sentimental animal.

We just had time to dab our eyes with cold water when the bell rang again. I was worried to see it was the messenger from the shop.

'You've come too early,' I said. 'I shan't be ready before tonight.'

He gave a sly smile and waited a moment as if to enjoy my alarm. His lined cheeks crumpled up with mischief and I would readily have banged the door in his face, but he took an envelope out of his wallet and said:

'Happy birthday, Miss Karin!'

I thanked him off-handedly and tore open the envelope. It was a word from the manager confirming his decision to raise my wages. Without being rich, I would be distinctly more comfortable. My happiness went to my head and I shouted 'Happy birthday!' to the messenger who was just mounting his bicycle. He burst out laughing.

'Marie,' I called out to the baker's wife as I shut the door, 'my life is changing.'

'But I told you that, Karin. After all, the war is over.'

'But the church bells won't all ring together. I don't ask as much as that, I'd just like to hear those of the Church of Our Saviour . . . I want to get away from here. I hate this room.'

Mrs Jensen's eyes goggled.

'Why? It's a lovely room.'

'The fact is I don't know what I'm saying because I'm so happy.'

And yet, with the manager's letter in my hand, I sat down and murmured:

'But not as happy as all that.'

'Not happy, Karin?'

'You couldn't understand. They've robbed me of my youth. And they won't give it back to me with money.'

There was another ring at the bell.

'You go, will you, Marie? I'm always afraid of something horrid.'

Through the open door I saw little Johanna advancing towards me dressed in white. Bathed in sunlight as she was, she looked like an apparition. Probably through shyness she said nothing as with a gesture of exquisite clumsiness she handed me a small bunch of roses.

'Johanna,' said the baker's wife, 'have you lost your tongue?'

'Let her alone,' I said. 'It's emotion, isn't it, Johanna? But we two don't need to talk to understand each other.'

And taking her in my arms I covered her pretty face with kisses. Far from trying to stop me, she smiled with a sort of complacency and even a trace of self-conceit. 'What a little flirt you're going to be,' I thought, 'but how lovely you smell!'

'How lovely she smells,' I said out loud.

'How lovely she smells!' exclaimed the baker's wife. 'I hope you've not put on scent, Johanna!'

'Not at all,' I protested. 'It's the natural smell of her skin. She smells like fruit. Youth smells like fruit, young people . . . haven't you noticed, Marie?'

'No,' said the baker's wife with a sudden firmness that seemed to me suspect, because, since her virtue was by no means irreproachable, she was afraid of her husband and did not like the turn the conversation had taken.

'Oh,' I said, laughing, 'I just said that for something to say, but I've a present for Johanna.'

And opening a drawer in my chest of drawers I took out – rather to my regret, I must admit – a coral necklace that I used to wear as a child, and kneeling down before the future flirt I fastened it round her neck. Those pink beads against her fair skin reminded me with a sort of violence of what I myself had been at the age of ten. I suddenly saw myself in a garden, happy, my hand in my father's, and he was calling me his favourite girl and telling me the names of the flowers as we went by them. I wanted to die.

'There,' I said to Johanna. 'You look beautiful . . .'

'Why are you still kneeling, Karin?' asked the baker's wife.

'You're right, I'm silly this morning,' I said, getting up, 'and as it's my birthday I'm going to put on my lovely sapphire.'

This precious jewel, which was lying in the same drawer as the coral necklace, had come to me from my mother. She had worn it in the days when she was happy, but I hardly ever put it on. This morning, however, I slipped the delicate little chain round my neck and fastened it.

'Oh,' cried the baker's wife, 'how beautiful you look with that jewel! May I see?'

With shining eyes she came right up to me and touched the stone with the tips of her fingers.

'It suited my mother even better,' I said, not without a twinge of melancholy.

'Don't look sad, Karin. I've made you a big vanilla cake full of almonds. Do you like almonds?'

There was a ring at the door. I ran for refuge into the kitchen.

'See who it is, Marie,' I said imploringly. 'I don't want to talk to anyone. You can say what you like.'

Through the closed kitchen door I soon heard a buzz of voices that sounded like a polite but cheerful argument, then Marie came and gently knocked. I opened the door.

'It's the schoolmaster,' she whispered, closing the door behind her.

'I've nothing to say to the schoolmaster, Marie.'

'Even so – Karin! He's such a nice man . . .'

'Tell him I'm ill.'

She left the kitchen and I heard the bell ring yet again. This time several people came in, and, looking at the window over the sink, I wondered whether I could not jump into the street and escape this queer ordeal of meeting my past enemies . . . Above all, I could not endure the thought of the forgiveness that they probably came to grant me, but suddenly I felt ashamed of my cowardice and bristling with indignation I opened the door.

I flatter myself that at that moment I looked like a Fury, because suddenly the cheerful chatter came to an abrupt end and in a dreadful silence I heard a hard clear voice – my own – addressing that group of eight or ten visitors:

'What are you doing in my house?'

In one glance I recognized the pork-butcher's wife who had persecuted me for four years with silent and enduring hatred, the ironmonger's wife who used to spit in front of my door every Sunday night, the jeering postman with his nasty cackle as he slid the letters into my box, an elderly gentleman with cheeks the colour of wine-dregs who had always waited for me at street corners with ambiguous intentions, three jovial boys from the high school, and, near the door and somewhat sheepish, a large and stiff-necked personage with a face as pink as a brick wall – the schoolmaster.

The situation seemed to me as spectacular as could be desired, and I relished my anger, for it was evident that I inspired fear in the whole gathering. With what inner jubilation did I let my eyes wander over those astonished faces, passing from one to the other, though not without a tigress's smile.

'Well then? Isn't anyone going to speak?'

As if my smile were infectious, I now saw it flowering uneasily on those silent lips, then finally one of the schoolboys threw his cap in the air and cried:

'Don't look so fierce, Karin! We're not going to eat you!'

The great burst of laughter that greeted these words (rather artificial as it was) took me unawares, and I stupidly started to laugh too, out of nervousness. So they then advanced towards me in a common impulse, their arms outstretched, their eyes shining with joy like people who have been forgiven, for the fact did not escape me that they had come to apologize (not grant me forgiveness, as I had supposed), to apologize for having shut me up for four years in a prison of silence and solitude from which I was emerging aged and frustrated. With an instinctive movement, I slipped behind my long work-table and, avoiding all those hands, stood with my back firmly to the wall. It was at this moment that the schoolmaster detached himself from the group, leant across the table and gave me a smile redolent of *kindness*.

'Karin,' he said in a sweet voice, 'today we have rediscovered our little siren . . .'

'Oh, no!' I cried, 'I'm no one's little siren. If you've come to talk to me like that, you can get out!'

He gave a start. His jaw fell, leaving his mouth open, and the pink of his cheeks turned to purple. With a huge shrug of his shoulders he pushed aside the people standing near the door and went out. His departure was greeted with mocking laughter by the three schoolboys and with collusive murmurs by the others.

'Come on, Karin,' coaxed one of the boys as he leant over the table, 'you're too pretty to be unkind. Please let's make peace.'

He was attractive with the great gold lock that fell over his eyes and his greedy lips. I smiled in spite of myself, when all of a sudden I felt my face and hands go cold. At the far end of the room, and, as it seemed, coming out of the kitchen where the door was still open, I saw someone: Ott.

It really was Ott, I was not dreaming, and all the more like herself in that she was dressed as a man. Thus clothed, she betrayed her real nature. Motionless and smiling, she raised her hand to greet me. I felt faint and collapsed into the armchair near the long table.

'What's the matter, Karin?' asked the baker's wife.

'Nothing, Marie. Leave me alone.'

'But you're white. Do you feel ill?'

I didn't even realize we were addressing each other in the familiar second person singular, for terror had overwhelmed me in one blow. I heard my visitors chatting away together and saw as in a nightmare the tax-collector's wife and the pork-butcher's wife walking about my room with the free-and-easy air they would have had if I had been absent or dead. I remained silent. 'Then is going mad like that?' I asked myself, and wondered what asylum they would shut me up in. Not in the one where my mother had been. That would be too terrible. For the time being I must pretend to be normal and I tried to talk to one of the school-boys who had said something to me, but what? I had heard nothing for the last two or three minutes.

Marie walked round the table and with a smile indicated Ott, who was advancing towards me. I grasped the baker's wife's hand and squeezed it with all my might.

'No,' I said in a voice I did not recognize.

Then she shouted at me as though I were deaf:

'It's Ib, poor Miss Ott's brother.'

I felt the room going dark and suddenly that absurd thing happened over which I had no control: I fainted.

When I came to myself, with my cheeks tingling from the slaps administered by the baker's wife, I heard a soothing voice saying:

'It's the emotion. Poor dear Karin, she's so happy to have found us all again!'

By now the room was full of people. Because the door was open, anyone who wanted to came in. As though through a thinning mist, I vaguely discerned formerly hostile faces now riven by the wide smile bestowed on the acquitted. There was a monumental cake on the table, built in the shape of a tiered pyramid, white with icing-sugar, and topped by one thin pink candle that the tax-collector's wife was in the act of lighting. My eyes were riveted to the little flame quivering in the air that came from outside. Was it going to go out? For a moment this question seemed to me crucial.

A hand was placed on my shoulder and I heard an almost childish voice gently saying my name. Lifting my head, I saw Miss Ott's brother regarding me gravely.

'Happy birthday,' he said.

He had his sister's eyes, her prim mouth, her pert nose, and I felt my throat go dry because it was like a hallucination, this unbearable likeness to the dead woman, but in the depths of his eyes something else could be read that I had never known in Miss Ott: the innocence of a new-born child.

'Happy birthday, Karin,' he repeated with a smile.

I stammered:

'You're Miss Ott's brother. In looking at you I feel I'm seeing her.'

'My poor little sister,' he said. 'She would have come too. She liked you so much. Will you kiss me? It will be as if she herself were kissing you.'

With an effort of my whole being I stood up and took him in my arms, then, losing my head, I said in French:

'I killed your sister.'

'Yes, yes,' he said laughing.

His regular teeth were still white despite what must have been his forty years, and his face puckered up, giving him the disquieting look of an old baby. It was obvious that he did not understand a word of French so that my rashness involved no risk, but the sentence that my lips had uttered relieved me and yet again tears formed on my eyelashes. Then Ib made a childish gesture that overwhelmed me: he put out his hand and clumsily stroked my cheek.

'Ott,' he said, 'poor little Ott, she's now in heaven, you mustn't cry.'

And he kissed me. His rather slack yet fresh skin against my burning face gave me a feeling of slight discomfort. But I let him have his way with me nevertheless. Then suddenly a resounding voice beside me made me jump. It was a schoolboy, the most dashing of the three, who had come round the table and wanted to put his arm round my waist.

'Come on, Karin,' he said, 'let's kiss.'

I pushed him away.

'Not you,' I said, 'not everyone.'

He laughed stupidly. At that moment there was a sort of movement all around me and even behind the table which no longer acted as a defence. I turned away from the schoolboy whose breath was heavy with drink on my cheek, and in my confusion clutched hold of the person nearest to me.

'Ib,' I cried, 'help me.'

But it was not Ib. To my stupefaction it was Emil.

There followed the faint beginnings of a scuffle and I felt Emil's hand clasping my shoulder to draw me towards him, then with a bound he jumped over the table like a demon, and it really was a demon he reminded me of owing to that ardent and implacable element emanating from his whole being. For a moment or two I could not see him, then suddenly there he was in the middle of a group that he was roughly pushing towards the door. There were jeers and protests but his harsh voice rose above them, the voice usually reserved for cattle:

'Get out! Everyone out!'

The women protested a little, while the men, who were naturally more cowardly, filed meekly in front of this robust young man who precipitated their departure with great shoves of his shoulder. Only two of the schoolboys tried to return but resounding thumps soon put them back on the right path.

A scream arose above the tumult. It was the tax-collector's wife not unreasonably claiming the rights over the cake.

'We've all clubbed together to offer it to Karin,' she cried.

I raised my voice in my turn:

'You'll come and eat it with me later.'

And I added shrilly:

'Thanks, thanks to everyone!'

For at last they had tried to obliterate a shameful past, not mine, but theirs. The sinner had become their judge. There lay the intoxication of that sublime moment, but there was another when the door closed on Emil and myself, now alone in the room.

He had certainly changed: he was stronger and also more handsome. In his white twill trousers and pale blue shirt which showed the top of his chest, he seemed to me the picture of our Danish youth in all its conquering and provocative aspects. And yet other people might not have noticed him. His great dark wide-apart eyes seemed to be reflecting a fire. Indeed they shone with reflections of red and gold that I had never seen in anyone but him. But this was not his only peculiarity: his wide, full, boldly drawn mouth had the colour of raw meat which could be displeasing, just as his neck-line could put people off, and his arms emerging from his rolled-up sleeves. You could imagine him behind an old-time cart. I wanted to soften this strength by love, but I was also afraid of it. However, another surprise awaited me.

For a few moments we looked at each other in silence, not without smiling, and there was embarrassment. I thought he would throw himself on me as in the past with the extreme shamelessness of his age, but no, he said nothing. My uneasiness grew. With the passage of time and the trials I had endured I, too, had changed, but in another way. In his eyes it might seem that youth had left me. I saw he was hesitating, then in a voice he tried hard to make pleasant he said my name:

'Karin . . .'

I said nothing. He brought his face near mine and I felt his breath on my ear and my neck while he put an arm round me.

'Karin, will you be my wife?'

I was so dumbfounded that I could not answer. We were both standing near that ridiculous cake. To tell the truth, I had imagined everything: the physical ecstasy, the half-sincere words of love, the promises, all of it in the bed, behind the screen, as in the past, but what I had not foreseen was a proposal of marriage beside a set piece. The word 'marriage' affected me like a cold draught and it is shaming to have to write that I shuddered. Slowly Emil took away his arm from my shoulders and I heard him sigh sadly.

'You're not answering, my little Karin. Does that mean No?'

'Not at all,' I said, touching his chest with the tips of my fingers, 'but I didn't expect . . . I must admit it, Emil. Will you let me think about it?'

'For how long? Two hours?'

'A day.'

'A day's a long time, but I'll wait.'

His look of a disappointed child touched me and I was tempted to say Yes simply to see his brown rustic-god's face brighten. In the light that fell straight on him, his hard, high cheekbones took on a vermilion tint, and his large pupils glowed with the strange fire that fascinated me.

'I've changed, Karin. I'm no longer the mad boy of two years ago. You'll see how sensible I am.'

'I don't know that I like sensible boys very much,' I said with a smile.

'But I love you, Karin. The sensible boy is also mad with love.'

'Where would you take me to live, Emil?'

'In the country, to my home. My parents are dead, the house belongs to me. It's one of the best in the region.'

And I at once imagined a dining room impregnated with a farm smell. The confirmed town-dweller in me glimpsed countless impossiblities, hours of tedious solitude, visits from neighbours with booming voices, age, lines on my forehead and Emil's, old age . . .

'No,' I said out loud.

He took my hands in his and I had the feeling that all the warmth of his body was passing into mine, all its hungers and all its dreams.

'Are you refusing me, Karin?'

'I didn't say I refused, I was thinking of something quite different. Put your arms round me, you donkey.'

He kissed me, and that was all. My arms, that I had knotted round his neck, fell down to my sides and, hardly perceptibly, I drew back. A sensible young man was just what he had become. With me, in any case, he maintained what is known as a correct attitude. However, he did give me another kiss, quick and irreproachable. I looked with astonishment at his small head, at once delicate and brutish, that used to explore my body and haunt my nights. Without knowing what I was saying, I heard my lips ask:

'Do you still run after girls, Emil? In Copenhagen . . .'

'I don't run after them anywhere.'

'Aren't you interested any more?'

'No. I'm only interested in you.'

'You're lying. You've always had fire in your veins.'

'I've changed. I've become sensible, I tell you.'

'Has anything happened to you?'

'No. I've had everything I wanted. Now it's over. What I want now is to live with you.'

Seized with impatience, I let myself subside into an armchair and look at this placid young man who remained standing. He rather clumsily buttoned his shirt-sleeves, then his collar.

'You don't look as if you're glad to see me, Karin,' he said at last.

'I'm amazed.'

'Why amazed?'

'I've the right to be amazed if I want to, haven't I? I like being amazed.'

'You're making fun of me, Karin.'

'Not at all. I'm thinking of the past.'

'Oh, the past . . .'

Had he not been so handsome, I would have told him to leave the house, but I could not help admiring him, I admired his strength, his broad shoulders, the curve of his back – and above all his face, a dark, knowing face, not at all the face of a fool. There was something I did not understand.

'Why didn't you come and see me earlier?' I said.

'I couldn't get away from home. My father and mother were ill, and I had to look after everything.'

'When did you lose them?'

'My father, eight months ago. My mother just recently.'

'Did you love her?'

'My mother? No.'

'Sit down. It makes me nervous to see you standing.'

He took a chair and sat down on its edge while a silence descended on us which I deliberately allowed to go on.

Finally I said very softly: 'Today my life seems to be changing: it appears that I'm no longer the German Woman.'

'You were never the German Woman for me, Karin. Remember?'

'You mean your secret visits? I'm touched by what you say, believe me, but I'm curious, I want to know why you chose today to pay me such an important visit – in fact to ask me to marry you. Don't tell me it's because it's my birthday.'

His face turned suddenly red, which brought it a new charm, but he spoilt the effect by a false laugh:

'No. I admit that I've never known the day of your birthday. That sort of thing doesn't mean much to me.'

'Nor to me. We're agreed on that point. Then why, Emil?'

'Why?'

'Why did you come this morning with everyone else?'

'It just happened like that, Karin. I was surprised myself.'

'So you knew nothing about what was being prepared? Your aunt Marie had told you nothing about it?'

He got up abruptly and I suddenly saw the quick-tempered man I would be living with if I said Yes.

'All these questions, Karin . . . What are you trying to get at? I don't understand a word of what you're saying.'

'Let me explain. It's very simple: you're lying.'

He pushed back his chair, which fell over without his noticing.

'Karin, how dare you?'

'Would you like me to talk to you now or wait till tomorrow?'

My icy voice seemed to calm him a bit. He glanced at the chair and picked it up rather sheepishly and I realized he was wondering whether he would benefit by waiting. I knew so well what was going on in that Danish head.

'If it's about the answer to the question I asked just now, then I'd rather hear it at once. I love you too much to endure uncertainty.'

'Why do you love me?'

'But, Karin, why do people fall in love? I just love what you are and I'm happy when I see you.'

'Not at this moment, surely? At this moment I must seem unbearable to you. And I'm going to go on being so for a bit. Will you sit down? You're going to hear why you came this morning and why you want to marry me. There must be no interruptions. Agreed?'

He nodded. I leant slightly towards him and went on gravely with my speech.

'This morning, Emil, I've been rehabilitated in people's eyes. They've decided to wipe out the past and I've again become . . . you know what? Respectable. You wouldn't have to be ashamed of me any more if you married me. No, don't move. In addition, though you don't find me as seductive as in the past – be quiet! – you remember we got on pretty well together, behind that screen, and so you tell yourself that I'd be perfectly presentable as the mother of your children.' A moment earlier he had been red, but the blood had left his cheeks as quickly as it had rushed there, and I had in front of me a pale man and a dumb one, and one who was trying to control himself so as not to beat me.

'So am I to understand that the answer is No?' he asked in a hollow voice.

I raised my eyebrows, feigning surprise.

'No? But I haven't said No. Not yet. How can I know what I'll be thinking in a moment's time?'

It was my turn to get up and I did so with the slowness of a queen. If he had struck me at that moment I would have understood, but he was keeping his acts of violence till after the wedding. It wasn't a lover but a husband who was grinding his teeth in front of me, and when I say 'grinding' I mean it: I could hear the noise perfectly – a noise familiar to me, for I was one of those women who provoke such primitive reactions. In a gentler voice I added:

'I won't keep you any longer now. Come back tomorrow, if you want to. We'd decided on tomorrow at the beginning. Let's keep to tomorrow.'

He took a step back, then turned round, opened the door, and went raging off into the street. I saw his angry little nose disappear beyond the window and at that moment burst into rather forced laughter.

'He doesn't love me,' I said out loud, 'but he'll come back.'

For a long time I questioned myself about the answer I would give him. The arguments for and against waged war in my mind with that mixture of absurdity and common sense that leads straight to indecision. If I said No, was I letting an unhoped-for opportunity slip through my fingers? And if I said Yes, was I agreeing to become a neurotic country-woman? And anyway, did I really want to marry?

So as to think better I sat down in front of my cake. It looked stupid spiralling upwards as far as the tiny coloured-paper flag. A tower of Babel made of sugar – that's what they offered me by way of consolation for four years' humiliation and sexual abstinence. And now that I wanted a man, life was offering me one, and a fine specimen at that, whom I was on the point of refusing. Was I going to be hard to please?

As for thinking, I did not know how to think, I had been nothing but emotion since my childhood, like so many women whom men will never understand because such women are not interested in their masculine logic with its arrogance and inadequacy. I picked up a pair of scissors lying there, plunged it into the base of the cake and cut myself a mouthful. It was delicious, flavoured with vanilla which gave it a taste of innocence, a detail that could only depress me. My life seemed to me the most lamentable failure. For a brief period of uneasy happiness in 1939, what endless days of shame and rage!

I settled down to do some work, for one must live, or pretend to. My hand was sketching the face of a little girl when suddenly the bell rang – rather timidly, or so I thought. A glance through the peep-hole and I opened. It was the baker's wife. She threw herself into my arms.

'Karin!' she cried, 'what did you say to Emil? He's in a terrible state.'

'Really?'

She pushed back a coppery lock that was brushing the end of her nose.

'Yes, he came into the shop like a madman. Luckily, I was alone there. And do you know what he said?'

'How could I know? I haven't got second sight.'

'If Karin doesn't want me, then I'll never marry. That's what he said. He looks to me like a man who's going to do something silly. Do you know what I think? Perhaps he's going to kill himself.'

'Oh?'

'Is that all you have to say?'

'Yes. For the moment I don't see anything else to say. But don't worry. Emil won't kill himself.'

'Take care!' she said, raising a melodramatic finger.

'Emil's too fond of beer and bank notes to kill himself. And pretty girls too, no doubt.'

'He doesn't like pretty girls.'

'Nonsense! But this is interesting. Won't you sit down?'

She seated herself opposite me.

'A slice of cake, Marie?'

Her face brightened.

'In a minute or two I wouldn't say no, perhaps with a little cup of coffee . . .'

'I see that you like the good things of this world. You're a real Dane, Marie.'

While talking I had gone into the kitchen to put the water on to boil.

'So,' said I, off-stage, 'your nephew doesn't run after girls any more?'

'No,' said she, likewise. 'He's settled down.'

'Settled down!'

'Yes, settled down.'

I re-entered the room.

'Your nephew is a hypocrite, Marie. People don't settle down at his age.'

'Yes, it can happen. My father married at twenty-five and has led an exemplary life.'

'Do you mean he's been faithful?'

'But of course, Karin!'

'Don't get cross. Your father was a completely calm man. But Emil wasn't at all calm when I knew him. You see?'

'I don't know what you mean.'

'Well, I do. I was in a good position to know. You sent him to me, Marie. It was sweet of you, and I've never forgotten it. For two days and nights he made me happy. He was wonderfully gifted – Emil. Not for talking, but for other things! For other things there was no one to match him. So when you tell me he's settled down . . .'

I don't know what got into me to make me talk like this. My flight into the past was both terrible and delightful. By a caprice of my memory, and as if in a hallucination, I saw again the nakedness of that man whose caresses I had so savagely desired.

'I remember the first night. Here, in this room . . . He had knocked over the lamp without breaking it, and there it lay on the carpet, giving out a very sweet, strange and disturbing light . . . I saw his shoulders shining against mine . . . His great golden arms . . .'

At that moment something happened whose meaning became apparent to me only later. I had the conviction that a voice was talking to me softly in the silence, a silence which was beyond the noise of my words as a desert is beyond a city. 'Why are you saying all that?' it asked.

I stopped. Looking down at the baker's wife I met her concentrated gaze from between eyelids brought close together by curiosity, and suddenly this woman disgusted me as I disgusted myself, but it only lasted a moment.

'I'm talking nonsense,' I said sharply.

'Not at all!' she protested, disappointed at the interruption. 'But surely you must see that you are as attached to him as he is to you. He is just as handsome as he always was.'

'Leave me, Marie.'

'Do you want me to go?'

I did not answer. She stood up, rather clumsily, and tried to think of something to say. Her little-girl's face told me plainly that I had offended her and this pained me. I wanted to kiss her, less, I must confess, to make up for my fault than to hold a human being against me, tenderly, and so keen was my desire to love that I would have clasped the tax-collector's wife in my arms had she been there instead of Marie. This absurd thought made me laugh in spite of myself, and I threw myself into the arms of the astonished baker's wife.

'What's the matter with you, Karin, what's the matter with you?'

'I don't know, Marie. It's been like this since this morning.'

'You want to marry Emil!'

'No, no, I don't. Quick, a handkerchief. Go and fetch me one from the chest of drawers.'

I collapsed like a lump into an armchair and remained quite still until the baker's wife returned with a handkerchief. Then I took the little cambric square from her hand and immediately blew my nose.

'You're not happy,' she said with a great cry of compassionate grief.

'Oh no, we're not going to start again, Marie. Run to the kitchen and turn off the gas.'

I could not tell her that emotion had paralysed my legs. After a moment another cry came from the kitchen.

'Your saucepan's ruined, Karin. It's leaking.'

'It doesn't matter. Take another and make us some coffee, really strong coffee, coffee to kill us, suicide coffee!'

By now we were both laughing like mad women, but for the last moment there had been someone in me who wasn't laughing – and how can one express these things? With what words? They do not exist.

Once again I saw the baker's wife dash into the kitchen where she got busy while shouting back to me phrases whose meaning escaped me. I shouted back at random:

'Yes!'

She guffawed.

'What a funny answer! I asked you where the sugar was.'

'Marie, forgive me, I've no idea what you're saying. The sugar is in the cupboard.'

She came to me and took my hand.

'Tell me, Karin, what's the matter with you?'

I made no answer and she disappeared again, afraid no doubt that the second pan would suffer the same fate as the first one, then a period of time passed by during which I knew neither where I was nor who I was.

At last I saw the baker's wife sitting opposite me with the coffee pot and the two cups placed on the round table.

'So, Karin, you don't want to talk to me?'

Her pink and golden face seemed to be coming towards me and going away from me as in a mist. I had the sensation of dizziness we sometimes have just before sliding into sleep. Something had happened to me, I was sure. I had had what is so correctly called a blackout. In an instinctive gesture I stretched out my hand towards the young woman, who took it at once.

'You must drink your coffee,' she said. 'That will make you feel better. You nearly fainted a second time, Karin.'

'It's all exhaustion, emotion, Marie.'

'Poor Karin,' she said, wiping her eyes.

Foreseeing a new deluge, I sat up, leant towards her and kissed her. She smelt of bread. I had never noticed that before.

'Now we must part, my little Marie. I'm going to try to sleep.'

'What about the coffee?'

'You drink your coffee. I don't want any more.'

'I've already had one cup. But I'll have another – and a slice of cake.'

'Have as much as you like.'

'Oh, you're so kind,' she said vivaciously, then arming herself with a knife she allotted herself a generous piece of cake, taken from the upper regions of the edifice so as not to endanger the equilibrium of the imposing ensemble.

I could not help watching the frivolous little person enjoying her treat while throwing me glances full of gratitude.

'Why don't you want to marry Emil?' she asked between two mouthfuls.

I shook my head.

'Such a handsome boy,' she said, her mouth full and her eyes cast upwards.

I waited patiently until the feast was over before I got up.

'Marie, we must say good-bye now. I've got my work and you've got your customers.'

'Oh, Johanna's looking after the shop, but you're right all the same,' she said throwing herself into my arms. 'Thank you, Karin, you're an angel.'

And her face drew near, now exhaling a scent of the cake's vanilla.

'All the same,' she said, 'you'll be sorry about Emil.'

'I don't think so,' I said and gently pushed her towards the door.

As soon as I was alone I wanted to get back to my pencils, but my hand was so heavy that I could hardly guide it, and my mind was elsewhere.

Suddenly I left the table and went to draw the curtains of the three windows to darken the room a bit, but how to prevent the midday sun from hurling itself against those walls . . . Those cretonne squares offered a derisory barrier to the all-conquering light which seemed to let out cries of joy. Then I decided to close the shutters and thus obtained an agreeable half-light rather more conducive to thought. I would have liked it to be night already, I wanted to hide.

Why? If I had been able to answer that question I would have known what I was made of, but there was something in me that eluded me. I no longer knew what I wanted, though I knew what I did not want any more. A curious thought occurred to me.

It had been at the back of my mind for a moment. Pushing my table to the right, I put it back in the place it had occupied two hours earlier, and then I remained motionless at one pace from the point where someone had stood the night before. A buzzing filled my ears and I let myself slip down on to my knees. It was this that I had been wanting to do for the last few moments.

'You who were there last night,' I murmured, 'oh, be there again!'

My heart was beating wildly. For an instant I thought I was going to be heard, but no, there was no one.

So I had been mistaken. Yet, no. My recollection was precise. But it seemed very naïve to suppose that kneeling down in the same place would inevitably attract the invisible presence. This was not the way that what believers call grace was obtained. There were God's good pleasure and his unfathomable preferences.

How long did I stay on my knees? I have no idea. Without having the slightest sense of praying or the desire to do so, I was nevertheless talking to him who had talked to me the night before: 'I'll put back the table where it was just now, so that no one may trample over the place where you were.'

Now I was listening. The murmur from the street which came to me through the shut windows in no way disturbed the silence reigning within me. Talking had become pointless. In a sort of dizziness that annihilated the world around me, one single thought had formulated itself in my mind: 'I want to love only you, even if you're always silent and even if I never see you.'

Was it the weight of this love that was overwhelming me? I leant forward so that my forehead almost touched the floor, and although the presence was not there as it had been yesterday, the memory I had of it was like another presence. Joy took the place of certainty. 'You are in love with God,' an inner voice told me, 'in love with Roger's God.'

Time passed.

'Roger's God is also Karin's God,' I said softly.

Shortly afterwards I went out though the idea of eating had not even entered my mind. Gross as the comparison may seem, I felt light-headed as if I had been drinking – a thing that in fact never happened. In this state of mental intoxication I saw things with quite other eyes. I saw the splendour of the world. I saw it especially in the leaves of the lime trees whose branches were exactly like clusters of light, for there were rivulets of sun from the top to the bottom of these trees that nobody looked at. I talked laughingly to the children I met in the avenue. I saw the beauty of the world reflected in their eyes, too. It all seemed like a revelation, then the habitual suspicion descended on me to tarnish my strange happiness: 'You're raving, Karin, this is how it all begins.'

I had the feeling that my knees were giving way. A bench a little further on seemed like a haven and at last I sat down, as conventionally as possible, instead of lying flat out as I would have liked.

An old woman came and sat beside me, smiling and talkative. All her remarks, inspired by the fine weather, were predictable enough, and she followed them with little childish laughs, but I gave her no encouragement to go on. How could I have? I felt incapable of uttering a word and doubtless the old woman took me for a foreigner, for she finally fell silent too. There were ten thousand wrinkles on the flabby skin of her face and her fat round hands which she had put on her knees like useless objects were speckled in the manner of all the potatoes she had peeled in her life. She was now reaching the end of her days and was admiring the light, as I was. Perhaps that woman had been adored. In an irrepressible impulse of curiosity, I examined what she was wearing and could not help admiring the decency and simplicity of her get-up, her navy blue dress with a pattern of tiny white flowers and her narrow straw hat yellowed with age and encircled with a black grosgrain ribbon. Everything seemed to indicate that she was a country-woman, but she had more dignity than many of the inhabitants of Copenhagen, and I felt a desire to say something kind to her, instead of which – to my horror – I felt an explicable fit of the giggles take hold of me.

I was on my feet in a second and walking away as quickly as possible to conceal the disconcerting merriment that was convulsing me. I forced myself to walk at a more natural pace and to stifle the laughter trembling on my lips.

By chance this aimless walk soon landed me near the town hall where the woman with the sunshade announced fine weather from the height of the tower. Three o'clock struck in the warm air and the sun drove the shade to the base of the walls. Not many people were about. They were all on the beach at Klampenborg and one could safely wager that a third of the population was lying stomach-downwards on the sand and the second third was lying stomach-upwards. The rest had stayed behind, kept in town by age or some sort of inhuman office, but as for me, I was free.

'Free!' I suddenly exclaimed with a gesture that was observed by a street-sweeper engaged in earning his living with a wise economy of effort. Though he was over sixty, he winked at me.

'I'm free too,' he said leaning on his broom. 'If I can be of any help to you, miss . . .'

I gave him a nice smile and turned the corner of the street. The idea of allocating a holiday to myself had suddenly come to me. Take advantage of the weather, I too . . . On the other side of the long avenue I was in, I saw the Klampenborg tram. There was no question of going and exhibiting myself on the beach, but there was nothing to prevent me from wandering in the woods as in the past.

Climbing into that out-of-date conveyance, I chose one corner seat, then another, as capricious as a schoolgirl, an indulgence I could allow myself for at the moment I was alone. I would readily have started singing, but some other people got in and soon we were off.

The journey seemed short. I felt I was rediscovering my Denmark (after all, it belonged to me a little . . .). There really was love in the air, even in that horrible tram as it ground along on its rails, and I was in a hurry to reach Klampenborg. My joy was mixed with an almost unbearable impatience. I felt like a girl running to a rendezvous. A rendezvous with whom?

I pushed this question aside more than once, but the answer was too simple for it not to come to my mind finally. A rendezvous with Roger, of course. Tears welled up in my eyes: Roger was over and done with.

He was over and done with, but now in the woods I endeavoured to rediscover the pathways we had followed when we were young. The budding foliage softened the light around me and I had the pleasing feeling of walking along a vast tunnel – but I was alone. The birds were in full throat, singing happy little tunes that broke my heart. I imagined what might have been and discovered I had a romantic soul. The years-old dead leaves rustled under my footsteps and spread a faintly rank odour which I breathed with delight because it brought back my childhood. With all my strength I addressed myself to the past as to the real refuge against grief. If Roger had been there, he would have talked to me in his way about the trees, about the sky. Things became more beautiful under his gaze. I looked for the place where I had told him that I loved him in my own language and without restraint, certain that he would not understand a word, and now, alone, I continued my declaration, I made my avowal of love to a ghost, but this time in French, a French lacking our fine Scandinavian wildness.

Twigs crackling under someone's footsteps silenced me. Others besides me were profiting by the good weather to stroll in these woods, sometimes with dubious aims in mind. Without hurrying too much, I set off towards the road, then towards the big hotel, whose presence was heralded from afar by the blare of an open-air orchestra.

People were having tea on the terrace overlooking the beach and I wondered if I would dare let myself be seen in such a blatantly public place. The customers were there as on a stage: I would be recognized, perhaps shown out. This had already happened to me somewhere else. But today I felt bolder because of the morning's collective visit – and then I was ashamed of trembling.

So I walked in the sun towards the hotel's imposing façade and entered the foyer where pages were chatting in low voices near the reception desk. Could there be anything more ordinary? The lift was on the left and on the right the main staircase. In front of me, across the dining room, I could see the terrace full of people. I made my way there with a firm step when suddenly there unfolded in my mind a sort of little speech as smooth as a professor's lecture: 'Here's our Karin who is herself again, freed from her mystical fancies, sensible, intelligent . . .'

'Here's our Karin . . .' I was not used to talking to myself in such a ceremonious way . . . The words made me smile and I stopped dead. A head-waiter was coming towards me and, with the slightest inclination, asked me what I wanted.

'To take tea on the terrace.'

He opened a glass door and like a sleep-walker – for in all this there hovered an element of the unreal – I chose a table a little apart.

I now had the real unreal in front of me: the beach whose sand was disappearing beneath some hundreds of bathers with skin of an as yet uncertain tan but promising to turn into gold or bronze when the heat really came. Apart from a few obscene old goats, it was all the youth of the town that was there, rather like rows of soldiers slaughtered at one go and in perfect order. I had before my eyes everything that Danish beauty could show at its loveliest – naked, of course; yet not entirely: total nakedness is chaste, whereas these boys and girls concealed from one's eye only what was needed to exacerbate desire, but our theories of modesty do not take such subtleties into account. However that may be, this static display of blond flesh produced a stupefying effect and gripped at one's guts. If I had ever thought myself mistress of every sensual surprise, I could now say good-bye to that illusion.

A tray laden with all sorts of cakes was set before me and I shook my head, then nodded, while hands spread a cloth on the table, after which a saucer, cup and teapot appeared, but I was hardly aware of them. All I remember is the ridiculous detail that the orchestra was playing the overture to Mendelssohn's *Ruy Blas* with rather absurd *brio*, and doubtless I would have forgotten that but for the violent contrast between the fury of what the music had to say and the cataleptic indifference of the bathers on the beach.

I will be told that for a Danish woman this spectacle was not new. But it was for me each time I was permitted to enjoy it. In view of the ostracism in which I lived, for years now when in Klampenborg I had never ventured to go near the hotel, whereas today I thought I could give myself over without scruple to the delicious tortures of lust. 'But you're still young,' I said to myself, 'and there's no doubt that you attract men, in the street. All that is for you, Karin.' I jumped as if someone had spoken to me. 'Look,' went on Karin talking to Karin, 'feast your eyes on that multiple wonder. You won't suffer long. You'll have your share. Just imagine . . . you thought yourself on the point of becoming converted like a heroine in some edifying film . . .'

This last thought made me smile. In those frightful books categorized as Christian novels we do in fact see the main character return to morality with all the meekness of an automaton. By means of more or less camouflaged trickeries, the author prepares the way for the triumph of religion in the final pages when a clergyman appears . . . or a priest in the confessional like a spider in its web. This was the way I viewed that sick-making literature, but I was not the type to be caught in the fine meshes of Catholicism. I congratulated myself on having a solid independent head on my shoulders (Lutheran by nature if not by faith) and on being here to have tea (I poured myself a cup) while at the same time surveying this young and splendid humanity offering itself so generously to my eyes.

I was in agreement with myself that there was something unsettling about it all. What I was looking at bordered on the hallucinating because of its extent and multiplicity. Yet I knew that when night fell all those men and women would tear themselves away from the sand, disappear into the bathing-huts and re-emerge vulgarized by their clothes. Then night would follow with its artificial lights, and for many of these creatures, having lost the mythological grace bestowed on them by the sun, there would be the routine assignations with all the predictable motions, with nothing to disguise the horror – yes, the horror – of *the thing*.

The horror? What horror? Suddenly I felt myself in the grip of former revulsions. Can one be attracted by the very thing that repels? I was unable to answer this question, but I would have liked the goal of love to be tenderness, and I repeated this word within myself like a sort of prayer against the erotic folly of man.

The orchestra now launched into a one-step and various people started dancing on the terrace. With the tips of my teeth I nibbled one of those delectable crisp pastries which I believe no other country can produce, and I was brooding on what I was going to become in my new life when a man approached my table, bowed, and asked me if I would do him the honour of dancing.

Here, I think, a novelist's pen would be more suitable than mine to describe this character, but I am not concerned with fiction. Sufficient to know that the unknown man looked pleasant and more than pleasant: seductive. Above all – this remark may produce a smile – his way of walking was a delight. Most men don't so much walk as propel themselves forward, while this one moved with a natural grace and elasticity that irresistibly suggested dancing. Was he handsome? I didn't ask myself the question for he was more than that. Had he been younger he would doubtless have exhibited himself on the beach with all Copenhagen's narcissists, but in view of the little lines round his eyes and a hint of sagacity in his bearing, I gave him thirty or even thirty-five. Rather tall, with broad shoulders and an admirable figure, his silhouette against the pale blue sky had a precision and elegance that would have been a painter's joy – and then there was that way of walking . . . but I do not want to drivel on. His transparently grey eyes in his slightly tanned face looked at me with an expression that was already a caress. Could anyone be more stupidly susceptible than I? However, I had the good sense to answer, not without disdain:

'But I don't know you.'

He displayed a row of perfect teeth.

'Nor do I know you, but you are far too pretty for me to resist the temptation of telling you so.'

A very faint Central European accent lent charm to this little speech, delivered – I could not help noticing – like a well-learnt lesson. I stood up, left my seat, and a moment later we were dancing.

'Did you think I was going to make a scene?' I asked when in his arms.

I was talking like a little girl, I was talking too much, I could not stop myself. It must have been because of those eyes my soul seemed to be losing itself in. One ought to protect oneself against the specific magic of certain gazes. There are eyes in which one swims as in a lake. So pure, so alluring are these mysterious waters that the desire to lose oneself in them is irresistible for natures such as mine, enraptured by gentleness. For a few minutes which may be numbered among the most intoxicating of my life, I was in love with that man whose name I didn't even know.

Under cover of the music he guided me imperceptibly towards the far end of the terrace.

'What's your name?' I asked him.

'Do you really want to know? Don't laugh. My name's Aloysius, but I prefer to be called Louis. Here everyone knows me by the name of Mr Louis.'

'*Oesterreichisch?*'

'*Oh, nein.* There's the blood of several countries in my veins and my name is quite unpronounceable. Mr Louis is enough.'

'Slav?'

'Yes, a bit.'

He was pressed tight against me and his hands were just touching my neck with such a soft caress that I shivered with pleasure. His eyes became more loving and I suddenly read a question in them which made me lose my head entirely.

'Tell me what you're thinking,' I murmured.

'Ah, that can't be said in words,' he replied in the same tone, 'but the advantage of your country is that one can kiss where one likes without upsetting anyone. Isn't that so?'

How could I have resisted? Almost swooning, I closed my eyes and felt his hand behind my neck. When I opened my eyelids I saw in the gaze of the unknown man something that sobered me up at once, a cold, hard determination whose meaning was only too clear: desire.

'Of course we're going to dine together,' he said in my ear.

'I don't know. Do you think so?'

In spite of everything, he was so attractive and could put so much cajolery into his smoke-coloured eyes that the indescribable vertigo came over me again.

'Yes, I do think so, darling. I'm going to drive you back home and at eight o'clock I'll be ringing at your door.'

'I'd rather go home alone.'

At that moment the music stopped and I made as if to return to my table for the prosaic detail of settling my bill, all of which I explained to my companion.

'Leave it,' he said with a bewitching smile, 'I'll look after all that nonsense. Will you give me your address?'

So I gave it to him and he wrote it down in a little notebook with golden edges.

'You've forgotten just one thing,' he added, stroking my cheek with the tips of his fingers, 'your name, my beautiful.'

'Karin.'

'Is that all?'

'That's all, because I live alone and you just have to ring.'

'I like Karin,' he said, jotting it down in his notebook.

'You like the name?'

'Tonight I'll explain what I mean, dearest Karin.'

'Will you call a car for me?'

We went down three steps leading to a gravel drive, and there, in front of the hotel, while the porter was whistling for a car, my conquest pressed me against him without the faintest embarrassment. I flushed with annoyance and broke away.

'You won't be cruel with me?' he said in French.

'Do I look cruel?' I asked in the same language.

'Extremely,' he said, 'but I love you as you are.'

It was he who shut the car door and he stood with his fingers to his lips until I had gone.

In the taxi I had a presentiment that this adventure which was taking shape would be more than just a brief affair for me and that I would suffer. From all the evidence Louis was not the type to look for a solid liaison. He must somehow be held. The little inside mirror cast back the reflection of a woman worn beyond her years.

Fifteen minutes later the car stopped without my noticing.

'I hope you're not feeling ill, miss?' asked the driver as he opened the door.

He was still young, with a pleasant open face despite a brick-coloured complexion, which, however, emphasized the brilliance of his beautiful, blue, vacant eyes.

'Not in the least,' I said, opening my bag. 'How much do I owe you?'

'Three crowns precisely.'

An idea I am ashamed of crossed my mind while I was fumbling for change.

'Why did you ask me if I felt ill?'

'Because you had your eyes shut as if you were ill. I saw in the driving mirror.'

'I hope I don't look ill,' I said, laughing.

'Not any more.'

'Anyway, it was nice of you to be worried about me. Look, I can't find any change after all, I have only a fifty-crown note. Can you change it for me?'

'I think so.'

A big wallet appeared in his heavy red hands.

'Take four crowns,' I said. 'It was a long run.'

'Thank you, miss.'

Once I had stuffed the notes into my bag I said in a weaker voice:

'Would you mind helping me get out?'

He opened his mouth in astonishment and held out his two arms.

'There,' he said, 'I was sure you weren't well.'

I got out, leaning slightly on his shoulder, and acted the part so well that I ended by believing it. I realized what a huge element of lying there was in all this, but I could not see a man without giving way to the desire of knowing what he thought of me. Today, above all, I needed reassurance.

'How kind you are!' I murmured in his ear when he had helped me reach the door of my little house.

'With such a pretty lady as you, it isn't difficult, you know.'

His breath smelt of drink, but I let that pass. I had had my compliment, however routine it was, and straightening up I slid the key into the lock.

'That's all right,' I said in a colder voice. 'Thank you. You're very kind.'

In an instant I was over the threshold and had shut the door with a bang. Through the peep-hole I watched the driver's astonished face and was sorry I'd been so brisk. 'He'll get compensations elsewhere,' I thought. 'He's what they call a fine figure of a man with all the coarseness that involves, be he taxi-driver or ambassador.'

And now all I had to do was wait for my appointment. It was a quarter past six. That meant a long time to wait, but I had things to do. First I threw off my clothes and plunged into a warm, lavender-scented bath. I could almost have slept under the caress of the water as it relaxed my body, all tense with emotion. With an eye that I tried to make merciless, I scrutinized myself from my breasts to the tips of my toes and noted yet again that I looked better naked than dressed. On Klampenborg beach I would not need to fear comparison with anyone.

I got out of the bath and dried myself, after which I did my hair with the utmost care.

The sun was going down when I had finished and I went to choose a dress. Choose is not the word for I took the prettiest with no hesitation, the pale blue silk one which emphasized the (artificial) glow of my complexion and the gold of my hair, which was definitely my own. 'Come,' I thought, 'you're not bad, my beautiful!' That's what he had called me and I found it rather silly, but charming too.

In my room I walked up and down in front of the mirror and smiled at myself ten times, twenty times, my head a little on one side. Who could say what the evening held in store for me? Great happiness, perhaps. I decided to consult the cards on this point and spread them out on the side table. A glance at the grandfather clock told me I still had three quarters of an hour to kill.

'Dear cards,' I said aloud (one always has to talk politely to cards), 'tell me the truth: shall I be satisfied with my rendezvous?'

But the cards refused to answer. I had always been told that they remained silent on certain subjects touching on the improper. I put the question another way:

'Shall I go to bed in peace at the end of this lovely day?'

This time the answer came, but it was ambiguous. However, its general drift seemed clear: I was in love, and someone in love is never at peace. Again I thought of that man's eyes, and of the coaxing way he had gazed at me while his fingers stroked the back of my neck and my throat, but it was best not to recall that dizzy moment. I wanted to stay very calm. It was five to eight.

Had I given him my address? Yes, of course I had. He had himself repeated it to the taxi-driver with that inimitable accent that endowed the most ordinary words with an absurd sort of poetry. I tried to say it again like him: '*Chauffeurr* . . .' – it was a polite but slightly disdainful tone, preserving the necessary distance. '*Chauffeurr*, take the lady . . .' Perhaps he was an aristocrat in exile. It didn't make any difference to me, naturally: I made fun of titles. But still . . .

Eight o'clock. Two minutes past, to be exact. I got up and put away my cards in the drawer of my work-table, with my pencils which had been idle all day. Tomorrow I would ring the manager and explain that there had been a little celebration at my home. He might even have heard about it . . . He was so well disposed towards me now, the manager. I think he rather fancied me, but as regards that, look out! No indiscretions!

Expecting a pleasure is a pleasure in itself, up to a point. One is anticipating happiness. Once the happiness begins, it is on its way out, so one can justifiably wish expectation to be prolonged a little, not *too* much. Now it was ten past eight. But had a Danish girl any right to demand punctuality? I mentally gave my stranger a good half-hour's leeway. Suddenly the bell rang. At last . . .

In the state of extreme nervousness in which I then was, I could hardly unfasten the safety chain, my hands were trembling so. I then let two or three moments pass: he must not see me in that state. Then adopting an air of indifference, I opened the door.

Why did I not faint with the shock? It was not he, it was the baker's wife and Miss Ott's brother. Smiling in the doorway, they looked at me as if they were playing some trick, she in her pale blue dress and wild hair, he in a black suit rather too tight for him and his face lit up with joy. It was the face that made me recoil in spite of myself: the resemblance to his dead sister was even more unnerving than that first time, and a sort of panic seized me.

'We wanted to surprise you,' said the baker's wife with a great laugh.

'Yes, surprise you,' said Ib, waving his fingers in the air like a baby.

'We've come to spend the evening with you, my little Karin. It isn't good for you to be alone. Why don't you say something? Aren't you pleased to see us?'

They came in, jostling me affectionately as I was barring the way, and Ib closed the door.

'It's just that I'm expecting a visitor,' I said at last in a flat voice.

'Well, don't worry, we'll hide in the kitchen when she comes,' said Marie, clapping her hands. 'She won't stay all night, will she? Or is it your Frenchman, by any chance? Oh, *how* indiscreet I am.'

'No, Marie, it's someone I'm going out with. So you see . . .'

'Very well, when the bell rings we'll vanish into the kitchen.'

Instinctively I went and stood behind the long table, in that corner which was like a refuge against the enemy.

'No,' I said, 'it's impossible.'

'Oh, Karin,' said Ib with a gesture of supplication which he tried to make comic, 'don't drive us away!'

I looked at him with horror and made no answer. I would have put my hands to my head, except that I didn't want to mess up my hair. I glanced at the grandfather clock. It was eight twenty-two. I sat down and indicated the armchairs to the two intruders who were now watching my behaviour with the beginnings of uneasiness.

'Aren't you feeling well?' asked the baker's wife. 'Shall I make you a good cup of coffee?'

'A good cup of coffee!' echoed Ib, sticking out his chin and joining his hands together with a smile.

'No, thank you. But you may stay.'

They could stay because there would not be the ring at the door I was waiting for. I knew it now. That had happened to me once or twice in my life: someone had not arrived, and the moment always comes when the girl who's waiting suddenly knows that she is waiting in vain. Truth to tell, I had known it since eight, but I did not want to admit it.

'Oh, how kind you are!' exclaimed the baker's wife.

'So very kind!' said Ib.

Half getting out of her chair, Marie took on a conspiratorial air and whispered:

'Will you let us make a little coffee for ourselves?'

I nodded my assent and Marie let out a little cry of delight. Then she resumed her mysterious air and whispered:

'And some cake? Could we have a little of that too?'

'Oh, anything you like, Marie.'

Without losing a moment, she and Ib went into the kitchen, while I, with a rather unsteady step, went and lay on my bed. In the state I was in I could not care less if my dress were creased. Dizziness made me see the furniture swaying around me, the grandfather clock leant towards the windows, which, themselves, tilted in the wrong direction. I closed my eyes. It now seemed that the whole house was slowly revolving like the big wheel at the circus I used to go on as a child. 'Perhaps I'm going to die,' I thought. 'Oh, if only I could go now, like this!' This discomfort lasted several minutes, then I heard Ib and Marie coming back into the room and putting cups and saucers on the side table.

'Karin!' called the baker's wife.

I heard myself answering from the depths of a tunnel:

'Don't bother about me, I'm resting.'

She came round the screen and took a look at me, open-mouthed.

'Karin, there's something wrong.'

'No, it's nothing, Marie. You go and drink your coffee with Ott.'

'Ott?' she exclaimed.

'Ott!' echoed Ib. 'Why are you talking about my dear Ott?'

'Forgive me,' I murmured. 'I don't know what I'm saying, and I'm tired. I meant Ib.'

Ib came to my bed and looked at me fondly.

'You were thinking about my sister,' he said. 'Ott is always with me like a guardian angel, because she's with the angels and she sees us, I'm sure she sees us on this earth.'

He became more lively as he spoke and his eyes shone like the dead woman's when she was touched to the quick.

'Of course she sees us,' said the baker's wife and she took Ib by the arm.

Though she, too, was moved, she did not forget the water on the stove.

'Let's go back to the kitchen. There's the coffee, my little Ib.'

'Poor Ott,' he moaned, 'she would have been so happy to eat cake and drink coffee with us! She liked her coffee very strong, as in Italy. She'd never been to Italy, but she knew an Italian lady who sometimes made coffee for her the way they do down there. It was called . . .'

He fumbled.

'Ib!' cried the baker's wife from the kitchen.

'I'm coming. Do you need anything, Karin?'

'Leave me,' I murmured, 'I'm tired.'

While running to join the baker's wife he suddenly exclaimed: 'Espresso! I remember. Espresso!'

He shouted that foreign word with joy, like a cry of victory. Lying on my back, I stared at the disc of light thrown on the ceiling by the lamp on the table and I imagined that it was a sort of sun that was killing me, or killing something in me. Because my unknown man had not come, life seemed to have lost all meaning. I could not see anything in it but the will to make others suffer: one was born for unhappiness.

After a few minutes Marie came back with Ib.

'How are you feeling, Karin?'

'I'm resting, but that light bothers me. Do you mind moving it?'

Ib grasped the lamp and with a burst of laughter placed it on the carpet, almost under the small table, so that the screen completely hid it from me and I saw the room in a mysteriously gentle light that reminded me of Emil's first visit.

'Oh, Ib, you're so funny!' exclaimed the baker's wife.

'It's a very good idea,' I said softly. 'Leave the lamp where it is and don't make too much noise, I'm going to try to sleep.'

They settled down chuckling like children and I heard them whisper in a clatter of knives and forks. I could not see them because of the screen, but the large, vague shape of their shadows was thrown on to one of the walls. From time to time they laughed with their mouths full, and once they thought I was asleep their whispers became louder and louder.

'We did right to come and keep her company,' said the baker's wife. 'She isn't well.'

'No. Poor Karin . . . Perhaps she's been working too hard.'

'Shall I cut you a piece?'

'Yes, do. I've almost finished this one.'

'I have to be careful to cut it at the top, though that means that the slices are thinner than at the bottom, but if I cut too low, whoosh! the whole thing will collapse.'

They burst out laughing, their hands over their faces to stifle the noise of their merriment, but their laughter exploded between their fingers. I guessed all that without seeing it.

'What's the time, Marie?' I suddenly asked.

A slightly embarrassed silence followed because they thought they'd wakened me, then Marie said in a voice she tried to make natural:

'It's nine, my little Karin.'

'Nine o'clock exactly by the grandfather clock,' said Ib.

'Is your visitor late?' the baker's wife asked.

I waited a moment, then had the strength to say fairly gently: 'They won't come.'

'Perhaps they'll come another time,' said Ib cheerfully.

'Won't you drink a little coffee with us, Karin? It's very strong, it'll pick you up.'

'No. But I'll tell you what I *would* like, I'd like you to tell my fortune with the cards.'

'But I don't know how to tell fortunes, Karin.'

'Cards belong to the devil!' put in Ib.

Marie got up and came round the screen.

'My little Karin,' she said, taking my hand, 'I'm going to tell you what you need: a handsome husband like my good Emil.'

Standing in the half-darkness, she looked like a statue blackened with charcoal. Only her golden hair, caught in a ray of light, flamed at the top of her head.

I made no answer.

'It's so sad, an empty bed,' she said after a moment.

Another silence, then in a muffled but distinct voice I murmured:

'Go away, Marie.'

She looked at me a moment without saying anything. I imagined all the shocked astonishment there must have been in her pale eyes.

'Karin,' she said at last, 'are you annoyed?'

'No, but I want to be alone.'

At that moment Ib pushed his head round the right side of the screen:

'Would you like me to sing you my little Norwegian ballad?' he asked with a troll's smile. 'It's the one my darling sister liked so much.'

'No, thank you. Some other time.'

'But it would give me so much pleasure!'

'Very well then, just one stanza,' said the baker's wife, 'a short stanza that doesn't amount to anything, can he, Karin?'

And she sat resolutely at the foot of my bed. I hadn't the strength to protest. Almost immediately from behind the screen there rose a thin pure voice which in the silence described the spiral of a nostalgic song whose plaintive notes trembled a little as they went higher. The tune was as familiar to me as the words which praised the mystery of giant pines bordering silent lakes and the blue sky as limpid as a clear conscience. I could not help listening, bewitched by the pure voice gently crooning in the half-light, then suddenly I had had enough, enough of this situation at once sentimental and full of foreboding, enough of the rather foolish innocence of that song, of the dubious complicity of the lighting shed by the lamp under the table, and in a sort of bound which made the baker's wife jump I leapt out of bed.

Marie stood up and the singer fell silent.

'What's the matter?' they asked in unison.

'Nothing. What's the time? Put the lamp back on the table.'

'It's twenty past nine,' Ib said, and he bent down to get the lamp.

And now, somewhat dishevelled, I rubbed my eyes in the brightness. Marie looked at me in some admiration.

'How lovely you look in that pretty dress!' she said.

'I detest it and will never put it on again.'

'You're wrong, but you ought to be wearing that beautiful sapphire you had on this morning.'

My heart seemed to stop beating as my hand went to my throat. 'The sapph . . .'

I let out a cry.

'Marie, I can't think what I've done with it. Help me to find it.'

'Have you been out today?'

'Yes, of course. I came back towards six, I took a taxi.'

This recollection slightly eased the tight feeling in my chest. I had undressed, so I must have put the jewel down somewhere without thinking. We would certainly find it.

'A sapphire!' said Ib. 'They're so pretty!'

'Help us look,' the baker's wife commanded.

So all three of us set to work to search, they as if it were a parlour game, I with death in my soul, for I was beginning to guess the awful truth. On all fours on the carpet, Ib lifted up the skirts of the armchairs, disappeared under the tables, not without emitting childish laughs that gripped my heart, and sudden exclamations that gave me cruel false hopes. Marie, bent double, giggled stupidly in the footsteps of the elderly child who pointed to pins and matchsticks hidden between the floor-boards.

I dragged myself to the bathroom and got on my knees to explore the corners of that little area. As I was miserably lifting up the woollen bath-mat, a thought came to my mind which I knew at once to be unworthy: 'If I find the sapphire, I'll be converted.' And naturally I found nothing.

When I returned to my room the baker's wife raised her arms to the ceiling and let them fall again.

'Nothing,' she said.

'Where's Ib?'

'He's gone out to look in the street in front of the house.'

The front door was still open. I shrugged my shoulders and sank into the armchair beside the telephone.

'Give me the telephone directory, Marie. There, under the little table.'

'What are you going to do?'

I turned the pages of the thick book without answering and dialled the number of the Strand Hotel at Klampenborg. I was not kept waiting.

'Strand Hotel.'

'I'd like to speak to Mr Louis.'

'A moment please. Who is it speaking?'

I hesitated. Then:

'Miss Karin.'

'Ah, Miss Karin . . . Hold on, please.'

A superfluous recommendation. I was clinging to the receiver as to a rope above an abyss. There was rather a long silence, then:

'Hullo, Miss Karin, we have no one of that name staying at the hotel. Can you give me the gentleman's surname?'

'He told me that Mr Louis was enough,' I said in a strangled voice, 'and that everyone in the hotel knew him. He was on the terrace this afternoon. Tall, dark, dressed in white.'

'Tall, dark . . .'

'Yes, that's right. A foreigner.'

'A large number of clients come and go on the terrace, Miss Karin. Ah, yes. A porter has just told me that he noticed him. A moment, please . . . In white?'

This question was not addressed to me, but nevertheless I answered it with a kind of desperate fervour:

'Yes, in white!'

There was another moment in which I heard a mumble of voices, then:

'Hullo, Miss Karin. That gentleman left almost immediately after you, in his car.'

'In his car!'

'Yes. Hullo, hullo, Miss Karin!'

'Yes.'

'We were pleased to see you again after so many years. Allow me to point out that you forgot to pay for the tea and the cakes you had on the terrace. Five crowns, including service.'

'The tea . . . I thought . . . Very well, I'll settle up.'

I let myself fall back in my armchair. The receiver was still dangling at the end of the wire.

'Well,' said the baker's wife, 'what's happened?'

'The sapphire . . . Stolen by someone . . . while I was dancing with him.'

Suddenly my nerves gave way. I began shouting and waving my hands and feet about and must have looked utterly absurd. Ib came dashing in, drawn by the noise; he was holding a pebble in his fingers.

'Karin!' he shouted, 'don't be too miserable. Look at this pretty stone I've found between the tram-lines. You never see any like that.'

'Go away!' I cried. 'Oh, Ott!'

It all suddenly seemed like a supernatural revenge on the part of my enemy.

'Ott!' exclaimed Ib. 'She'll find your sapphire, Karin. I'll say a good prayer to her this evening. And one day she'll come and fetch you.'

'Take him away, Marie,' I implored.

The baker's wife drew herself up and adopted an air of importance.

'We must ring the police,' she said.

'No! No! Just go away!'

And I buried my face in my arms on the back of the chair and began howling. Ib and Marie must have been frightened, because through my wails I heard their whisperings and the noise of their footsteps going towards the door.

Once I was alone, I calmed down, for truth obliges me to say that when the spectators had gone I was still suffering, but in another way. Perhaps I might not have broken down like that if those two idiots had not been there as an audience, and yet I certainly was not play-acting this time. At all events I had got rid of them, above all got rid of Ib, who terrified me.

I stood up, went to dry my eyes in the bathroom, and took a long look at my face. 'That is what one looks like,' I thought, 'when one has let oneself be fooled by a thief because one's no longer in the first bloom of youth and has believed in his compliments.'

'My beautiful,' I said out loud.

The words sounded strange in the silence. I said them again while observing the way my mouth opened, and in a natural voice that was a delightful imitation of the one I had used to ask the stranger my German question, I repeated:

'*Oesterreichisch?*'

'*Oh, nein.*'

He had said that with an irresistibly seductive smile, and he had added:

'There's the blood of several countries in my veins.'

It was then that the stupid thought had occurred to me that I was dancing in the arms of a prince. What an adventure if he married me ... And in a spirit of abandon I in my turn had smiled my most captivating smile and murmured:

'Slav?'

'Yes, a bit.'

His fingers had run so lightly over my neck. He had seen perfectly well that I adored him and that this was the right moment to open the clasp of my little chain, while his other, bolder, hand had caressed my throat and collected the sapphire. As for me, I was shivering like an idiot at the approach of desire, while he ...

'Bastard!' I said aloud.

What he had done was so cowardly, but then men are cowards. They have the coarse courage to march towards the enemy and get themselves killed, yes, but our courage is of another kind, not to be dwelt on now. I lifted the receiver and dialled the police.

They listened and took notes without giving me much hope. And the staggering thing was that, in answer to their questions, I asserted that my thief had dark eyes and fair hair, whereas he had dark hair and blue-grey eyes. It was the memory of those eyes that caused my sudden change: I suddenly wanted to put them off the scent, I was incorrigible, others would say incurable. To put it briefly, infatuated.

I spent that night wandering the streets. They were almost deserted. It was fine, and as usual Tivoli attracted most of the strollers. The deliciously warm air charmed one's senses and despite my sorrows I enjoyed the sweetness of the moment. I too could have strolled in the great public garden, but had I gone there too many things would have taken me back to the summer of 1939 when I was drunk with love for Roger – for there was always Roger.

I avoided the great thoroughfares where I would risk unpleasant encounters, and walked my neurasthenia in the area around the Church of Our Saviour. There was no ulterior motive in that itinerary. I went to the place where I thought I would be most tranquil. Above all, I was fleeing from my room, where the accumulation of unhappy hours had installed a hostile presence.

In the silence of the night I heard the noise of my footsteps on the stone. The mass of the cork-screw steeple rose above me as far as the stars, which I gazed at until I felt almost giddy, as if I were going to lose my balance and fall from a height. They seemed to want to say something, but what? Their pull was certainly over the nameless part of me, but the part whose reality I was vividly aware of, and they were saying . . . In that position, with my head thrown back, my neck started to hurt. What they said was that nothing was important. That was what their message seemed to be, if a message existed.

I sat on a bench in a corner of the market square and, with my hands clasped behind my neck, tried to read something else in the black depths. Something else . . . Either a blind indifference, a boundless, an infinite indifference, or else joy, a joy far beyond words and extending in all directions as far as the end of space. In those unimaginable stretches there were thousands upon thousands of other stars. I was up there, not here.

I stood up, a little dizzy, but calmer. The memory of Roger, who long ago had had his room a few yards away, seemed so remote that I had the feeling that it belonged to someone else's memory rather than mine. The same was true of the sapphire and the man who stole the sapphire. I no longer believed that all that was true. 'But tomorrow you'll believe it,' I thought, 'so you'd better put an end to it all bravely, like your father. I'll close my eyes and in death I'll see all those stars.'

My steps led me towards that point on the harbour where I had sat with Roger. I say 'led me' advisedly, for they had a will independent of mine. I followed them.

Soon I was there and I sat down under the trees. On the other side of the water the lights of the town twinkled in a continuous line, but no sound reached me save the lapping of the ripples against the boats almost at my feet. I would have just had to stand up and proceed to the edge of the quay, then a little bit further, as we go down a staircase in the dark. A moment of suffocation, then peace, the end of all suffering on earth. My father had done that, a little further to the right, beyond that great barrier with the iron chains which I could see if I leant forward a little. So I would dare to do it, too.

A man and a young woman passed near me, made as if to sit down, changed their minds. He whispered something that made her laugh, and both laughed as they went off, and as they walked they kissed.

I stood up. One step forward, then another . . . I had not the courage, I was a coward. I had to sit down again and wait for courage to triumph by means of a sudden decision.

I fell asleep. In my dream I saw a young man sit down beside me, an officer in grey uniform. I said: 'So you've come back?' To which he replied: 'In a fashion, Karin.' I looked at him and already he had another face, one that I recognized: 'It's you! I thought you were down there!' He shook his head. '*Russland,*' he said. 'You were so handsome!' He laughed, but it was still another who laughed in his place, someone I also recognized, a very young man this time, almost a boy, so that my memory made me somewhat ashamed: he had lied about his age on joining up, I had told him he looked like a drummer, he had pursued me, implored me. Now, his too-staring eyes looked at me without blinking and his lips were pale. I asked him: 'And you, where have you come from?' I saw rather than heard the name *Russland* forming on his lips. He gazed at me with his blue, expressionless eyes and murmured: 'Do you want to go to bed with the dead, Karin?'

I woke up. Now everything filled me with fear: sleep and what is hidden in sleep, the night, the world, the lapping water, solitude, and above all myself; I was afraid of what I was capable of doing. Can one flee from oneself as one flees from a town?

It struck eleven. It was from the spiral steeple that this broad solemn sound fell and it made me shudder. I had to get away from this dangerous place beside the water that gently called to me . . . I got back to the market place, then to the streets.

At the end of one of these there was a glass telephone booth. I entered it and flicked over the pages of the directory. Luckily I had my little bag in my hand. I inserted a coin and dialled the number, but as soon as I heard the ringing tone I hung up and the coin was returned.

'No,' I said. 'Not that.'

Now I was outside, laughing out loud, even bent double in an access of mirth. I could not stop laughing. Also the picture I conjured up struck me as extremely comic: that person probably asleep whom I was going to pull from his bed in attire that I fancied as very odd.

I laughed so loud that from a still open window on the first floor of a house a voice of happy complicity reached me:

'If it's as funny as all that, tell us about it, won't you?'

And I saw a boy in shirt sleeves leaning over the window-sill, then the head of a woman outlined against his shoulder. I hurried away.

While I was walking along the avenue leading to the port, I noticed a car moving at the kind of slow speed that arouses suspicion: I was being followed. I was not mistaken. Opposite my house, on the other side of the road, the car stopped and a young woman got out. Plainly dressed, though not without a touch of elegance, and almost pretty, she came towards me, smiling:

'Miss Karin.'

My hand was in my bag to pull out my bunch of keys.

'What do you want?' I asked coldly.

'A minute's conversation.'

'I'm sorry, but I haven't time. And anyway, who are you?'

'Oh, excuse me. My name's Ursula Janning. We have a friend in common. A friend, or perhaps I should say an acquaintance: the baker's wife, Marie.'

'That doesn't explain . . .'

'I know, Miss Karin, but Marie is very fond of you and she dropped in on me just now. I'm sorry to hear that you've not been well today.'

'I? I've been perfectly well.'

I was now slipping the key into the lock. The unknown woman

placed her finger-tips on my hand as if to restrain me in my gesture.

'I only ask a minute, Miss Karin. I've come to help you.'

'It's quite unnecessary. Good night.'

With a speed that I was the first to be surprised by, I entered my house and banged the door in Miss Janning's face. 'Who is she?' I asked myself, peering through the peep-hole. Her face was lit up on one side by a street lamp and seemed to me less engaging than just before because she was not smiling: the eyes were hard and the chin a bit too determined. After a moment's hesitation she turned on her heel and crossed the road. Once again, I began laughing.

'That crazy Marie sending me her chums!' I said out loud. 'Soon I'll have the whole town on my heels offering apologies and wanting to perform little services.'

In my haste to get into my house I had forgotten to switch on the light. I found the switch, which I turned on with an impatient hand, and the light made me blink. I felt as if the room were jumping at my face. The carpet was my enemy. The curtains too, though not so much. That seems a bit strange, what I have just said, but it has a meaning. Everything has a meaning.

Now I could laugh out loud to my heart's content, and cry if I wanted to, howl, or dance with the unknown man of Klampenborg – but without him. That too had a meaning much too long to explain, and anyway no one ever understands anything. Out of curiosity I stuck my eye to the peep-hole. The car was still there, on the other side of the road, and Ursula Janning was at the wheel. Seated beside her was someone else, a fairly strong woman, or so it seemed to me. I became angry. I suddenly opened the door and shouted:

'What are you waiting for?'

There was no answer, but the car slowly started up only to stop again a little further on. I shut the front door with a bang and, as on every evening, turned the key twice in the lock.

'There,' I said to myself. 'Peace at last!'

But I was not at peace. I was frightened. Oh, not particularly frightened of that woman or that car, but frightened of everything, of the ceiling, the street lamps, the North Sea, the earth revolving in the sky without our knowing why, of myself too, a little. I was frightened of doing what I ought not to do.

For instance, making a telephone call at this hour of the night, eleven-thirty by the grandfather clock. But I was going to do that odd thing all the same. I sat down beside the small table and the clock said: 'No – no – too – late – too – late – no – Karin – no – too . . .' I picked up the receiver and dialled the number, the one I had dialled just now in the glass booth. My hands were damp. I waited. The ringing tone echoed in a room that I imagined as white as a cell, with an iron bedstead. Once, twice, four times – eight times . . . There was no one there. I was going to hang up when I heard:

'Hullo.'

My surprise made me cry out.

'Hullo,' repeated the voice that I knew, the voice that I needed to hear.

'It's I, it's Karin.'

'Good evening, Karin. Is there something the matter?'

'Oh, I'm disturbing you, I've woken you up.'

'That's of no importance. What is it?'

'That silly letter I wrote you . . . Will you forgive me?'

'There's nothing to forgive, Karin. Your letter didn't surprise me.'

To my great embarrassment I began crying. What touched me was this man's goodness. Even though he was an emissary of the pope . . .

'Forgive me. I'm rather unnerved. I wrote such silly things.'

He asked very gently:

'Karin, what do you want to say to me?'

'I'm worried, I need someone to say something to me, someone to talk to me.'

'Don't be worried. No one wishes you harm.'

'There's a car in front of the house. There are two women in it who seem to be waiting. One of them spoke to me just now.'

'Do you know her?'

'No. She accosted me, she pretended to be interested in my health. It was as though it were for my mother.'

'What do you mean, Karin?'

'They shut up my mother. First they surrounded the house, then they came with honeyed words, then they asked questions.'

'Karin, go and see if the car's still there.'

I put down the receiver, went to look through the peep-hole, then came back.

'No,' I said, 'it's gone.'

'If it were serious it would still be there.'

'Perhaps it'll come back.'

'Karin, you're a sensible person, but your imagination leads you astray.'

'I don't want to be alone.'

'You're not alone, Karin.'

'May I see you?'

'Tomorrow, yes. Tomorrow afternoon after five.'

'Not before?'

There was a hesitation.

'Tomorrow morning before seven o'clock mass. But wouldn't that be too early?'

'Why did you say I'm not alone? Did you mean that God is always with me?'

'Yes.'

It was my turn to hesitate. My eyes fell on the place where no foot should be set and which I had protected by moving my work-table.

'Can one feel his presence as one feels the presence of a human being?'

The answer did not come at once.

'Karin, without realizing it you're asking me a very difficult question, but I can tell you that, yes, it can happen.'

'Can one be sound in one's mind and yet have the certainty of that presence?'

'Of course. Many saints have had it.'

Doubtless he suspected something, for he added:

'But there's always the possibility of illusion with humdrum people like ourselves.'

'Illusion . . . It should be impossible in certain cases. Can one talk about experiences of this kind if one has had them?'

'It's better to keep these things to oneself. Now I want you to go to sleep. Till tomorrow, my little Karin. Be in peace.'

And he rang off. I called him back immediately.

'Why do you leave me alone when I need someone to talk to me about God? The Lord wouldn't have done what you've just done.

Don't you understand that I can't hold out any longer? I'm calling for help, I'm calling on God for help, and you who are there in his place, you just ring off!'

This outburst was received with both calm and humility.

'I think you're right, Karin. So tell me what's worrying you.'

I was unprepared for such a straightforward reply and lost my head yet again. To my own dismay I said in one breath:

'I was the German army's girl during the whole of the occupation. Did you know?'

'Karin, I know what everyone knows, but the only thing that matters now is the sorrow you have for your faults.'

'What good is that? It doesn't change the past. And anyway I'd begin again tomorrow if I had the chance.'

'You'd begin again?'

'Yes, I know myself. I'd begin again.'

'You don't really know. And then,' he went on with the faintest hint of irony that betrayed the Dane, 'we must hope that you won't have the chance! But pray to obtain the contrition that you lack. Then peace will be restored to you.'

'Contrition?'

'A sorrow such as breaks your heart. The human heart has to break so that God can enter it.'

This phrase coming to me in the middle of the night had an extraordinary effect on me: far from seeming harsh, it seemed to open a whole world to my eyes and I realized I needed this divine severity.

'God enters the broken heart,' I repeated.

'That shouldn't frighten you, Karin. God isn't frightening.'

'I'm not frightened. Now you're speaking a language I can understand.'

My heart began beating violently as if to bring about this mysterious breaking, and without another word I rang off.

And now an exhaustion overcame me as if I had climbed to the top of a steep mountain. I hardly had the strength to drag myself to bed and I don't know how I shed my clothes, but suddenly I found myself lying between my sheets with all the lights out, and sleep came at once.

It was still dark when I woke up with the jump of someone whom one has touched on the shoulder. I tried to remember a dream whose last shreds were fading from my memory, and all I could recall was a silent crowd through which I tried to push my way, and it was these efforts to get ahead that dragged me from sleep.

I groped in the darkness towards the end of my long table and there I knelt down on the bare floor. Why? I felt that in a state halfway between wakefulness and sleep, a dream was continuing within me, and I shut my eyes, all ready to fall asleep again, but I didn't want to sleep. What I was looking for was the presence. Perhaps in the darkness and silence the nameless one would come back. Perhaps by talking to him I would draw him to my side, and I uttered in a whisper some words that came to my lips of their own accord:

'Be there as you were the other day. You who can do anything.'

I waited, but there was no one, I was talking to myself. Then I bowed right down, trembling in the cold in my nightdress, my forehead touching the floor. Something held me back from saying aloud what I had in my mind. He would be able to read my thoughts. 'Don't you know that I love you? I've done wrong more than any other woman in this town. That isn't a reason for you to stay away – just the opposite. Remember the woman they wanted to stone. I would have preferred to be stoned, don't you see? But they killed me in another way. They have killed me through not punishing me by violence. Real death would have been better than the living death into which they cast me, the death they invented for me. Their forgiveness has come too late. Now I'm lying at your feet, O Christ, my last and first love. Come to me. How should I talk to you so that you will answer me? How long must I cry?'

The tears came of their own accord and washed my face. There was no one, absolutely no one, near me. After a few minutes I got up and turned on the lamp. The room reminded me of someone whom one surprises while sleeping, and who suddenly stares with wide open eyes. Reality was here: the stupid furniture, the striped chintz, and that sugary ruin, the baker's wife's cake.

My first need was to take an aspirin tablet and get into bed, then I turned out the lamp. Once again the darkness, this world full of things . . . I saw myself kneeling, and then prostrate, at the other end of the room. What a sight I must have looked! Was I really losing my mind? Yet the day before I was sure there had been someone. Suddenly I had the feeling that a voice was talking to me. Was it my own, the voice of my rather delirious thoughts? No. It said this and repeated it softly with no sound of words: 'Why do you look for me outside when I am in your heart?'

I stayed a moment motionless, stupefied, then I got up and, hesitating yet again, knelt down:

'Lord,' I whispered. 'Jesus!'

But I could not say anything else but that name, and I repeated it twenty times.

The morning's mail brought me a typewritten letter. Even before I opened it I knew whom it was from:

'*My little Karin,*' it said, '*by the time you read this, I'll already be on my way to South America where I'm going to try to re-make my life. After what happened between us, I realized in time (I hope) the whole extent of my error in believing I was called to the monastic life. I still have the faith, of course, but I feel I'm no longer the same person and I'm giving up a sacrifice that perhaps was never asked of me. I loved you, Karin, and I still love you. In my dark night you were a sort of apparition, and it was the memory I had of you that upheld me in the long period of captivity, but there's something that I cannot conceal from myself. The hope of regaining happiness with you suddenly failed, not through your fault, but through mine. Last year I received an offer from Brazil where I hope they may be able to make use of my architectural skills. It's pointless to tell you how much I'm suffering. Perhaps you wouldn't believe it. Henceforward I'm going to live with a scar, the one I received in the adventurous wood. Let's try to forget quickly. I wasn't able to re-make my youth. I'm ashamed and I'm fleeing. Go and see the priest I told you about, he will perhaps help you regain the faith I so madly misused. I'd like to talk to you lovingly, but love is dangerous, it would rob me of the little courage I have left. One last time, I look at you, and now it's over, all is over for me, youth and joy. All that remains is the love I gave you and that I still have. Roger.*'

This letter seemed to have been written years before by someone I did not know. I let it fall to my feet and looked at it for some time, fascinated in spite of everything by a sheet of paper that spoke a language henceforth incomprehensible to me. It was as though a dead man had written to me. And yet at the bottom of that typewritten page was the living, hand-written signature that would have made my heart leap three days earlier. After a few minutes I picked up the letter and tore it very gently, first in one direction, then in the other, then threw it into the waste paper basket, without emotion, but with the sense of a slightly sinister gesture reminiscent of the shovelful of earth of the final farewell.

That day my work was bad and I had to begin almost all my drawings again. Time passed, I don't know how, both slowly and quickly. The idea came to me of opening at random my mother's Bible in the hope of finding a magic text, one intended just for me, but I could not understand what I read. There was a veil over that book.

Towards four I set out for the Catholic chapel – walking slowly and ceaselessly asking myself what meaning my behaviour could possibly have. The sky was grey and the air much fresher. I looked for a ray of sunshine in vain – everything was dull and glum again. Faces closed up as I passed, and the houses became like people who hunch their shoulders and imperceptibly turn away. I suddenly felt a violent desire to die, to kill myself like my father, because nothing meant anything. That was it: nothing meant anything. One must stop breathing, throw oneself into the water.

On reaching the chapel, I started up my silent laughter. To push open the door of a Catholic church was the height of that nothing that meant nothing. Doubtless there were degrees of nothingness. I went in. The chapel was empty.

But not quite: an old woman in black, bent double with devotion, and rather frighteningly still, was praying at the end of one of the benches, her head raised towards the altar. She held my attention only for a moment. I looked around me in an attitude of defiance, which I soon abandoned in obedience to heaven knows what instinctive politeness. What rather disconcerted me was that the engaging impression of mystery that I had had the first time here, was lacking today. The sullen light from the sky did nothing to transmute the stained-glass windows, whose crude and violent colours now seemed hostile. Only the silence retained its potency, and I finally sat down in one of the benches fairly distant from the altar.

There was something new on the altar. In front of the little house there was an object imitating the sun, a white disc surrounded by sort of rays and all of it mounted on a base shining like gold. What kind of idolatry was a thing like this in aid of? That was what I asked myself, not without a hint of pity for Catholics and their oddities.

What was I doing there? Nothing. I was resting, I was tired, bending over a little with fatigue – and with despair, yes, with despair. That was the word I muttered in the imperturbable silence whose waves closed over my voice as if to drown my words.

There was no question of seeing the priest, and I was about to go when the chapel door opened and someone came in.

It was a girl, almost a child, wearing a light blue frock with short sleeves that left her pretty, rounded arms bare as far as the elbow. She passed close to me and I noticed her rather dim-witted profile (better say innocent), but pretty too, and her mass of black glossy hair, such as I had never seen before, spreading over her shoulders and down her back with a sort of magnificence. 'That one,' I thought as I looked at her, 'will find any husband she wants.' Just as she was she would have troubled the unhappy Ott, but why did I think about Miss Ott? The girl walked slowly towards the rail in front of the altar and there knelt on both knees on the linoleum patterned with imitation tiles, then bowed deeply before the little sun.

Something happened in me. I did not find her ridiculous and I did not even find what she was doing ridiculous. She at least did not believe that there was no meaning in anything. For her, that white disc meant something. After a few moments she took her place on a bench not far from the altar and began praying with a rosary between her fingers. How pleasing to the eye that idolatress was! Up to a certain point, but only up to a certain point, I understood Miss Ott's infatuations. And to think that one day a man's, perhaps a lover's, hand would fondle that marble-white neck, those arms, that whole body that was now untouched . . . Strange thoughts crossed my mind, some of them impure and for me quite new in their unexpectedness. I decided – why not? – to speak to this enchanting person when she went out, to catch her as she passed. I would ask her absolutely anything . . .

She took her time slipping the beads of that endless rosary between her pretty, patient hands. Finally she made a large sign of the cross on her chest and went and knelt again before the little sun, then got up to go out. It was then that I accosted her, but what to say?

'Excuse me,' I said in an undertone, 'but may I ask you a question?'

Her perfectly oval-shaped face turned towards me. Everything in her features breathed ignorance of life and of the body, and yet what greediness in her full lips contradicted by the magnificent and astonished eyes!

'A question?'

What could I ask her? Even before I was aware of speaking, my tongue had articulated totally unplanned words which nevertheless poured from my mouth with irresistible force.

'You look so serious, how can you adore that metal object, when after all . . .'

The fine eyes opened wider and I heard this rejoinder muttered with horror:

'Leave me alone, please. You're mad.'

Mad! Something reeled within me and I felt as if my mind were caught in a blinding light.

'Forgive me,' I stammered, 'I express myself so badly . . .'

After a moment's uncertainty the girl moved away two or three paces and I then said to her in an imploring voice which certainly did not seem to me my own:

'You must listen to me. I'm very unhappy.'

She stopped and looked at me in that indefinable way assumed by people – even the best – when they think you're going to ask them for money. I went on:

'As I'm not a Catholic myself, I was puzzled by what you were doing, I would have liked to understand . . .'

She gave a smile that wiped out the bad thoughts I had had.

'That monstrance contains a consecrated host,' she said more gently.

'A host . . .'

'That little white disc. Where the host is, Our Lord is too.'

'You don't see him.'

'Faith has no need to see.'

I wanted to ask her something else and made a movement with my hand, but she turned her back and went out quickly. I still had in my ears the sound of her sensible, if rather emotional, voice, with intonations that were not of our country, though she had no accent.

Advancing towards the altar – not without an inexplicable distrust – I looked at what she had called the monstrance. The object, admittedly, was rather beautiful, but there was a sort of defiance and conceit in the way it shot forth its golden rays. Here I recognized the Roman pride that makes us Protestants bridle. Then finally the host and its extreme whiteness ... 'Where it is, Our Lord is too.' Strange. He was there and two yards further on he wasn't there. I would more readily have believed that he was everywhere and I regretted not having produced this argument to that self-assured young lady.

With a confident step I advanced towards the rail enclosing the chancel, but there I stopped, not daring to go further. And the foreign voice whispered again in my ear: 'Faith has no need to see.'

'If you are there for that girl,' I said very softly, 'be there for me too.'

Ought I to kneel down like the old woman a yard or so away from me? For a while I resisted, then, my face blushing and my heart pounding, the proud woman knelt. What was happening? I could not say exactly, but suddenly I felt calm and happy. I was especially struck by the sudden serenity. It seemed that all fear had disappeared from my being, as if a great wind had swept it away. For the first time I felt sheltered from all misfortune and sadness, but this delicious halt in time did not last.

At the back of the church the door opened. It was then that my heart began beating harder; it seemed to want to tell me something. I guessed that the man in black was there and that he was waiting. And finally turning round, I saw him kneeling with his eyes fixed on the altar. Then I stood up, and as if he had been waiting for this signal, he too stood up and went to open the sacristy door through which I passed, not like a dreaming woman but like a woman in a dream, and as in a dream I heard the door close behind me. An inner voice whispered the words I feared: 'The trap.'

Instinctively I looked down so as not to see the man in black. There was dust on his shoes and I looked in vain for the cassock he had worn before. He was wearing black trousers from which the crease had gone owing to long use. I do not know why it shocked me to think that the priest had abandoned the rather absurd garment which, nevertheless, set him apart from other men.

Looking up, I met his pale eyes, where I thought I detected severity.

'Karin,' he said simply.

'You knew I would come,' I said without really thinking what I was saying.

'I was expecting you, Karin.'

'This is beginning rather like a conversation between lovers,' the incorrigible Dane inwardly remarked – she whom I could not silence.

I suddenly blushed and took two steps towards a chair into which I collapsed. In order to hide my blushes and confusion, I buried my face in my hands, a gesture perfectly suited to the circumstances. 'Lord,' I thought, 'spare me the ridicule of saying embarrassing things!' Between my fingers I saw the priest sit down in the other wicker chair about a yard away. I smelt the smell of polish again and, lowering my hands, saw once more the big yellow doors of the cupboards, then the cross over there on the wall.

'Talk if you want to,' said the priest, 'or say nothing, Karin. I'm here to help you see things clearly and find peace.'

He said these words with a reassuring slowness and in his eyes there was the tenderness I found it so hard to resist.

'I want to ask you a question. Do you believe that where there is the host in the golden sun there is also truly Our Lord who spoke to men?'

'Yes, Karin.'

'I believe it too,' I said suddenly.

The face of the man in black lit up with a smile and he let a few seconds pass before he spoke.

Then I wanted to break the edifying silence with an unexpected and exaggerated remark.

'Basically,' I said, throwing back my head, 'I've fallen into a trap.'

'A trap, Karin?'

'Don't misunderstand me. When Our Lord gambles with the devil to save a soul, he can sometimes cheat.'

'This time again the devil has lost,' he said, and he took hold of both of my hands as if to kiss me, but he did not kiss me, and I left.

PART FOUR

20 April 1949

Fear not those who kill the body
and cannot kill the soul . . .
Matthew, x, 28.

As she finished writing these last lines the light was failing and she could hardly see. Outside, the noise she knew so well came in through an open window, the distant roar of a tram and, close by in the avenue, voices and sometimes laughter. It was the time when she usually switched on the big lamp on her work-table, but now she preferred to stay in the twilight, to see the furniture in her room disappearing, the sofa, the small table, and at the far end of that long room the grandfather clock whose enamelled dial could dimly be seen – the whole context of her long boredom. Yet she was sorry to have nothing more to write and her motionless hand still held the pen.

Suddenly she stood up in the brisk way that was natural to her, opened the drawer and slipped in the last page of her manuscript.

'Finished!' she said. 'Finished for ever. I'm going.'

But going where? That was not important. Get out. 'Get out of this novel,' she thought with the irony that had enabled her to endure her ordeals. 'Escape the edifying ending.'

She laughed and lit the lamp. Everything reappeared in its tyrannical ordinariness and she felt a moment's fear, faced with the unavoidable hell of the solitude that was always ready to gather her in and close her round. For years and years there would be that furniture, those walls, those windows. Middle age, followed by appalling old age, would still find her there, diminished, vanquished.

'Oh no,' she said quickly. 'Not I, not Karin. I'll go into a convent, I'll sing hymns, I'll find the one who stood here for a moment, I'll be happy with him – with him alone . . .'

For a few minutes she talked out loud, in the grip of a sort of ecstasy of adoration in which her amorous past intermingled with memories of a believing childhood. She saw herself kissing the feet of the Saviour whom she was clasping in her hands so that he would not go, she saw her long hair pouring over that white flesh and delicate bones, then suddenly, in a sudden and violent hallucination, she saw the scars and let out a cry. They were terrible scars, swollen and discoloured, and from them there trickled almost black blood dividing on the skin like torn ribbons. She cried out again, and the vision disappeared.

By an effort of the will she walked towards the window, shut it, then drew the curtains. She saw her hands trembling on the folds of the heavy material and it seemed to her that they were not her own, but little by little her fast-beating heart became calmer and a great sweetness took possession of her, a strange sweetness that was almost like a burn. Karin felt this heat throughout her chest for a full minute, and she stayed motionless with her eyes closed so as to preserve the inexpressible joy. 'To die. To die now,' she thought. But already the burning was going away. In the place of the woman of a few moments before, transported into another world, there was only the everyday Karin, pulling the curtains with her habitual movements, as on every other evening. She was dumbfounded – enraptured and disappointed at the same time. 'What's the matter with me?' she asked herself. 'What happened?'

She went out. The light was disappearing from the sky and the street lamps were lighting up in the town, making a long sparkling line on the other side of the port. Beneath the trees in the avenue, where she was, there was still a half-light, but it was deepening from minute to minute. After a moment's indecision she went towards the quay, deserted at this time, without knowing clearly what she wanted to do. Perhaps sit down near the water whose lapping continued like a conversation in the dusk. Less than fifty yards away was the bench where she and Roger had sat. She wanted to go there to tell him, the absentee, what had happened to her, because love for him flowed back into her heart in spite of herself. Could one love a man and love God at the same time? This question which flitted through her mind did not disturb her, she felt too happy for those interior discussions that lead nowhere. Everything spoke to her of other things, the rows of painted houses, the masts of the little boats rocking from left to right, and even the uneven stones each one of which was familiar to her, although she stumbled from time to time.

Once she almost fell. An arm caught her by the waist and for a brief moment she thought it was Emil, but a hollow mocking voice soon undeceived her:

'*Fräulein . . .*'

Karin freed herself and leapt back. She had been followed. Thick-set, with broad shoulders, the man did not move and all she could see was his silhouette in the twilight when suddenly the street lamps on the quay lit up and she shuddered. The unknown man was looking at her with a wide smile revealing yellow teeth. His face, of a coarse simplicity, was seamed with lines which looked as if they had been traced on the reddish skin with the point of a penknife. A black sweater and a pair of velvet trousers without creases clothed a powerful and uncouth body. Karin did not move, as though fascinated by all that was sinister in this encounter. 'It's not possible,' she thought, 'it isn't true.' Suddenly she pulled herself together and asked:

'Why do you call me *Fräulein*?'

'Don't you understand German any more?' said an ironic, almost polite, voice behind her.

Turning round, she saw a youth dressed in pale blue linen who was looking at her, his hands in his pockets. His narrow, greedy face inevitably recalled an animal watching its prey with cruel pleasure. When she tried to move away, he jumped to one side without taking his hands out of his pockets and barred her way.

'Not so fast, my pretty one. We've got some things to talk about.'

'Let me pass,' said Karin in a strangled voice.

At that moment the boy's accomplice approached her from behind and placed his enormous hands on the young woman's shoulders. With an instinctive movement she suddenly bent and managed to escape, but realized that in her panic she was running towards the edge of the quay. Shaking all over, she stopped.

The two men walked towards her unhurriedly, a small distance apart, so as to prevent her from escaping should she try to pass between them.

Now she thought of nothing but staying alive. Her teeth were chattering with terror. She moved along the quay first, two yards from the water. The men followed her with the same even steps that made them so terrifying.

'You needn't be frightened,' said the younger of the two

in a soft and treacherous voice, 'we won't hurt you, quite the opposite.'

'Of course I don't want to hurt you,' continued his companion, 'only you must be reasonable and co-operate nicely as you did with the Fritz.'

While walking they got nearer to her and she quickened her pace along the waterfront and so close to the edge that she dared not run.

'Can't be done, you'd get a mouthful,' said the young man. 'You'd do much better to come with us, my beauty.'

Karin opened her mouth to call for help but found she no longer had a voice. Not a sound came from her throat. Then she remembered that Miss Ott had been unable to shout when, standing in the passage with the door wide open on to the landing, she, Karin, had ironically encouraged her to call the neighbours.

She began to run first one way, then the other, hoping in this way to confuse the two men, but the younger anticipated her movements and followed her closely. With a sudden movement she knocked against a big metal ring and, losing her balance, fell into the void.

The surprise tore from her a howl, releasing her voice. It seemed to her she was falling slowly, as in a dream, and suddenly, with a deafening crash, the icy water opened and closed over her head. Once, her teeth clenched, she came up again to the surface with a single thought in her whole being: to live; then her strength gave out and she sank without a struggle.

On the quayside the two men stared at the water for a moment or two. The younger whistled very softly to express his disappointment.

'Tonight,' he said, 'she'll be able to have fun with the dead.'

'Let's not stay here,' said his companion. 'Let's meet up at Tivoli.'

And they separated at once and disappeared.